THE SEVEN SIX-GUNNERS AND MULE MAN

A WESTERN DOUBLE

NELSON C. NYE

WOLFPACK PUBLISHING
— EST 2013 —

The Seven Six-Gunners and Mule Man
Paperback Edition
Copyright © 2022 (As Revised) Nelson C. Nye

Wolfpack Publishing
5130 S. Fort Apache Rd. 215-380
Las Vegas, NV 89148

wolfpackpublishing.com

Paperback ISBN 978-1-63977-951-2
eBook ISBN 978-1-63977-950-5

THE SEVEN SIX-GUNNERS AND MULE MAN

THE SEVEN SIX-GUNNERS

THE SEVEN SIX-
GUNNERS

ONE

IT DIDN'T SEEM like any handful of months could have made so much difference in the way a place shaped up. The huddled blobs of buildings appeared almost to have settled against each other like an armlock of staggering men in their cups. They sure as sin looked punier than they had to me last winter when I'd come through here chasing cow thieves. Even in the dark they had a scurvy of dilapidation that came at you like a smell.

Made me think first off I'd got turned around. I hadn't. This was Allen Street. There was the Crystal Palace and Hatch's, the Alhambra and the Occidental and, across the way, the Grand and Cosmopolitan hotels and Warner Brothers' huge barn of a store. Tombstone, all right. I sat back in my saddle trying to make out what had happened.

One big difference was the astonishing quiet.

Tombstone had never been modest about noise. The bang and reverberating boom of its stamps pounding raw ore into powder had served merely to punctuate its other rackets. This had been a bull roarer of a town, never shut down and crammed with carousals, horseplay and bickering. Where were the Cousin Jacks and the cowboys, the shouts and drunken laughter, the crash of jerked pistols and the damned fiddle squeal the five abreast riders that had torn through these streets?

It was hard to believe I was in the same place.

Lemon halos of lamplight gleamed uncertainly behind the grimed windows of maybe a dozen establishments. A paltry nothing beside the glare when forty thousand leaps of flame had turned the night skies red as paint and guns had blazed around the clock as hordes of shouting sweaty fools had schemed and cursed and toiled and brawled over the gangrenous metals ripped from this earth.

Tradition of that kind rooted deep and not likely to be snuffed in eight short months. Not even the Earps had very much changed it, rough as they'd been in the wink of their shooters. Nor Curly Bill Brocious and all his hellions or even Burt Mossman, fierce as he'd been.

So what could have turned this town so still? It was like a plague had swept the place.

I came out of the saddle, standing stiffly down, the slanch of my glance darkly quartering the street. A window flapped someplace in a lift of the wind but no talk prowled the raddled gloom.

Ducking under the pole, I stepped up on planks that were frazzled by rowels and the track of sped bullets. As far down Allen as a feller could see the street was an abandoned aisle of stacked shadows. Gave a man a queer turn, no getting around it.

The place had been called too tough to die. Yet just

over there, against the slant of racks, two horses stood hipshot asleep on their feet where only last winter half a hundred had been.

Had me fighting my hat, I can tell you.

A dim sheen of light leached through unscrubbed windows at either side of the Oriental's doorhole. Outside this deadfall, about where I was standing, Luke Short had killed Charlies Storms one night. Scarcely ten steps beyond, behind that corner, Buckskin Frank Leslie had shot Billy Claibourne. The town was pocked with such reminders. Boot Hill, up yonder, was crammed with old bones and if there was one thing I wasn't hankering for it was to have mine added to that moldering pile.

I'm Flick Farsom, happens you've been wondering. Late of the Lincoln County War that busted up Murphy Dolan, killed Alex McSween and just about finished Old Man Chisum who had figured to be about the biggest damn thief ever to come out of Texas.

I could of stayed over there I guess if I'd wanted. The Kid was dead and Lew Wallace had give out a blanket pardon to get things patched up as best he could. But old animosities have a way of hanging on and I had just about got my belly full. A gent doesn't cotton to putting in his whole time with his back to a wall.

Like enough I'm what you would call a rolling stone. Fiddlefooted, some have said, and they're probably right or were when they'd said it. Man gets tired of that after a while. What I'd really been hunting these past several months was a good quiet place where I could drop out of sight. When a gent knows little beyond cattle and guns, finding a hole he can cram himself into just ain't so danged easy as might be imagined.

I'd gone to Texas, plumb into the brasada which is country where brush gets so thick and stout you pack an ax just to get yourself through. Happened some others seemed to have got the same notion, some of that Jingle bob crowd that had rode for John Chisum. Would of been a short life if I had hung around there. I moseyed clean north to Kansas.

I tried breaking horses. But when a ranny gets hip deep into his twenties he can't take that kind of thing like he used to. I drove stage for a spell, halfway figuring to stick till a couple damned fools in the rain one night stepped out of the dark with lifted rifles. Toting them fellers in had soured me some.

Colorado that had been. Now I was down to the bottom of Arizona, said to be the wildest west of Forth Smith. It didn't look wild to the clabber headed chump who had told Major Murphy he'd just as like shoot Billy the Kid.

I wasn't figuring to step into another jackpot like that.

The Oriental's louvered doors, agleam within that shadowed entrance, spilled yellow light across the walk's gray planks. No piano trinkled out, no clink of glass or conversations. Only thing I could see, looking in, was the bent over shine of some jasper's bald head.

Few lessons had been ground deeper into me than caution but nobody, far as I knew, would expect me here. It was all very well and even smart to be careful but this kind of thing, given into continuous, could turn a man into a goddam rabbit.

Squaring my shoulders, I pushed open the doors.

The place was only a little less embalmed than I'd figured. No need to line up to get your boot on the rail. This baldheaded joker evidently the apron appeared to be anchored to the sober side of the bar. The games were closed, dust enough on the green cloths to make them seem gray. Only other person I could see, besides this jigger holding down the mahogany, was a black-haired female with the top of her bent over a beer at a table.

Neither of them bothered to see who'd come in.

The remembered pictures still looked down from the walls, cheap and tawdry in the lamp's feeble light. All the corners was filled with shadows. Even the mirrors looked foggy and dull.

The barkeep finally got up off one elbow. "What's yours, Mac?"

"Being's you've asked me, bourbon," I said. "What's come over this town?"

He set out a bottle, put a glass beside it from a mound of the same behind him. "Old age, I reckon." He wagged his forehead against braced knuckles and paraded his teeth in a prodigious yawn. "Catches up with the best of us."

"Where's the Earps?"

"Gone. Cleared out. Lock, stock an' barrel."

"You don't mean to tell me." I picked up the bottle, took a considering squint and thought what a sight that must have been. On a par with the Hebrew children quitting Egypt. "Whole town go with 'em?"

"There's a few hangin' on. Don't ask me why."

"Place," I said, "looked pretty lively last winter."

He gave me a closer scrutiny. "You musta been through early. Before the water got into 'em." He shoved a hand toward the bottle. "You goin' to drink that stuff or..."

The hand hung fire while we eyed each other. "You mean," I said, "all the mines have closed down?"

"All the ore worth workin' is plumb under water. An' like to stay there if you want my opinion."

"Oh, it's not that bad," a crippled codger piped up, limping in from the back with a broom and bucket. "Plenty of folks still around. Not a sportin' crowd, I'll give in to that, but once they git things opened up again"

"That'll be the day!" The bald barkeep snorted.

The old coot set up his broom like a hitching post. "Now, Ollie, you got to admit they're workin' on it. That engineer from the T. M. & M. said"

"His job holds out just as long as the hopes, an' you can bet your bottom dollars he ain't about to cut himself off at the pockets."

"Len Mosslin claims the Old Guard mine and the Bunker Hill will both be goin' by the end of the month."

"He say which month?"

The old man, shaking his head, limped off and the baldheaded Ollie, dragging a rag across his bar, said like Moses handing down the twelve stones, "Them mines is plumb finished."

"What about pumps?"

He threw up his hands.

"Well," I said, picking up my glass, "maybe they'll open some new ones."

It was no skin off my butt. Some fellers just naturally rub a gent wrong, and this contentious old codger with his windy pronouncements had about took my mind clean away from good sense. The woman piped up then. "Work... is it work you're looking for?" she asked.

I tossed off my drink. "Just passing through."

But I could feel her eyes.

I picked her up in the mirror. Pretty pert proposition. Hair as black as the ace of spades. Black eyes, too. Mexican or Basque might even be Spanish. I'd seen her land before in dives but something about her was somehow different, and it wasn't the pride because a lot of them have that.

Or make out to have.

There was paint on her mouth but her clothes had some class and her skirts was too long to have been much around a bar. In the glass our eyes swapped a couple of looks and it was like she had put a hand on my shoulder. Then her glance pulled away.

She finished her beer. She got the shawl off the back of her chair and stood up. And she knew how to stand to let you know what she had was every bit of it real and oiled for action. She fixed the shawl over her hair, took up her reticule and left.

"Dames!" the barkeep said, rolling his eyes.

"Reckon a man could find him a room in this town?"

"You kiddin?"

I dropped some silver on the bar. "Old Dick Clark still around?"

"Them fancy Dans was the first to go. Then the pimps an' their whores an' the hard rock crowd." He hoisted one side of his lip like a horse. "What'll you give fer this place, cash on the barrelhead? C'mon, name a price."

"I'm just huntin' quiet not a coffin," I said.

* * *

OUTSIDE IN THE DARK, crossing the planks toward my dun, I marveled again at the way this wild town had so suddenly tamed. Anyone predicting such a change last winter would have been laughed at for loco.

It kind of made a man think.

I was still wrassling it around when I went under the rail. Coming up, straightening, reaching for the reins, a voice someplace in the shadows said, softly, "Just a minute."

It was her.

She stepped out from behind my horse but not so far as to come into the light. A smell of crushed violets lifted off the dark shape of her. "Would you take a job, Mr. Farsom... if you got out of it what you wanted?"

I looked at her, hard.

"How'd you know my name?"

I couldn't tell what she was doing in the dark for all I knew she might be pointing a gun at me. She didn't answer straight off. Then she said, holding her voice down, "I have an uncle at Lincoln. I was there when the Kid got out of that window."

I said, "I still don't see"

"They were expecting you to shoot him."

"But..." I said, kind of riled and impatient, "How'd you know *just now*?"

"I remembered your voice."

Some guys, I expect, would have been some set up a looker like her. Alls I could feel was that mess I'd got into. There might be those holed up in these parts that would damn well like to see me planted. I said, "What kind of a job?"

She come a step forward, likely figuring her near-ness would work some advantage. Or maybe she come for a closer communion, having no thought of the hungers she stirred. It was too dark to see, where she stood, what her look was.

The stillness got thick with the chirring of crickets.

"What sort of job?"

"Well ... nothing," she said with her breath so close herded I had to crane over, "nothing that would bother a man like you."

"Gun work," I growled on an outrushing breath.

She knew me all right. She held quiet for a bit, maybe turning it over. "I don't imagine it will come to that? All I want is... protection. You will help me, won't you?"

I eyed the dark shape of her, the distrust still on top.

The throaty sound of her reached out, curling round me stronger than wine. She said, "Write your own ticket," and the words rang a bell, chousing up thoughts a man my age shouldn't of took no stock in. That crushed violets smell of her was like warm hands sliding through my guts.

I pulled back, thinking I had better hit leather, better dig for the rules the way I'd been minded. But like a damn nump I kept right on standing there.

What come off my tongue was the kind of fool talk you'd expect from a kid. "What are you scairt of?"

"That's just it I don't know."

I kept staring.

She dragged in a deep breath. I watched the way it pushed out the front of her.

"It's just a feeling." She sighed. "Cold fingers running up and down my back."

I had some fingers that would like to do that. "Where is this job? What's it pay, and".

"About forty miles. In the Davis Mountains."

"Never heard of 'em."

Sounding bitter, she said, "The lonesomest hole I ever got into. Nothing but rocks and snakes and cactus. A place God forgot and never bothered to finish."

"When do we start?" I said, feeling better.

TWO

I MUST HAVE BEEN BORN with the simples. I should have got clean away, just as quick and as far as a fast horse could take me. My steeple never had been crowded with bells but even a chap in three-cornered pants might of savvied this dame wasn't up to no good with her perfumery and paint and all that clack she had given me. Why, those damn Davis Mountains wasn't even on a map. But alls I could think of was the isolation of it a place that had nothing but rocks, snakes and cactus. It figured to be just the hole I was hunting.

There was, of course, one other thing that had considerable to do with my foolishness her. I reckon I don't know a great deal about women, but it wasn't just her looks. There was other things too... the queer land of breathless way she spoke, the husky sound of her voice even the way she stood, and the half glimpsed things that peered from her eyes.

Lavender gloves came almost at her elbows. Lithe and slim she was in a quail colored dress that fit tight at her neck. Her waist I could of got my two hands around and did when I helped her into the rig, a kind of two wheeled cart or cut down buckboard the like of which I had never seen before.

We got started straightaway. She was hoping, she said, to get home in time for breakfast. Climbing onto the dun I followed her out, content to ride behind for a spell but planning, even then, to be up on that seat with her before we got done.

This I mention to show you the state I was in, lally-gaggin along with my head full of wool and never a thought for what direction we was headed. I did get to wondering what her father might be like. Certainly he figured to be a pretty big man.

It was right about there, with all that craziness in me, that the first disquiet began to rub at my attention. For all I knew he could be poor as Job's turkey.

The night wasn't so dark now we'd lost the lights. About ten million stars was winking down. Even without no moon a feller could make out well enough where he was going. She handled that team like she'd been brought up to it.

Nothing strange about that. Most women raised on a ranch could handle horses. Yet it did seem queer, her being off like this so far from home all by herself. This was a gringa fashion and she didn't look gringa not even in this starshine.

Odd, too, where I'd found her. Guzzling beer in a saloon.

Plenty of Mexican girls did that, but not the kind that come from big holdings. No hidalgo or don would put up for a minute with having his women folks carrying on so common.

Sure, she might have run off. Some of those girls was wild as March hares.

I got to working back through the things she had said, surprised to find so little to catch hold of. Big thing I come up with was her being so frightened yet she hadn't said that, not in so many words, She hadn't actually said 'ranch' when you come right down to it. Hadn't told me her name. Alls she had said was I should call her Lupita. I thought back to the look that had come along with it.

The rattle and clank and the clopping of hoofs didn't rush up so loud now we'd got off the shale. We was down in a kind of broad trough, a sort of canyon, with the thorned wands of wolfs candle showing on the slopes among a scattering of pear and greasewood. The lean bright sickle of a moon glowed like silver about one foot above the wall's ragged rim.

We'd been riding some longer than I'd figured by this sign, and the chill of the night was beginning to leach into me. "What's the name of this place we're headed for?"

I watched the turn of her head as she came half around. She didn't answer right off but kept looking like maybe she was rolling something over in her mind.

Whatever she saw, I got the notion she liked it. Her teeth flashed. "Silver Spring," she said.

"A ranch?"

Again she seemed to take longer than was needed. "I suppose," she said, "you could call it that. We don't have any cattle."

"Not a *sheep* spread, is it?"

I heard her silvery tinkle. "We're running horses."

What there was about that to make her laugh I

couldn't see. But it was plain enough, even to me by now, she wasn't the kind to talk a guy's arm off. Way she measured out information you'd have thought it was gold sliding out of her fingers. "Mustangs?" I said.

I caught the glint of her teeth as she touched up the team. Good horses, that pair. Matched bays. Looked like Morgans.

The moon got up. I found the north star. Begun to seem like we was headed southwest, though it was hard to pin down what with twists and all the dodging and turning we done to keep from ramming into rocks. Way this girl handled the ribbons was a" caution. She seemed to know where she was every bump of the way. Myself, I couldn't even begin to see a trail, neither wheel marks nor horse tracks. When I mentioned this she said it was the winds. "Loose sand through here. Always shifting and changing."

"This the only way in?"

"You don't have to worry. We're not going to be lost."

Well, lost was what I'd come out here for and it begun to look like I'd come to the right place. I said, "This ain't the Jornada, is it?"

"Not really." She spoke up quick enough answering that, but she hadn't just give it to me right off the cuff. She appeared to measure every word, to look askance at every question. The queerness of it begun to dig through the spell of her nervousness.

As the night unraveled the terrain got rougher. The whole stretch of this country seemed to lay on some slant like in time before man it had someway faulted, like it had started to flop over and had given out midway.

I hadn't spotted one light in all this riding. Hadn't seen any cows. Usually a man would turn up a few, even in hardscrabble landscape like this was. Couldn't everyone be cattle barons. Small independents, the one man layouts and greasy sackers, generally figured to latch onto whatever was too sorry for the big spreads to bother with barrens like this where a man pretty near had to go to hell for water. But if there was anyone ranching this end of the cactus they was sure some shy about letting it be known.

Nights in the desert, where you've got any land of altitude at all, even in the hot months can get surprisingly cold. This one was, with a chill wind pouring down off the rimrocks. Even through my brush jacket I could feel the teeth of it nipping at the ends of me. I asked Lupita if she wanted my fish.

Shaking her head she got into a kind of short waist length coat that looked like a Confederate shell jacket that she pulled out from under the seat. "I'm not really minding it," she said, tugging a lap robe over her knees.

I debated getting into the slicker myself, figuring it would turn at least the worst of this wind that was beginning to blow now in grit laden gusts. I pulled the wipe over my nose, deciding to tough it out for the sake of having a more easy access to my guns, the one under my leg and the pistol riding my hip. By which you will see I was not entirely easy in my mind, though I hadn't yet got around to taking conscious stock of it.

"How did you happen," she asked presently, "to be around Tombstone?"

That was a pretty open question and not one generally asked in my circles. "Just sifting around." I shrugged. A woman, of course, was like to ask anything.

"You know how it is with us rannie. Just natural born drifters.

What's beyond the next hill always seems more fetching than the dirt you got under your toenails."

We rocked along for a spell without no more talk while the unrest that was in me began to build up some. I've been, I suppose, what you might call a trained observer. This could likely be said for any of the bunch that come out of that Lincoln County fracas. Rolling rocks over some poor fool, digging out graves for gents that got careless, had taught plenty of galoots the value of keeping their eyes skun. Still, I wasn't actually suspicious. It was habit, I guess, that was sawing my nerve ends, and becoming a disquiet that was gradually beginning to scratch at my notice.

I didn't climb onto that seat like I'd aimed to. I put in my time looking over the country and it was something to look at, all standing on end. Rock and sand and saguaros and cholla about as desolate a region as I'd ever got into. How she found a way through with that wagon was something to marvel at, for it didn't look like you could hardly get a horse through.

Along towards morning, with the stars turning pale and a fresh wind stirring, I come out of my silence to rub at cramped muscles. "You got much of an outfit at Silver Spring?"

"We'll be there pretty quick. You can see for yourself."

I done some hard looking, done a mighty mort of it, but alls I could see was the damned rocks and cactus. They was all over everything like flies round a sorghum spill. Then we dropped down into a sort of walled valley and there was this outfit smack dab in front of me.

THREE

IT WAS ABOUT AS WELL HID as the needle
somebody lost in a haystack. Even close-up like this you
had to stare twice before you realized what you was
looking at was buildings, so clever had they been
blended with the rock faces tumbled behind them.
Holed up here a feller wouldn't need no dog to let him
know when company was coming. A gopher couldn't
hardly scratch up there without the sound of it raveling
through this gulch. For a timid gent it was the finest
kind of setup, the one spot of color being the green of
the cottonwoods hung out over the house.

Against the door stood a man with a rifle which he
didn't put up until Lupita waved. He didn't come off
the porch even then. He stayed where he was in blue
shadows until she'd drove up and stopped by the steps.

"Morning, Fred. Weren't getting worried, were
you?"

She loosed a flutter of laugh and got down, peeling
off her gloves while she stomped some of the kinks from
her legs. "I've brought back some help. Meet Flick

Farsom," she said, waving me up. "A good man with a gun. Flick, shake hands with Fred Oakes. Fred's the boss here at Silver."

He looked me over. I done the same by him. He was probably well into the shank of his forties, dark and bony with a crooked nose whitely ridged with scar tissue. He was built like a stilt. There was a harshness narrowing the displeased search of his stare.

"Grub on the table?" Lupita asked, like it went clean over her head that he was riled. "I could gobble a catamount, hair, claws and all."

Oakes didn't reach out to grab my paw, just stood there meanly sizing me up like a steer he was minded to put on the block. Lupita grinned. "Guess you two will be wanting to talk." She went up the steps and into the house, pulling the plank door shut behind her."

"You the Farsom," Oakes said, "that was mixed up with Murphy?"

"I worked for an L. G. Murphy at Lincoln."

Oakes chewed at this for a couple of minutes, not showing what he thought, not saying nothing either. If he was waiting for me to back off or put up some line about getting the girl home at this time of morning he didn't know as much about me as he let on.

He was gaunt enough to get through a knothole. He had a brushy stubble of gray bristle on his cheeks and the knobs of his hands thumbed onto his shell belt. He said with a bullypuss stare,

"You any kin to Curly Bill Brocius?"

I shook my head.

"Ever met him?"

"Not to know it. Heard he was dead didn't Earp kill him?"

He give me a dark look, his unwinking stare as hard as a gun snout. "Did he?" Rasping a rope scarred fist across his whiskers he wheeled, still scowling, and moved towards the door.

"This Brocius," I said, "a particular friend of yours?"

Oakes stopped like he'd heard the cock of a pistol. He didn't come round, didn't get up much wind, but the language he used wasn't no kind for ladies. He chopped it off sudden. "Wash bucket's around to the side."

I can take a hint if it's put to me right. I went around to the side.

When I come back, freshly scrubbed and with my hair slicked down, he was waiting in the door. "We'll tie on the nosebags." Stepping back for me to pass he followed me in.

It was a rangy sort of room, long and lean like Oakes himself, filled with the shadows that come down from the walls. It had a cubbyhole kitchen off to one end and doors leading out to the other parts of the house. A checkered cloth was on a big table in the living room proper; benches anchored to either side of it would have seated a crew of twelve. "Set down," Oakes said, "an bite a biscuit."

The girl had shed her coat. She was at the stove with her sleeves rolled up, filling the place with bacon and coffee smells. I chucked my hat in a corner and got onto a bench while she fetched a heaped platter and come back with the Java. While I was turning over my eating tools Oakes settled into a chair at the end.

"Dry summer," he said, fixing a napkin into the

neck of his shirt. "How's it been where you come from?"

"I ain't needed webbed feet."

The girl poured our mugs, turned back and fetched the biscuits. She passed Oakes the platter. He took four of the eggs and about half the bacon. There was two eggs left. I took one of them and three crisps of meat. We all got biscuits. They was stacked three deep and flat and hard as crackers.

"This the whole of your, outfit?" I said to Oakes.

"I ain't got much help an' that's a fact. Hard to git hands to stick in this country. No neighbors," he said with a dry little grin that some way, I figured, was aimed at Lupita. "Pretty quiet."

The girl tried to stir up some conversation. Oakes' grunts wasn't aimed to encourage it much and I had notions of my own to sort out. When it seemed like I wasn't getting anywhere I started packing my pipe, the old blackened brier I'd carried since Lincoln. The girl's glance touched my face. "More coffee?"

"All right."

Oakes, when she got up to fetch it, was folding his napkin. He held out his mug. "I'll take some of that."

I put a match to my Durham. "What's the name of your iron?"

"Don't rightly have a name."

"It's a picture brand," Lupita said from the stove. "Cover anything. I knew a man once used to call it the 'Cyclops'."

Oakes got up with his eyes like baked marbles. He didn't look at the girl. Never looked at me either. Just scraped back his chair and stomped off through the door.

I found the girl's eyes. "He'll get over it," she said, and poured me some Java. "He's like a bull to get along with till he's had his second snort."

She set the pot back, considered me a moment and then sat down in Oakes' chair. "There's probably some things about this deal you won't like but if you play your cards right...."

"I'm weaned," I said. "You can speak right out."

She smiled. "Fred's sour and suspicious and kind of set in his ways. He's had a lot to contend with"

"He don't want me here."

"Give him a little time," she said.

I scratched a match and puffed for a spell. For some reason she liked the idea of my being around. I was some considerable of that notion myself but it hadn't grown into no mote in my eye. If Oakes was against it, it wasn't likely I'd stay. Girl or no girl. And if he was engaged in moving other gents' horses he was flirting with something I didn't want any part of.

"Fred isn't grabbing them," she said, "he just grazes them."

"You can kick as high for a sheep as a goat."

Red lips pulled away from her teeth. "And you were the one that would just as like shoot Billy."

"*I* got over that craziness."

"Sure of that, Flick?"

I scowled at the swirls of smoke floating around me.

"You didn't claim amnesty from Governor Wallace. Your name wasn't posted in the lists of those pardoned."

"Never done anything to be pardoned for."

She just sat with that pussycat grin.

I puffed some more. "You calling me a owlhoot?"

Her eyewinkers flapped. She peered at me brightly. "Guess you'll admit there are those that would."

I come onto my feet, shoved away from the table. "Thanks for the grub...."

"Do you *have* to be a fool?"

"I ain't goin' to be no monkey on a stick!"

"All right. Go on. Clear out," she said, like I didn't have sense enough to blow my own nose. "When Chisum's hands, or some of McSween's bunch, catch up with you out in the dark some night just remember what you had here."

I scooped up my hat and reached for the door. Like a nump I looked back. "What was that?" I said.

"A place where the devil himself couldn't find you."

She had me cold.

* * *

SO FAR AS I knew there was nobody after me, but a lot of ill will was still blowing around and she'd put her finger right on it. Bounty hunters was prowling the hills, the rim rocks was filled with master less men. Some of the soreheads out of that Lincoln County War would be a heap overjoyed to line their sights on a man who'd helped spoil a good thing for them. It was a time to tread lightly and there was plenty of us doing it.

When I got outside Fred Oakes was stowing a fresh chaw in his jaw.

His eyes come around like the wheel of a hawk but his voice when he spoke sounded friendly enough. "I've got some stock you might break if you can stand a little dust." He even dredged up a grin before he spat. "You want to look at 'em?"

I couldn't see where it would hurt much to look.

"All right," I said, with the most of my thinking still back in the house. She'd said I could get out of this about what I wanted and, while I figured that was probably spreading it thick, it did seem like the attractions ought to more than offset any edges of unpleasantness growing out of Oakes' dabbling in other folks' horses. I didn't even know he was doing it. About all I could see for sure was that she seemed pretty anxious to have me around.

A man couldn't be expected to get on his ear about a thing like that,

"Fetch your horse," Oakes said. "We'll cut out a couple fresh ones."

Chances was I had him all wrong. He'd had a good thing here, all alone away out in the cactus with a woman as good looking as Lupita.

Following him back through the rocks it did come, over me to kind of wonder what was between them. Probably she'd hired him to run this place. Nobody would ever take Oakes for no Mex.

Just as it looked like we'd about reached the back end of this gorge or gulch or whatever it was, we come into a sort of clearing where there wasn't any rocks for pretty near a hundred feet. This was where they had the corrals, three rails high, laced with ocotillo and bound at the uprights with rawhide cured with the hair on. There was two of these pens, roughly oval, the biggest being about forty foot across and; at the moment, empty. The other one had three horses in it. There was a bunkhouse built into the face of the cliff behind.

"Ropers," Oakes said, indicating the horses. "That

grulla there is mine. You can throw your hull on either of the others."

It was pretty good looking stock, nothing fancy but as good as you'd find on a working cow spread. I would say they'd average forty dollars apiece, by itself perhaps a bit more, for Oakes' grulla which had a long underline and considerable muscle. I said, 'It looks like that mouse might git up and go."

Oakes got a bridle and went in and fetched him out. The horse was docile as a kitten. While he was saddling I got the gear off my dun, all but the bridle which I left on to hold him. I took a cotton rope halter and went after the buckskin which, in this part of the country, is generally called a bayo coyote. He wouldn't let me even get near him.

I come back and got my grass rope. The horse didn't want no part of it. He ducked and turned and weaved and twisted, always keeping some part of the other one between us. There wasn't no chance to get a shot at his head. "All right, son," I said, "you asked for it," and made an underhand cast he stepped right into. He stopped quick enough then. I brought him out on the halter, cinched up, turned my dun in and put up the bars.

"Where you grazing this bunch?" I said.

Oakes grunted. He sure wasn't one for wasting words. We climbed into leather and he led off past the bunkhouse. I didn't see nothing but rocks back there. It looked like the end of the line to me, but each time I figured we'd reached it another twenty feet or so would open up off at a tangent, shut in by rock walls that pretty near pinched together over us but kept leading on, deepening and dropping till I lost all sense of direction.

"This place got a name?" I said.

Oakes didn't even bother to grunt. He never turned his head, but presently, when the walls widened out enough for me to come alongside, he said in a kind of offhand way, "What we're on is an old smuggler trail. Then bones you been seein' come from Mex'kins an' burros. Been a passle of 'em killed here."

"Indians?"

His lips got to moving but all you could hear was the swush swush of hoofs plowing through deep sand.

I seen right then he was some kind of nut. Not far enough yet off his rocker maybe to be playing with a string of spools, but no sort either any gent would pick to be ramming around in country like this with a six-shooter strapped in easy grab of his fist.

A loony and her penned up with him away off here! Small wonder she had said I could write my own ticket! It was plain enough now, her wanting me around.

Then I wasn't so sure.

When I peered a little closer some of them pieces didn't fit as snug as might be; some began to push up wrinkles from being squeezed in where perhaps they didn't go. Last night she'd been free of him clean over to Tombstone. Why had she come back?

FOUR

I GOT the chin off my chest and took a sharper look around.

The sides of this canyon didn't offer much help. They was mostly rock with the rims away up so dad burned distant what sky I was able to glimpse looked bluer than Yukon ice. I could even make out a dim scatter of stars though the sun must have been well up. Down here the walls was maybe thirty foot apart with the trail antigodlin among whopping slabs and chunks cracked off through years of frosts and heat. In the lavender tinge of this shadowed passage where the horses' breaths spewed out like smoke my jacket felt right down good.

A man, I reckoned if he was in good shape and was desperate enough might be able to crawl himself up out of here, but he sure wouldn't be getting no horse up them walls.

It was things like this that had ahold of me but back of these what you might call surface activities was a hard deep core of churning thoughts. Like sniffing hounds they was dashing about with such wriggling and clamor I wondered Oakes didn't notice. *Why had she come back?*

If the girl had been a prisoner how had she managed to slip away? And why hadn't she kept on going?

I couldn't fit her into this deal.

There's been malice in what she'd said about the brand. Oakes had gone stamping off in a fury. If he'd been working for her that could figure to make sense, and I could even see if they had a good thing how he would feel some riled at her bringing me in. But if it was him she was afraid of why hadn't she said so?

The more I poked and pushed at the business the less any part of it appeared to add up. A man could get just as far toting beans, boots and buttons. The trail took another of those sudden twists, widening some and still definitely dropping. A platter shaped valley begun to open out, looking lemon where the sun touched waving rolls of knee deep grass. There wasn't no sign of a building but there was horses scattered all through it. Must have been pretty nigh onto a hundred of them, some of the wilder ones flinging up their heads red roans and bays and sorrels and duns, as fine looking a bunch as a feller could ask for.

"A little potbellied," Oakes grinned, "an' rough from being out, but nothing' a few feeds of grain won't cure."

"A mite light for cow work," I said, looking over those nearest. "Them dish faced ones might have Arab in them."

"What you reckon they'll weigh?"

"Thousand, maybe. That blood bay with the snip won't top nine hundred."

Oakes fetched his glance back, nodding.

"How many you figuring on breaking?" I said.

"Many as you got time for."

I considered them again. These were short tailed horses. Taken in conjunction with the dished faces I had noticed, it seemed reasonable to suppose they were pretty well bred. "Ain't none of them acting like they're uncut studs."

"Mares an' geldin's," Oakes said, watching me. "You don't have to finish 'em. Green broke's all I want. Sooner the better."

"What's it worth?"

"Dollar a ride."

I looked at him then. I looked at him hard. The going wage for green broke learning a bronc to start, stop and turn was five bucks a head. Took about ten rides if you figured to get the job done.

I thought about Oakes and them eggs he'd ate. "What are they," I said, "gold plated or something?"

"All I know is I've got 'em to board. Only thing I got in 'em is what feed they've put away. You want to stomp 'em or don't you?"

"What's to prove I'll ever get paid?"

Oakes' eyes fanned around. He didn't bust into no flock of explanations. "You'll git paid," he said, "one way or another," and sent his horse jumping on up ahead.

Putting rides on broncs, like I mentioned before, ain't the easiest way in the world to make a living. That double pay looked good but a heap unlikely; and I still hadn't nothing but his word I'd collect.

I tagged along, uncommitted, to see what else he might decide to turn up.

After about ten minutes of eating his dust I come onto a hogback and, staring beyond, took in all that was left to be seen of this trough. Off there it pinched in, squeezing away through the gut of a pass that had a fence thrown across it.

The fence was cut brush stacked on end and held in place by a pair of stout ropes that had been wove through it. A girl was there, just in front, straddling one of them dish faced roans, both feet in the stirrups and a .44-77 Sharps across her lap.

That kind of gun ain't the sort you look to find in the hands of no woman. Without you know what you're doing it can lift you straight back into last week. It can knock down a buffalo at twelve hundred yards.

I couldn't guess, on that horse, how tall she might be but I could see enough, right from where I was then, to figure she wasn't no kind to write home about. She had on a man's hickory shirt, an open coat over it, her legs stuffed into a man's faded Levi's and a black flat crowned hat chin strapped to her jaw. I halfway thought I might be looking at Belle Starr.

It was the clothes, of course, and that authority she was packing.

Time I come up to where Oakes was talking I could see my estimate was somewhat short of doing her justice. She was in that first maturity that follows girlhood, with quick green eyes and red-gold hair, a faint suggestion of freckling across the bridge of her nose. But I'd been right about one thing. It showed in the glance she slanched across Oakes' shoulder.

"Farsom," he said, hearing me come up, "this here's my niece, Dimity Hale."

I took off my hat. "Pleasure, ma'am."

"Hello," she said, and turned back to Oakes. "I'm ready whenever you are."

Oakes' dry smile showed he got the message.

I put my hat back on, feeling about as comfortable as a bundle left on the parsonage doorstep. Oakes said, "You'll find water an' grub cached behind that red rock. I'll see that you get some more when it's needed."

He picked up his reins, kneed his horse around, the girl wheeling after him.

"Just a minute," I said. "Ain't you getting a bit ahead of yourself?"

His glance come around.

"I ain't said yet I'm hiring on for this deal."

He brought the grulla back with the lids of his eyes squeezed almost shut. "Well?"

"You got some threes and fours in this bunch. You want them broke, too?"

"I told you once. Everything you got time for."

"On the spreads I've worked they never touched anything younger than five. You're paying the same all down the fine?"

"Dollar a ride."

I give him back look for look. "I'll want that in writing."

He sat there so long with them dark eyes staring I was half expecting to see him go for his gun. But all he finally done was nod. "You'll git it," he grunted, and went larruping off. The girl never did look around. Not once.

* * *

THEY LEFT me with plenty of thinking to chew on. They left me so filled with notions I was about half minded to haul my freight. Then I'd remember what I had here. I'd remember Lupita. And while I stood bogged in the guff she had given me I would find myself staring at the face of Oakes' niece and the whole sorry go round would start up all over.

That Dimity female could sure rough a man up. She hadn't left me no more pride to, set down with than a range dick could sift from a sack of shucks'. Between the pair of them they had me so graveled I couldn't by God have told dung from wild honey.

I took a slow ride around. There wasn't no pens here and no stuff to make pens. There wasn't no land of shelter if it come up *a* storm. Just me and them broncs and the lemon curl of last year's grass. And the goddam quiet piled up so thick you could pretty near cut it.

I rode over to the red rock and had me a look at the grub situation. About enough for a week. The cache was a box built of planks set into the ground and covered over with rusty tin. I didn't see no water, but I knew there had to be some someplace and knocked around on Oakes' buckskin till I found it, a seep oozing out of the trough's far wall, dribbling down through green slime to collect two foot deep in a slab of red sandstone that was rimmed with gray clay. This clay, darkly damp, was all chopped up with hoof tracks, some of them still wet. Wasn't no green anyplace around but that puke on the wall.

I got me a drink and let the buckskin dip his muzzle.

There was still a little shade coming down off the cliff. Once the sun climbed into the top of its swing I could see that this trough was like to heat up considerable.

It was warm already.

Getting out of my jacket I folded and tucked it into the roll with my blankets and parkers and a half mile of tarp. I was traveling light, as they say over in Texas.

While I wasn't putting all my eggs in Oakes' basket it did look to be about time I got to work. I left my rifle there too to get it out of the way and, taking down my rope, shook out a loop and looked around for a target.

The first bronc I worked was a hammer headed moro, the only blue horse in the bunch. Then I rode two sorrels and an apron faced bay. It was damned sweaty business handling broncs in the open without no chute or squeeze or pen or nothing to cramp a horse down to. Time I got off that bay I was ready for a rest.

When I'd cooled off some I got me a drink. The more I thought about the wages Oakes had offered the less likely it seemed that I would ever collect them.

The whole deal smelled. All the way back to where I'd met up with Lupita. Even the way I had been sucked into this.

And yet there wasn't a thing a man could rightly put his finger on. Nothing, I mean, that mightn't be made to appear perfectly reasonable. Even Oakes out here plumb alone with two fillies. But the stink persisted, and smelled like trouble big trouble.

Take this caballado, for instance. One horse may look pretty much like another, but not to a man who'd punched cows for a living. There is as much difference in horses as there is in people. Really top horses are about as scarce as top hands, the percentage shaking down to about one in twenty. Yet this bunch Oakes had here, near as I could tell from looking, wouldn't number probably more than a dozen that shaped up below being mighty fine animals. Clean limbed, close coupled, sound of wind and long on bottom. For size, for muscling, for the way they handled themselves and stood, there wasn't a jughead in the lot.

That just wasn't natural. A kid could have told you this bunch was hand-picked. Small hoofed, thin legged, bright eyed every one of them. And every last one of them packing the same brand.

I got up off my heels and stepped back into leather. The buckskin whickered, shaking the flies away from his face. The shadows was building out from the wall; we had about three hours left to go. My appetite was beginning to catch up with me but I reckoned I could maybe top off a couple more. Shaking out my loop I eased in on a roan. We had quite a chase with him ducking and wheeling back and forth through the pack before I could get a clear chance. He stopped like he was shot when that rope snapped around him. Smart. The whole bunch was. They'd been roped at before.

But they hadn't been ridden. It was fight all the way. That bronc had more tricks than a dog has fleas. He stood like a stone while I was cinching the rig on I hauled his head around and swung up. Then he jumped sideways, dropped his bill and started pitching. He sun fished and twisted, swapped ends and pump handled. He tried to run out from under me. When he finally give up I couldn't of lasted another jump.

I cuffed him around for another few minutes, yanking the sonofabitch this way and that. He savvied all right, acting meeker than a kitten. I got off him then while he knew who was boss.

We scowled at each other and I couldn't help laughing. You could almost see the notions wheel through his head.

Don't let nobody tell you a horse has no humor.

I pulled off hackamore and kack and slapped his lathered rump. He threw up his tail and went squealing away to join the others.

He bad sure took it out of me.

FIVE

I WAS up the next morning at first crack of light, putting together a breakfast over a fire of dried horse apples. I hadn't got must rest, though sleeping on the ground come just as natural as breathing. I was stiff and filled with groans from that jouncing but it was the things in my head that had made me so twisty.

That Squabble O brand Lupita had called 'Cyclops' was the only iron these broncs was marked with, and I'd have bet any chance I had of collecting it had come out of Mexico. Probably come in a hurry from some big holding like Valdepenas or the hacienda at Nacozari. Stolen, of course. Run up this smuggler's trail and left with Oakes for board and breaking. It wouldn't make no difference that I hadn't stole them if some of those long eared sons of generals with braid all over come up here and found them.

If they'd of been took recent there'd have been more sign. They'd been here long enough anyway to put on pot bellies from eating cured grass.

Despite the number of things I didn't like about this

deal it was still a fair setup for a man hunting cover no getting away from that. Or from thinking of those two females living under one roof alone with Fred Oakes and whatever he was up to.

I was scrubbing sand in the skillet it and a bent fork being the only eating tools I'd found when I remembered Oakes asking if I was kin to Curly Bill. What I wondered, had prompted that notion? It wasn't the sort of question a man would ordinary ask.

Curly Bill, if you don't know it, was about as rough as they'd come in this country. A Texican. A loud laughing clown with black hair and smith's shoulders, quick on the shoot and with no more scruples than you'd find in a snake. Dead now, they said, killed by Wyatt Earp someplace in the brush; but a little bit back, when I'd been riling John Chisum on behalf of Murphy Dolan, Curly Bill in this region had been the kingpin bandido and had rode sometimes with forty men at his back.

No kind of guy to stamp your boot and yell bool at. All the owlhoots at this end of the catclaw had owed some manner of allegiance to him, and he had sure cut a swath with his stealing and shooting. He'd took cattle wholesale from both sides of the line. He'd killed a mort of smugglers' and sacked several towns, including Matamoras. John Bingo rode with him and the Clantons and McLowerys. He run off Army horses but there was nothing cheap about him. He come and went at his own sweet will. He'd even dabbled in politics, voting a batch of chickens and pigs and, by God, got away with it.

Now here was Fred Oakes wanting to know first pop out of the box if I was kin to him.

I chucked the pan back into the grub box, caught up

my bridle and went after the buckskin. I'd left him hobbled for safe keeping so I didn't have to tromp more than a mile to come up with him. I fetched him in and put my rig on, kneed the wind out of his gut and took up the slack. I rode him across and let him wet his whistle. Wrapping a knee round the horn then I got out Durham and papers and twisted up a smoke while I looked the outfit over.

I didn't spot nothing I hadn't seen before.

The sun was beginning to gild the far wall. The air was sweet with the smells of grass and horses and the sky overhead was a clean bright blue. About as peaceful a view as a feller could ask. The things on my mind didn't look so dark now. There was probably nothing wrong with Oakes a fuller acquaintance wouldn't set straight.

I shook out my loop and got to work.

* * *

THREE DAYS SLIPPED BY, the weather staying clear, the nights continuing cool and the grub getting lower in the red rock cache. The job progressed, moving a little faster now that I'd got in the swing of it.

Nineteen of Oakes' broncs had a good work behind them and I was topping the twentieth about the middle of the morning when some of them others set up a racket of nickering.

I couldn't catch me no look. The clown between my knees was trying to drive all the bones straight up through my noggin. When he finally jumped off the dime and took to weaving I had all I could do to keep from losing the leathers. I thought for sure my head would tear off. It was like some bastard had the back of my belt and was shaking me same as a wrung out bar rag.

Then the damn bronc stuck his bill in the ground. While my teeth was shifting he slatted his sails and hopped for mama.

I went through the air. I come down, throwing up dust like a plow with my chin, all spraddled out and piling up in a heap.

When I finally got my face pulled clear it felt like half my joints was unhinged. Probably looked that way too if you could seen me trying to get up out of it. I didn't hardly know one end from the other.

I'd forgot about the nickering. Alls I could hear was this roarin like a big wind rushing through me. All I could see was a whirling of ground, yellow grass, sky and horses.

Then they flopped into place. I heard the laugh and, twisting my head, seen her settin there shaking like what I had done was the funniest ever Oakes' sorrel-topped niece, still in pants and still lugging that chunk of artillery.

"You'll wet your britches," I said, "an' I hope you do!"

It wasn't no way to talk to a lady. I didn't give a whoop if she. whirled straight around and went back to Oakes with it. I looked for her to.

Her cheeks fired up but all she done was set there.

She didn't look furious or even insulted, nor was she ignoring me like she had when her uncle was around.

She suddenly chuckled. "You git hurt?"

I reckon I did look pretty foolish. "Generally," I

said, "I pass the hat about now," and watched to see if it would fetch back the grin.

"Hat?" she said.

I limped over and fished it out of a pear clump. "Just an old Farsom saying. How long you been with your uncle?"

She pushed a dangle of hair from her face and continued to stare while I picked out the stickers. A queer one, all right. You might have reckoned by her stare I had two heads or a tail, maybe. "The old man," I said, wanting to shake her, "Fred Oakes."

"Oh. I've always been here... pretty near, anyway. He isn't my uncle not really."

I must of looked blank. "Fred found me," she said. "Near some burnt wagons. I guess I wasn't much bigger'n a minute."

It was my turn to stare. "Mean he give you a home? Raised you up?" It sure didn't fit my picture of Fred Oakes.

Her green eyes, widening, darkened. "He wants you back at the house."

"What for? And where's that grub he was supposed to send out?"

She did smile then, somewhat meager like and doubtful. She said, and it was like Fred Oakes himself talking, "I'm not in the business of answering questions. You better climb back on that bronc or you never will be able to do anything with him."

Didn't help my temper none to be reminded. I got my rope and went after him.

I should have known better than to think I could ever get near enough on foot. Feeling like a fool I had to come back after the buckskin and get up on him bareback.

Time I caught the bronc and got back in the saddle Dimity Hale was halfway to the cliffs. This was a four year old and some set up with himself for having dumped me. He tried to fling me off again as soon as I got on him. Then he reached around to bite off my leg.

I worked him over with hat and spurs. The more he bucked the worse I used him. He was tough as a white oak and twice as ornery as any mule. I began to wonder if I was going to make it.

When he quit the girl was clean out of sight.

I was mightily tempted to ignore Oakes' summons. My job, as laid out, was to put rides on these horses; I wasn't being paid to run errands for Oakes. But he had sent the girl after me. Maybe he'd changed his mind about the deal. I looked around for the buckskin, found he'd gone frisking off with a bunch of them others. Swearing, I put the hooks to the bronc.

He took off like a bat out of Carlsbad. I cuffed him with my hat and got him pointed at the cliffs where they come together in that trail the girl had come in by. He must of figured to run out from under me. He had plenty of speed, I'll say that for him.

The girl was waiting just beyond the first bend. It was plain she didn't much approve of what she saw "What are you tryin' to do kill him?"

"I thought you was in a hurry," I said.

She give me another of them long cool looks and without saying anything started her horse on past. I put out a fist and grabbed her arm and the snout of that Sharps rammed me hard in the belly.

I let out a grunt. I let go of her, too. Her eyes looked green as two pieces of glass.

"When I want to be pawed I'll tell you," she said. "Now get on back to the ranch like Fred told you."

There didn't seem to be much else I could do, not with that rifle staring down my throat.

* * *

MY RETURN to Silver Spring was done a heap quicker than the way I had left, but it wasn't no ride I hanker to look back on. I didn't have much time for thinking. Twice the damn bronc tried to take off a leg by scraping me into the sides of the walls.

By the grace of good luck most of the hide he took off was his own, but that didn't keep him content for long. He tried a dozen times to get his teeth into me and every time he made his move I put another lump on his jaw. I had to watch him all the way, every minute, with the chances odds on that before he got through he would pile me up in spite of all hell.

He had lather all over by the time we got in. You'd of thought, the way he was using up energy, he'd have been plumb docile. He was wet as a cow's tongue but when I swung off damned if he didn't try to slam a hoof into me. I jumped for the porch with the halter shank, sloshed it twice around a post and left him there tied solid. I knew one thing for sure: he had all the ride I aimed to put on him!

I wiped the blood off my lip and sung out. When nobody answered I put a fist to the door.

"You don't have to break it down," Lupita called. "Come on in and take the weight off your feet."

I pushed open the door. She was over by the cupboard putting dishes away, but the first thing I seen was this guy with the gun. He had it pointed straight at me, teeth bared, the eyes looking like burnt holes in his face.

SIX

HE WAS BACKED AGAINST A WALL, a stringy wisp
of a feller with a weak chinned jaw, fright stretching the
skin tight as vellum across the bones of his skull beneath
its thatch of red hair. The gun a gambler's pepperbox
begun waggling in his fist like the tail of a nervous cat.

Lupita screamed. "Not him you fool! That's
Farsom, Jake's hired hand!"

Indecision spread like cracks through his stare but
the revolver's yawing focus never quit my shape till
Fred Oakes, sounding disgusted, growled, "For Chrissake, Brace, git aholt of yerself." Only then did its
muzzle grudgingly dip toward the floor.

My tongue rasped over two mighty dry lips. The
nearness of it put claws in my stomach. A kind of wild
fury begun to pound through but, before I could scrape
up enough spit to cuss, a board someplace retched out a
thin wheeze. In a quiet, thick carpeted with unspoken
thoughts, a second guy come limping in from the back.

Younger, this one, awkwardly unsure in his patched
hand me downs and runover boots. Not more, I put

him, than maybe sixteen, though big for his age. Tow hair showed under his hat's floppy brim, milky eyes, the merest nubbin of a nose. His pants was kept up by a twist of frayed rope. Between pants and shirt was wedged the notched butt of a nickel-plated pistol.

With him at my right and the redhead off to the plumb farthest left of where I might keep peeled eyes on the both of them it didn't seem no time to be flapping my jaw. Particular after I got a squint at Fred Oakes.

He looked like a man coming off a bad drunk.

Could have been the way that light struck across him pouring off the rocks. He kept rubbing together his goddam teeth the way a wormy cow might do and breathing like he'd just run a full four-forty.

He clamped a hand to the table and got out of his chair like it was a hard thing to do. He took time then to swaller.

"Farsom" he said, and cleared the squeaks from his throat. "Farsom, these here is friends from over the mountain. Cort Brace," he said, jerking his chin at the pepperbox, "an Alamagordo. Boys..." He grabbed for more breath with his eyes swiveling round like two bats in the buckbrush, "have yerselfs a good look at my pardner, Flick Farsom."

I could cheerfully have knocked the teeth down his neck. The he was bad enough; they weren't his friends, and, more to the point, I wasn't his partner. But the worst was putting that handle to my name. He hadn't no call at all to do that.

I never looked at the kid. Cort Brace the redhead in black coat and grimy linen stood froze to his pepperbox stiff as a gatepost. Nothing come through the gray cant of that stare.

For me, nothing had to. It went without saying if he'd been around at all he would know who Flick Farsom was, the part I had played in that Lincoln County shootout.

I took, a wrap around my temper.

The arrival of this pair had certainly upset Oakes. He looked to have aged ten years since leaving me out on that grass, though I couldn't see anything about a fool kid or this rablty tinhorn to put his wind up.

Calling him a liar wouldn't help any. It looked like I'd better string along for a spell Jill I could see where the play was headed. I wondered if these jaspers had come about the horses.

Lupita, with a sniff, went off to the kitchen.

Brace's hands when I looked back at him was empty. His glance slid away and with the barest of nods he went over to a window and stood there staring out.

The kid never give me that much even. Still glowering at Oakes he flopped into a chair. "I don't know why you had to drag him"

"I'll do the talkin'," Brace said. "You want to make yourself useful go out an' walk that horse you'll find tied to the porch."

The kid didn't look like he was figuring to go anywhere, but he got up when Brace turned and went grumbling out. I pulled the chair against the wall and tipped back in it, crossing my arms. Oakes didn't seem in much of a hurry to get at whatever it was he had wanted with me. Maybe all he'd wanted was to give these sports a chance to find out he wasn't quite alone.

I said to the gambler, "What's your interest in this outfit?"

They didn't either of them like it. Brace, at least,

kept the scowls off his face. "I expect," he said with a sly grin for Oakes, "I'm what you might call another of Fred's pardners'."

Oakes liked that even less by the look. I could hear Lupita moving around in the kitchen.

A man would of had to been deaf, dumb and blind not to feel the things that was poking their heads up. I would stick, I reckoned, till I got some chuck in me, then pick up the dun arid roll my cotton. Two girls and Fred and now this pair all holed up together was no kind of deal for any gent who aimed to put wrinkles on his horns.

Brace pulled out a chair and, straddling it, said, "Whatever happened to that girl you had here, Fred the one called you 'uncle'?"

Oakes pushed around the chaw in his mouth. "You'll find her, like enough, if you look."

"Well, now, I might just do that," Brace smiled, and got up. "That your horse outside, Farsom?"

"Belongs to the outfit."

"You object if I borry him?"

"Help yourself."

But, soon as he went out, I said Oakes, "You think that's smart? Putting him onto that girl?"

He stepped over to the window, come hotfooting back.

"Listen," he said, "I'll make this right."

"Don't waste your breath. Soon's I put a few beans in the boiler I'm cuttin' my stick. What about the girl?"

He grabbed my arm. "You can't go now not while I got that pair on my shirttail!"

I eyed him, quiet. "I can go any time I make up my mind to." I threw off his hand. I got out of the chair.

"God damn it," Oakes snarled, "will you listen a minute! Them sonsabitches is fixin' to *kill* me."

"You should of thought about that before you run off their horses."

"Horses?" Oakes cursed. "Them goddamn broncs ain't got nothin' to"

"Neither have I. Ain't aimin' to, either."

From downwind someplace come a flutter of hoof sound. Oakes, with his eyes looking big as slop buckets, whirled and run from the house.

Lupita come from the kitchen. "Flick... Fred's right! That pair mean to kill him before—"

"Guys don't go round killing other guys for nothing."

She didn't look half so cuddly as she had. She was scairt, all right. You could see it in her stare, the way her breath jumped. "What do you figure I can do?" I said, watching her.

"You got to keep those fools from killing Jake."

I said, "You mean Fred, don't you?"

She'd been excited, of course. Her nod acknowledged it. "I won't lie to you, Flick. His real name's Gauze he was in on those Skeleton Canyon massacres. I was afraid if I told you, you wouldn't come out."

There ain't nothing like making a clean breast of things for disarming a man if you got the right shape for it. I could pretty near hear the wheels going round behind that little girl look she'd dug up for me.

Jake Gauze. Well, it figured. One of Curly Bill's bunch, I didn't wonder he'd been riled when she come dragging me in.

The red lips grinned. "Didn't I tell you," she laughed, "you could write your own ticket?"

Maybe my look wasn't bright as it should of been. She said, coming nearer, "It wasn't Jake wanted you, it was *me*," and held her mouth up.

"Reckon you better spell that out."

The black eyes blazed. "Lupita don throw herself at *any* man, hombre!"

A guy could believe that. With them lumps of warm flesh joggling around like ripe melons she didn't look to need to; but a feller would of had to been dumber than me... I backed off for more air.

I could feel the old Adam climbing through my blood. It was plain what she was offering. Question was *why?*

She come right up against me and I never moved a finger.

Breath whistled out of her. "What are you a mouse!"

"A man could get hurt reachin' for something like that," I said, hot around the collar.

She spun away from me in scorn, flouncing over to a window looking out across the porch. Almost at once she put her back to it, still angry but seeming someway desperate. "You've got to stay."

"Give me one good reason."

She said, "Don't you feel like you owe him anything!"

"He's had good measure from what grub I've et."

"You're impossible!" she blazed. Then her eyes winnowed down. "Would you stay for a sixth?"

"A sixth of what?"

Fred Oakes come in. Before she could move he'd cuffed her hard across the face, force enough in it to send her reeling against the wall. "You goddam slut!"

Seldom have I seen such fury in a man. He fetched his stare around to me. "No matter what she told you them horses ain't in this you're not gettin' a one of 'em! Understand?"

I felt like telling him what he could do with them horses. Then I got hold of myself. A man could look pretty foolish trading insults with a loony.

"Never mind," I said. "I'm gettin' out."

Still watching me, he scraped the back of a hand across his cheeks. "I hope you brought your walkin' shoes."

"What's that supposed to mean?"

"Means we're afoot. Goddamn kid run all the ponies outa that pen. Choused 'em to hell an' gone off down the canyon!"

SEVEN

HE WATCHED me with a slippery grin, peering from the door when I stepped out to have a look for myself. I went far enough to know this wasn't no bluff he'd put up.

It appeared I was pretty well stuck with this deal; they had run off my dun along with the rest. Remembering the hours it had took to get here I wasn't even about to put hope in a shank's mare. If there'd been nothing else, saddle boots plain wasn't built for hiking.

Which ain't to say I'd give up by a jugful.

I went back to the house.

Oakes or Gauze or whatever his name was, was still in the doorway picking his teeth with a sharpened match. He turned and went in and come out with a chair. He put his butt into it cool as you please and, tilting back, propped his legs up. That grin had again got the lips off his teeth.

I hunkered down by a post. He wasn't looking at me but off towards them rocks masking the mouth of the canyon where he'd shown me the bones he'd said had come from dead smugglers.

If this was Jake Gauze it was a cinch he'd helped kill them.

I considered him slanchways, wondering what he'd found to be tickled at. Not ten minutes back he'd been so wild and mixed up he'd took his hand to the girl and knocked her half silly, and all on account of he had jumped to the notion she'd been about to deal me a share in that bronc pool. Before that he'd been half out of his pants in the conviction that that pair had come here to murder him. Lupita apparently had thought so too, yet there he pat as smug and complacent as a frog on a lily pad waiting for flies.

Either he hadn't been scairt but that didn't make sense. He'd been scairt, right enough. He'd come back from the corrals mad as a drunk squaw, howling them two had put us afoot. In a towering rage he'd lit into her. Between that business and this grin on his mug was just a handful of grumbles. Was it something he'd got out of her while I'd been gone? Or was the damn fool chuckling because I was stuck here?

A little time slipped away, maybe a couple or three minutes.

Oakes hitched over on one hip. "How you doin' out there?" He made it sound real chummy. "Shapin' up pretty good are they?"

"Soon's I can get me a horse, I'm clearing out," I said.

"*I* wouldn't count too much on it," he said, sounding smug again. "That tinhorn, Brace, ain't no amachoor, you know."

"He ain't no horse breaker, either."

Oakes peered at me, scowling, not getting it. I jerked my jaw at the rocks. "Ain't that him on the saddle?"

The legs of Oakes' chair hit the floor with a thump, but he didn't get out of it. Like me he just stared, holding silent. Then he laughed.

It was something to see, if you like watching cripples. That old pepperbox wasn't in sight at the moment and not much of Brace, belly down like he was. The kid, with the chin plumb nudging his brisket and the reins of Oakes' horse hoisted over one shoulder, looked to be furnishing most of the power for this travel, sloggin along on his runover boots and apparently not caring if school kept or not.

"Have an accident, boys?" I called out, cheerful.

The kid never lifted his eyes off the trail, never paused, swerved or nothing, but Brace quit groaning long enough to curse.

They come into the yard and hauled up by the porch. We could see then what ailed him. He was a sure enough mess. The shirt was half out of the back of his pants and from shoulder blades down to the backs of his knees he was practically plastered with silverspined cholla.

"Just goes to show," I said, "what can happen to a gent that takes another feller's horse."

Oakes had been having himself a real time admiring that slob with all the cactus stuck in him. Now he broke it off short, all the breath wheezing out of him. It was a toss-up which looked the meanest, him or that kid.

Brace said, "You going to for Chrissake stan' there all day?"

The kid flung down the reins. "Yeah," I said, "you better ease him off."

I didn't notice much wrong with Brace's talking talent except his remarks run to pretty lurid language. Alamagordo looked meaner than a new sheared sheep. "C'mon," he snarled, "git down here an' give me a hand!"

Oakes stayed where he was, and me with him.

I thought for a minute the kid was going to go for his pistol he was so goddam mad. But Lupita come out and, ignoring the both of us, tossed him a pair of fence cutting tools. "Try these."

Even with them pliers Brace alternately howling and swearing the kid took pretty near a plum half hour to get enough room cleared for hand holds. He worked till the light got too poor to see by, and then with the tinhorn folded over his shoulder staggered onto the porch.

Brace swearing a blue streak what time he wasn't groaning.

The girl held the door. "Put him in that back bedroom." She followed them in.

I looked at Oakes. "What have they got on you?"

He forted himself up behind that scraggle of whiskers, hunching there like he was glued to the chair.

I got out my pipe. Trying the bowl with my thumb I put the fire to it while I tried to decide if I should take Oakes' horse. It was a powerful temptation. I was pulled two ways, knowing I'd probably never get a better chance. I could take care of Oakes a tap from my gun barrel would hold him quiet, but what about them two fillies? Same thing must have been in Oakes' head. He got up sudden and, stepping out of reach, said, "I'll put up that horse," and was off the steps before I got my legs under me.

Probably just as well. I don't reckon I'd of got far, worrying over them females. They weren't my lookout but after seeing the way he had swung on Lupita I wouldn't of felt right just up and going off.

Something else got to chewing my tender disposition. What if Oakes, out of sight, piled into that saddle and kept straight on?

I was minded to go after him. Fact is I was on my way when this other notion hit and brought me, scowling, to a standstill.

Might be best to let him do it. From what I'd seen it appeared a heap likely if he yanked his picket pin Brace and that kid would be right on his tail. No trouble at all then for me to grab a horse; and if the girls wanted to leave I never doubted *that* part, I could mount them up too.

Lupita come out again. "Flick is that you?"

She looked tall against the lights. She was a damn attractive woman.

I went back. "He's took off," I said, "to put up his grulla. If his feet's cold enough he may skedaddle and you'll be rid of him."

"Flick you've got to stop him!"

I guess the lights showed my astonishment. She said with the words tumbling over each other, "I know it sounds crazy but he mustn't.... Call it a woman's intuition. Something in here" She clamped a hand over her bosom. "You've got to stop him!"

"Well... I thought you didn't want him killed?"

"Hurry!" she cried. "We can't let him get away!"

So I went peltin towards the corrals, all mixed up

in my head but doing her bidding, distrusting the woman but infected by her urgency. She certainly knew Oakes better than I did. If she wanted him around...

I didn't, as it turned out, have to go at all. I was busting around the last of them rocks when his voice come against me like the rasp of a saw. "Whoa up! Strike a light!"

"Farsom," I told him, feeling ringy and foolish.

"Figures," he said, coming up with a chuckle. "Reckon you thought I'd took out."

I wondered if he'd seen the gun in my fist.

"Well, no harm done." He patted my shoulder, turned me back towards the house. "You don't want to take all my wife says fer gospel."

* * *

I MUST of choked hard enough to be heard clean to Roswell. I turned cold and then hot, the heat swirling over me, remembering the way she'd took hold of her bosom.

Oakes nudged me into motion. "She's wrapped smarter men than you round her finger. Old game with her, playin' boys fer suckers."

We tramped on in silence.

I was thankful for the dark and filled with a mighty burning.

"You'll git over it," Oakes said. "Once bit, twice shy. A good thing to remember."

I was remembering plenty.

He didn't say no more till we come into the lights. Then, kind of under his breath, he said, "You want to play this smart, let her think you stopped me. Mebbe, given enough rope, she'll tip her hand."

"If she's that kind."

"They broke the mold, after her. Wouldn't surprise me none if it turns out she sent fer Here, let me go ahead. You keep right behind me."

I thought at first she'd gone inside but she was still there, waiting, backed into the shadows between two windows.

Oakes, ignoring her, went on in. I'd of done the same but her hand, snakin' out, latched onto my arm. "Flick." She drew me into the shadows. I could feel her breath on my cheek. She said, "Was he?"

"He didn't quite make it."

She said softly, "Thanks," and hugged my arm. "I'll make it up to you." She pushed me toward the door.

The perfidy of her nearly turned my guts. But for her I might have ridden out of this mess. In the Bible they had a name for her kind.

I shoved her out of my thoughts. She went into the kitchen. I looked over at Oakes. "Think he'll five through it?"

Oakes was sprawled in a chair with a glass in his fist. Looked like his mind was a hundred miles away. He was a hard man to like but I could almost feel sorry for him, being tied up to a dame like that.

The door to the back bedroom was shut but you could hear the occasional skreak of a bedspring through the interminable murmur of Brace's moans and mumblings. Alamagordo said presently, sounding fed up, "Either hold still, by Gawd, or pick the rest out yourself!"

I went back to the porch and dug out my pipe, but

the smoke was no good. I kept thinking about Lupita, about her lying eyes and her lying red mouth and calling myself twenty lands of a fool. But supposing, I thought, it had been him that lied? that she wasn't his wife!

I got up and knocked out my pipe. She was probably what he had called her; all my experience endorsed it and there had been real conviction in the sound of Oakes' voice.

Jake Gauze she had named him, a fly by night vulture; but all I had was her word for it, a woman I'd come onto in a Tombstone deadfall, a harpy who preyed on a man's natural feelings to entangle me in this damned web of hate and treachery.

I grinned, a little sheepish. I guessed that was piling it on pretty thick. From what I had heard of him, if Oakes was Jake Gauze he could probably make out to take care of himself.

I got to pawing around. It was astonishing how little I was able to turn up, aside from the fact the man had had a bad name. He'd been with Curly Bill or certainly had been named with him, Old Man Clanton, Ike and Billy Clanton, Tom and Frank McLowery, John Bingo, Jim Hughes, Joe Hill, Rattlesnake Bill, Charlie Thomas and Charlie Snow, in that canyon massacre that had sometime in July of '81 wiped out Don Miguel Garcia and his smuggler train, only one 'handsome stripling' getting away to tell of it. Loot from this foray was held at seventy-five thousand in Mexican silver. A month or so later the gang had gotten wind of another and even bigger expedition bound for Tucson by way of that trail. When Jim Hughes arrived Curly Bill was in Charleston. With no time to fiddle around getting word to him,

Hughes set the stage himself, rigging an ambush with the outlaws over ninety thousand in Mexican money plus thirty-nine bars of very solid gold. Gauze was figured to have been in on this, too. It was, even by repute, the only other dido with which I could connect him.

Now another idea got hold of me.

When Oakes had come in like the wrath of God to send Lupita banging into that wall, I had figured it was because he'd reckoned she was cutting me in for a sixth of them horses. Could have been jealous rage. Or he could have jumped to some conclusion that had nothing to do with her or them broncs like maybe his cut of the swag from them killings. If he still had it.

I had to admit this didn't look a heap likely.

Outlaw money is quick to the pocket and, generally speaking, even faster spent. Plenty figured they would pile up a stake but few of them done it; not even Jack Ketcham. John Chisum that I had quit for Murphy Dolan had taken a mort of cattle out of Texas but he probably couldn't rub three dimes together now. Jesse James had died strapped, Cole Younger and Quantrill likewise. Old man Clanton and he had been a shrewd devil, had been pretty near stony when a bushwhacker bullet come along with his name.

Still, it didn't look reasonable when a man stood off for Oakes to have got in such a sodpawing fury over a jag of broncs he'd said himself didn't belong to him. If a man had put enough trust in his wife but Oakes hadn't talked like he put any at all in her.

I went on in to find him still in his chair. His eyes looked so glassy I thought remembering that tumbler he had got himself plastered, but he come out of it hearing me and, scowling, made some attempt to pull himself together. Twisting his head he bellered, "What the goddam hell have you done with the grub!"

From the region of the stove there came a racket of pots and pans; she'd been keeping it warm, apparently, waiting for Brace and the kid to come in. She must of had it ready because she come right in with it two platters of sow belly and half a kettle of ham hocks and beans. "Pull up a chair," Oakes growled, and done likewise. By the time we were settled she was back with the Java, pouring the mugs and darting looks at Oakes slanchways.

He shoved out an arm when she turned back to the stove. "By God, fer once you'll eat with me!" She stood with hands gripped together, dark eyes on him, nervous. "But Fred... we've got guests...."

"I never ast 'em here! Now get onto that bench and put some grub on yer plate."

Smiling stiffly she climbed over it and got her legs out of sight. I reckon she was furious but if she was it didn't show. Strain, pulling her skin tight, was the only difference noticeable, that and the fact she spoke only when talked at. Oakes chewed noisily, shoveling food to his face as though he'd news a bad famine was just around the corner.

Mostly Lupita kept her eyes on her plate. Once when she looked up I winked. "Brace say how he come to pick up that cactus?"

She didn't wink back but said civilly enough that, according to Alamagordo, they'd run onto Dimity Hale in one of the canyon's narrower twists, that before either one of them could open their mouths she'd whipped up that Sharps and loosed a blue whistler. All that saved Brace was the brass horn of my saddle. The bronc with that blast and the slug's shock of impact had stuck his bill in the ground and heaved Brace like a flap-jack into a five-foot clump of spined cholla.

This account of Brace's misadventures appeared to have put Oakes in somewhat better fettle. His belly shook. "That Dimity!" he said with every evidence of admiration, the fervence of which was not lost upon Lupita.

He looked around to grin at me.

"Guess you reckoned old Fred a pretty sorry bastard sendin' two like them off to badger that girl, but I knowed what I was doin'. She coulda killed Brace jest as easy. Matter of fact," he scowled, "I figgered she would was kinda hopin' she'd ventilate the both of 'em."

He had certainly give me something to remember. I hid my ire behind a lift of Java, but one thing was plain as the hump on a camel. Any jasper as twisty as that would bear watching.

When I glanced up again his look was filled with listening.

Took another couple heartbeats before I picked up myself the faint *clop clop* of a walking horse that finally whittled to a stop someplace out beyond the porch. From Oakes' frozen look I knew it wasn't Dimity.

He had both hands spread flat against the top of the table.

EIGHT

HE LOOKED like a gopher about to pop in its hole.

A door, creaking open, sounded raucous as the top being pried off a coffin. A thump of feet come towards us. The gambler hove into sight, dethorned, sponged off and swelled up in his clothes with the courage he'd apparently augmented from a bottle.

He smelt like Saturday night at Big Emma's. His glance, darting over our faces, bugged a httle as he sniffed at the stillness. With his nose coming up like a rabbit's he stopped so short the kid, limping after, rammed into him.

Brace, shoving the kid off his elbow, in the fog of his libations tried on a grin for size. "Well!" he exclaimed, blearily blinking. "You can't raise a ghost without you grab hoi' of han's."

"Ghost..." Lupita stiffened. In the whiteness of her cheeks the staring eyes was black as coals. "What ghost?"

So choked was her voice I had to guess at the words.

The crazy tinhorn whacked his thigh. "The ghost of

Curly Bill!" he chortled, and flung back his head in a gurgle of guffaws.

Something almost frightening got into the feel of the thickening quiet. Across it come a hail from the dark more a flutterous whisper it sounded to me. "Hallo-o-o the house!"

Thin as a thread, horribly bloating, the call crept and curled through that jumpety hush. Then the question, "Someone call me?"

You'd of swore Oakes had petrified. Not a breath moved in nor out of him.

Leather squealed under shifted weight. Come a tinkle of spur chains, feet slapping ground, inescapably nearer. These come after the Voice, one by one, to circle and join in their romp of the room.

Sweat stood out on Oakes' lip like rain.

Feet stomped across the porch, knuckles thumped. "You all dead in there?"

Again Oakes astonished me. "Come in, Bill," he growled, pushing up from his chair.

Lupita clutched at her throat.

The man who came in was a swaggering dandy with a fierce black mustache and a good-natured grin. A handsome devil with a real air about him.

There was gloves on his hands. While he was peeling them I took a sharp look. Brown pants he wore over the tops of bright boots and a brown frock coat open all the way down. A blue cravat bound the stand-up collar and there was the carriage of him, too, his importance an observable quality as plain to grasp as unquestionably his, as the feet inside those fine Justin boots.

A wine colored weskit embroidered in yellow was

tight buttoned over his chest, with a length of gold cable swung from pocket to pocket above the soft blaze of a turkey red sash. One other item no eye would of missed was two bone handled sixshooters pouched in brown leathers, strapped so they held back the skirts of his coat.

He said, 'Tour servant, ma'am," with a whimsical grin, his bow of an elegance not to be matched except by the charm of some Mex hacendado. With his hundred dollar hat rucked under his arm he shut out the night and come back to us looking as completely at ease as if he'd been made, blood brother to everyone.

I wondered how many of this outfit knew him. Oakes sure enough. Probably Lupita though she seemed, I thought, somewhat less than delighted. One thing I'd have bet: he was *not* Curly Bill. He had the mustache, and more guts than John Chisum who could stare down a mountain cat, but his hair didn't have as much curl as a Injun's his whole build was different.

He tossed the hat carelessly not two foot from the gambler who jumped back in such alarm I had to grin in spite of myself.

Every move this hombre made was done with a sort of flourish. Put me in mind of one of them play-acting fellers. His voice was strong and deep as a snake oil peddler's and, just now with his stare swiveling back to Oakes, so bland new butter wouldn't melt in his mouth.

"Come, come, good host. Make me known to your friends."

Something more felt than seen passed between them nothing a guy could put a handle to.

Oakes' sigh was the kind that comes out of old dogs. "You know my wife..."

"Know that one, too. Pink Cort Brace." The feller's grin skewered .the tinhorn with a contempt so plain you could pretty near taste it. "Sort of figured he'd probably put in here for water."

Whatever had brought these people together and never for a minute did I think such a bunch had just happened to turn up, he was giving the gambler a chance to get out. Maybe it wasn't the whole shape of his meaning, but this much stood out public as paint.

Seemed like Brace thought so too, the way he colored.

Oakes, with his lip skun back a little, nodded. "Gent to the left there's my pardner, Farsom 'Flick' they called him in the Seven Rivers country. Kid come with Pink." Oakes' stare cut around. "Boys," he said; on an upswing of breath, "meet Bill Ivory," and sat abruptly down.

The man peered at him, concerned. "You ailin'?"

"Nothin'," Oakes grumbled, "I can't make out to put up with."

Ivory's eyes let go of him and, ignoring the kid, wiped a look over me. "You buying into this?"

"Does it make any difference?"

His cold grin flashed. He took his look at the girl. "And how are you, Mrs. Oakes?"

"Feeling pretty fair till you walked in."

Ivory chuckled. "What I've always liked about you. Straight as an arrow, sharp as cut glass." He dropped a hip on the table, little imps of mischief jumping up and down behind the glint of that glance. "Any luck?"

She flounced off to the kitchen with a wriggle and a scowl, but not before I'd seen the fury that was in her.

"Be a cruel waste to have a woman like that folded

over her sewin' like a hog with its throat slit." Above the twist of his grin Ivory's bold look shuttled across the blobs of our faces. It didn't seem like to me he was more than half funning. "By the way," he called after her, "where at's that filly you been fetchin' up for Red? Filled out any, has she?"

Lupita said, cool enough, "Better ask Pink. Way I heard, she ran him into a cactus."

Color plowed into Brace's face. Bill Ivory laughed but Oakes appeared deaf as a gatepost. Ivory winked. "What does a feller have to do to get fed here?"

"He has to be around," Lupita spat, "when its ready!"

Brace muttered, "Reckon I'll turn in," and turned for the hall.

"Door you're hunting's over yonder," Ivory motioned.

"Better take a blanket. Gets right down chilly up here before morning.

The kid, who had got up to follow, looked around with a scowl but Brace kept going.

He was nearly to the hall when Ivory said real soft, "I'm taking that room myself. Steer away from it."

Brace, snarling, come around and, yanking open the door, stomped off across the porch so mad you could pretty near hear his teeth crack. Alamagordo, looking puckered around the edges, limped along in his wake.

Ivory stepped through after them and, just out of sight, called, "You there, kid! Put that horse in the corral. Rub him down good and see that he's grained. When you get that done I want some hay forked to him."

He stepped back in and closed the door.

I expect it was pretty plain what I thought. Under his mustache I seen the gleam of Ivory's teeth. "You can't bake a cake without you break a few eggs."

I could of said several things, they was right on my tongue. But how he treated that kid wasn't no skin off my butt.

Oakes, across the room, was deep sunk in his rocker-sunk, by the look of him, in more ways than one/ Ivory, considering him, scooped up his hat, He said towards the kitchen, "Anybody wants me I'll be in that back room." And he went off down the hall.

Not until we heard the door shut did anyone move. Outside, unseen, the hoofs of a horse made solid but diminishing lumps of sound against the empty growl of Brace's cursing.

Lupita stepped sober faced out of the kitchen, hauling up by Oakes' chair. "You better tell him." she said.

Behind the deep crevices of shrunken cheeks Oakes sat like a mummy.

Impatience came into Lupita's black stare. "You can't hold them off without help!" A wildness got into her tones, "You better do what you have to while you've still got the—"

"Keep your voice down, you fool!"

He looked alive enough now. No matter what they were or had been to each other, it was plain her worries wasn't bothering him none. You couldn't see that look he give her and stay very solid with any other notion.

He got out of his chair and stood uncertainly silent, obviously trying to pin down what I thought. Now he nervously pawed at his scraggle of whiskers. "Reckon you kin see I'm in a pretty tight bind."

"You've sure put me into one."

Oakes, scowling fiercely, took a turn about the room. I couldn't tell, when he stopped, if it was me he was eyeing or something in his head. "How much," he said, "would it cost to put your gun on my side of this deal?"

"What's it worth?"

I could see he was worried, but even with the fright working on him he was minded to drive as stiff a bargain as he could. "Let's hear your best dollar price."

Telling him where he could go wouldn't help none. I didn't think they had swallowed that 'pardner' stuff, but I was here. And I wasn't fool enough to think they'd let me clear out.

Not, anyways, if they could help it.

I had some sharp thoughts on that subject too, but there was a heap more to this than a bunch of stole horses. "Either there's something around here them jaspers is after or they figure you're onto something they aim to be let in on."

I could see greed struggling with the fear in Oakes' look, but it was the girl that tipped his hand. She said with the words tumbling over each other, "It's the Curly Bill plunder, two wagonloads of it! All them saints he rode off with. A cigarbox of diamonds he got out of the vaults of that bank in Monterey. Thirty-nine bars."

"You bitch!" Oakes said.

"Look at him!" she cried. "You don't have to take my word for it, *look at him!*"

The rims of Oakes' lips was the color of dust. A

horrible hate was pouring out of his stare. He was so red in the face, so swelled up with rage, it was hard to put anything past him right then. Yet his voice, when he spoke, was flat as a mill pond. "You heard her," he said. 'I'll split it right down the middle."

NINE

HE MUST OF TOOK me for being still wet behind the ears.

Buried treasures and maps was all over this country, likewise fools to go with them; but this Curly Bill plunder, if there was any truth to it, explained a heap that had been gnawing me. The big thing, however, that come over me right then was that Oakes wasn't figuring to split this with anyone.

You couldn't take in the scowl, and the cocked ugly shape of him, and come up with anything different. He had the look and the sound of a Simon-pure believer; and his wife was in it clean up to her lying mouth. I seen the bob of her head and her eyes, big and earnest. "A man couldn't ask for one fairer than that." She said it like Moses coming down off the mountain.

I was minded to laugh in their faces I was riled enough to.

She put her oar in again. "With a stake like that a man could do just about anything he wanted he could get plumb out of the scrabblin' country." When the mood was on her she could make things shine. "In Nicaragua or Chile you could both be kings."

I guess she figured this to clinch it. But alls I had to bet with was my fife, and with the five of them against me I didn't need no peace twig to see it mightn't last no longer than a June frost in Tucson. I said, "How much'll half add up to?"

I guess they pegged me chump enough for anything. Oakes put another hold on his breath. "Countin' the images," he said, "an that altar stuff, the whole thing'll figure to run at right aroun' three million."

Maybe I didn't look properly impressed.

His cheeks got dark and puffed up again. He did have the wit to keep his voice down, but you could tell by the way the words tumbled out he wasn't scarcely two jumps from going off his rocker. "It's there, every goddam bit of it! That Christ an the Virgin is both solid gold! Forty sacks of coins, gold an' silver mixed took a four horse team just to haul..." His eyes turned black and then jumped to mine sly like. "A cigar box crammed with diamonds! Ninety thousand Mex dollars in rawhide aparejos, thirty-nine bars of gold bullion."

"You sound powerful sure."

He clamped his choppers and stared like a bull snake. It come over me then I wasn't going at this right. "All right," I said, "but the trick is to find it. Let's see your map."

Lupita cried fiercely, "He don't need no map! He was there with Zwing Hung when they buried it!"

Oakes, snarling, nervously peered toward the hall. "You want that sonofabitch back in here?"

A shine of sweat lay across his flesh. His eyes was

like hot iron banging into her but she held her ground, giving him back look for look.

I said, "If you know where it's at why ain't you dug it up?"

"Because he's scairt," Lupita sneered, "Earp never killed Curly Bill."

"Never killed him..." I looked at him and then her again.

"He thinks Bill's still alive!"

'Is he?" I said, and Oakes, his stare hating her, testily growled, "You ever hear of 'em findin' his body?"

"But they shot it out"

"You know that, do you?" Oakes pinned his glittering eyes on me. "I put in three months pawin' through that brush. *I* never found him."

We stared across a clatterous quiet.

If Earp hadn't killed him where had Brocius gone?

I'd been trying to drop out of sight myself. I hadn't left no plunder, real or imagined. I wasn't a quarter so well known as he'd been. "Well, if Wyatt didn't kill him," I finally said, "and there *was* any loot, he's probably dug it up himself."

"Sure," Oakes snorted. "Dug it up barehanded an' packed it off in his pockets!" He peered at me contentiously. "You in this or ain't you?"

"He ain't," Ivory said from the shadows of the porch.

The surprise of it held Oakes rooted in his tracks. Lupita's blanched cheeks showed the depths of her fright, a spread of worry, the mounting flush of a furious anger. "How'd you get out there!"

Ivory chuckled. "Get rid of this feller if you want to stay healthy, Fred."

Quiet closed round us, black and deep. Chunk on chunk it rose and grew till a man scarce could breathe from the thickening of it. The feel of his eyes put the cold shivers to me. "Get rid of him tonight or he'll be got rid of for you."

TEN

"YOU TALK brave as hell standing out in that dark!" That was me, and nothing come back. You couldn't tell if he was gone or still out there.

I started for the door. Lupita, grabbing me, dug in her heels. "You want to get yourself killed!"

"If that was the answer I'd be dead right now."

Oakes, scowling, nodded. He smeared the sweat across his cheeks. His wife, turning loose of me, ran over and slammed the porch door. She put her back to it, glaring. "No tellin' what he'll do if you keep pushing at him!"

Mad and scared, her bosom heaving, she made a picture no feller with a eye for a woman could scarcely overlook.

Oakes, sunk back in his chair, was staring nastily. Then, his look finding me, he said, blowing his breath out, "Mebbe you better roll your cotton." He dug a handful of crumpled bills from his jeans and, never moving his look, flung them onto the" table. "This'll take care of any time you got comin'."

I didn't say whether it would or it wouldn't.

Down the hall I threw open the first door I come to, went in, shoved it shut, and stood in dark that was blacker than stove shine. When I could make out the blobs of bed and bureau I seen a heap more I should of thought about sooner. Sometimes you wonder how crazy can you get! It wasn't the greenbacks I'd left on that table but the chance I'd passed up to climb out of this jackpot.

The goddam room didn't even have a window! And no way of keeping the door like it was without a man put the bureau to it. I wasn't about to let them hear me doing that

A man's pride. But pride was all I'd got to show for the reckless years I'd put into a saddle. Sure, I had talents good hand with horses, fast with a pistol. But all that last ever fetched a man is bullets.

I slumped down on the bed and took a look at myself. The things I seen didn't noways come up to the view I'd had of me. When you scraped away all the goddam twaddle I was as wild to get hold of that plunder as anyone.

I finally got around to hauling off my boots, dropped them one after the other with a jingle and thump. I sat a fidgety spell, hearing house sounds and crickets, the banged down clatter of a sash Ivory, likely, back inside. Come the yammering of a coyote and, presently, Oakes and Lupita shuffling past in the hall. A door opened and' shut, and not even this hid away their caustic bickering.

I scowled and glared and thought some more about Ivory. Three million bucks takes a heap of getting used to. If it boiled down to no more than half that much there would still be plenty... for one guy, anyhow. Course there was bound to be some dying, maybe a powdersmoke payoff with myself odds-on choice for prime target.

I pushed this aside, hooked like the rest with clamorous notions of what I could do with even a piece of that plunder. It's easy to scorn greed in others, but I wasn't one to do the scorning. I wasn't counting on nothing, but it couldn't hurt to wonder what a man could do if it come to him. I sure wasn't figuring to catch me no sleep, not after what Ivory had said right in front of me.

Pure bullypuss bluff. He'd of bit and not barked if he'd been aiming to be rid of me. Still, I lifted my gun from leather before stretching out to wait for daylight.

Half a hundred things must of wheeled through my head as I laid there twisting, unable to get comfortable. Combinations I would have to watch out for as this bunch wheeled and dealed to get leverage. Wasn't a one you could trust to pass up the lion's share if he could hit on some way to get at it without being like to turn up his toes.

I clean forgot Dimity Hale in this thinking, but not Lupita, never her husband if that's what Fred was. These were what a man had to work on, Oakes' fright and hate and Lupita's stupidity, the man hunger in her and whatever else kept pushing her into the path of Oakes' fury. These things could be used and Bill Ivory would use them. He was the one I would have to watch out for. I remembered his eyes, the cold savvy they showed, the grin that never got out of his mouth. Here was the dangerous one, not them other two.

Brace and that kid was just a couple of twisters, bad

enough maybe backed into a corner but nothing to worry a man who'd been around. Stamp a boot and Brace would scuttle for cover. Alamagordo might be more stubborn, but stubborn was a horse I knowed how to handle.

Those broncs had taken out of me more than I'd reckoned. I'd of swore I never closed my eyes, but it seems I did because the next thing there was somebody out in that hall, setting each foot down quiet as a mouse.

I could feel it. Something about stealth gets into your bones.

He must have took off his boots; there wasn't a sound. I had to make myself breathe. Probably had his ear to the door, standing there listening, trying to make out if I was asleep. I done my best to convince him.

I waited and sweated, and then I knew of a sudden he was no longer out there.

I come off the bed still holding my pistol and stepped catfooted to the door in my sockfeet, listening again and then easing it open. It wasn't so black out there as inside but the hall was filled with a curdle of shadows and a current of air coldly lapped round my ankles, a warning that someone had opened the porch door.

I went forward, moving careful. I still hadn't got to the end of the hall when a board skreaked horrible under my foot. I waited till the jumpety sound of my heart quit banging my ribs, then slipped into the room where the table and chairs was.

It was dark, too, and considerable colder but not so blamed black I couldn't spot that open door. Whoever I was after must have gone outside, or was this only what they aimed for me to think? A come-on, maybe?

I stretched my ears while my eyes probed the shadows.

I moved to the doorway, searching the yard with no better success, the rocks and the dark blocking me off from too much of it. Then I picked up some sound, a murmur of voices that seemed to be coming from the direction of the corrals. I supposed I ought to step out there but stood suspicious, irritably uncertain whether to go or stay put.

I didn't want to come up with any cats that curiosity had killed. That business outside my room, the open door, them voices, could all be intended to pull me out where some gent with a gun could snuff my light. At the same time I was impatiently conscious it might be some deal I wasn't to know about.

The only thing I was sure of was that, if I stayed put, I might learn which of the ones in this house had gone out there. Actually I wasn't even sure of that; there was nothing to stop them getting in through a window. If it was Ivory out there and he was sure as hell my favorite he was apt as not to come swaggering cool as you please right on past me.

And there was still the back door. A man could look mighty foolish crouching over this mousehold while the sport he was hunting come in at the back.

I was minded to burn the bridge and go out there when a flutter of motion something more sensed than seen yanked my stare to the start of that trek through the rocks. The talking had quit and the shadows was piled so thick over there all those broncs I'd been stompin' could have taken cover in them. If the goddam moon would of only come out...

I sucked in my breath. Already the night was

turning gray along the rim. In another couple hours the sun was due to show unless the sky was overcast, and I reckoned it was by the smell of that wind. All we needed in this deal now was a drizzling rain to make everything ducky.

Looking back at them rocks I let out a soft grunt. There was something coming out of that forest of shadows, a two legged something, and coming straight on.

I got away from the door. Gun in hand, I backed against the wall where the murk was thickest, figuring when he come through the door to be able to gauge his size and put a name to him.

I heard bare feet cross the planks of the porch. A deeper black got into the opening, then the door was pulled shut and I still didn't know. I lashed out with the gun, felt it strike, heard a gasp and the lurching thumps of somebody staggering. Something clattered on the floor. I reached out blindly, wildly grabbing, got a fistful of cloth and felt it burn through my fingers, tearing. Then he was loose of me, gone down the hall, the sound of him lost in the rush of my breathing. I didn't even hear the goddam door shut.

I stood balked in front of the room Ivory'd taken from Brace and that feisty kid. All I could hear was the roaring pound of the blood slogging through me. It made me furious to come so close and end up with nothing.

We had made enough noise to wake John Brown, but nobody showed. I was halfway back to find out what had clattered when I realized I still had that cloth in my fist. I mighty near flung it down in disgust. It was only a scrap, and to prove anything it would have to be matched with the shirt it come off of. I couldn't see much chance of him letting that happen. I shoved it into my pocket, put the gun away, too.

I stood thinking a while, both ears cocked for trouble, then went on, thumbed a match and seen the glint winking back at me the glint of a five inch blade with bone handle. That's what he'd dropped, and it was sharp as a razor.

Snuffing the match I stooped, got the knife, and went back to my room with it, closing the door mighty careful behind me. It was the kind of dagger that fit into a case, perfectly balanced, somewhat short for close work but just right for throwing. I wondered how many more was around and when he would try to put one of them into me. I pushed the frog sticker under the bureau, dug out the cloth and scratched another light.

ELEVEN

OTHER THINGS CAN MAKE a man stupid besides pride.

Don't ask how long I stood there. When the match got to cooking my fingers I dropped it, still seeing that twist of cloth I had hold of even after I couldn't see my own hand.

It hadn't come off no shirt I'd laid eyes to. Looked like calico ripped from a dress a hard thing to think when you set it beside that blade I'd picked up and the time and the place and that gabble of voices. Who had she come from with a knife in her fist? and where was he now?

I was minded to look at that blade again, but even as I hitched up myself to go after it the remembered grin of that damned Bill Ivory took my thoughts down another track. Nor all her wiles couldn't turn me away from the picture of her out there with him darkly cuddled in them rocks. She was capable of it. On the porch tonight almost under Oakes' nose hadn't she squeezed my arm and give me the eye? She had no more morals than a goddam rabbit!

How else had that bunch come onto this place if somebody hadn't passed along the word? Oakes sure as hell never sent out no invites! Young as she was, time was getting away from her. Maybe she was tired of waiting on Fred. Maybe she reckoned he never would dig it up without somebody prodded him.

Still, a guy like Bill Ivory... I couldn't see no woman wrapping *him* around her finger. If she had started this rolling it was Brace she'd probably sent for. Then she'd happened onto me, probably scairt when he'd fetched in that kid with him; it was after they'd come she'd started giving me the business.

Ivory had been here before. Oakes had said, "You know my wife," and Ivory had asked, "Where at's that filly you been fetchin' up for Fred?" Brace had been here, too, and he had asked about the girl, gone off hunting her... Oakes telling me later he had hoped she would put a blue whistler through him.

Feller as tricky as that could have slipped outside after his wife was asleep, or after he figured she was. Him and Ivory probably caused some noise... that bunch of stole broncs maybe. He hadn't come before about no legend of plunder; he wasn't the kind to have left without getting his hooks on it. This had to be something new with him. It struck me he may have been watching Cort Brace. Hell! He said he'd figured Brace would probably put in here for water!

It didn't make no never mind. A jasper like Ivory could just about smell loot. Come to that the whole push could. I'd smelt something myself I remembered uncomfortably.

But she wouldn't kill Fred. He was the goose who knew where the eggs was hadn't she said to me, and in considerable of a lather: *You got to keep those fools from killing Jake!* Just because she'd dropped that knife on the floor didn't prove she'd just come back from using it. Probably slipped out to gab a spell with Brace...that knife likely hadn't been in her hand till I jumped her.

I didn't think in them shadows she could have known it was me. She might even have thought Bill Ivory'd got hold of her. The more I woolled it around the more tangled it got me. The smart thing, I figured, was to go out and have a look. It was pretty damn sure I wouldn't catch no more shut-eye.

I shoved the rag in my pocket, shucked the spurs off my boots and, carrying them the boots I mean, eased open the door. It was still plenty dark and quiet right now as the bottom of a pond. By considerable effort I missed the creaking board. In the sitting room I stopped for another look and listen.

If there was anything to see I certain sure missed it. Crossing the planks of the porch, balancing myself with a hand against the steps, I got into my boots.

A thin sliver of moon only made the dark chunks blacker. Half Lew Wallace's army could of been hid out in them shadows. That bed I'd give up begun to look pretty good. So would three million I reminded myself even a chunk of it, but the thought didn't help my breathing none. It didn't help me neither to suspicion that Ivory was out there somewhere waiting with his grin for a good clean shot.

Except for the solid black of the cliffs, things at a distance you couldn't pick out at all. Even where the gloom seemed piled chunk on chunk, there wasn't enough to it to hide a man proper at scarcely less than ten paces a sight too damned close to have to fight it out with belt guns.

I don't know why I kept picturing Ivory; it was a heap more likely she'd been out to see Brace or, just maybe, that kid. And even if it was Bill Ivory she'd been with I had no reason for supposing he'd be there now. There was something about that cold-eyed potato that kept jumping around through the tramp of my thoughts like I'd seen him before and that didn't make much sense when you looked at it. A jasper like him a feller didn't forget.

I thought she'd come from the direction of the corrals, from the rocks anyway that hid them. It would of been some assurance to have come onto her tracks but I wasn't about to strike any matches. I was in the rocks now, trying to creep my way through and still, if I could, keep from adding my bones to the ones Oakes had showed me. I was in a fine lather, I can tell you. Only reason I didn't have hold of my pistol was I reckoned it would show up like a tin roof.

The further I went the harder it got to put one foot down ahead of the other. It's a wonder I didn't turn back. I wanted to. It made a mort of sense, but I had to see, if I was able, what she'd run with a knife from.

She wouldn't of been much beyond them next rocks because the pens, I figured, was right there behind them; and, probably, Brace and the kid. And maybe Bill Ivory just waiting for me.

I would sooner of took a beating than step around them rocks, but I knew I had to do it. The dark slid up around my chest and lapped around my neck like water, cold and black as a cartload of stove fids, and the quiet got thick enough to chop with an ax. He was there, and he was waiting, though I didn't straight off see him.

What my stare latched onto was this crumpled up blotch all spraddled out like a bunch of dropped clothes. A stiff, of course. You don't have to get down and rassle them around to know when a guy ain't got no pressing use for boot jacks.

I was right about him waiting but wrong about the pens. It was the next rocks they was back of. It was when I looked to find them I seen Ivory's teeth grinning out of the shadows. He said, powerful soft, "Scratch a match an roll him over."

He must of thought I couldn't tell skunks from house cats. I said, "You want him over, turn him."

There was a heap of ugliness breathed into the silence while I fished out my pipe and thumbed fresh smoking. It done me good to feel his temper and know Flick Farsom, by grab, had outfoxed him. If he'd been going to shoot he'd have shot in the first place.

It was this, and him holding his voice down, that woke me up to who had the choice. For some reason he wanted to keep this just between him and me. I should of looked that part of it over more careful.

I seen him folding his arms. He said, "You know who this is?"

"Don't look like Fred Oakes. Bony enough, maybe, but..."

"Ain't Brace, neither. You reckon it's that kid?"

I took another squint. Then it come over me what he was getting at.

Ivory nodded. "Looks like somebody else has

bought into this. You got any notion how he got here, or when?"

I shook my head.

"You reckon he just sort of stumbled into it?"

Both the place and the time was against it. "Maybe," I said, "we better look for his horse."

"What I want to know," Ivory said, "is who got him here."

I could feel the black drill of his gaze boring into me. All the good feeling had turned to bile in my throat. From here on out he would be watching his chance to get rid of me.

For all I knew he may have got rid of this guy.

I said, "Could be he just happened by and dropped in, some old friend of Fred's."

Even to me it didn't sound likely.

"There wasn't no horse sound," Ivory said. "I got here just as whoever dropped him cleared out. Wasn't no sound at all."

"Then how"

"The breath was still whistling out of him."

It put a cold shiver through me. Watching him that way, seeing him plainer, it come to me that daylight wasn't far off. "If they knocked him down with a gun barrel..."

Ivory said, "It wasn't no gun barrel."

"But if there'd been a shot..." I stopped, silent, staring, as. Brace and the kid stepped around the boulders that blocked us off from any sight of the corrals. I thought Alamagordo was going to walk right into the corpse before he seen it. Brace, a little ahead of him, turned handily aside but the kid, when he spotted it, stopped so short he had to throw out both arms for balance. Ivory, watching, kept his notions to himself. The kid said, "Jesus!" and his eyes looked round as marbles.

Brace was trying too hard. It just wasn't natural he should be so near and never once bat his glance in that direction. "What's the row?" he growled testily. "You goin' to wrangle like cats on a back fence all night?"

He knew better than the kid did what was there. But they hadn't been listening, or been together long, else Alamagordo would of played the same tune.

Brace done his best. As though just waking up he kind of stiffened in his tracks, let the jump of his stare be drawn behind him and down. Ivory, not waiting for any more, said, "Turn him over, and let's have a look at him."

The light was bettering fast. The tinhorn looked like something hacked out of cardboard.

"Go on he won't bite," Ivory said. "Hurry up, I'm gettin' hungry."

You'd have thought, the way he stood, Brace couldn't bring himself to bend. But he done it, turned him; then shot up to twist away, puking, and I didn't much blame him.

There was a gaping slash beneath the stiff's chin, dark with blood, where his throat had been cut. It was the kid's skreaky voice that put the name to him. "Billy Grounds!" he gasped, and his face was wet with the sweat of terror.

The hair on the back of my own neck stirred. Billy Grounds had been killed several years ago during a fight at the Stockton ranch.

TWELVE

MUST BE SOME MISTAKE, I thought, scowling at the shaking shape of Cort Brace, wondering how much he knew about this, wondering which and how many of us would be picking up cards from this deal tomorrow. Cold and sharply sliding through a churned up welter of floundering confusions was the feel of my arm squeezed against her bosom, the clatter of that blade and the gravelly sound of her wildly shouting, "You got to keep those fools from killing Jake!"

I couldn't help thinking this was one way to do it.

Ivory said to Brace in the same kind of tone he might of spoke about the weather, "You still packing that pig sticker you used to pare your nails with?"

The gambler jerked up his head in a disbelieving stare. He might not have been no picture of innocence, but shifty or not he looked plenty affronted. "You think I could do a thing like that!"

"Somebody done it." A cruel amusement crinkled Ivory's mouth. "For three million smackers any one of us could and I ain't countin' out Jake or that double-breasted whore. Now get out of those boots."

I noticed the cold in the widening quiet that abruptly appeared to be everywhere about us. In this gray light it must of seemed like to Brace, with them hard eyes cracking into him, he didn't have the chance of a snowball in hell

Shivering, whimpering, the rabbity face of him twitching and jerking, he got down on his butt.

"The other one, Sweetheart. The one with the knife in it."

Visibly wilting, Brace switched his hold.

"I don't think he done it."

Above the black mustache Ivory's look reached across in a hard, searching scrutiny. "Someone asked for your notion?"

I don't know why I should of took up for Brace except it was the remembrance of what was under my bureau. The tinhorn had known, before he'd come butting in, what they was going to run into. Look at the way he'd stepped around that stiff!

Now he'd got off his boot. The hilt of a knife stuck out from it plain. "Still reckon he didn't do it?"

Without the patronizing mockery oozing up out of the sneer of that question I might have turned loose of Brace, remembering the girl. But Ivory's assumption of always having the answers to everything graveled me. "It don't have to follow, because he's got a knife, Brace used it to cut that whipporwill's throat."

"You got a better prospect?"

The smugness of it woke me like a hoof in the gut. I'd been took like a kid, led by the nose and oh, sweet Jesus!

Bully Brace was just a dodge Ivory'd used, a strawman set up to coax past locked faces any knowledge of suspicions we might think to hide away from him. To me it was the measure of an inexcusable carelessness my own, because I'd marked Bill Ivory the first time I'd seen him as a lobo among the foxes, a real plumb hombre, a Ketchum romping with a bunch of fool Sam Basses.

He seen how I felt, enjoyed every bit of it. The sly goad of his chuckle nearly pushed me past the last grab of caution, so goddam mad I could cheerfully of belted him. One thing it done nothing could of dragged me out of this now. I meant to beat that son of a bitch if it killed me.

Fred Oakes come round from the house, snatched one look at that face up stiff and cringed like he had took a mortal hurt. He went a fish belly white, staggered back a couple paces with his jaw dropped down like a hoof shaper's apron. He pulled a shuddering breath and tried to scrape himself together.

"How about it, Jake?" Ivory said smooth as silk. "Cort allows you've run with most of the bad boys. You got a handle for this feller?"

Oakes' mouth worked but nothing came out of it. On the ground Brace reached for the boot he'd took off. Ivory said, "You're not goin' anywhere," and hooked the boot with a foot clean out of Brace's reach. "Well Jake, speak up," he grinned. "You ever seen him before?"

It was cold in them rocks but the glint of sweat could be seen in Fred's whiskers. He wiped the hands against his pants. "Billy Grounds," he wheezed, shuddering.

Ivory considered him. "Didn't I hear Grounds was killed in that ranch fight at Stockton's?"

"The dead walk in these hills," Fred groaned. He grabbed a fresh breath with the hate twisting through him so naked you could hear it. "You might try kickin' him up like you done that greaser down to Uvalde. Go on kick him. Couldn't be you're scairt of a dead hant, could it? The great king..."

Ivory caught the old coot such a clout in the face I half looked for his fist to come out the other side. It didn't, of course didn't make much improvement to Fred's looks, neither. Blood spurted from his nose, brightening up his whiskers as he went reeling back to come down hard on his butt in a jounce of loosed air.

I looked for the old fool to break right out and bawl. He brought a hand from the dirt, whimpering like a cur no more than it touched the pulpy wreck of his beak. Staring at the blood he hauled himself to his feet. "All I said"

"I heard what you said," Ivory told him, spider soft. "Now get on up to the house and set out some grub before, by God, I really work you over."

* * *

THE GRUB WAS all fried up and waiting, which was probably what Oakes had come out to tell us flapjacks and sowbelly and a great heaping platter of warmed-over frijoles. Fred's wife had done herself proud, she truly had. But anyone who looked to find a welcome mat out was going to have to put on his fine print cheaters.

Oakes didn't come tramping in with the rest but cut

off around to the side where the spring was. Since he might have a pistol, though he'd left off his shell belt? I rather expected Ivory to order him back. He never even looked to see where Fred was headed for.

After we set, set down and everyone had dug in or was fixing his grub to suit, Ivory said, "Eating, with me, is a solemn occasion. When I put on the feed bag I don't take kindly to people junin' around."

She give him a bitter look but set. It didn't have no effect on her tongue, though. "Where's Fred?" she demanded.

"Can't you stand for him to be out of your sight for ten minutes?"

Before she could fly back Fred came in. He hauled up his chair. His nose looked powerful painful, but he'd scrubbed all the gore out of his scraggle of whiskers. He pitched in without speaking after Lupita, still riled, had filled his plate It was plain she was busting to sound off some more but with Ivory leaning into his food like he was I guess she figured it was best not to bother him.

Maybe you're thinking it was strange, after the deal Oakes had offered half of everything split straight down the middle, I hadn't taken up for him when Ivory hung that fist in his face. First place, Fred looked the kind that in a bind would offer a man the moon if he had to. Bets made on the strength of any deal with him would be plum off, I figured, the minute he got out from under.

I suppose I might of put in my oar if Ivory, instead of popping him, had made a stab for his pistol. As things turned out I was plenty content to rock along with the rest. I'd be having my turn with him soon enough without bringing anything on premachoorly. I wasn't even to myself ready yet to admit there could be any doubts which of us would bait coyotes when the smoke rolled away.

There wasn't much question about Ivory's caliber it ain't barking dogs you got to watch out for. Back of his grins he was rough as a cob. Touch iron around him and you'd be like to have to use it.

Oakes didn't appear to be overly hungry. The girl, too, only kind of picked at her food. The kid ate strong, his spare time being divided pretty even between surly glances first at Ivory, then at me. Brace's hands shook so bad he finally give it up. When we'd left that corpse Bill had fetched along Brace's boot had it setting right up on the table beside him. When he swabbed out his plate and set back, I done likewise.

He was a cool one, all right. He could beat around the bushes or come straight at a thing blunt enough to make a stone twitch. Now, passing out the smiles, he said, 'We didn't none of us ride out here to hunt mosquitoes. Before we bring this meeting to order you got any thoughts, Jake, you'd admire to unload?"

Fred's eyes flapped around like two flies in a bottle. "I don't guess," he got out, "you'd be settin' no store by my gab if I had."

"You got every right to speak if you want," Ivory said, teeth shining. "In a deal like this its best to all be equal partners, poolin' everything we know. That way we can be sure no one's cheatin'. It's share and share alike or we come right up against them plain hard facts we seen out there in the rocks. Beckon none of us is anxious to feed the buzzards. Long's we act like gents there won't nobody have to, if you get what I mean.

"Now, we've got this boot," he said, picking it up,

"and we've got that stiff." He slid the knife up and down a few times in the leather. "Boot belongs to Cort, we all seen him get out of it; so it's reasonable to figure this Arkinsaw toothpick's his too. I'm not sayin' he killed that feller. If the jigger's Billy Grounds... hell! Mebbe the guy ain't Grounds at all. The dead may walk in these hills like Jake says, but I would personal want a little more than his word for it. Thing I'm tryin' to bring out is, if we don't want corpses stacked up all around we better make out to be a mite more cooperative."

Brace, by the scowl of him, had picked up the message. Oakes settled deeper into his chair, but all it got out of the kid was a sneer. He sure picked the times to expose his ignorance.

What I wanted myself was another look at that blade not the one in Brace's boot but the knife someone lost in the dark of the hall when I'd struck out with my gun. I knew it hadn't been Oakes'. I wasn't sure it was his wife, but that cloth I'd yanked loose hadn't come off no shirt.

So unless it was Lupita, it must of been Dimity Hale. She could easy have ridden in, I thought. What was harder to figure was what she'd been up to before she had fetched the corpse. It could explain how he'd come into this deal. It didn't account for everything though his condition, for one. Had he arrived as dead freight? Quick or dead he must of come on a horse and what about the muddle of voices I'd heard just ahead of whoever had slipped into the house?

Every trail a man took brought him back to that knife and it might, even in daylight, be clean as a new pin. First chance I got I meant to look.

There was a heap in this deal I couldn't latch onto. I

was riled and excited and crammed with frustrations, but of one thing I was pretty well convinced. If Oakes was Jake Gauze, and this dead guy was Grounds, there was sure as hell some kind of plunder to be had and it wasn't far off.

THIRTEEN

"WELL," Ivory said. "What's it going to be, dog eat dog, or a little sweetness and light?"

He flashed his tough grin, settling back, crossing his arms. Didn't seem much doubt what the upshot would be. Greed and envy and fear was coming out of Brace like water from a rusty tub. Hate shone like a lantern in Lupita's bitter stare, and Fred Oakes didn't look much happier than a weasel with his backend caught in a bear trap.

Only the kid looked to have any spunk and, as usual, he picked the wrong time to parade it. He said with his lip pulled into a snarl, "You think we're dumb enough to swaller that?"

A cheap crook like Brace would have swarmed all over him. Ivory laughed it off. Big and easy, he said, "Believe what you like but give it a try. There's plenty in this for all of us. I know you're thinkin' I been fixing to grab the lion's share. Well, I just plain can't, and you can't neither. Nobody here by himself is goin' to do it."

He slanched the brash glint of his shrewd stare

around. "We got to be practical. With all of us pulling together, and everybody watching everybody else, there's a pretty fair chance we can all come out well-heeled. I leave it up to you."

He had a real talking talent. I suspect there was other things up his sleeves that he would probably trot out when it suited him. He slipped the knife from Cort's boot and run his thumb along the edge in such a offhand show you couldn't help thinking. I seen Brace shiver.

Fred's wife squeezed her eyes shut. When they flew open she said, "I'm for poolin'."

"Figures," Oakes sniffed. "I notice them that's got the least is generally agreeable to addin' to it. How do you vote, Farsom?"

"Reckon I'll have to string along with the lady."

His stare raked Brace and the kid and come away. I suppose he found the situation intolerable; he showed his contempt. "All right." He glared at Ivory. "Where you figure to go from here?"

Bill, putting the knife back, hauled the lips off his teeth. "Why, Jake, old horse, we're leavin' that up to you."

The only think Oakes' face give away was his temper.

Ivory, watching, lazily smiling, said, "You're the nearest thing to Curly Bill a man's like to get his hands on now."

"Let me work him over," Brace said. Nobody paid any attention to Brace.

"If there's anything buried and Fred knows where it's at," I put in, "why ain't he dug it up and took off?"

"Yeah," Alamagordo said, "how come?'

Ivory chuckled. "What would the rest of you do in Jake's boots if you had it in your heads Curly Bill might be lurkin' just around the next rock?"

Brace showed the whites of his eyes. "That's crazy!" the kid cried. "Wyatt Earp emptied a shotgun into Bill at Iron Springs..."

Oakes showed the snags of his yellowed teeth. 'You help bury him? You was there, I presume?"

That meanness come into the kid's look again. "Plenty others was there!"

"Well," Fred said, "you think what you want an' I'll do the same." He scrubbed a hand through his whiskers, took his look back to Ivory. "The unvarnished truth of the matter is I wasn't around when that plunder got buried. I don't know no more about it than you do."

Lupita, whirling in a rustle of skirts, grabbed onto Bill Ivory. "He ain't spent all this time around here just to keep hid out from any bunch of damned stranglers!"

"Say! That's right," the kid grinned, "Jake Gauze was s'posed to been strung up, wasn't he? Somethin' about a horse..."

"And Grounds, that's out in those rocks with his throat slit, was supposed to been killed in that Stockton ranch fight," Ivory purred. "And Zwing Hunt, you'll remember, is said to have been buried at the mouth of this canyon in a scrub oak's shake. Accordin' to his uncle over at San Antone, that ain't so at all. By his tell Hunt come clean back to Texas where he died a few weeks later after gulpin' out this yarn of buried plunder."

"It ain't no yarn," Lupita said waspishly, "it's the God's own truth! He even made a map! Jake's got..." Stopping, startled, she clapped a hand to her mouth.

"Now," Ivory smiled, "we're getting somewheres. Not that I put any great stock in maps. If it comes to that I got a couple myself. But with Jake bein' close as he was to Curly Bill..."

"Grounds was closer," Oakes said, getting up. "Bill never buried it. He give that chore to Grounds an' Hunt, which is why Zwing let out fer Texas like he done. All Bill knowed about where the stuff was is what they told him. He was powerful anxious to come up with those boys. Facts is, he was huntin' them when he ran into Earp at Iron Springs."

"And it's your contention Earp never killed him?"

"Think what you want," Oakes said, glaring. "The Tombstone *Nugget* offered ten hundred dollars fer a look at the body. Nobody ever walked off with that dinero. Nobody ever turned up Bill's bones. If he's dead where's his carcass?"

The kid, I seen, was staring hard at Bill Ivory. Brace, too, was looking uneasily nervous. Had I missed my bets? Was Ivory really Brocius? Even allowing for the changes time might have wrought I still didn't think so. To my mind Ivory wasn't right for the part. In lots of ways he was I reckoned, but Oakes would know. If this feller was really Curly Bill, Oakes was a heap better actor than I was ready to admit; and I found myself considering Lupita. If Ivory wasn't Brocius, who in the devil's name was he! While he may not have fit my ideas of Curly Bill, he fit a heap less the role of shoot and fly gunslick. Too shrewd he looked, too smooth and deadly.

Oakes said abruptly, "If that stiff is Grounds, whoever made meat of him either didn't know him or never looked beyond his nose. Because why? Because, aside from Zwing Hunt that we can take it fer gospel is sure enough dead, he was the only jasper still afoot that knowed where the plunder was planted."

Consternation climbed into the look of Cort Brace. Lupita turned livid. Alamagordo, the kid, begun throatily to curse, opening and closing his fists in balked fury while he glowered first at Ivory, then, wickedly, at me. It was plain he figured, in what he used for a mind that one or the other of us had done Grounds in. Yet it was him that had put the name to Grounds first and Oakes that had confirmed it.

Ivory, apparently plowing the same furrow, took hold of Fred with a narrowing glance. "You said the guy *was* Grounds. Now you say *if* he was Grounds. You can't have it both ways. Is he or ain't he?"

Oakes pawed his whiskers. "I thought first off he was. But..."

"Now you ain't so sure. That what you're trying to say?"

Fred looked confused. Ivory said, "You better look again then. Come on. You, too Farsom."

I didn't know Billy Grounds from Adam's off ox but it didn't seem to be the right time to argue it. I followed Fred out, Ivory trailing behind us, Brace and the kid wheeling through the door after him. Brace said, "How's about givin' me back that boot?"

Ivory, with the book tucked under an arm, never turned his head. His eyes, when I looked back, was bright and watchful as a magpie's. Was it me he mistrusted or Fred? Probably, I suspected, both of us. Brace looked minded to reach for his gun, eyes wild and scairt enough for pretty near anything. It was the look of the kid that really gouged me. There was a chessycat grin pulling back his lips as he come limping after us.

I heard Ivory closing up. We was into the rocks, twisting and turning, following that snake's hips wiggle of a path, and he was sure not figuring to be treated to no surprise. Fred, I thought, you could pretty well figure. That kid was the one had me fighting my hat. I'd of give something to know what he found so damn funny.

It was getting hot fast with the sun beating down like the flat of a hammer when I rounded a twist and walked hard into Fred, grabbing onto him for balance. He grunted as the breath flew out of me. Then I seen what had stopped him and turned rigid as he was, eyes stiff with shock.

You ain't going to guess what was there, so I'll tell you. Nothing, by God, but a empty path and that dark gob of blood. The sound of stirred up flies, and Bill Ivory back of me sucking his wind showed he seen the same things. Just the rocks and the dust and that blacked over muck where Grounds had got his throat cut. The corpse was gone.

FOURTEEN

ONE THING COME into my head straightaway the face of Dimity Hale, and I sure as hell hated it. Scowling and squirming wouldn't butter no parsnips. It had to be her. No one else had the chance, we'd been all cooped up together in the house.

More I thought about it more convinced I. got. She could of pulled him into this; greed wasn't just for the bastards, it could break out in anyone. And even if she hadn't had just stumbled onto him out of the blue, it was her had took Grounds away from here.

Nothing else made sense... unless you could make out to believe there was more of them. I plain couldn't do it; and no more did I figure Brace and that kid, or Ivory either, had just happened to show when they had. Place was too well hid, too unhandy to get to. These rannies, I'm damn sure, were sent for.

Brace, I suspected, had been sucked in by Lupita; maybe not the same way she had got me out here, but the fact that she had was a step toward believing. Fed up with Fred, half out of her mind, she'd likely figured with his help to grab what she could and light out for new pastures. She'd have ways to get at Brace, no trouble there. She was the kind to tie more than one string to her bow, which was where I come in. But when the gambler showed up with the kid she'd got scairt that was the way I sized it up anyway.

Grounds was something else. According to Oakes he'd been the last man alive to know for a fact where the plunder was planted. Ivory, on his own word for it, had been expecting Brace. Both of them had been here before. There was nothing at all to show Grounds had ever been here, no reason for him being here now unless it would be the Curly Bill loot.

Had Oakes sent for Grounds? Before these others had turned up he might of. Fred might know just enough to feel likely he could talk his way into a pretty fair slice of it. Only Fred and the kid appeared to know Grounds by sight. The kid hadn't killed him not to my notion. Brace, when he'd come onto us before, had already known there was a stiff laying there, and Brace had been packing a knife. But one of Fred's women had had a knife on her too, the one I'd picked up and shoved under my bureau. And I was pretty sure now the one I'd grabbed was Lupita, but that didn't mean she had used it on Grounds. Had Fred cut his throat?

Behind me Ivory said, "Well!" and repeated it. Nobody else seemed to have wind enough. Brace and the kid fanned out beside us. "Now that he's got up and took himself off," Ivory said in Fred's direction, "you come any nearer to putting a tag to him?"

Oakes scarcely grunted, looking more than ever like something put out to keep the birds off the crops. Ivory's mouth, tightening up, shaped its cold thin grin while his eyes got narrower and darker till a gusty breath fell out i of him. His voice when he spoke was considerable changed. Temper was scratching through, giving out in rumblings of impatience. "You think I been talkin' to hear my head rattle?"

He reached out then quick, uncoiling like a cougar, and the slap of his hand back and forth across Oakes' cheeks was like the flat of a board coming against a mare's behind. "By God we don't have to keep you alive!"

It brought Fred back like nothing else could have. The loony look went out of his stare. He stumbled off a couple of teetering steps, got hold of his balance and stood there unwinking.

Ivory's eyes looked as bleak as two bullets. "Now I'll ask you once more to put a name to that corpse."

"It was Grounds, right enough," Fred grumbled.

"You send for him?"

"No."

"Well, somebody did. And I'll tell you something else. He was dead as a doornail. So unless you got more of Bill's gang cached around..."

"Jesus Christ!" Oakes said, desperate, "I never even knowed he was here, damn it!"

"Then that Hale filly moved him. Where is she?"

Oakes licked his lips. "She's supposed to be out there watchin' them broncs."

"Farsom," Ivory said, "go find her." Never taking his look off Fred, he growled, "Throw some feed to whatever's in the pens and see can you turn up the nag Grounds come in on." He stood there a moment with his eyes flattening out. "While the rest of us is waiting we'll be studying Jake's map."

Oakes, scowling ugly, headed back the way we'd come, Ivory herding the other two after him. Going on to the corrals I dumped grain in a nosebag and hung it on Fred's mouse.

There was only one other horse in sight, probably Ivory's, a three stockinged roan. I shook him down a armful of hay. Neither my dun nor any of the others the kid had run out of these pens had come back; and while I was standing there I reckoned it might come in handy was I to take along this roan. Be a really good chance for me to get plumb out. And if I pushed along the broncs I'd have the makings of a stake and I wouldn't have to risk being carved up to get it.

It was the most sensible notion I'd had since gettin' here, but of course I wasn't about to run out on three million dollars, nor anybody else. No matter how many horses was left to climb onto.

I grabbed a handful of mane, stripped off the bag and slipped my bridle onto Fred's big grulla. I got a blanket on his back, added my saddle and worked out the wrinkles before yanking the trunk strap. I thumped a knee against his belly and took up the slack. The old skate grunted like he'd rollers in his nose.

I went back and cut for sign, finding about what I'd reckoned I would. I seen where she'd hoisted him onto her horse. Lucky Grounds wasn't bigger; even so she'd had her hands full the way that horse had kept sidling around trying to get away from the blood stink.

Pretty soon I come onto heavier sign where she'd added her weight to what the horse had to carry. These tracks I followed through the dust of the gut. Wasn't no place else she could go from here but off down canyon to where I'd worked them broncs. I was too anxious to come up with her to waste any time hunting around for Grounds' horse. Settling back in the leather, half fried from the heat trapped between these walls, I let Fred's horse pick his gait through the shale and bleached bones left behind according to Fred by dead smugglers.

A creepy place and a hateful one. I was glad enough to have better things to ponder, like what I would do with my share of the loot if we found anything and I could get clear with it. Wasn't likely to be easy; wouldn't none of that bunch give a inch without he had to.

Brace's rabbity face come into my thoughts, and the kid's mean look and Jake, Fred Oakes, or whatever his name was, and the scairt jiggly ways of his unstable wife. Wasn't a one of them to be trusted any further than you could throw them. But they was all of a land compared to Bill Ivory. Fume and stew like a basket of snakes, twisting and hissing and showing their fangs.

They was beauties, all right, but Ivory was the one I looked at the longest. Fear didn't have no holds on that tiger. What he figured to do he would do if it killed him.

I kept coming back to this same notion. It was the others a man would better keep both his eyes on. Till the plunder was found I needn't worry about Ivory. I would as soon have forget about Lupita but I couldn't.

Her or Brace was to my way of thinking the most likely agents for what had happened to Grounds. I wanted another good look at that knife before I'd be satisfied which had done it; and maybe not even then, for there was always Fred Oakes. Fred had mighty sure known him.

He might of fixed it so Grounds would pop out here. It wasn't impossible. And if he'd got what he wanted maybe more if he hadn't, he was in pretty deep. He had the pushiest reason, but Lupita and Brace was the ones with the knives. At least Brace had sure as hell had one. And he was twisty, conniving but no more than Fred's woman. It give me a turn to remember the feel of her snuggling up to me, hugging my arm. I'd plumb forgot all about that.

* * *

WHERE THE RED sandstone walls opened out around the broncs in that waving lemon carpet of grass she was standing, watching, with the wind in her hair, with it slapping like shot through her man's hickory shirt. She made a sight I can tell you, slim as a boy except where her breasts was.

She didn't call, didn't wave, never backed off a foot, just kept standing there waiting with that Sharps in her hands, watching me come up with her sea green stare hard and bright as jagged glass.

"Far enough!" she sung out before I got in good belt gun range. "You got somethin' to say you can say it right there, then turn that nag and git back where you come from!"

Didn't seem like she was minded to waste much breath. In my thoughts she hadn't been so sharp, nor half as handsome as she looked right then. I said, halfway riled, "Bern's I've rode clear out here you might at least listen."

"Just come right out with it. I can hear you."

"What I come to say was for your ear alone, and if that's the best welcome you got you can keep it." Saying which with a soowl I yanked the grulla's head around and was fixing to beat on his ribs with my heels when curiosity, like I figured, got the best of her.

"Just a minute!" she called.

I looked over my shoulder. "If you can't trust me," I said, "let's forget the whole business."

She'd half lowered the rifle but she could bring it into line with my name mighty quick. I reckoned she had plenty of reason to be cagey considering the sort of folks she'd be used to, rimrock riders and drifting gunslicks, Oakes and Lupita and tinhorns like Brace. You could see she was weighing remembered indignities against the risks of letting me nearer.

I said, disgusted, "I never bit you before."

"You never got no chance. That's Fred's private horse you're forkin', mister. He'll lift the roof clean off the rafters."

"There's a new, bigger dog barkin' back there now. Oakes ain't piping the tunes no more."

"What you done shot him?"

"Ma'am, this yelling is ruinin' my throat."

Way them eyes stared back would have shook a brass monkey. My clothes felt like I'd been out in a dew. "All right," she nodded, "peel out of that shell belt. Loop it over your horn. Now git off that grulla and come up slow."

It was plain enough she wasn't no fool. What wasn't so sure was how far she'd go if something I done throwed her into a tantrum. There ain't many things more crazy to prod than a itchy fingered female crouched back of a firearm. I say I kept this in mind every step of the way. You'd have thought Polite was my middle name.

She let me come up to within ten foot. "That'll be

fine," she said. "I guess we can hear each other plain enough now."

For all that her voice sounded cool as a pig on a platter of ice there was a prickle of sweat across the top of her lip and I could see a pulse thumping in the hollow of one cheek.

Her tone got impatient. "You goin' to stand there all day?"

"Ma'am," I said, mighty edgy, "what'd you do with him?"

"If you're speakin' of Grounds I buried him, what else?"

* * *

I DON'T MIND TELLING you it give me a turn, her talking so offhand about that corpse. Made me narrow my eyes, trying to read her better. "How'd you know what his name was?"

"He ate here last night. Said his name was Grounds and he'd come huntin' Fred."

"Say what he wanted with him?" She shook her head. I said, "Come up, you mean, from the San Simon?"

"He come through the fence."

"That's all you know about him?"

Her eyes swept my face, and I could almost of swore I seen the glint of hidden laughter. "How much do you know?"

I was under a strain, of course, and confused. I growled, "Accordin' to Fred he was the last guy" and stopped, staring furious.

"Oh, you don't have to hide it. I know all about that

mule team of plunder." A small, taunting smile struck across her mouth. "Poor Fred, I guess he'll never git over it." She stepped back with her eyes, green as grass, opening wide. "Don't tell me you been took in by it, too!"

I peered at her uneasily. The rush of horrid thoughts through my mind come unsettling and raucous as a stampede of cattle.

"You honestly believe Curly Bill's still alive?" She put back her head in a fine show of scorn. 'You figure he's trampin' around through these hills still tryin' to come up with a treasure that never existed outside them crazy dreams of Zwing Hunt? A cigar box of diamonds! Forty aparejos crammed with Mexican silver! Bars of bullion! Plaster saints made of solid gold! Farsom, you astonish me I never would of guessed you had a noggin full of pigeons."

FIFTEEN

I COULD of took open laughter just as easy. I was sick as a man can afford to get, feeling mean all through and horrible used. I reached for my pipe, jerking away the hand in a haze of red fury so violent it shook me. I had to clench my fists to keep them from trembling. And then, needing something to hit, I snarled, "You callin' Lupita loco, too?"

"She's got it bad as Fred," Dimity said.

"And how do you explain Billy Grounds showing up? One of the pair that"

"I'm tryin' to tell you. Grounds never buried a thing in these hills."

"You're wasting your breath. Grounds wouldn't come"

"That's just it," she insisted. "He did. He come up to show Fred the whole thing was a hoax. Him and Zwing Hunt made it up for laughs.

"Some laugh!" I said, bitter. "I don't believe it."

Color jumped into her cheeks and ran out. Her

finger curled white round the grip of that trigger. "Be a fool then! Go on and git yourself killed!"

"I don't see Brace"

"That tinhorn!" she looked her contempt. "Cort Brace ain't got sense enough to blow out a lamp."

"You lumpin' Ivory in that, too?"

"Ivory!" Her eyes opened wide. "Has he been back?"

"He's took over this deal."

She stood post stiff for about six heartbeats. The rifle sagged in her hands. "Flick I'm scairt."

"I'm astonished," I said, giving her back some of her own. "Ain't that somethin' of a comedown f"

"Be still!" She chewed at her lip. There was almost a sadness to the look of her then, a kind of defeat that seemed unbearable. I had a crazy impulse to reach out and grab her, and probably I should of. Then her glance swept up. Her face cleared like magic. "Of course!" she cried. "He's come after his horses."

"If you're meaning these broncs," I said, glad of the chance, "you can forget 'em right now. He's talkin' treasure and offering shares to anyone who'll help him lay hold of it."

Half shut eyes hid away her thoughts. But she wasn't licked yet. It was in the way her chin come up, in the hard-edged way she pushed out her words. "Fred'll never do it!"

"He'll do it," I growled. "He'll either do it or die."

Her hand caught my arm. "You don't understand!"

She looked mixed up and frightened, like only just now was she coming to grips with this. She said, terrible earnest, "That treasure's Fred's life."

"Thought you claimed there wasn't no treasure?"

'In Fred's mind there is."

"You bet!" I grinned. "He sure ought to know. He was with Curly Bill when they throwed down on them smugglers, and Christ knows how many other deals, too."

Her eyes was bigger. Her fingers was like steel hooks on my arm. "Flick, you've got to help him!"

"*Got* to?" She must of seen something of what I was feeling. She let go and stepped back, her face strangely different. She started, timid, to put out her hand. "Flick...?"

Whatever was eating her she pushed it aside and, though the jumpety pulse was still beating her cheek, she spoke cool enough. "You've got to make them see there isn't any plunder."

"And how do I do that?"

"Convince Ivory."

She was perfectly serious. I seen right then she didn't know Ivory. I didn't know the sonofabitch either but I could see well enough no remarks of mine was going, even partway, to turn him around. Whoever he was, wherever he'd come from, he was here for one thing. It looked to me like he'd get it.

"Now you listen," I told her. "Thing for you to do is get clean out of this. Pronto! You and these broncs if you don't go lallygaggin' 'round picking daisies, can be halfway to Christmas before that bunch ever finds out you're gone. Go on," I growled, "start roundin' 'em up while I'm pullin' this fence down."

Figuring I was being a heap more noble than the girl had any call to expect, I was hiking for the brush Fred had stacked across the trail when some half grabbed notion jerked me about for another look. Her eyes met mine. She hadn't moved an inch.

"Don't you savvy plain English?"

"Fred's been good to me."

For a moment I glared, too whipped to cuss. The idea of a shoot and run bastard like Jake going out of his way to be good for anyone looked about as likely as a growed bull in bloomers.

The wind shouldered into me, snapping out the manes and tails of the broncs, scooting off like shadows through the twisting folds of that flattening grass.

There was no sense trying to talk him down to her. I could still snake her out of this, taking her myself, and if we sent these nags pounding down the trail it looked a fair enough chance with one horse between them, they would never catch up. But was that what I wanted?

I stomped back to her, scowling. I didn't want to see her hurt, wasn't anxious to think of her being around when Ivory begun to turn rough and get ugly, which he sure as hell would and mighty quick if Fred balked. But I didn't crave either to be left out if it happened she was wrong and they come up with that plunder. I didn't see how she could possibly be right. Brace I could discount same as she did, but a feller just couldn't look at Ivory and believe it. Conviction lurked in every twist of his grin.

She watched me out of a wooden face. The Sharps still hung at arm's length from one fist and the other was halfway up to her throat, dangling there like a hawk in the blue. She must of sensed...her woman's intuition must have told her I wasn't going along with her notions.

She didn't yell or cuss, tear into me or nothing. Her

eyes, big again, got dark and glimmery. Her raised hand dropped like a gut shot duck.

"Flick." The word come out of her thin as a whisper. I watched her swaller. "I'm so terrible helpless." A land of shiver ran all the way through her.

I stood there, scowling, knowing what she was up to, feeling the heat piling into my cheeks and not able for hell to get my talk going. There was an ache in my arms I tried to snort it away. I had a chance in this deal to come out fixed for life, and only a nump would pitch it aside like a busted pot on account of a woman he didn't scarcely know even. It was Fred she was worried about, not me! Fear had got her backed into a corner. *Pity her, sure, but don't let her push you out of the boat. She's trying to help Fred. You can see that, can't you?*

It was why she had told them lies. I said, bitter, "Fred don't need you or me to speak for him. Did you send for Grounds? Was it you got him out here?" "I never laid eyes on him before last night." Then why was she watching so breathless and bright? "Why'd you move him?" I said, almost hating her. "How'd you know he was there to be moved?"

"I was worried." She begun twisting her hands around the snout of that Sharps. "You'd of been too, knowin' Grounds had gone up there to tell them the truth. I didn't know about Ivory, but Brace had been creepin' around here before, mumblin' at Fred and actin' like"

"Fred! Why are you all the time calling him Fred? Don't you know he's Jake Gauze?"

Her eyes never said whether she did or she didn't. "He was one of the bunch that jumped them smugglers. A cow thief and horse thief!" I said, warming up to it.

"A murderin' killer what's spent half his life dodgin' hemp and sheriffs' posses!" Her eyes was like glass. "You got proof of that, have you?"

"Go ask his wife!"

She skinned back her lips. I never ketched what she said, it sounded like *pooda*. She grabbed a fresh breath. "When I got to the pens I could hear someone arguin'. Just the sounds is all, not what was said, not who was talkin'. I piled off my horse I didn't know what to do scarcely. It was awful quiet when I got into those rocks. It was powerful dark. If I hadn't stumbled over Grounds I probably wouldn't of known he was there."

"How did you know I mean, know it was him?"

"Scratched a match."

"Some surprised, wasn't you?"

"I was terrified."

"But you got your horse and packed him off."

"I couldn't just leave him like he was a piece of waste paper!"

"No skin off your nose. You hadn't never seen him till a couple hours before."

She give me a careful look. "You don't believe that?"

"I'm trying to get at the facts," I said. "If a jury ever gets called in on this."

"Well... I didn't just go fetch my horse. I heard talking again when I got back to the pens. Before it had seemed to be off towards the house... like where I found Grounds maybe. This talk was coming from behind the corrals. Two men it sounded like, arguin'... I think one was Brace. He was pretty excited."

Probably Brace and the kid. I said as much, adding, "Ivory wouldn't let them sleep in the house." It come over me then. The first voices, the ones that had pulled her into the rocks, was the same ones I'd heard back at the house Grounds and whoever had used that knife.

I said, "You better not tell no one else about this."

She went still, darkly staring. Then her jaw dropped a little. Some of the color leached out of her cheeks. "You mean?"

"That feller might get the idea you could name him. Might make up his mind not to take any chances." I considered her grimly. "I think you'd be smart to get the hell out of here."

She got that stubborn look back on her face. "All right," I said, "stay if you got to, but at least keep away from the house."

"They'll know he didn't walk off by himself!"

"You'd of been a heap smarter to have thought of that sooner." I swore then, disgusted. Brace or Lupita. Either one of them could of killed him. From the way Dimity had curled back her lip when I had mentioned Fred's wife it was plain there wasn't no love lost there. And Brace...

I remembered something else. The way he had looked stepping around that corpse, and my thinking how unlikely it was he should miss stumbling into a thing he didn't know was there. And her telling me now about him sounding excited. He'd be excited all right if, in the flare of that match, he'd seen her crouched over a dead body her that had run him into that cactus. He was weasel enough to use it, too.

"Stay here," I said, "and—"

She never let me finish. Shoulders back and jaw hitched up, she come right out with it. "I'm goin' back with you."

"Christ," I snarled. "You want to get yourself killed!"

She paled again but she didn't back off. "I can't put my life ahead of Fred's need."

"Don't talk like a fool!" I seen her eyes flatten out. I said, more reasonable, "What the hell can you do?"

"I don't know, but I can try. If I can just make them see there's no loot to squabble over..."

Man might as well argue with the shadow of death.

SIXTEEN

I CAUGHT up a horse for her, saddled it. We started.

She hadn't spoke a word since. I hadn't, neither, but there was plenty of words locked back of my teeth. About the worst thing she could do was go back there, deliberately putting her life in my hands. For that's what it come to. Making me responsible, compelling me to help whether I was minded to or not.

It was blackmail, slicker than slobbers.

Straightaway she'd seen I wasn't taking hold of that "No plunder" foolishness. So she'd pegged me for tough, a gunhung drifter, a main chance bravo, light on scruples and long on greed. She'd likely been plenty acquainted with such in the time she had spent on this place with Jake Gauze.

I've said she was smart. She was proving it now; a country girl who walked and talked and rode like a man but thought with the crossgrained mind of a witch. Hell what else could I think, knowing what she was up to? She wanted Fred helped and didn't care who she got killed in the process.

A harsh judgment, sure but no worse than she'd give me. Greed, she figured, would suck a man into anything. She was so convinced she didn't even look around.

I was powerful minded to upset her calculations, if only to by God prove that she was wrong. Serve her right if I yanked the grulla's head around and rode straight out of this jackpot! She pegged me right, you'll say, or I'd have done it.

Well, I didn't.

It was two hours to noon and hotter than a blister when we rode through the slot and come up to Fred's corrals with nothing between us and the house but them rocks.

She "swung out of her saddle. Still mad, I followed suit. I was in a ringy mood and both them, caballos knowed it. Stripping off the gear I choused them into the nearest pen, and took after her. They ought to be rubbed down and cooled out. Knowing this didn't improve my temper, but I had no time to fool with them. She was off through the rocks like a bat out of Carlsbad.

Cort Brace in his socks was setting on the front porch and she was climbing the steps when I come in sight of her. She had more guts than you could hang on a fencepost. She went straight on in.

I paused on the steps to wipe the sweat off my hands. "Ivory, picked up the guns?" Brace, hiding his hate, shook his head. "Pretty sure, eh?"

Something curled like smoke behind the gambler's stare. My eyes let go of him then and I went in.

All the rest of them was there, hunkered like buzzards round a broken legged skunk, the skunk in this picture, of course, being Fred. His whiskered jaw was sunk on his chest and the quiet would of stuffed a place ten times as big. Everyone else had their stares on the girl. She had her back to the door. I couldn't see her face but I could see Ivory fine.

He said, "I don't give a damn who slit his throat. What I want to know is why you moved him."

"I already told you why," Dimity said. "He was dead. So I buried him. Ain't that reason enough?"

"Not for me," Ivory growled. "You claim he ate with you last night. You claim he rode up here to tell old Jake there never was no treasure, that him and Zwing Hunt made the whole thing up." Considering her, still with that bullypuss grin, he said in an easy teasing way, "I'll put it to you straight. Even if there wasn't no plunder, you think a guy like him would come clean up from Texas on a fool deal like that?"

"All I know is what he said."

The quiet come back.

"You going to stick with that story?"

"It's not a story. It's the truth."

Ivory said with a trace of impatience, "The truth as you know it, mebbe. What'd he say about the map Hunt made when he was dyin' back there in Santone?"

"Never mentioned a map. He said the whole thing was a joke him and Hunt made up for laughs."

"He may of told that to you; he knew a sight better than to try it on Jake. I tell you, girl, I've checked this out. Curly Bill did sack Matamoras. They come out of Mexico with two four horse wagons loaded with plunder. From a bank they stuck up in Monterey they got two bulgin' gunny sacks crammed with money and a cigar box full of diamonds. From the cathedral at Matamoras they carted off full-length life-size figures of Christ and the Virgin Mary... *solid gold.* I talked with the priests.

"Now listen to what Zwing Hunt told about it. This come straight from his uncle. 'One of our men who'd been shot in that bank job kicked off at Davis Mountain and we planted him by Silver Spring. Five hundred dollars in gold was his cut. He'd damn well risked his life for that money so we buried it with him. It's in a tin can at the head of his grave."

Brace, who'd got up and was standing in the door, was pretty near drooling. His eyes stuck out like knots on a stick. Oakes hadn't moved. Lupita's stare was bright as brass, and the kid had both ears out at least a foot and forty inches'.

I stepped against the wall trying to catch Dimity's look and Ivory, like he was her big brother, said, "So you see that pins it down pretty definite. Look outside and what do you see? Silver Spring and that mountain back of it." His bold stare slanched a glance at Fred where the old coot sat like he was hacked out of wood, and come back to me with a knowing wink.

Dimity said, more stubborn than ever, "That doesn't change anything. You knew this the same as Fred. What nobody knew except Curly Bill, maybe was that Grounds and Hunt made it up for a joke. You've got Grounds' word for it."

Brace scowled. "Grounds is dead."

"That's right," Ivory smiled. "All we've really got, ma'am, is your words that Grounds come up here to set old Jake straight, which make about as much sense as Jake, here, thinkin' he can hog the whole works."

They all started talking at once then. They made

enough noise for a convention of coyotes. When they reached for fresh breaths, Ivory, cutting in, said, "If I'm allowed a suggestion, how's about the women rustlin' up a little grub? Shouting and swearing won't butter no parsnips."

Dimity cried, "This whole thing's ridiculous!"

"Not much point to it," Ivory said, "when all you got to do is go out there and dig."

That fetched to their faces some pretty startled looks. Kid said, "Where?"

"Well, myself I'd favor spadin up around that spring." Ivory grinned with open amusement. "If the dead man's there with his can of gold I would say Hunt pretty well knew what he was oratin' about." He settled back with a chuckle. "What do you think, Jake?"

If ever I seen hate it was on Fred's face then.

Ivory laughed.

The girls went off into the kitchen part. I said, "Hunt must've left some kind of instructions."

"He's supposed to've wrote out some. You can find as many different versions as maps. I talked to the uncle," Ivory said, smiling. "That Mexican trip come ahead of the Skeleton Canyon rub outs, the way I got it from him. That last bunch of smugglers the gang wiped out was really loaded. Big mule train. Supposed to been ninety thousand in Mex'kin money and thirty-nine bars of gold.

They buried this by three live oaks at the mouth of Skeleton Canyon.

"Few days later still according to Zwing's uncle Hunt and Grounds fetched a wagon driven by a Mex and moved this swag to the pit already half filled with the loot they'd brought up out of the south. Teamster was shot and dumped in on top. They burned the wagon."

Brace with a glassy look was rubbing at the soreness them cactuses put in him. Alamagordo scowled.

"By the uncle's tell," Ivory's tone turned gruff, "on this map Hunt made he set down in positions the mountain, the springs, the place where they burnt the wagon, a rock with two crosses and an X for the spot where the plunder is buried." With his grin spreading out he said bland as butter, "Jake has the map. Why not get him to give you a look at it?"

Oakes seemed to settle deeper into his clothes and all the lines of his face run together. He was trapped and he knowed it, and finally pushed himself up. Not looking at nobody he mumbled, "I'll git it."

Like something on strings he stepped around the table. Brace, jumping up, said, "I'll go with him."

Ivory's eyes pushed him back. "Jake's not about to run out on his friends."

He could of said *Where would he run to?* What he actually added across that cold grin was, "Not while we got Dimity Hale."

Fred tried hard but you could see him wilt. He might of carried all the weight of the world on his shoulders, his steps was that shaky. Lupita, stirring something at the stove, twisted her head to eye the whipped look of him shambling past. He mumbled at Dimity. I seen her startled face when she turned. She looked about to argue. He muttered again. She backed off out of sight. A moment later her arm come out and something passed from her hand into his.

Oakes come back and dropped the dog-eared folds of a paper on the table. Brace snatched it up, the kid at his elbow. I didn't go over, didn't even watch them smooth it out against the wood. I was staring at Ivory, grudgingly giving him the respect that was his due.

How could he have known? He couldn't, of course; it had to be a guess. But a man who could guess like that... His eyes laughed.

"This don't help too much," Brace said, looking up. He was plainly disappointed. The kid said, ugly, "There ain't no dimensions."

Ivory nodded. "Didn't figure there would be. Stood to reason. Jake, if it had been so simple as that, would of had it and flown. Hunt give his uncle a few extra notions that wasn't put down as a part of that map. He said the gang played poker in a cave on Davis Mountain said they bathed in the waterfall and that with glasses they could see from the mountain clean into New Mexico."

"Ain't no waterfall here," Brace said in a nettled whine. He looked to hold Ivory personally responsible.

Ivory grinned. "When you go after treasure what you need's imagination. That's why Jake ain't done no better than he has."

They stared at him, angered, then turned to glare at Oakes. "I bet," the kid said, "this ain't even the place! I never heard of no Davis Mountain!"

"I expect we'll find out about that when you dig."

The gambler and the kid was still grumbling over Hunt's map when the gaff in them words begun to scratch Brace. He jerked up his face in a glowering stare "Ain't you goin' to be diggin' too?"

"Oh," Ivory smiled with his usual offhand easy assurance, "I might turn over a shovelful mebbe. Any proper alliance has a place for everyone; a simple matter of talents. A place for lookers, a place for diggers"

"And what," the kid growled, "do you figger to be doin' while the rest of us is sweatin'?"

"Using the talent I'm contributing, of course."

"And what would that be?" Lupita asked from the kitchen.

Ivory put up a finger and tapped his head. "Imagination."

"It sure has brought you a far piece."

"Thank you." He bowed with an audacious flourish.

Fred was keeping out of this. Brace looked affronted. "If that means," the kid rasped, "you'll stand around doin' nothin'."

"Somebody's got to be boss," I said. "So long as we're all getting a chunk of what's found."

"All that freely contribute," Ivory coolly said. "There's obviously got to be some basis for shares. Brace and the kid, here, with picks and shovels. Jake's furnishing the map and...other particulars. Farsom his pistol." His look, brightly amused, passed on to Fred's wife. "And what will you be furnishing, my dear?"

"You son of a bitch!" Lupita said whitely.

"Tsk, tsk," Ivory clucked. "Such talk from a lady."

I got up from my chair. Not a pair of eyes shifted. I stepped around Fred and tramped off to my room, remembering the look of her when Oakes had told Ivory Grounds had been the only man still afoot actually to know where the plunder was planted.

I went in, shut the door, and shoved a hand under the bureau. Pure carelessness; I might of pushed into the fangs of a rattler. Way it turned out there wasn't anything under that wood but my hand. Like Billy Grounds, the knife was gone.

I don't know how long I stood there. When I got back they had the grub on the table, the smells of it curling up off the plates in a stillness that suddenly caught at my notice.

Brace was having some trouble with his breathing. The kid's cheeks was flushed. He come onto his feet looking meaner than gar soup. "How much," he snarled, slamming his words into Fred, "did they lift off that mule train of smugglers?"

"Ask his wife," Ivory said. "She was part of that train, the only one that got away. The 'stripling'." He laughed at Fred's look. "Lupita Garcia, the old Don's daughter."

SEVENTEEN

THAT SURE AS hell tore it, far as Fred was concerned.

It was enough to knock anybody off his perch, to get told in such fashion his wife was the daughter of a guy he'd helped murder and no telling how many more of her kin. I thought to Betsy he would bust his surcingle. His face begun to bulge. I moved in quick, figuring to get hold of him before he done her a mortal hurt.

Ivory, eyeing him slanchways, chuckled. "Jake won't touch her. Be same as admitting he fixed Grounds' clock."

I wasn't too sure about that, thinking to myself he might be selling Fred short, but it soon become evident he had yanked the right string. By degrees Oakes sagged back into his clothes. The wild look finally quit his face. He dropped onto the bench like a man with the ague.

Lupita, while the rest of us was staring at Fred, had time enough to iron out her looks, and done it. Most of what Ivory had said made the kind of hard sense a feller couldn't get around, tying in so many of the things that had stumped me and that maybe had been gnawing at

Fred off and on. It was her had killed Grounds. I was sure of that now.

You had to admire her gall. She done what she could. Looking scornful at all of us she passed Brace the meat and, with her lip curled back, said, "What kind of yarn have you figured out for Flick?"

Ivory flashed his teeth, helped himself to the hashed browns and reached across for the plate Brace held. "Long as Farsom and me understand each other there's no point proddin' up facts that might embarrass him."

That there was mighty few facts of that sort to be prodded made no difference at all. By such a slick gabble of words he had crippled opposition, making it appear him and me was buen amigos, that anyone figuring to put a spoke in his wheel would have me to reckon with.

Without promising a thing, he'd got us so worked up so filled with frustrating suspicions, there was hardly a chance we'd get together against him. Covert glances was passing around thick as bugs when Fred said, gruff, through the squirmy quiet, "What you figger on doin' if diggin' around that spring don't turn up nothin'?"

"You better just hope it don't come to that."

The stillness got thicker. You could tell by his look Ivory wasn't about to stand for much foolishness.

Dimity from the first had hardly been more than picking at her food. I seen her chin come up, and dug eyes hard into her trying to head it off. She said bound and determined, "If you'd half the sense God give to a gopher you'd know mighty well if there'd been anything around Fred would of had it dug up and spent long ago!"

Ivory grinned.

Brace growled, "Fred ain't the spendin' kind."

And Fred himself, prodded finally into speech, heaved another bitter sigh, grumbling, "Let's git on with it."

He pushed up from the table, the kid and Brace following. Lupita's look stayed fixed to her plate; but Dimity, coming off the bench, bewilderedly cried, "You surely ain't serious?"

"I expect," Ivory said, "Grounds found it so." His glance picked up Fred's wife. "You got anything more to contribute?"

She watched him sullenly, eyes twin pools of seething hate. At the door Brace twisted his face to whine, "You makin' me dig without no boots?"

"You can swing the pick."

Stepping over to the stove, never turning his back, Ivory pushed in Brace's boots and set the lids back on. He shoved the point of Brace's knife into the joint of the oven, snapping off half the blade, tossing Lupita what was left in his hand. "I can break an arm or a leg just as easy." Motioning me ahead of him he stepped onto the porch.

But Dimity wouldn't leave it there. She had to come storming after him. It scared me and I guess, Fred too, when she grabbed Ivory's arm.

Must of been the one he'd trained for his gun work. White as chalk he snatched it out of her grip and come clean around like a shot stung bear. I tell you, by God, he looked plumb loco with the spit fuzzin' out around them teeth and his eyes blazing wild. I reckoned for sure he would knock her down, and I couldn't of moved to save my soul.

Oakes, too, stood froze and, like the rest of them,

about as much help as a .22 cartridge in a twelve gauge gun.

Ivory hauled a deep breath. Some of the stiffness let go. Terrible quiet he said, "Never touch me again. Never put your hands on me."

We stood there like fools with them eyes biting into us.

With a bark of a laugh he motioned us on. My throat was so dry I couldn't spit even.

* * *

LIKE I MENTIONED BEFORE, no Davis Mountains was on any map of this country I'd looked at. There was some named Davis over in West Texas, but nothing about them tallied with Hunt's story. I'd been all through them. No waterfalls over there. Far as that went there was none around here, though Fred's wife had called this place Silver Springs and right off had told me it was in the Davis Mountains.

Fred rounded up a shovel and a oak handled pick and Brace and the lad squared off and went to digging. I stood in the shade of a cottonwood with Ivory and watched Fred hunker with his back to a rock. He looked as near natural as I'd ever seen him.

It must have been powerful hot working out in that sun with all the rock trapped heat swirling round, but for the first hour or so them boys kept hard at it. When they finally knocked off to get some ginger back into them Brace, red as fire, flopped flat on his belly, plopping his face right into the spring.

"Better go easy on that," I said.

The kid come out of his soggy shirt and Brace,

getting up with the front of him dripping, declared, "At this rate, by Gawd, we're like to be here till Christmas!"

I said, peering at Oakes, "You sure this is the place?"

Looked like his mind was a million miles away, squatting there dribbling dirt through his fingers.

"It's the place," Ivory nodded.

Brace swore, scowling at Fred. "An' who's to say he ain't already been dug up?"

"Maybe Dimity's right," I said.

"And maybe she figures to save it for Fred." Ivory's look toughened. "Get on with your digging."

The kid spit on his hands. "I'll have a go at that pick." He took a hard look around like he was trying to discover the best place to begin at. They had already worked clean around the spring.

Steps sounded back of us. It was Dimity Hale and behind her, coming through the rocks, was Lupita. Alamagordo, scowling, asked if she had any ideas on the subject. Fred's wife said, 'You're not deep enough. Put a little muscle in it."

The kid got down in the pit, spit again on his hands, begun swinging that pick like he was going for China.

Ten minutes later while he was resting his strength, Brace, working back of him, shoveled out some bones. Ivory, scrambling down, squatted over them.

"Chest bones," he grinned, lifting one to show us, whacking the earth from it. His glance come up with a plain satisfaction that curled into a scowl as Lupita's hard stare drew his look back and down. Out of the shoveled away dirt he picked a moldering length that must have come off a leg.

Didn't take no crystal ball to know a thing of that

kind wouldn't be mixed in with ribs without this ground had been stirred up before. His look found Fred. He got out of the pit. As Oakes come to his feet Ivory shoved the bone hard against Fred's breast. "Old man, you better talk fast," he said.

Fred shrunk back, waggling his head. Wouldn't of surprised me none if Ivory'd gone to beating him with it. Then Dimity run up, pushing reckless between them. Eyes blazing, she cried, "You ought to be ashamed, bullying a man old enough to be your father!"

Ivory glared. Dropping the bone he spun around, the leap of his glance searing Brace and the kid. "See if you can turn up that can!" he snarled.

The gambler wiped his streaming face. The kid took the shovel and started poking around, turning over the broken dirt, scraping through it. Oakes let Dimity lead him off into the shade. He appeared more stunned than scairt or guilty with his jaw hanging open and his shambling steps. I seen his wife and Brace exchange quick looks as Ivory, scowling, jumped into the pit and commenced impatiently to scuff around with his boots.

Then the kid, bitterly swearing, reached down and come up with a bent and rusted tin that any fool could see had once been a can like the kind they had buried full of gold when the guy was planted. You could see plain enough there was no gold in it now.

We all looked at Fred as the piece of scabrous metal thudded harsh beside his feet. The eyes jumped around in his cheeks like dying fishes. Even Dimity looked shaken.

"Tomorrow," Ivory said, "you're going to show us where you put it."

EIGHTEEN

THIS WAS one of the things about Ivory that scared
you his uncanny habit of cutting straight to the facts'.
He'd dig up these remarks that first rattle out of his
mouth looked loco, and next thing you know we was
seeing the God's awful truth of them. Like Fred, and
Hunt's map. Like Lupita being the daughter of that
murdered boss smuggler. She was one, by grab, I figured
to swap words with. But I could see getting to do it
wasn't going to be like falling off no log.

One of the things I wanted to know was what she
had got out of Grounds before she had put that knife to
his throat. Was it her had brought him here? I wanted to
know too where that knife was now, but more than
everything else I wondered why Ivory had left this
bunch of galoots heeled. Worked up like we was it
seemed a crazy damn risk he hadn't needed to take.

Fred I noticed, though he looked like a man stumbling around in his sleep, managed handily to stay
within reach of the big man's stare. Part of the time,
while supper was getting, Dimity was off with Fred's

wife out of sight, but while I could see her she never opened her mouth.

After we had got the grub stowed away and I doubt if anybody knowed or cared what they was putting into them, the whole shebang set around in the glare of that big front room like they was holding a wake or a séance or something. And every time I looked at the girl she was staring at Fred like a dying calf. She looked worse than he did.

Wasn't nobody doing any great amount of talking. Brace mostly looked at his bootless feet. I guess all of us was thinking more or less about that plunder which according to Ivory Fred would be showing us first thing tomorrow, wondering maybe if he'd called the turn again. Probably wondering too if there would be any chance of getting Fred off to himself for a little bit.

Some such notion may have been gnawing Fred because when Ivory, stretching, finally quit his chair, Fred shot up like he couldn't do it quick enough. "I been thinkin'," he said to me, "if you got no objections, I'd as like spend the night in that back room with you."

Alamagordo stared. Ivory showed his sour grin. Lupita's lips come together like the jaws of a trap. Fred's eyes frittered around not looking at nobody when Ivory took off his hat and said slyly, "Ain't nervous, are you?"

"Hell," Brace said, "I don't mind settin' up with him."

Ivory chuckled. "Sure, he'll take care of you. If it'll make you feel better you could leave your door open." Then he looked at the kid. "I'll leave mine open, too, and," his glance picked up Fred's wife, "be a good idea if you left one of these lamps lit."

Brace turned ringy. The kid's lips cracked away from his teeth and an oily shine come over Fred's cheeks.

"What are you trying to do," Dimity cried, "scare him to death?"

Ivory's stare come up off his hat. "No call to talk rough. If there's one thing all of us share in this place it's the high regard we got for ol' Jake. Ain't that right, pardner?"

Oakes' stooped shape stiffened piece by piece. He had enough sense to keep the fright off his face, enough savvy not to beg, but it was there. You could smell it.

Dimity's mouth came apart and you could read in her eyes she suddenly knew what Fred and all the rest of us had saw: that without some kind of miracle popped up she was staring at a man who could mighty soon be dead.

Now was the time, if he ever meant to do it, for him to come straight out and make the best deal he could with whatever information he'd been hugging to himself. But all he done was stand there.

The look of that girl got to be too much for me.

"I ain't sleepy," I said. "Go on and get your rest, Fred. I'll be settin' right here. Nobody's goin' to bother you."

* * *

THERE WAS A PRETTY GOOD CHANCE, when you come right down to it, I might be setting there forever. Though I called myself seven kinds of a fool, the look I got from Dimity spread a tight warm glow inside me.

She went off to bed. Lupita, wheeling into the hall after her, slipped me a kind of bullypuss stare; then the rest of them, milling, commenced straggling away. I turned my back, knowing Ivory was watching, and went around snuffing lamps till there was only one left. This I picked up, and turning it low, set it under the planks of that big stripped table where its funnel of light, fanning out across the floor, filled the length of the hall with a dim lemon glow.

Now the upper half of the front room was dark. I pulled Fred's chair off to one side and stood there a minute, uncomfortably aware of that open porch door. The far right corner of the room had no window. I dragged the chair over there.

This put a wall to my back, door and window off to the left of me, table to my right and the hall dead ahead. But the shine of that lamp come straight at my eyes. I went back, turning one of the benches over.

Now my chair was in shadow. Fred's door was open; Ivory's, too, but if anyone stepped into the hall I could see them. I bent by the table, turned the lamp down some more, then went back to my chair.

I wiped the sweat off my face. Ivory's light went out.

The place quieted down. Sounds drifted in from the night, the chirk of crickets, the cry of an owl. Twice in the next hour I caught myself nodding. You might think with all I had on my mind the last think I'd have to watch out for was sleep, but I'd got none last night, I'd fought those broncs all day yesterday; it was beginning to catch up with me.

The next time I pulled the chin off my chest there wasn't a snort or a snore, not even the shriek of a settling timber. There was no sound outside, and that wasn't natural.

I took hold of my pistol.

The quiet got so loud it put an ache in my ears. I could see the length of the hall and there wasn't no door in that end of the house nothing going outside, I mean; but Ivory's room had a window. He had used it last night... was he using it now? Which room was Dimity's? And what about that kid? Was Fred still in bed?

Questions my damn head was full of them. The back door, I remembered, opened out of the kitchen, the alcove part I couldn't see from my chair. Maybe, I thought, I'd better look in Fred's room, if only to make certain he was still there and breathing.

I got out of the chair, carefully working the kinks from my neck and shoulders, standing there then with the gun in my hand. I eased out of my boots, finally setting them down, and looked a long time into that lamp lighted hall. Two things I could do: go look in Fred's room or stay right where I was. Before I done anything something moved in the kitchen with a Indian stealth; more a hunch, I guess, than any definite sound. I was pretty near scairt to twist my head, but I done it.

And saw not one thing I hadn't looked at before.

Just the same there was something. The lampflame was climbing up one side of the glass and a suction of air was running over my feet. Like a door had been opened.

Hardest thing I ever done was go out in that kitchen. Door was open, all right clean back against the wall. Maybe this was what had roused me. If it had been open very long the flame in that lamp would have blackened the chimney.

You're right I was stalling. Maybe any guy would that had a lick of sense. One of this bunch, while I'd been pounding my ear, had slipped outside... or was this what they wanted me to think? Some hoax set up to get me out of the house? Brace, or that kid, might not be so cute, but Ivory could have rigged it. And so could Fred's wife. I could see plain enough no matter what I done would probably be the wrong thing.

The need to look into that hall overpowered me, or maybe it was Dimity that turned me around. I was already moving when a snaggle of whispers stopped me cold in my tracks. Every hair on my scalp stood up and I spun, gun lifting, to stare into the night.

Too black to see, but there was somebody out there. Two of them, anyways. One was furious, apparently threatening, savagely angry. There was whispers again, the sounds' of a scuffle, the crack of a hand flat and hard against flesh.

I went out, crouched low, trying to get the shapes of them against that murky sky. The dark bulk of the canyon wall was too near. Somebody gasped. There was a flutter of motion. Booted feet beat a clatterous retreat through loose shale. I fired into the racket, no yell frittering back.

Pistol flame jumped from the house's far corner, the whine of that bullet singing bitterly close. No time for thinking. I went down on one knee, drove two shots at the flash. Somebody screamed. I leaped up and run toward him, cursing, gun lifted.

He was down, all right. I could see the dark blotch of him. I pulled up, brassy mouthed, fighting vomit, the ragged thud of my heart the loudest sound in all that clamor. The runner had hid himself in the confusion, the night was suddenly shouting with eyes.

I backed off, fading away from that place, anxious and dreading what I'd find in the house, knowing I'd better get in there quick. No good hunting for the one that hadn't run. I cut in toward the kitchen, hearing the gabble of voices, still hearing my heart, too. The back door was open. I went in fast.

Dimity, in the hall, come around at one swipe, her eyes big as sauce pans. She was dressed and standing not an arm's length from Ivory who, though bare to the waist, had a gun in his fist. I kept hold of mine, too.

We peered at each other while the quietness piled up, Ivory finally breaking it. "You do all that shootin'?"

I sloshed into my boots, bent and got the lamp out from under the table. Eyeing Fred's closed door I twirled up the wick. "He's gettin' his clothes on," Dimity said.

It didn't strike me at once, what an odd thing it was that Fred, of all people, should have peeled off for bed. I made a bet with myself that nobody else had. Dimity's eyes, narrowing, darkened. "I thought you were going to stay in that chair."

"Seems a lot of folks did. Where's the rest of this outfit?" I shoved my glance at Ivory.

He stared, eyes flattening, hefting his gun. "You sound kind of proddy."

I give him both barrels, blunt enough to stop clocks. "There's a jasper outside won't be wantin' no breakfast. There was two others out there I didn't catch up with."

His look come full open. I heard Dimity gasp. One of the shut doors cracked, Fred's wife popping her head out. "You damn fools going to caterwaul all night?"

Shoving past Ivory I got a fistfull of night rail, hauling her out where we could all have a squint at her. She come scratching and swearing, looking madder than hops.

I slammed her into the wall. "You goin' to talk, by God, or have I got to rip it off you?"

Even Ivory looked startled. You could tell by the fit of it she had all her clothes on.

Her eyes was like daggers. She slanched her look at Fred who had just that minute come up. "You going to let this bastard insult me?"

"Could he?" Fred said.

"All right," she snapped, rounding back on me, "if a girl has to go she's got to, don't she?"

Dimity's cheeks fired.

Ivory smiled, watching us. "Who was with you?"

"No—"

"Powerful lot of mutterin'," I said. "You always wrassle with yourself when you step out to squat?"

She went up in smoke. There was blood on my cheeks when they dragged her off. She called me every damn name she could put tongue to.

"Someone," I said, when she run out of breath, "took off like a twister. Then a gun by the corner of the house opened up pretty near had by name on it, too! I fired at the flash. You want to go have a look at him?"

"Bound to be either Brace," Fred said, "or that kid."

"They bed down in the house?"

Ivory shook his head, switched his look, to Lupita. "You want to sing a little now?"

"It was Brace," she said sullenly. "He knew who I was it was him put me up to marryin' Jake. He's been at me to get his hands on that map."

You couldn't tell what Fred thought. I figured about a quarter of what she said might be true. "And tonight?" Ivory purred, "What'd he want with you tonight?"

The red lips curled. "That crystal ball of yours broke down?"

He cracked her across the face so hard her head banged into the door frame. Part of her hair come down, the marks of his fingers showing livid on her skin.

You'd of thought after that she would have called it a day, but all he'd done was turn her more wild. Her nostrils flared like a trumpeting horse. "You son of a bitch!" she cried, tearing into him.' She made a grab for his pistol and he struck her again this time with the barrel of it. She went legs over elbows, fetching up in a heap.

She come onto one knee. I seen the blood mixed into the spittle on her chin, but she had guts by God, you had to give her that. She wasn't one to let a little hurting cramp her style. "What's the matter, mister?" she snapped at me. "You glued there or somethin?"

I couldn't get enough wet in my gullet to swaller.

"Never mind!" she snarled, and got onto her feet with that hair every whichway, eyes burning out of it. She hawked up a frog and spit it square in his face. "You been blowed up so much by them pelados you run with I guess you think, Fisher, you really are a king. Hell, you'll cut just the same as any other two legged bastard!"

I seen the flash of a knife as she flung herself at him. Flame jumped from his fist. She run right into it.

NINETEEN

ONCE A THING'S over a man can generally figure what he ought to done different, and it was that way with me. Perhaps Fred's wife had used up her luck getting clear of that Skeleton Canyon massacre. Maybe her course was laid out and decided before ever she'd come to Silver Spring but I couldn't help thinking if I'd been a shade quicker, or jumped that devil when she first lit into him, I wouldn't be feeling quite so draggletail mean.

With the smoke whimmerin' round through them clattering echoes we stood like bent sticks, scarce breathing, frozen eyed, hamstrung by the truths confronting us.

Wasn't a man in that room hadn't heard of King Fisher, or could doubt this was him now she'd put the name to him. The fancy clothes, the slick deadly feel of him that grin and the gun, had figured too bright in things told round the cow camps. He rated with Thompson and John Wesley Hardin, a gun slamming galoot who killed without quarter we had the truth of that, too.

We knew or anyways I did it was Brace outside" that had been doing the jawing, that lit out through the shale the minute I'd showed. We had Lupita's word for it, and this put the kid at the corner of the house. I hadn't a doubt it was him we would find there. I was more concerned now to discover where Brace was.

"Hold up." Fisher growled as I started for the porch. "Where you off to?"

"Brace," I grumbled over a shoulder.

"I'm givin' the orders here," Fisher said. "You want to stay healthy you better remember it." His eyes was like a pair of baked marbles. With that gun in his fist I hadn't much choice. "Stop right where you are," he said, and I done it.

Sure I had a gun in my hand. He grinned when he saw me reluctantly let go of it. His glance slanched over Fred and the girl. "Pretty soon Jake's going to dig up that plunder. Just to make sure we all know where we're at I'm dabbin' a loop round this Hale filly's neck."

* * *

WHEN FIRST LIGHT spread its sheep's wool gray behind that jagged rim to the east Fisher levered himself up out of the chair. Walking past Dimity he got hold of the rope, nipping the loose end of it over a rafter, hauling in slack till he had her right under it. He give a couple of tugs that fetched her onto her toes, eyes weighing Fred watching me even more before, thinly grinning, he let go of enough to let her heels come back down. "Expect you know what'll happen if things don't come off accordin' to Hoyle."

He was all through fooling. Any nump could see that.

First thing he'd done after getting the noose round her was to take Fred's pistol and then lift hers, thrusting them into the pockets of his coat. He broke the blade of Lupita's dropped knife, told Fred to find a shovel and put her underground as though getting her out of sight was like to fix anything.

With her over his shoulder Fred stumbled out. Taking up the lamp I followed. Like a dog on a leash Dimity came after, Fisher, with the guns, bringing up the rear.

A change had set in. It was like a smell on the air.

The West in its time had managed to live with a heap of things, some of them violent, a few downright bad. But no part I'd heard tell of had so far been able to swaller a killed woman. What had happened to Lupita was gnawing pretty sharp. Like the scratch of sand it stayed harsh in our thinking, each guarded look, every breath we drew, isolating Fisher, setting us against him as nothing else could.

He seen it, too. It was why he'd disarmed us, it was back of him putting that rope on Dimity. He'd had to have some way to keep us in line but he sure didn't look to be putting much trust in it. His stare jumped around like a boxful of crickets.

Killing that woman kept chewing on him. He couldn't forget it. When we come to that corner and didn't find the kid I thought for a minute he would bust his britches.

Maybe I looked as flabbergasted as I felt. Fred was

the only one that didn't seem bothered. He stood with his wife hunched over one shoulder and looked like he hadn't no more mind than an idiot.

Fisher snarled, waving his pistol. "Git that lamp down where we can see somethin'!"

"Here's where he stood," I said, pointing out the marks. There was a scuffed place just past them. I pointed again. "Looks like blood."

Fisher poked out a finger, sniffed it and nodded. "Guess you knocked him down, all right." His glance, weighing Dimity, moved on to Fred. "Hell," I said, "they ain't been out of your sight."

He eyed me a while, stabbed a squint at the sky. "Take a look in the bunkhouse."

We trailed through the rocks filled with our thinking. The shovel they'd used to put Grounds away stood against the poles of the nearest corral. Fisher tossed it at Fred, motioning me on.

The bunkhouse was dark. Packing that lamp like I was, and no pistol, I expected any minute to get shot clean loose of my everlasting soul, but nothing happened. We come up to the place. I kicked open the door.

No sign of the kid. But Brace was there, all shivers and shakes.

"On your feet!" Fisher barked.

Eyes rolling, Brace come out of his blanket.

"All right," Fisher said. "What'd you do with him?"

"Never touched the little bastard, as Gawd's my witness he was gone when I got there!"

"Gone where?"

Damn fool was so scairt you could hear his teeth

clacking. "C-c-leared out, I guess your horse is g-g-gone, too."

Fisher spun Dimity round and shoved her out through the door. At the corrals the truth of what Brace said was apparent. The only horse there was Fred's big grulla. He tromped up to us, nickering, put his head over the poles.

I switched the lamp to my other hand. Fisher's look was black as thunder. "All right, Brace. You pile on this mouse and go fetch in those broncs Jake's been holdin."

"Broncs?" Brace quavered. "What b-b-broncs?"

"You'll find 'em. Just foller your nose. And don't be all night." Fisher's look turned impatient.

Brace's rabbity face was covered with sweat. Great drops stood out on his narrow-boned cheeks. His Adam's apple worked like the float on a troutline. "B-but—"

"Look!" Fisher growled. "Do this right and I'll take care of you."

Brace swallowed noisily. Swallowed again.

"Jump, God damn you!" Fisher cried, tipping his gun up.

With a frightened squawk Brace went through the poles. Fisher waved Dimity and me toward the sound of Fred's digging.

And now here we was, turning over thought we'd been through a hundred times while day come bumbling towards us out of the night. Fred hadn't spoke all the time we was waiting. Dimity's eyes was like burns in a bed sheet. She finally roused to tell Fisher wearily, "The only thing Fred's dug up is post holes."

Fisher's face showed his scorn.

I said, "But what if she's right? What if there ain't no goddam plunder?"

"What's he got all them pack saddles for?"

The stillness filled with our unspoken fears. Beyond the east window the darkness curdled, become gray as fog. Stringers of it swirled across the porch and pearl gray floating puffs of it swooped in to curl around us like the gnawing of our thoughts.

Fisher said, "Here they come," and the gulch was loud with the racket of horses.

TWENTY

THROUGH EVERYTHING else even the cold shaking shivers of what I felt for the girl, I kept going back to what had happened at the corner of the house. There was a fuzziness there, black sliding into black, beyond the bright burst of that muzzle flash. It was the lad right enough nobody else showed hurt, and I'd seen the dark blotch of him there on the ground.

We'd found blood, and then boot marks. Still it kept nipping me... something unfinished, something pushed aside, lost in a welter of more striking impressions. That kid wasn't tough, he'd only wanted to be, and the light had been bad. If all I'd done was wing him he would of sure enough bolted soon's I went in the house. With Fisher's horse gone there wasn't much else a man could think.

Brace's reedy voice come out of the murk.

"Come in," Fisher growled.

The tinhorn showed up, flapping over the porch in what was left of his socks. His eyes goggled round. He sleeved the drip off his chin. "I didn't g-git all of 'em..."

He run a hand round his collar. "S-some got away but what I got is shut up in them p-pens."

"You done fine," Fisher nodded. He put his pistol away, hard stare drilling Fred.

Fred's look cringed away. He worked his jaw up and down. When the words finally come you'd of thought they'd been hauled all the way up from China. "I'm ready."

Fisher, grinning, took hold of the rope. I grabbed at his arm. "You figurin'," I said, "to leave her tied to that rafter?"

"You got a better way to keep him in line?"

Fred said, husky, "I won't make you no trouble."

"I will," I said, "if you don't git that rope off her."

His look banged into my face like a fist. I don't know why he didn't shoot me right then. The whole top half of him swelled. He jerked himself loose and rared back like a scorpion, hand hooked to pounce for the grips of his pistol. His stare in that quiet was like slivers of glass.

Maybe mine was, too. For seconds hand-running we stood there with the sound of the wind crying through them rocks and nobody batting so much as a eyewinker. His hand fell away. "All right," he said, laughing it off, "you make your point." He flipped the rope off her neck. "Now get out there with Brace and saddle four of those broncs. Whatever's left throw pack rigs on, and don't take more than two weeks to do it."

* * *

BY SIX O'CLOCK WE was ready to start. Brace and me, mounted, had each of us a saddled bronc to tow and twenty-three others, decorated for packs. You might of thought we was fitting out to go to the moon.

"All set," I grumbled with my look quartering over them. You never seen so many walled eyes in your life. One good sneeze and the whole humped, foot stomping, headshaking bunch was like to go kiting off in forty directions.

The girl come out first. Then Jake looking like he'd been pushed through a knothole; then Fisher, spurs flashing, red scarf at his waist, both bone handled guns and that big silver buckle standing right up between the pushed back skirts of his coat. He got his grin working again but it didn't get up into his eyes any to speak of.

Dimity said, "Hadn't I better throw together some kind of a meal?" Fisher shook his head. "You can eat when we get back... if Jake keeps his mind where he better had."

"Which way we headin'?" Fred asked, inscrutable.

Fisher grinned. "Don't think I've gone at this blind, old man. I been up on that mountain. Damn good view. You can look straight across the San Simon Valley, see right into New Mexico without a glass. I found the cave where that bunch is supposed to've played poker. Some graves up there. If it's all the same to you I believe we'll mosey west."

Dimity said, startled, "But Silver Spring—"

"That's the thing about Jake, he's cute," Fisher said, "real cute. Handy with a runnin' iron, too. He can work things over till an ordinary pilgrim couldn't tell Plymouth Rock from Sittin' Bull, and work God damn! The bones he's moved..." He let the rest of it go, staring hard at her. Then his eyes grabbed Fred. "I don't know what's between you two I don't give a damn. Just get this straight: every time you steer us wrong there's goin' to be something broke. That clear?"

Fred jerked his head.

"All right. Git goin'. Git up there with him, Farsom."

Only thing I found to feel good about was I had my gun back between my legs, the horse I'd rode in here from Tombstone on Lord, but that seemed a long while ago! Fred was on one of them green broke broncs, gingerly steering him off through the rocks.

At the pens I come up with him. "This ain't no time to be playin' games," I said. "All the loot in hell ain't worth her losin an arm or a leg for. That son of a bitch means just what he said."

You could head the broncs shuffling along behind. Fred never turned, never opened his mouth. I suppose I was pretty near beside myself. "If he harms one hair of her head," I snarled, "you better get ready to meet your maker that's a promise!"

Still not bothering to say anything, he led into the twisting pinch of them walls on the trail down canyon where he'd showed me the bones. I seen a mighty good chance I'd be leaving mine here. If by killing Lupita Fisher'd welded us closer you sure couldn't tell it. He had the whole bunch buffaloed. That kid had showed sense getting out when he could.

If he'd got out. For all I could tell maybe Fisher had killed him, cracked him over the head and shoved him into some hole. He'd been out of my sight long enough to have done it.

Only thing I knew for sure was I'd hit him. Blood... we'd all seen it. But if he hadn't been hurt bad enough to stay put and Fisher hadn't had no hand in what happened, maybe, just maybe, he hadn't took off. Might be the gimpy fool had hid out, hoping someway to get the best of us yet.

Which was all right with me. He hadn't no gun, but a rock, moved right, could do about as much damage in a place like this. It was nothing but wishful thinking, I reckoned, but I begun to perk up, peering around with more notice, hugging to my hopes what I could do with a diversion.

This whole country was dry powder dry. Even the dusty weeds, what few you could find, was stunted and brittle, falling apart like cracked glass no more than you touched them. In the gray pall kicked up by so many hoofs almost anything might happen if a man stood ready to take a little risk.

I was ready, right enough, but my hands was tied long as Dimity was back there with Brace and Fisher. I kept scouring the rocks for some sign of that kid.

The trail, crooked here as the track of a snake, kept wriggling and winding back into the west. We was headed, I figured, to where I'd worked them damned broncs. They seemed to be doing pretty fair for the moment, coming along without much fuss. Like Fred, up ahead, with his jowls on his shirtfront. I wondered if he'd thought what might happen if they bolted.

I had some other crazy notions in the next couple miles Fred, too, probably. I couldn't tell what he was thinking but I sure had my eyes peeled. If Fisher was right this old coot could be desperate. And then he scared the hell right out of me.

We'd just come round one of them gooseneck bends and there he was, putting his mount at the wall, twenty-five foot of it straight up and down, the bronc raring back and him slapping the hooks in for all he was able. I said, "For Chrissake!" I thought he'd gone off his rocker, booting that bronc at a clump of dwarf cedar that was all you could see between him and that wall. And next thing I knowed, by God, they was gone I mean plumb out of sight like they never had been!

I reckon my eyes damn near rolled off my cheekbones.

Back of me them loose broncs was coming up in their pack rigs, and back of them Fisher, and what he'd said would be happening first time he figured he was being crossed up. I was sure enough in one hell of a sweat and it didn't help none when Fred, impatient, growled, "What're you waitin' on?"

I looked all over. I didn't get down on my knees and flippers but alls I could see was these cedars growing out of that great chunk of stone. Then his voice come again, 'Push 'em into those bushes!"

If it was hard for me to accept the idea, it was harder still to sell the facts to them broncs. They kept wanting past, trying to get to their bedgrounds. With all that churning and pawing the dust got so thick it was like trapped in the middle of a twister. They didn't break past but not a damn one would go into them cedars. Alls I got from my cuffing and swearing was heads and tails going round and around, and the racket we raised you could of heard clean to Chloride.

I was on the third trip around with my assortment of cusswords when Fisher come larruping out of the dust and, assisted by Brace, with rein ends and romal began shoving them through. "Drive 'em into that brush!" Fisher shouted. It come over me then what a kettle of fish we'd of had on our hands if Fred had figured to skin past this hid crack. Made me so weak I pretty near puked.

About the time Brace was waving the last bronc through I got back enough steam to wonder what had become of Dimity. Spinning around in the leather fetched a look from Fisher that would have set corn to popping. "You can forget that kid he's probably halfway to 'Frisco."

I didn't disentangle him. I figured I might just as well be agreeable. "I thought," I said, pulling the wipe off my mug, "Fred was clean off his rocker when he piled into them bushes. Mind tellin' me how you got onto it?"

You could see he was tickled. Tapping the crown of his hat he said, "Brains." Then he pointed, "That's Davis Mountain up there, first thing I had to make sure of. Cave's there, and the graves. Soon's I got a look at Hunt's map I knew we was in the wrong canyon; things he described simply wasn't there."

"But the spring"

Fisher grinned. "By Hunt's description there was *two* springs remember? I've poked around. This puddle Jake calls Silver is the only piece of water you can find in this gulch. Had to be another canyon; they climbed the mountain to look into New Mexico, so it had to be close. Somethin' else he didn't have was that waterfall. Sure, it might have dried up but there should of been signs. There ain't nothing south, so it had to be a canyon running into Round Valley."

"How'd you know Fred would turn it up for you?"

"It had to be close. If he hadn't made his move inside the next mile I'd of tackled the girl. I was here a couple months ago, fetching these broncs seen then he was sweet on her." His grin toughened up. "That makes two of you." He waved me into the cedars. "Better catch up with them."

You could see the opening behind them now that some of the brush had got twisted and trampled. I trailed Brace through. First thing I seen was Dimity up there by Fred hanging onto the horses. She must have gone through while I was fighting that dust.

Brace pushed up the stragglers.

This place didn't look much different than the other except it was greener and maybe, right here, perhaps twenty foot wider. Pretty well haired over. Juniper and live oak mostly. I said to Brace out of the side of my mouth, "You reckon that kid really did cut his stick?"

With his dirty bare feet sticking out of them stirrups all scratched up and clotted he didn't look like nothing a man would put much stock in. His watery glance slithered around. His nose twitched, he snuffled and tugged down his hat to get him out of the sun. "That boy," he confided in his pipsqueak whine, "hadn't no more guts than a junebug."

His lip peeled back and he said, resentful, sounding righteous as hell, "All blat an' no bottom. Even before you loosed that blue whistler the little sidewinder was all set t' crawl off an' leave us!"

Reaching out, Fisher poked him with the end of a finger. "Ride up there with Jake and keep your eyes skinned. And send that girl back."

Pink Cort Brace. An elegant title, I thought, watching him, for as mangy a rat as you would ever find. Then I looked at myself, wondering by how much I assayed any higher. We was all in the same boat... except maybe Dimity, I figured, eyeing Fisher.

He grinned at me sourly. "Keep right on hoping. Maybe you can hope Brace out of his pepperbox. Get up there now and keep these broncs moving don't string 'em out or you'll hear from me."

Dimity come past as I kneed the dun away from him. Our glances touched. I got the notion she was wanting to say something but she reined on by without never a word.

I got the broncs closed up, not chousing them none. Glancing back, I seen Fisher had a rifle across his pommel. I don't know what the hell happened to mine, guess he lifted it probably when he got rid of them others.

The walls was widening out. It was getting hot in here with that sun beating down. There wasn't much dust. Things was moister in here, the broncs breaking their way through a tangle of ash and sycamore. I kept scanning the walls for a way up out of it without finding nothing a goat could use even. I begun to wonder about Fred. Didn't look like anyone had ever been in here.

In the next quarter mile we got a lot more elbow room. You couldn't see the mountain, but through the leaves of the trees and where it was open there seemed to be places where a feller on foot if he kept his wits about him might get up that east climb.

About the time I noticed the broncs slacking off, Fred stuck up a hand. We seen him waggle it at us. Fisher said, "Hold 'em," and, scowling, pushed on with the girl. She was one thing he wasn't about to forget.

Even I could see the excited look on Brace's face. Fred's jaw flapped as Fisher come up with them. I like to ruptured a ear trying to catch what he was saying. Fisher, after a minute, stood up in his stirrups and took a long look around. Shaking his head he pulled aside, waving them on.

I could smell the damp before I got up there. "Silver?"

Fisher shrugged. "We'll know pretty quick. Ought to be a burnt wagon a hub, anyways. Might be nothin but spokes. Keep your eyes peeled."

He pushed after the others.

He didn't have to tell me. Maybe it hadn't showed like it had on Brace's face but he was plenty keyed up. Three million smackers!

"Jesus Christ!" I said, and looked around for something I could use to turn the tables. Nobody had to tell me a damned thing. Once he come onto that loot he'd have about as much use for the rest of us as a gray squirrel would have for a load of them minnie balls.

TWENTY-ONE

IT WAS Dimity found the next of Hunt's clues.

She had her bronc out a ways from the others; trying, I reckoned, to get enough room to think in, lally-gaggin along like a sorefooted turtle.

The tinhorn and Fred had pulled ahead a good piece and it was my notions she might be figuring I'd catch up. Seemed like Fisher might be hugging the same idea. He was staring straight at her when she hauled to a stop. Right away he was reining Fred's grulla over, with the old man and Brace twisting round in their saddles.

"Gum Spring," he called.

She must of had good eyes. It was nothing but a green-scummed seep maybe two foot across and just about buried in a clutter of granite chunks off the rim.

"Boys," Fisher grinned, "we're gettin' close." Their excitement was contagious. Even Fred, I seen, was beginning to breathe hard. It was like I was perched on some high bare place hanging on by two toenails in a buffeting gale. The glare was sky and sun, probably two thirds fright. The reds and grays and maggoty yellows, with the pale greens shimmering below and above, was the whopper thorns I had fell among that could without half trying rip a man to the bone. It was like I was wide awake in a dream, bare naked and everyone around me dressed. Even the smells was louder, like the hot iron stink coming off that fried ground. It was like I had seen the end of the world and no one but fools could talk my lingo.

Time had about run out. They was going to come up with this goddam plunder. All at once I knew I could feel the grate of it between my teeth... and something else, coldly wicked, like bright little wires boring into my back.

It done me no good to look. There was nothing to see but the rocks and brush and that white crack of sky. Just the wriggle of heat writhing up through the catclaw. Nothing at all I hadn't peered at before.

Fisher waggled an arm. "Forget them broncs. Get up here and help us hunt for that wagon."

I toed the dun over, being careful not to let my glance stray towards Fred. It didn't make no difference. "Old man," Fisher said, "you been in here. Where is it?"

Fred looked like he'd reached the end of his rope.

"Well?" Fisher snarled. Each strike of his stare was like a coiled rattler, wound up and ready.

Fred went back a step, cringing. He'd got off the damned bronc. His eyes crept to me. The knuckles of his hands where they was wrapped through the reins couldn't of been squeezed no tighter.

Fisher's hard stare tramped over my face. I expect all of them was watching sure felt like they was. A wild fury clawed through me and I come off the leather, straight up in my stirrups... and seen the black snout of that unwinking rifle.

I dropped back, all the rage and the shame of it bottled inside me.

What Fred said I never heard. If Fisher laughed I never noticed. Hoof falls and the screak of saddles presently cut through what had hold of me. I seen we was on our way again, still pointing north, riding through gravel as the canyon bent east and the look of things changed, the walls pinching in, the floor strewed with granite, brushy with reefs of manzanita and catclaw that ripped at our pants legs and tore free, slaty green. There was yucca, too, and pincushion pear, and jumbles of cholla reaching to prod the unwary. Then the view loosened up and Fisher grinned. "There's your waterfall."

I didn't see no water. Just a nest of black rocks heaved up out of the ground in a tangle of broken sticks and dead weeds, and Brace's jaw hanging open. Like the rest I followed Fisher's look to the rim. 'It ain't runnin' now," he said in that told you so voice. "But there's where she come from and here's where she hit."

We was in a dry wash I seen that much. And, against the east wall, the mark of high water. I see Fred staring like a hard hooked fish. If ever a man looked sick it was him.

Fisher herded us on. I glanced back a couple of times and seen Fisher's teeth. Wasn't nothing else to see but them loose broncs clattering after us. Though I quartered both rims, every patch of brush, each crack and cranny without spotting a thing, the notion kept gnawing. If the goddamn fool didn't hurry it up...

It was Fisher and his guns that finally opened my

eyes. All the way from Fred's place I'd been determined Alamagordo would someway get the best of him and save us. But why should he? What did he care about Dimity, or even Brace? No skin off his butt if Fisher gunned the lot of us. The kid was after that plunder and alls he had to do was keep out of sight, wait till we found it, then step in and pick up the pieces.

These was the plain hard facts.

You might shut your eyes, talk all around, but when the last chip was down they was what you had to reckon with. Fisher wasn't going to split that loot up with nobody. No help from Brace. Fred ... well, the fact that he'd showed us the way through them bushes pretty well spoke for him. Any help to be looked for was going to have to come from me, and there wasn't any question but what Fisher figured likewise. Not once had I caught his eyes off me.

It was Brace discovered all there was of the wagon. Two spokes, an iron rim and what was left of a hub. He got them out of the wash. It wasn't surprising we didn't find more. The hub had been half eaten by fire.

The girl looked at Fred like she couldn't believe it. I suppose I had known all along Fred was Gauze. If I hadn't I certain sure should of when he'd parted them bushes.

I had thought when Fisher gunned Lupita it would bring the rest of us closer together. Nothing I could see give any evidence of this. I couldn't afford any more wrong guesses. Gauze, despite the girl's unwavering loyalty, had to be looked at for what he was, a coyote, bold and cunning enough among dogs and women but a mighty sorry sight now that a wolf had sat down on his doorstep.

Brace had a pistol, if I could get my hands on it. He still had that pepperbox he'd poked in my face the first time I'd seen him.

Why had Fisher let him keep it? A whim? Or out of the vast contempt a man of his caliber would feel for a tinhorn? Fisher wasn't a fool; there'd be more to it than that. It probably give him a laugh.

I could see how it would. Curly Bill in his time he'd been another who'd took a heap of fun out of fools, had frequently pulled some pretty wild stunts for laughs. More likely, I thought, Fisher'd left Brace his pepperbox to make, him feel useful, to make him think he was counted on, a part of the boss man's plan. A Judas steer. A kind of pardner.

Why not? That way he could get some use out of the feller. He already had; he'd got his broncs rounded up, the horses he'd had Fred pasture to have them handy when the time come for riding off with Curly Bill's loot.

"Now, Jake," Fisher said, "you get out Hunt's map an' take another look at the positions of these things we've got pinned down. Get them firmly in mind. The next job we're givin' you is to dig up the rock with the two crosses on it. We're countin' on you taking us pretty much right to it."

He showed his teeth. Gauze stood there a minute, then he climbed on his horse with the sweat popping out of him and, never bothering with the map, let off up the wash. He had the look of a man on his way to Armageddon.

Fisher waved me after him, then the girl, leaving Brace and himself to bring up the rear. Near as I could figure, from what I'd seen, we might have as much as a mile to go. We was headed straight in toward the mountain now, coming up from the west. Dead ahead of us it was, the bare rocks sticking out of it like busted ribs.

Maybe, I thought, he'd let Brace keep it in the hope it might push me into showing my hand. Wasn't a chance with him watching I could get the thing away from Brace. Any try I made would give Fisher the excuse to put me out of this deal for keeps. I didn't .see, however, that I had much choice.

Ain't a prospect many dwells on, not being around anymore for Java. Dying is for others, never for yourself. What was it like to cash in your chips? Was there something really waiting for a man beyond the quick?

I hadn't thought much about it, didn't figure to find any time for it now. Something had to give, and soon, or we was done for.

Fisher still had Dimity up at the front but she'd been dragging her feet again. Brace wasn't two horse lengths behind, Fred abreast and me maybe fifty foot nearer the hard shape of the rifle.

There was a dispirited droop to the look of her shoulders that told better than words the kind of thoughts she was stuck with. She set that bronc like a sack of oats, all the jounce gone out of her. My eyeballs quivered, I could feel the breath piling up in my throat. She was nearer already to Brace than she had been.

It come over me like a bundle of sticks, she was shaping a play to get hold of that pepperbox. Near scared the goddam fiver right out of me.

It just might work if I could keep that big...

I pulled off to the side, rolling a smoke while I set there. Up he come, curious as a cat and twice as leery. "What do you reckon you're up to?" he says, swiveling that rifle to where with one squeeze he could puncture my tintype. "I give you your orders."

"Only one thing," I said, sidling my horse around to where his eyes couldn't take in the both of us. I seen his suspicion, the wicked jump of his muscles.

Brace's yell climbed like the squeal of a shoat. Fisher'd come too near to back off in time now. My foot hit the rifle just before it went off, tearing it out of his grip.

Then I was onto him, slugging and falling as the weight of my dive took him out of the saddle.

It was hard where we fell. I caught the worst of it. Pain roared through me like the rip of barbed wire. He squirmed loose, rolling clear. I tried to come off my back but it was like that rock had busted my shoulder. That damned right arm wouldn't mind me at all.

Frantic, I come onto one knee. A heap of things come into my mind I even seen my old man. Then the world exploded in a burst of white sparks.

TWENTY-TWO

MUCH AS ANYTHING, I reckon, it was the jolting finally roused me; the lurch and roll, the sagging twist, the nerve nagging churn of continual motion. Takes a while, sometimes, to catch up with yourself. The swush of hoofs beat through my head. Hairy legs, a lathered shoulder and heaving ground took up most of the view. I was folded face down across the hug of a saddle.

I wasn't right sure I wouldn't just as like be dead. I'd never had such aches. I seen the hands flopping around. I must of looked at them half a mile before I noticed they was mine. I wiggled the fingers, first the left then the right. I was kind of surprised to find that both sets worked. Then I remembered Fisher. When I couldn't stand no more of it I got myself up into the saddle.

He must of beat the bejasus out of me. I hung on with both hands, and when the dizziness passed there he was, right alongside of me. He said, "I figured, by Gawd, you was smarter than that."

She was up ahead with a stick thrust between her back and her arms. They had her hands tied again. Fred was bound, too. I could hear the grunts of the climbing horses. The side of that mountain wasn't a quarter mile off.

The collapse of our attempt at turning the tables had restored all his confidence. You'd have thought by his tone he had that loot in his pockets.

Brace, when Dimity had jumped him back yonder, had snatched out his pepperbox and then, what with the horses acting up and trying to fight off the girl, had dropped the damn thing. It was lost now, gone down a crevice. Only guns in the crowd was the ones in Fisher s holsters and the rifle he'd picked up and had back across his lap.

He said, "I'm tellin' you this so you'll know where you stand." He made it real plain. "You want dirt thro wed into their faces just try something else. It ain't going to take more than two of you to load it."

I guess he had a right to feel good.

The east wall petered out against the side of the mountain. It was climbable here, the glare broken up by the shadows of ash and sycamore. Above was fire and piñon and, in between, the blue black green of juniper. It stacked high for looks with the light filtered through that leafy tangle of branches.

It was here Fisher found the rock with two crosses.

* * *

WE SPENT HALF an hour lolling around while he sized up the place, studying Hunt's map and estimating distances. A dozen times he jumped up to poke around, not saying a thing, just looking.

I thought if he would only put down that rifle... but

he never did. He never come near enough. Unless Alamagordo took a hand in this go-around we had come to the end of our rope it sure looked like.

Fisher, stepping back with his eyes cold and mocking, said, "That kid ain't going to copper no bets. I busted him over the head back yonder."

Something seemed to let go inside Fred. I seen all the lines of his face run together, and the clothes hanging to him looked more looselike than ever; and I wondered if he had made with the kid the kind of a deal he had shoved at me.

"Brace, get the pick," Fisher said, thinly smiling, "and a couple of shovels off that apron faced roan."

Dimity sniffed. "You're wastin' your time."

Beneath them bold eyes Fisher's grin was like velvet. "You fix your mind on stayin' healthy, anything harder than that I'll take care of." His look bit at me. "Grab up that pick and get over there where you can touch those two crosses."

I felt like a man walking over cracked ice. When I come to the rock he said, "You see that old slide?"

"You mean against the west wall?"

"Sometimes I wonder how I ever done without you. Now, accordin' to this map, Bill's plunder ought to be about midway between where you're at and that slide."

I couldn't sight too good with all them trees sticking up. "You want I should find how many steps it is?"

"Just start hikin'. I'll tell you what I want."

I went around the first boles making sure he was able to see me. The next was a sycamore, two foot through. I could feel the sweat rolling down my back. "While you're wonderin'," Fisher purred, "just recollect what can happen to that girl if I squeeze this trigger."

The son of a bitch thought of everything.

"Bight there ought to be about right," he said presently. "Lumpy, ain't it?"

"You think all this chaparral's got growed over it?" I growled, disgusted. "Some of this stuffs two inches across."

"Some of it's dead, too. Start swingin' that pick."

Just bucking that brush was a chore in itself. The ground was like flint and lousy with stones, some bigger than melons. A lot of that growth was green and springy and the goddam thorns didn't make it no easier. When I stopped to. mop sweat I'd broke up a patch about ten foot square.

Fisher waved in Fred and Brace with the shovels.

He still had the rifle in the crook of his arm. I peeled off my shirt. "All right with you if I go fetch a drink?"

Eyeing me hard, he said to Dimity, "Get him the canteen off Jake's grulla."

"Tied up like this?"

"It ain't me that's wantin' it."

She finally got up. Her feet wasn't tied. But her hands still was. "Try usin' your teeth," Fisher said with a chuckle.

I hoped she wasn't going to try nothing crazy. You couldn't tell what that bastard would do. He might shoot to cripple. He might kill her flat out. He had a mighty short fuse and it was already smoking.

I thought back to Lupita. Guts she'd had and a terrible patience, and all she had done knocked hell west and crooked in one squeeze of the trigger when she come up against him.

Who could forget the bright red of her courage or the twist of her look in the flare of that pistol?

The pound of it shook me. I almost cried out when she come to Fred's horse, so wild was my fears, so fierce my imaginings. The moment she stood there seemed to go on forever while my guts shrunk and trembled. My mind yelled *Don't do it!"*

When she caught the canteen's strap in her teeth I didn't know whether to shout or swear. I was frantic, I tell you, for a look at his face, but all Tunstall's horses couldn't of turned me then. Her eyes was clear and hard and bright when she passed him with her head held high and come to me through the glare and the shadows.

"That's far enough!" Fisher sharply called while still there was most six strides between us. "Let it go and step back. He can pick it up off the ground if he wants it."

It scairt me the way she fought his will. Then her shoulders sagged, the canteen fell, and she stumbled away with a kind of sob.

Fisher grinned. "Get your drink."

I got off the cap and filled my throat. Then I tossed it to Brace and took up the pick. They had the hole pretty well shoveled out. There was nothing, it seemed, I could do but get at it.

When they cleaned out again we was down two foot. Fisher come and peered in. I tried to think how I might get an edge on him. I seen the glint of Brace's eyes, the scowl on Fred's cheeks. I poked a look up at Fisher. "You think it's deeper'n that? Try it with your foot."

"Cut away that east back a little more," Fisher said.

It was hot stubborn work. Wasn't a breath of wind stirring. The sweat dripped off my nose and chin, off the lobes of my ears and the points of my elbows. You couldn't get him into that pit on a bet.

When I knocked off to ease my aching hips I got that feeling again of being watched.

I rubbed at my kidneys and straightened up slow, taking a long look around. Only eyes meeting mine I could find was Fisher's. Bright as a hawk's and flatter than fish scales.

A bark of a laugh come out of him.

I scrambled up from the hole. The slant of his rifle stayed right on my brisket. "Look," I said, glowering, "we're down better'n two foot. Why don't we try the other side of that rock?"

"Because the mark's over here."

We glared while the quiet got thick enough to chew.

"I've about had my fill of your mulishness, Farsom." The bore of his gun shifted blackly to Dimity. "Git back to your diggin'."

What the hell could I do? He seen her importance. He savvied how it was, knew the threat was all he needed. I went back to the pick. The worst of it was I had this damnable hunch that before he was done he would knock off the lot of us.

Someone else in his place would of maybe been satisfied once he'd grabbed onto what he had come for to set us afoot. But not this whippoorwill. There'd been no call for him to kill that kid. Grounds' death I had laid to Fred's wife because a knife seemed her style, and because she'd been out. But he'd been out too been practically standing right over him!

Killing was his trade. And, as he'd proved with the

kid, he wasn't the kind to leave someone camped on his backtrail.

I banged the pick into that guff like it was him I had under me. I could still feel them eyes, though nothing I come up with offered any real hope this deal was like to get better. A chance could be made, but if it didn't take care of him Dimity would catch the same dose he'd give Lupita. No matter what I figured he was half a step ahead, and no damn way I could see to get up with him.

The fury, frustration the wild bitterness in me, was sinking that pick to the haft every stroke, breaking the ground up in chunks when I freed it. *Whunk* it would go; then the whole sound was different it drove into something that turned it and held it, mighty near wrenching it out of my grasp. Brace had the canteen tilted with his head back, froze with the water bobblin' over his shirt. Fisher, shoving past him, peered down at me, excited.

"Sounded," Fisher said, "like you went through some kind of"

He must of seen his shadow stretched across the floor of the pit. A second shadow, violently whirling, sent an outflung arm lamming straight for his head. You wouldn't of give Fisher, with that rifle in his dewclaws, any part of a chance. Yet he come around, letting go of the rifle, dropping into a squat, the swish of that arm crazily sailing above him; and there was Cort Brace with his round, frightened eyes of a rabbit off balance, the water still sloshin' in the canteen dangling from its strap at the end of his arm.

A pistol blurred into Fisher's upsweeping fist, fire leaping out of it. Mouth stretched wide in a scream that never come, Brace went half a step back, both hands clapped to his belly. For the moment that he hung there his eyes looked big as slop buckets. Then his knees let go, he come flopping towards me, pushing a path through the dirt with his face.

I guess I jumped back, Fisher's pistol swiveling after me like a snake winding up for a second strike. Dimity screamed. The pistol flew from his hand. From behind and above us the crack of a rifle bounced off the west wall in a clatter of echoes.

We all stood there speechless. The wisp of a mocking laugh drifted down, ugly as gar soup thickened with tadpoles. "Want to try for the other one?"

Fred looked like he wasn't two steps from crazy. All the fires of hell was blazing in Fisher but he was foxed this time, caught flat footed with his back to a rifle and a shooter that had proved he needn't take no sass off anyone. Fisher had one chance, one hand fit to grab it, and no idea where the feller had spoke from.

Wild is one thing. Being loco is for fools and Fisher never was that. He could toss in his hand or get salivated. Way he got shucked of that belt was plumb careful.

Well, Fred had told us. Now we seen the living proof. Just the same I was some surprised when this burly six-footer limped into the open not so much at his dark beefy face as at the whacked off pants leg and the bloody rag twisted around that hairy thigh. Surprised because it was plain enough now I never had dropped that rattlebrained kid; it was Curly Bill Brocius I had put my slug into.

Never mind this was *him*. You had only to look at Fred or the froze disbelief anchoring Fisher in his tracks. If this wasn't enough consider his shape, the round swarthy face so often described, them black eyes and dimples and ragged shock of raven hair. The sureness of him, the bold clap of his stare. There never was another like Curly Bill.

Thinking about that hole I'd put in him I wasn't a heap more comfortable than Fred. By repute he was chancy as a shedding snake, and just about as chummy when paying back a grievance. But right then all his notions must of been hard tied to that treasure. His look was crammed with an immense satisfaction as he put us to clearing that plunder of dirt.

Like most tales of booty it had grown somewhat in the telling but there was more than you'd expect. Then two images, almost lifesize. A cigar box filled with precious stones not all diamonds by a jugful. Round a hundred thousand in negotiable coin, a half dozen chunks of melted down silver and forty-one bars of gold bullion. Enough to have kept most of us in chicken for a while.

Time we got it all loaded we was pretty well pooped, all but Curly who'd done nothing more taxing than push out his talk from behind the black bore of that screecher he carried.

While we'd been packing the stuff he had got himself onto Fred's chesty grulla. Fixing Fisher with his stare he motioned the rest of us back. "Mount up, sport. You're trailin' with me till we git some of the ginger worked out of this caballado."

He showed the rest of us his dimples in a parting grin. "A heap worse could happen if we meet up again."

MULE MAN

For RUTHIE,
who suggested one of the story's most scintillating
moments

ONE

FOR A FOOTLOOSE EX-RANGER who'd come out of that fight at the Hashknife with a bullet-made limp and some nightmare memories of Mossman's resolve to clean up this Territory, I guess you could say I had heard the owl hoot. Several wasted years had gone down the drain since Cap Mossman had turned in his badge and taken up ranching over in New Mexico and I had quit, too, to drift back to Half Step and a humdrum life of trading heirlooms for cash.

Broiling glare of the Arizona sun was scarce two hours from dropping back of the mountain when I rode into the plaza at Ajo.

The bad boys were beginning to ease back into this country, in spite of the Rangers, now that old Burt wasn't around to harass them. Once again gun sound was banging through the hills and dealing with tame Injuns made me think more than once of signing up for another hitch, bad leg and all. As one of Mossman's Rangers I'd come to spot the breed soon as I laid eyes on them and like an old fire horse, I could feel the pull of remembered excitement.

I had taken in most everything in sight time I pulled up Gretchen by the hitchrail fronting the assayer's office. Ajo was mining with a capital M. Cow outfits were in town, a sure sign of payday. Wasn't no big crowd lallygaggin' in the plaza, but tied horses and buckboards was thicker than flies on a spill of sorghum. I'd been aiming to get back to Half Step and tell my old man I wasn't cut out to be no counter-jumper, that routine chores couldn't never make up for the kind of a life I'd known with Burt Mossman.

To tell the plain truth I was bored plumb silly.

Getting out Durham and papers while slanching around one more cautious look I twisted up a smoke and set fire to it, rummaging my mind what I had better do next. I could eat and push on or—willing to risk a bit —could spend the night here and slip away first thing in the morning. What I purely wanted was to get myself home.

I hauled my weight into the saddle, ignoring the dubious look Gretchen flung me. Off to the left about a whoop and a holler was a near bleached-out sign spelling LIVERY; and that's where we ambled, up a gut-narrow alley that presently fetched us to a barn's hoof-tracked ramp.

An old duffer reluctantly got up off his peach crate. "Yeah? By the week or the night?"

"Expect one night'll take care of our needs. Give this animal a good feed of oats. Rub her down—proper." I peered around. "All right if she swipes a drink from that trough?"

"What it's there fer. Two bits ever' time she lowers her head."

"Water must be a heap scarce in this community."

I could see he was fixing to get on his dignity. "Never mind. She's worth it," I grumbled, and flipped him a cartwheel. "Where's the nearest grub for a two-legged specimen?"

"Buck, two doors down, can take care of your tapeworm."

Racked by saddle cramp I took myself back to the alley mouth, crushed the butt under a bootheel and stretched another long glance the full length of the square without latching onto anything to put my wind up. Place he'd touted said BUSTED CROCK, a two-by-four hash house right next to the stage office.

Getting out of my brush jacket, I slapped out the dust against the nearest wall. My gimpy leg was giving me hell; bullet holes don't cure up like an overnight cough...unfortunate. I didn't see anything showed a need to squat and reach. Place would liven up before long without any prodding. A few of those old varmints we hadn't shot and buried might recollect my face; something I'd forever have to be watching out for.

I mounted the porch and went on inside.

Five-six shapes held down stools at the counter. Only table occupied was in a corner by the window. A woman sat there over a half-finished meal. Preempting another halfway down the long room, I gave my order to the biscuit-shooter and made a careful point of minding my own business.

Carving up my steak, cramming my gut with frijoles, I couldn't escape the scrutiny I was getting from that dame, the feel of her probing my face, sorting out the rest of me. I put up with it long as I could and then, shelling out some silver, shoved back my chair and headed for the door.

Her heels tap-tapped behind me and I swung round on the porch with a smothered oath.

She put a hand on my elbow. "I'm Fern Larrimore. Could I speak with you a minute?"

I gave her a scowl, not wanting any part of this. "I don't usually," she said, "approach strange men in this fashion."

"All right. Let's get away from this door."

We moved down onto the walk; her arm slipped through mine. Not like a hustler, more like she had it in mind I might try to get away. "Would you tell me your name?"

"Corrigan—Brice Corrigan." We stopped in front of the stage office. "What's the problem?"

"That's just it." She looked at me undecided and puzzled. "I don't really know. It's just a feeling I have. Would you be free to take a job?"

"What job?"

"A sort of watching brief. You see, my brother's an anthropologist—interprets fossils and relics. He has a couple of months' leave from the university to see what he can turn up about those old cliff dwellers, the faraway ancestors of today's Pueblo Indians. Specifically, the Basketmakers—"

"I wouldn't know a Basketmaker if one jumped up and bit me."

A quick and brief grin streaked across the contours of that scrubbed-clean face. "You have the look of belonging. Jeff—my brother—has to have a guide, he knows nothing about this part of the country. He's out here to make a dig, nothing elaborate, a kind of probe is all, to see if there's anything here to be found. I'd like to hire you."

"I don't want to be hired. I'm trying to get home."

"Is your home around here?"

"No."

Her blue-green eyes kept trying to take me apart. A sigh came out of her. "Look," she said, "I've an uneasy feeling we're going to need more help than my brother is counting on...Whatever your business is, whatever your stipend, I'll double it."

I stared at her, astonished, yanked my glance off her face to throw another look around. More horse sound, more jabber, more movement in the plaza, more people sifting around and about over the rough plank walks. No ore wagons in sight but plenty of ranch rigs, a lot more jaspers standing around by the tie rails. I eyed the look of her again. Younger than I'd reckoned. Not much more than twenty, well-built but no beauty. "Why me?"

"Sometimes," she said, "you have to fight fire with fire."

She had a pretty sharp eye for a girl her age and a dude at that. She had me picked for a bravo, I could see that plain enough. "Figurin' to buy a..." I let it go, to say, disgusted, "This thing your brother's after. Some kind of loot, is it—buried plunder, that sort of thing?"

A rush of color came into her look, flushing some of the paleness out of her cheeks. A touch of resentment sharpened her voice. "Of course not! I've told you; he's an anthropology major, an assistant professor at a Chicago university. He's hunting for Indian artifacts, to learn whatever he can, to pin down the time these cliff dwellers arrived here from Asia and Siberia, the length of their stay and why they aren't still here. That sort of thing. This is very important. We want to know what their day-to-day life was like."

She said, more composed, "Jeff's got hold of a man called Harry Hatcher who grew up in this territory, knows all about it. Mr. Hatcher's going to show us the best places for a dig. He's told Jeff about some caves that have petroglyphs—he's been on digs before, understands what is needed. It's the men Hatcher's hired that makes me uneasy."

"This Hatcher, what do you know about him?"

"Only what Jeff learned from the bank—"

"Bank, eh? Bank vouch for him? Guarantee him, did they?"

"Not exactly. They say he's been a guide, takes out hunting parties. Took a party of archaeologists into the Tonto Basin—"

"And where is he proposing to take your brother?"

"Into the Chaco Canyon country."

"Pretty well into the back of beyond. Damn rough country, lady. No place to be draggin' a woman through—"

"Yes. That's what he said."

"But you aim to go anyhow."

"That's right. I've got a stake in this."

"Don't sound much like a woman's business. I wouldn't expect your brother would care to put you at risk. Let me get this straight. As I understand it, the reason you want to rope me in is because you don't like the kind of crew Hatcher's put together—"

"It's not so much the crew I dislike. It's this fellow Fletcher and another called Clampas. I don't like the looks of them."

"Have you told your brother?" I said. "What is it with you? Can't you talk to him?"

"I've told them both—him and Hatcher. Jeff only throws up his hands. 'Women's notions' he calls everything I point out. Hatcher says we have to understand this place where we're going is bleak, rough country, a maze of draws and ridges where anything could happen —wild and desolate. He thinks we might run into fugitives, renegades, even hostile Indians. He says we need men like Clampas and Fletcher as a kind of insurance. Jeff calls them 'rough diamonds.' He thinks it's all in my head."

"I don't think they'll want me along in that case."

Her chin came up. "Perhaps not, but I'm the one who is putting up the most of the money for this dig— my inheritance. Without my support there won't be any dig."

I looked her over again. I blew out my breath. "Lady," I said, "I've got to get home. I been away too long now."

She met my stare with a kind no man cares to get from a female. "Have I been wrong about you?"

TWO

SHE HAD ME THERE, no two ways about it.

Man could be a rightdown bastard, yet even the worst had to have some value of self to hang on to. Graveled me plenty to be pushed and shoved by the likes of this kid who had nothing I wanted and wasn't no better looking than the handful of others I'd left wailing in the past.

"Shit!" I said, and didn't care that she heard it. I felt meaner than gar soup thickened with tadpoles, too damned riled to keep a hitch on my lip. "Ain't it crossed your mind latchin' on to me could be jumpin' from the skillet straight into the fire?"

Just breath wasted. I said, "This brother of yours—where at will I find him?"

She half turned, lifting an arm with the ghost of a smile. "Over there at the hotel. With Harry. You going to play this my way?"

I charged off through the clutter of horses and wagons, too disgruntled to answer. She could think what she liked and to hell with her. I felt like a fool being choused around this way.

She wasn't two steps behind when I reached the far walk and stepped onto the hotel veranda, hating to think what damage this fine brother of hers could do pawing around in his greed for more facts. "Dudes!" I muttered, but this Larrimore filly with her mop of roan hair had a lot more to her than appeared on the surface.

I paused to say grimly, "Aside from this Hatcher, big brother, yourself and that pair you don't cotton to, how many others is roped into this deal? What's the size of your crew?"

"Well...let's see. Hatcher's picked up four men—"

"With me—if I go into this, that makes an all-over total of ten in this party?"

"Twelve, counting the Mexican handyman and cook."

I looked down at the dog sitting patient by her legs, a shaggy mixed breed of some sort, black and tan. "That dog goin' too?"

"Flossie? Certainly. I sometimes think she has more sense than my brother."

"This Hatcher, now. What do you think of him?"

"He's all right, I guess." She pushed hair off her cheek. "A little glib perhaps. Seems very knowledge-able, easy to get along with."

"Yeah. I bet. Who's assembling the supplies, the stuff you'll have to pack into that country?"

"Hatcher has that all taken care of. We're planning to leave first thing in the morning." Her glance swung up, openly curious. "Are we likely to meet the sort of riffraff Harry mentioned?"

"Can't tell what you'll meet up with these days.

There's riffraff anyplace. Far as Indians go there's actually no saying. Some of them's gettin' a mite touchy here of late. Come on, let's get at it."

I limped after her into the lobby. Stuffed animal heads decorated the walls. The floor held a scatter of Navajo rugs; club chairs were grouped about an oversize fireplace, and three paunchy gents in the garb of ranch owners had their heads together off in a far corner. Girl led the way toward worn leather chairs where two men leaning forward were engaged in what appeared to be an earnest conversation. They looked around as we approached. The one I reckoned to be Hatcher stood up fairly pleasant as Fern stopped in front of them.

"Jeff, I want you to meet Brice Corrigan, who'll be going our way. Brice, this is my brother, Jeff Larrimore. From Chicago."

Larrimore said, getting onto his feet somewhat surprised, "Glad to know you, Brice," and put out a hand, which I shook as a matter of simple courtesy. "Do you live around here?" he asked, curious, civil.

"Not too near, I'm afraid. My old man runs the trading post at Half Step."

His eyes changed a little but hung on to his smile. "That so? We're going north for a tour through the Basketmaker country, looking up the remains of what these Navajos call the Ancient Ones. University is sponsoring a kind of small dig."

"Big country." I nodded. "Rougher'n a cob."

"And this," Fern said brightly, "is Harry Hatcher, who will be in charge of the route and our crew."

"You been at Half Step long?" Hatcher inquired, shaking my paw.

"Born there."

"How are the natives around those parts? Any truth in the rumors I hear going around?"

"Could be. Some of them seem a mite restless lately. But I don't figure any trouble you run into can be charged up to natives. Renegades," I tucked in, "ain't confined to one color."

"True enough." He laughed. "Arizona's got their share all right. Did I understand Fern to say you're also heading north?"

"He's going with us," she put in without beating around any bushes. "I've hired him to round out our safari."

Through what had the makings of an awkward silence Harry Hatcher said with no loss of charm, "Glad to have you with us, Corrigan. Bigger the party the more likely we'll be to come through in one piece." Behind his bland mask he was giving the look of me a thorough going-over.

"You expectin' trouble?"

"Not at all," he assured us with a comforting smile. "Just one of them fellers feels it pays to be prepared."

Bobbing his head, Larrimore chipped in. "Harry's been around. I haven't turned up one person since I've been out here who knows as much as he does about the people we're trying to find—the Anasazi. All the Indians I've talked to just look at you and shrug. They don't know the first thing about those old cliff dwellers."

"Understandable." Hatcher nodded, confident smile enveloping Fern. "They have no written history, no way of bridging the gap of centuries. For all practical purposes the folks Jeff's interested in disappeared from this region about 1400 B.C., give or take a handful of fortnights," he said, much admiring his own wit, it seemed like. "I'm going to take him back where probably no other whites have ever been, right into the heart of that Basketmaker country."

He had the right line to take with young Larrimore. Fern's brother looked pleased as a cat with a fine plump bird by the tail. "Yes," he told me, "quite a bit of serious work has been done on the Pueblo peoples but they came later. First pueblo we know about has been dated no later than seven hundred and fifty, and that's after Christ. Practically modern compared with the aboriginal people I'm trying to get a line on.

"You see, what we need is more artifacts. We've a great need to understand more about primitive man. These Basketmakers come fairly close to being as near as we can get to early man in this country," he declared with conviction. "Near as we know now, they arrived here from what we call Siberia either during or immediately after the Ice Age."

Hatcher with his smile appeared to be in full agreement. "What we're trying to do here is a lot like hunting for the Missing Link, with apologies to Darwin. So little, truly, has been discovered you could practically" —he chuckled— "put the whole bundle in a teacup. Jeff hopes to embark on a voyage of discovery, wants to pioneer the forgotten world of the Anasazi and go straight back some twenty-five thousand years!"

Yep. You had to hand it to Harry. He'd come as near in tune with Larrimore as two peas out of the same pod. I thought to see right then at least a partial reason for the girl's disquiet. I wouldn't trust this Hatcher half as far as I could heave him. "Just what," I asked Larrimore, "are you hopin' to find?"

"If we can get onto the right location, I believe there's a possibility we can unearth some primitive tools and weapons, bones of prehistoric animals they've killed, artifacts used by them in everyday living—that sort of thing. The scientific community, the anthropologists and scholars, so far as these people are concerned, haven't managed to come up with the definitive answer."

Hatcher said, "We'd like to be able to pin down the source of whatever it was that drove these folks here from their former homelands. From wherever they came from, be it fire, floods, famine, pestilence, drought or whatever. An ambitious concept? Certainly. But Jeff feels strongly if he can come onto remains that haven't been tampered with—"

Larrimore cut in, fairly bubbling with excitement. "Harry thinks he can put me onto some graves."

"Where?"

"If I remember correct," Hatcher said persuasively, "it's someplace in the vicinity of Chaco Canyon. Lot of cliff dwellings back in that cut-up country."

"Cliff dwellings, sure," I said. "I don't remember any graves. I went through there several months ago."

Harry showed his smoothest smile. "You didn't get back far enough. There's places back there no white man's ever seen—"

"And what do *you* expect to get out of all this?"

Hatcher laughed. "Maybe I'd like a little piece of the credit when Jeff makes his big find. That's reasonable, ain't it?"

"You'll have it," Jeff said earnestly. "This could be a big thing!" He pulled in a gusty breath. "The pots, pans and bones of man's culture. Going back pretty near to the beginning!"

I hadn't no doubt he was sold on it, but Hatcher to me didn't seem hardly the kind to give a whoop about credit. He had to be in this for something more substantial if I knew anything about the cut of his jib.

The dog sprawled at Fern's feet had the look of watching Harry with a jaundiced eye, too. Larrimore, still flushed with enthusiasm, bit off the end and lit up a thin cigar he produced from a pocket of his silver-buttoned vest. "If we could get even one absolutely conclusive answer—"

"I think we've talked enough," Fern said. "This place is filling up. If you fellows expect to eat, you had better get a move on."

Harry nodded. "I guess we've got the subject pretty well covered. "If you're goin' with us on this jaunt," he said in my direction, "be down at the corrals by five o'clock tomorrow morning to help us load. Jeff's counting on an early start."

That broke up the conference. The girl, the dog and young Larrimore moved away.

Thinking a drink would go pretty good right then, I was turning around to go hunt up one when Hatcher thrust out a hand. "Let me ask you somethin', Corrigan. How'd you manage to work yourself into this?" His eyes, bright and hard, locked into mine. "Where'd you meet up with that girl?"

He plainly didn't like the way I grinned. "You look like a saddle tramp—a damn grubline rider!"

"Reckon that was it," I said. "Miss Larrimore's got a heap of compassion. Offered me a job, she did. An' being chock full of pity myself, I signed on. Just as simple as that."

* * *

TO KEEP AN EYE ON GRETCHEN—MAKE sure she wasn't tampered with—I talked myself into a deal with the livery keeper that got me the right to bed down in his hay-filled loft. I must've tossed and turned pretty near the whole night. Too many questions, too few answers, too many faces flitting through my head. I hadn't met the pair of hombres that had driven the girl into taking me on...

My thoughts jumped around to Burt Mossman. People claimed Arizona Rangers never looked back, but Burt was one who stuck to a trail like heelflies after a fresh-butchered calf. And I was mighty sure, too, Harry Hatcher hadn't missed my occasional limp. In this much time that leg should have cured itself. There was a heap of talk these days—and a heap of agitation, about this Territory getting to be a state.

A good few of the pictures flitting through my mind had to do with Fern Larrimore and this thing I had let her auger me into. Hell, a kid in three-cornered pants ought to've had more sense than let himself be prodded into this kind of trap!

No one had to tell me a ranny like Hatcher didn't give two snorts for Jeff Larrimore's Injun ancestors. Nor for Fern. No girl could compete with the kind of return that slick catamount was hunting! What he saw in this deal had to be real dinero, and scratch around as I would and damn sure did, I couldn't see big mazuma in old bones and pot shards.

I got down next morning to the corrals ahead of schedule, aiming to have me a plumb thorough look at what kind of a crew handsome Harry had picked up to make sure this deal went the way he intended. I saw with disgust there wasn't no answer there. Four of these five hombres was just ordinary cowhands of the twenty-five-dollar-a-month sort. The fifth, Turtle Jones, might be a cut above them, both in gumption and savvy, which to my way of thinking wasn't saying a whole heap. The other pair—the ones that had got Fern's wind up—was a different breed of cats, a breed I knew from the bootheels up.

Fletcher turned up first with a jingle and scrape of big-roweled spurs. His look showed the hardness long years had ground into him. Pale flaxen hair beneath a squaw man's hat and pale blue peepers above his sneering mouth. A short-barreled .44 was shoved into his waistband and he came striding through the crew like he owned the whole shebang. "What the bloody hell," he rasped at me, "d'you think you're doin' here?"

"Hadn't given it much thought. You the boss of this outfit?"

He stood like a coiled spring, tipped forward, hands working with his mouth pinched into a tight-rimmed slit. "That's Corrigan, Fletcher—new man we've signed on," Hatcher called. "Get off your high horse and help stow these packs."

"You hire him?"

"He was hired by Miss Larrimore and don't you forget it. Now quit pawing sod and get busy." Hatcher turned away to speak to a man who had just come into the corral where the pack string was being loaded with boxes and bulging gunnysacks. "Keep your eye on that fool. I want no trouble round here!" Then off Hatcher went, all smiles, to greet the Larrimores, who had just come up with their saddled mounts.

"Reckon you must be Clampas," I said to the man Harry'd spoken to. "Looks like we'll have a good day to get off on. I'm the new hand—Corrigan."

This Clampas—if that's who he was—would have had to stand twice to cast one shadow, so thin he was, so tall and gangling with that flat tough face above the wipe at his throat and the six-shooter slung at either hip. The gaunt cheeks twitched, amber eyes crawled over me like fingers and he flung away with a bridled impatience, never opening his mouth.

No wonder, I thought, the girl was uneasy. That pair was no kind to stamp your boot and yell *boo!* at.

I slanched a look round for Fletcher as Fern's black dog came sidling over to test the air at my legs. Reaching a hand down for sniffing, I heard Clampas demand of Hatcher in a grumbling growl, "How come that waddy ain't helpin' the boys load?" I didn't catch Harry's answer because just then Fern, stopping beside me, said, "Where's your mount?"

I cocked my head to where Gretchen stood on grounded reins. The girl's face showed a considerable astonishment. "You surely must be teasing. Nobody rides *mules!*"

"I been ridin' this one a heap of dry miles."

She stared, disbelieving. Even when I mentioned the mule and me went together and she couldn't have one without having the other, she couldn't seem to take it in. Gretchen waggled both ears in obvious approval and heaved up a sigh like a bunch of hailstones coming off a tin roof. Fern had to laugh.

I said, "Where's the cook?"

"Backed out." She looked provoked.

"Expect we'll manage to make do if we put our minds to it." I sent a look at the overhead. All along the horizon the gray blank of sky was taking on a pinkish tinge. We watched Fletcher and Clampas ride out of the corral. "You don't truly think,"—it come out too solemn—"I'm whacked from the same bit of goods as that pair?"

She got into her saddle and sat looking down at me. You had to like the way she wrinkled up her nose. "Expect we'll just have to wait and see, won't we?"

I knew her eyes were laughing but reckoned to glimpse a suggestion of warmth that hadn't been there before. Bitterly damning the notion, I sent an irritable hand across new-shaven chin and told myself there was enough on my plate without indulging that sort of foolishness.

Fletcher and Clampas rode off into the brush, the crew with the pack string swinging in behind, followed by Hatcher and the Chicago professor, young Jeff got up like Montgomery Ward's version of what the well-dressed Western gentleman will be wearing this fall. "Don't you think he looks real nice?" Fern asked.

Eyeing the flat-topped hat, white shirt, red tie, that cowhide vest with double row of silver buttons, sand-colored whipcord pants stuffed into knee-high boots with huge-roweled shiny nickel-plated spurs, I could only wonder.

"Very nice," I told her. "Time to get crackin'." Then I climbed onto Gretchen.

We went along in this strung-out fashion for maybe half an hour without no more gab.

Then abruptly she said, "What sort of work were you doing before we ran across each other—I mean, were you working for one of these ranches?"

"I was headin' for home."

"And before that?"

"Oh ... a little of this and some of that."

"You aren't very forthcoming, Corrigan."

"Ain't much I can say. Most of the time, like now, I been ridin' for a livin'."

Her glance was like a pair of hands digging into me. "Would you describe yourself," she persisted, "as—"

"Mostly I been what you might call fiddle-footed. Haven't stayed too long anyplace, I reckon."

"Tell me about your home. Was someone ill that you wanted to hurry back?"

"Reckon," I said, "they're healthy enough. I wasn't hurryin' particular, I just wanted to get there. Matter of fact I never knew my mother; goin' by what I've heard I guess she died pretty young. Old man's all right, never been sick a day in his life."

"Doesn't he get pretty lonesome?"

"Not that I ever noticed. Runnin' that tradin' post don't leave much time for lonesome."

"What does he sell?"

"Anything folks'll buy, I reckon: beads, food, flashy gewgaws, blankets—that kinda stuff."

"Doesn't he sell whiskey?"

"Not to Indians he don't!"

"Well, you needn't take my head off about it."

"They got a law against that. My old man wouldn't want to lose his license. Or any other privilege, come to that."

I could feel her studying eyes going over me. "I have

noticed," she said, "when you're not thinking about it you have a tendency to limp. An old hurt perhaps?"

"The leg got bit by a bullet."

Expect it come to her goddam notice the conversation was definitely adjourned. She rode off after her brother, who rode alone up ahead of us.

Country was beginning to show its teeth a bit now, not yet what you'd call rough but increasingly cluttered with rocks and such barbed growth as mesquite, yucca, Spanish bayonet and wolfs candle. An occasional saguaro reared its spiny length some thirty or more feet into the rapidly heating air above this sandy floor. The sharp spikes of hedgehog with their curled-up crimson blooms were generously mixed among the prickly pear, cholla, fishhooks and barrel cactus. I'd been living with such for the past couple weeks and paid them scant heed other than to yank the blue wipe up across my nose in the hope of filtering out some of the dust.

After a couple hours of reasonable progress young Larrimore in his grit-covered finery dropped back to share some chunks of his learning about things nearest to his heart, in especial the long-gone Anasazi, mainly Basketmakers of the earliest variety.

I said, "Let's hope you don't run into any chindis."

"What's that?" he questioned, twisting around to eye me, curious.

"Chindis," I told him, "are what Navajos call the spirits of the dead."

He gave that some study, considerable more than you might reckon it warranted. "But the Navajos aren't related to the cliff-dwelling Anasazi, nor to the people who built the early pueblos even. The Navajos showed up here a good while after the Basketmakers quit this region."

"If you're sure of that, tell me where they took off to."

This was evidently something he wasn't able to answer. It undoubtedly griped him but he brushed it aside. "I'll tell you something else," he earnestly declared. "Over the centuries both the Basketmakers and their near kin the Pueblos received and amalgamated continual additions to their cultural inventory. Such improvements eventually as stone axes and pottery, the hard cradleboard, permanent housing and that marvelous weapon the bow and arrow none of these luxuries had come to this country with them. They even learned to domesticate wild turkeys."

"What about the horse?"

"They knew nothing of horses. The Spaniards didn't set foot in America until two or three hundred years after the last of Basketmakers had completely disappeared. The term *Anasazi* in the Navajo use of it means simply 'ancient enemies,' "he assured me, "but why those old Basketmakers should have been considered enemies is completely up in the air. The two cultures, far as we know, never even came close to any confrontation. Indeed, how could this have been possible when the Navajos' arrival found this region up for grabs?"

"Do you reckon," I said, "if I had gotten here sooner..."

Jeff laughed. "Anyway, according to the best current advice on the subject, somewhere about two thousand years ago this primitive and extremely simple people lived scattered in pretty small groups over much of this region. In appearance and culture, they've been likened to the Australian aborigines—not that our present Indians bear much resemblance. It might surprise you to learn I've been told a man can step back seven hundred years and more just rounding a bend in some of those draws and canyons. Kind of grips you, doesn't it? These ancient long-abandoned ruins, I'm told, are mostly found in sandstone country, tucked away in caves and plastered overhangs."

"I expect we can promise to show you a few. Don't know as you'll discover a great deal you'll want to cherish. Might even come up with one nobody's seen except for those usin' it. There's still a few hostiles runnin' loose and, hard though he tried, there are still a few scalawags Mossman an' company never got their hands on."

He peered around sharply. "You honestly believe—?"

"Wouldn't surprise me a heap if we run into some pretty hard cases. Not red ones though. You won't find many Indians around those ruins—live ones, I mean. They don't consider such places healthy. Too much chance of scarin' up a chindi."

"Spirits? You don't imagine they really *believe* in such foolishness?"

"You bet," I told him. "Never mind. You've got a forty-sixty chance of stumbling onto some ruin nobody yet has ever blundered into."

THREE

HAVING FIXED my own grub times without count, I thought maybe offering my services as cook might take a little heat off my own situation so far as it applied to Hatcher and company. According about the middle of the afternoon I pushed a reluctant Gretchen into overtaking Fern where she rode with Jeff a broiling hundred yards ahead.

"How's the dust back there?" Jeff asked, swabbing a wipe across flushed cheeks.

"No worse than it is up here," I said. "What are you folks fixin' to do about a cook? I could patch up a meal if you can't do any better."

She kept whatever reaction she had under cover. "Turtle Jones has agreed to take over that department. Seems he spent last fall being roundup cook for Colonel Green's outfit."

"That's fine." I grinned. "Can't say I was ackshully lookin' forward to that sort of chore." After her brother rode off to rejoin Hatcher up ahead, I said to Fern,

"How long does Hatcher figure it's like to take to put Jeff where he can start his hunt?"

"He says he don't want to push these horses. That it most likely will take us five or six days."

I looked off through the smudge of heat and dust where the pack string plodded up a shallow draw. A couple of the crew were hoisting canvas water bags to put a bit of damp on their whistles. "You ever think to ask Harry what he hopes to get out of this?"

"Get out of it? You've already asked; we both heard what he said. What could he think to get beyond the fee he and Jeff agreed on?" Her stare seemed puzzled. "It isn't Harry you've got to watch. Why, Jeff thinks Hatcher is the luckiest find he could possibly have made!"

"Just what's he payin' Harry, if you don't mind sayin'?"

She looked at me intently, halfway shrugged and presently mentioned Hatcher was to get one hundred and fifty dollars a week to furnish crew and transport, locate a suitable spot for the dig and fetch all Jeff found back where we'd started from. Pretty good pay I was bound to agree, but someway it left me less than satisfied. I glanced at the dog ambling alongside Fern's mount with her tongue lolling out but still going strong and taking pleasure in this romp.

"And who picks up the supplies, the grub and what not?"

"Harry picked them up under Jeff's instructions; Jeff and I paid for them. Look—" she said, "I don't see the point to this. What are you getting at?"

"Nothin' wrong with the deal. It all hinges on Hatcher. If you can take him at face value, if you're satisfied the feller's no more than he claims to be, this trip could be duck soup." I touched Gretchen up with a spurless heel, Fern scrambling after us.

"I told you Jeff trusts him, sees nothing in Fletcher and Glampas to bother him."

"But you went out of your way to pull me into—"

"That's right," she said with no attempt to duck around it. "I'm afraid of those two. I don't like their looks, can't see why Harry, if it was simply a matter of running into something we hadn't allowed for, couldn't have found—"

"Yeah. You told me. He obviously picked them figurin' if we ran into gunplay, they'd be tough enough to earn whatever he's payin' them. Same notion you was fondlin' when you came after me." I considered her disgustedly. "What if Harry can't control them? Were they known to him beforehand? An' what do you suppose'll happen if he can't? If he decides to pull out?"

"If you want to back out—"

"Get rid of that notion. I'm not backin' out. Just tryin' to make sure you understand where you're at in this business. That's a damn lonesome country Harry's takin' you into; you better go into it with both eyes open. Your brother's a babe in the woods."

There was color in her cheeks, an angry sparkle in her glance. "You sound—"

"Never mind that. If Hatcher decides to pull out and leave you—"

"Leave us where?"

"In that wonderful place he's been talkin' about that no other paleface has ever set eyes on."

"We've got a contract with Harry. I don't see how he could pull out. The bank assured us—"

"If Hatcher's got other plans, that piece of paper won't stop him."

* * *

ABOUT AN HOUR short of sundown Harry threw up a hand. Declared we'd gone far enough for the start of this journey and would make camp here where these mesquites and ironwoods would afford some protection should a wind come up and start belting through this sand.

It wasn't a bad place. Plenty of dead wood for the fires and a small creek gurgling over gray rocks between moss-covered banks. Ample room to set up the tents, one for Fern and the other fetched along as a cover for our supplies. He told Turtle Jones to get busy with the small fire and fixings, and the rest of the crew to get our stuff off the pack string. Fletcher he picked to take care of the horses and Clampas he posted atop a rock with a rifle. He seemed to know what he was doing.

I took Gretchen to the stream and let her have a small drink. I considered the scanty forage as I rubbed her down with a piece of gunny sacking, then limped over to the bags of grain we'd brought along for the horses and dumped a couple quarts of oats into a nosebag for her. I didn't bother with hobbles, knowing from long experience she wouldn't stray beyond reach of my call. They had the horses, likewise with nosebags, penned inside a hastily thrown up rope corral.

With no chuck wagon to work from you had to give Turtle Jones high marks for the potluck meal he put together this first night. As Jeff remarked in the midst of our eating, "That chef we stole from the Waldorf-

Astoria has more than lived up to his great reputation," and handsome Harry cried, "Stand up, boy, and take a deserved bow!"

"Aw, shucks," Jones muttered with his cheeks firing up, "ever'thing come outa cans but them biscuits. If I kin ever git organized, I'll try to do better."

Most everyone sat around the fire that first evening singing old range songs to Alfredo the handyman's accompaniment on his mouth harp. Fern left Jeff to come and flop down beside me with her mop of roan hair, eyes brighter than the stars, that splatter of freckles across her nose hardly showing and denim-clad legs tucked snugly under her.

"Mighty well-behaved dog," I said, eyeing Flossie where she crouched nearby with her behind reared up, face on paws, glance fixed on me intently.

Fern laughed. "I think she likes you. Look—she wants to play! She almost never barks, she puts all her thoughts in body language."

"How'd you come to give her that name?"

"She's named after a girl I went to school with. She wasn't even weaned when I got her, just a pitiful stray I picked up off the streets. We had to feed her from a bottle. When she got old enough to eat from a pan, she insisted on me holding it while she lay stretched out across my lap. When finally I refused any longer to accommodate her she used to sprawl on the floor beside her pan—it was nearly a year before she'd eat standing up. See! She knows we're talking about her."

The dog rolled over on her back, watching me upside down, waggling her paws. "I don't think she'll let you but that's what she does when she wants her stomach rubbed."

I reached out a hand. Quick as a wink the dog ducked out from under it. "She's shy." Fern laughed. "Come on, Flossie. Time to go to bed."

We all turned in fairly early that night, myself finding sleep hard to come by, too many wild thoughts chasing through my head like a herd of spooked horses. Coyotes yapped back and forth across the moonlit distance. Crickets chirped and nighthawks swooped and between un-restful periods of dozing I tried to keep a weather eye on Clampas and Fletcher taking turn and turn about atop that twelve-foot flat-topped rock.

The night passed without untoward alarms or excursions. It was Jones beating a racket from his washtub with a ladle brought me out of my soogans while the only light in the solid dark came from the built-up breakfast fire. "Come an' git it!" he yelled.

* * *

BY MY FIGURING we had covered some thirty miles—perhaps a bit more than less—in that first day's travel toward an uncertain future. On this second day we did better. The horses' high spirits in the cool of that early morning and the exasperated shouts and cursing of the crew were not allowed to impede Hatcher's schedule and there was no lallygaggin permitted on the trail.

During most of the morning Fern rode ahead with Harry and her brother and I'd had plenty of time to sort out my notions had I been able to put my mind to it. There was always the chance Jeff was right about Hatcher though I couldn't persuade myself that was likely. The man was too glib, too agreeable, too obliging in furthering Larrimore's views and aspirations.

About Fletcher and Clampas I had no doubts at all. Until Mossman's advent this state had been more than rife with their kind. Cut-and-run killers of every shade and description had all but taken over the towns; stages were stopped, often ransacked and burned, rustlers and horse thieves made ranchers' lives miserable. Claim jumping had become the biggest business you could find in the outback. Some of these rascals had become so slick that, as Burt Mossman had been heard to declare, it took one to know one.

Burt's boys, the Rangers he'd been picked to head and organize, could not afford to wear any mark of their calling. Arizona was a gun-governed country and its Rangers looked just like anybody else. Tough and enduring, hard-nosed survivors on call night and day, loners by necessity.

The sun grew hotter as the day wore along; you dared not rest a hand on any piece of metal. An egg would have fried anyplace it was dropped, but we had no eggs and we ate in the saddle, ignoring the customary stop for noon. "We don't have to push these broncs," Hatcher said, "but on the other hand we don't want to waste a lot of time. Steady riding will eat up the miles and put us in the next camp with something still left in case it has to be called for." His quick stabbing glance brushed across sweat-streaked faces. "Keep your minds on your business and be damn careful with that water."

It occurred to me to wonder where Harry imagined he was bound for but I didn't figure it behooved me to put in my gab in the face of his authority. Unless he got on to himself before we squandered tomorrow, the schedule he'd laid out was going to come up mighty short. It crossed my mind Larrimore might like a look at Inscription House, a ruin so named for the seventeenth-century date chiseled onto it by some forgotten Spaniard. Jeff, I reckoned, wouldn't come within miles of it.

Hatcher was being only prudent in warning the crew to conserve their water. But I thought those very words showed the man lacked considerable of being near as smart as young Larrimore esteemed him. Nothing but sheer ignorance could get a man killed of thirst around here. This was Basketmaker country; as Jeff delighted in mentioning, they had lived in this region for hundreds of years and they certainly hadn't thrived without water.

Toward the shank of the afternoon Jeff dropped back for a powwow. Seemed a bit embarrassed about announcing what he'd come for. "Get it off your chest," I said. "You must've come back here for somethin'."

"Well...doesn't it look like to you Harry's going the long way around?"

"How so?"

"Hadn't we ought to be heading a lot more to the east than he's taking us?"

"Why not ask him if you feel strong enough about it? Ain't he the one you're payin' to get you there? He's the man you said was on back-slappin' terms with these environs."

"But you said," Jeff protested, "you'd recently come through the place we're supposed to be heading for."

"Some fellers say a heap more'n their prayers. Direction he's goin', there's all sorts of red cliffs—"

"But not the ones I'd figured to be finding." He looked a mite grim about the edges of his mouth. "I might be what you call a tenderfoot," he said pretty harsh, "but by cripes I haven't yet lost all my marbles! If you won't tell me, would you advise my sister?" He was some het up, no two ways about it.

Lifting one of those skinny cigars from his pocket, I bit off an end and fired up.

"Wouldn't want me to cramp Harry's style now, would you?"

He slammed me a long look and suddenly, spinning his mount, took off for the head of the line again.

Result of all this became immediately evident. A considerable commotion broke out up ahead. Dust churned as the whole file of horsebackers, pack string and all, stopped like they had run plumb into a brick wall. Angry voices sawed through the confusion. *"Where's that sonsabitchin' mule man!* "Hatcher shouted, and here he came with blood in his eye.

Pulling up so short his horse reared, snorting, right on top of me almost, his yell crashed out of a livid face. "What d'you think you're playing at, Corrigan! What'd you tell that goddam fool?"

"Seemed to think we'd got off our course, wanted me to confirm it." I smiled at him thinly. "Told him you was runnin' this outfit; if he had any beef he should take it to you."

The hot glare from those eyes showed him still a far piece from any kind of shape to be reasoned with. I thought it best to try anyhow. "Your contract," I said, "as I understand it, gives you authority to take this outfit in whatever direction you figure will best serve. So why not go on with it?"

"You trying to get me fired off this job?"

"*Can* he fire you?" I said to him soberly. "He's just

one dude against the whole push of you. Wouldn't think he'd get much change out of that."

"Maybe not," Harry growled after rummaging through it. "Just the same, you keep your damn yap out of this," and he went pounding off in a great rise of dust.

No telling what he said to young Larrimore but evidently, they managed to patch up their differences because not ten minutes later our whole line of travel bent off to the right.

FOUR

WE CAMPED LATE that night with the dark congealing round us and Jones in a temper, short of wood and with no water available save for what still sloshed in the bags on our saddles. Retried beans was heaviest item on the menu.

No sitting around the fire at this place, no grins or pranks. Mouth harps, singing and the usual big windies were conspicuous by their absence. Fern with Flossie went early to bed. Fletcher went up a palo verde with his rifle looking sour enough to curdle fresh milk and Clampas, similarly armed, went off someplace back of the rope holding down our remuda.

Nobody said one word in my direction, not even Jones showed a friendly face. With not the frailest notion what Hatcher might come up with as a suitable reprisal for giving in to Larrimore, I kept Gretchen handy and slept with a pistol under my hull.

We were up before sunrise and on our way within the hour, some of us half scalded with the heat Jones flung into that Java. The sky turned pink and the landscape brightened and the sun shot up in all its glory smack-dab into the horses' faces.

The country looked flat, stretching out long miles in its mildly undulant surface through its haze of brown dust.

Larrimore, despite any change he'd effected yesterday, appeared fidgety with visible worry lines about his stare. "Yes," Fern said when later she dropped back to ride beside me, "he was pretty upset. He had a terrible row with Hatcher when Harry threatened to quit and pull the crew out with him. I think what bothered him more than anything was having his faith in the man undermined. Jeff was banking heavily on Harry's ability to put him onto a real find."

"I expect they'll get over it. Hatcher's lettin' off steam; I don't reckon he'll quit. Not yet anyway."

"That," she said, eyeing me in some concern, "wasn't the impression I got from you yesterday."

"Just wanted you to consider the possibilities is all. I can't tell what he's up to; if it suited whatever's runnin' through his noggin he could leave you in a minute, but I shouldn't think he's anywhere near doin' it yet. And as for pullin' out with all hands, some of these boys might not see it his way. You can bet he won't leave before Jeff gets his dig started."

She looked a little reassured. "How big is this Chaco Canyon?" she asked.

"Pretty big. Some ten miles long and I'd guess about a mile wide between the walls. A heap of ruins in that space. Those old boys certainly built for the centuries. I've poked around in a couple—"

"Is there much there to find?"

"Depends what you're lookin' for. Probably find a

few pots but I doubt they'd be old enough to interest Jeff. He wants to get back to the beginnings of these people. I'm afraid any relics he might come across there, except perhaps the buildings themselves, probably wouldn't be things actually used by those Basketmakers —not the early ones. Best bet," I told her, "is to hunt them side canyons and gulches branchin' off it.

"All the towns—if you can call them that—along the Chaco itself were big places in their time. Most of them had several hundred rooms plus ceremonial chambers. Much like the pueblos bein' lived in today. Most of them—even those that haven't been looked over by folks in Jeff's line of work—have still had a mort of people prowlin' through them."

"Why would those gulches be less likely to be picked over?"

"Some of them ain't so easy to come onto, either deliberately hidden or screened by brush that's grown up through the ages. All the trees within ten miles of the Chaco were cut away and used up at different times by the builders. But get back in some of them tributary canyons and you're dealin' with buildings of sixty rooms and less."

I found her studying me curiously. "You sound as though you know as much about it as Harry."

"Can't speak for Hatcher. About all I personally know comes of observation. Anyone meanderin' over this desert learns to keep his eyes peeled. Same as Flossie," I told her, grinning down at her watchful sheepdog.

She said, "If Harry hasn't taken this job for what we're paying him, what do you suppose he's after?"

"Loot."

She looked considerably surprised. "Well...I know
—I quite realize the relics Jeff hopes to find and identify
would possibly be worth a little something to collectors,
but..."

"Some people would put up a king's ransom for
such things if they went back far enough in reasonably
good condition and had nothing broken out of them.
And the more rare the object the more they'll fork over.
Looting's an enticing and highly profitable occupation
for more people than you'd imagine."

"Now and again," she said like she was studying on
it, "you use words few persons hereabouts have ever
bumped into."

"Yeah," I said. "It's a damn bad habit I've found
hard to get shut of."

That night we camped alongside an arroyo where
Hatcher went down into an apparently dry wash with a
short-handled shovel he got out of the camp gear. He
didn't have to dig for more than five minutes hardly
before the hole began filling with water. Jeff allowed
we'd be more comfortable camping down in that wash
but Hatcher knew better. "A man can mighty quick
wake up drowned doing that around here. You get a
storm up in the mountains you've gotten twelve foot of
water in this wash."

While three of the crew and Fletcher was getting
the loads off the pack string the other two hands began
fetching the saddle mounts down for a drink. I dumped
my water bag into my hat and held it while Gretchen
cooled her insides, then anchored her to grounded reins
and went over and put up the tent for Fern. Jones broke
up a couple creosote bushes and got his fire started and
Clampas with rifle found him a station on the lip of the

arroyo, Hatcher going across to have a few words with him.

I pitched in to help water the pack string while somebody else busied himself setting up the rope corral and pouring oats into nosebags to hang on the horses. I rubbed Gretchen down with my piece of gunnysack and wiped out her nostrils. By that time Turtle Jones had a good bed of coals and was dexterously throwing together our supper which, praise be, tonight featured no retried beans, Alfredo the handyman scouting up wood.

On Hatcher's advice we went early to bed and once more with a pistol stashed ready for use I kept Gretchen by me in case of quick need. No breeze sprang up to whine through the straggle of wind-bent trees along the arroyo's rim where Clampas stood with his rifle. We'd have a late moon tonight and, by the look of things, a hot day tomorrow which most likely was the reason Hatcher aimed to be moving ahead of daylight. Being short on sleep I drifted off almost at once.

Something jolted me awake. Grabbing up my six-shooter I peered through the dregs of the moon's fitful glow to find Gretchen's whiskers not three inches from my cheek. Throwing off my cover I came onto an elbow. There was some kind of hubbub boiling up beyond the penned stock, punctuated by horse sounds and angry voices. Gretchen, sidling closer, softly blew out her breath. Fletcher's furious yell sailed through the racket.

"That goddam mule man! Told you to git rid of him! Prob'ly turned them critters loose a-purpose!"

I got out of my soogans, put a hand out to Gretchen.

Jeff came shoving out of the shadows. "What's the rumpus?" Beyond him Jones was building up his fire.

Catching up Gretchen's reins I headed for the corral and the group standing around that motionless huddle on the ground.

"What's happened?" Jeff demanded, singling out Hatcher.

"We're short one man and two of the broncs."

"Who is it?" Larrimore wanted to know.

"Ned Benson."

"Is he hurt?"

Fletcher's sarcastic growl said, "Why would he hurt? Hell, he's never been happier!"

"He's dead," Hatcher said. "Been walloped over the head."

I said, "How'd those broncs get loose from the corral?"

"You tell us," Fletcher snarled, starting toward me.

Hatcher thrust him back, hard eyes digging into me. "You got anything to say?"

Two of the boys stepped aside to let Fern through.

"Brice had nothing to do with this. You had Clampas on guard—didn't he hear anything?"

Hatcher's stare swiveled to Clampas. "Well?"

"Nary a thing," Clampas told us. "Whoever done this must've moved on bare feet."

"Maybe you fell asleep," Fern said, and Clampas snorted. "Whoever done this was Injun quiet."

Jeff's face looked troubled. Hatcher looked worried, near as I could make out in that uncertain light. I said, "What makes you think two horses are missing?"

"They're missin' all right. Soon's I spotted Benson I slipped in there an' made a count," Fletcher grumbled. Fern and Jeff exchanged a quick look. I said, "If someone was trying to make trouble for us, why stop with two horses? Why not grab all of them?"

Hatcher nodded. "Good point. Couple of Navajos probably snuk up on us someway."

"Come an' git it!" Jones called.

He'd beat up some biscuits and what he gave us to go with them was refried beans.

* * *

HARRY TOLD off a couple hands to bury Benson, made sure all water bags were filled and hustled us out of that place just as the sky was beginning to turn gray. He and Jones had gone through the supplies and none of the foodstuffs appeared to be missing, but the loss of Benson —not to mention two horses—had put a damper on our spirits. It was a pretty subdued outfit that got under way that morning.

Clampas dropped back to ride alongside me, but had nothing to offer in the way of conversation. After a couple of hours Hatcher came back and motioned Clampas to move on ahead. "This Chaco," he asked me. "How much farther do you reckon it to be?"

"Another couple days, if we push them a mite, ought to fetch us in sight of the south gap, I reckon. Thought you knew all about that canyon."

Harry's face put on a sort of rueful scowl. "Tell you the truth I ain't never been near it. There's red rocks lots of places. I was figuring, long as he wouldn't know the difference, to take him up into them Lukachukai Mountains. Figured he could dig there good as anyplace." He hawked up some phlegm and spit it off to the side. "How do you look at that business last night? Think it was Indians?"

"What about Fletcher? Heard him tryin' to lay it onto me. He wouldn't think no more about killin' a man than he would about findin' worms in his biscuits."

"Keep away from him," Hatcher grunted. "On pretty short notice I had to take what I could get." He kept looking into the swirl of heat haze ahead of where Clampas, lounging in the saddle, was riding point. "Country's changin'," he said. "Bunch grass and grama. Lot of rocks croppin' up—ain't none of them red though. You been through here before?"

"Don't rightly remember."

"Didn't somebody say your old man run a tradin' post?"

"He runs the post at Half Step."

"Doin' pretty good, is he?"

"Gettin' by, I reckon."

"You in that business?"

"Guess I'm too fiddle-footed. Too much settin' around. Too quiet."

"How come," he asked, "you don't ride a horse?"

"I find this mule more dependable. She don't spook so easy, for one thing."

Hatcher's stare wheeled around. "Man could get lost damn easy round here. Mile after mile it all looks alike. Can't see how them Basketmakers stood it. Dry as a brick horn."

"Expect it didn't used to look like this. Don't hardly ever rain here no more."

There was about Harry this morning a suggestion of something stewing in his craw which he wanted to get up but was making rough work of. Two-three times he'd cleared his throat, the gloom in his stare wandering over my face while he chewed on his lip with unaccustomed indecision.

Something hauled my thoughts away from him. Scrinching my eyes, trying to cut through the pack-string dust up ahead, I said, "Company comin'."

It jerked Hatcher's head up. We could both see them now. Jeff coming back with two other horsemen.

"Navajos!" Hatcher grunted, loosening the pistol in its housing on his hip.

When they came up, swinging their horses to ride alongside us, the older Indian, wrinkled of face and gray of hair, was energetically puffing one of Larrimore's thin cigars with every evidence of relish. Jeff with a glance at Hatcher said, "They want to know what we're doing here."

Harry looked them over and with hand on gun butt contemptuously spat. The younger Navajo's eyes turned hateful. I could see pretty quick this could get a little touchy. "We're huntin' old pots from the time of the Anasazi," I told the old man.

"I think you better leave," he answered. "This land," he said with a hand taking in everything in sight, "belongs to the People."

"Since when?" Hatcher challenged.

"Many years—"

"Soldiers say different."

Both Indians took a long look about. The older man smiled. "No soldiers here," he announced with satisfaction. "You go."

Hatcher smiled, too. A nasty thin-lipped grimace; and there was Clampas with his rifle coming down the line to join us. "This man," I said, putting a hand out toward Jeff, "is a friend to the People from a great white man's school far away. He'd like to take back some things—"

"All white men take. Too much take!" the younger Navajo growled. "All time take!"

We had all come to a stop in the sort of confrontation that could bode no good for anyone. Something had to be done before a bad situation piled up a worse hereafter. Clearing my throat I said to the old one, "This teacher," with a nod of the head at Larrimore, "is tryin' to find the Chaco. He wants to tell the men at his school of all the wonderful things built there by the people who left this land for the Navajos."

Those Indian faces didn't offer much encouragement. Cold sweat came out along the back of my neck. I waved Clampas back. "So if you'd agree," I said, "to act as scouts for this outfit and show us the fastest, most direct way to get there—"

"What you give?" Greedy interest was all over that young buck; and Jeff, catching on, held out his watch to the older one, who gravely accepted it, holding it up to an ear, smiling at the sound it made. The other Indian spurned such baubles. "You give tobacco? Blue stones? You give whiskey?"

I looked at him sternly. "Whiskey bring soldiers. We give tobacco. Frijoles. A tall hat for each of you."

"Give me a chew of tobacco now," the younger one demanded.

I reached into my pocket and handed him my plug, from which he took a great bite and threw the rest in the dust. "You give gun!"

There was naked envy in the way he was staring at the Sharps across Clampas's saddlebow. "No guns," I said, and he glared at me malevolently. "You already have a gun," I told him, pointing to the Henry rifle on his saddle.

"That gun no good." He thrust out a hand toward Clampas. "Give me that one!"

"Where do you want it?" Clampas growled without expression.

"Maybe so," the fellow said, grinning, "some Indian kill you."

"Have at it," Clampas invited, and elevated his Sharps to bear on the man at point-blank range.

FIVE

WHITE about the mouth Jeff said, "Put that down. We don't shoot people at a friendly powwow, nor while we're crossing Navajo land."

Clampas for a moment appeared to be of two minds. Before things got out of hand, Harry kneed his own horse sufficiently forward to blank out the threat. The old man, seeming unaware of the danger and smiling sadly at Larrimore, finally spoke. "What you say is good. Since I was no higher than your dog the white man has brought us nothing but trouble. I have not forgotten when blue-coat soldiers took the People away, but your heart is good." Still considering Jeff he sat quietly a moment, then abruptly said, "That we may live at peace I will take you to the Chaco."

The two Indians rode with Larrimore past the stopped pack string and forward to the head of the line. Harry released pent breath and looked at me with a shudder. "A near thing, that." His darkening glance found Clampas. "Stay away from that fellow." The laden pack string began to move, but in a new direction, still east but more southerly. Clampas rasped a fist across flushed cheeks. "We'll have to watch that buck," he told Hatcher. "We ain't outa this yet by a long shot."

It was obvious Harry agreed. "Have to post more guards at night. Long as they're with us. Old man's all right, but that younger one might be brash enough to try and stampede the whole string."

"Could fix him up with a accident mebbe."

Harry gave him a sharp look. "Don't even think of it. That old duffer looks like to me he might have a bigger than average say hereabouts—in Chaco too for all we know."

"You're probably right," I said. "We sure don't want to fetch the whole tribe down on us. You heard what he said about white men and trouble. He's peaceable now; we ought to do our best to keep him that way."

Clampas slapped the butt of his Sharps disgustedly. "Pamperin' them bastards won't buy you nothin'. Put it into their heads you kin be pushed around an' by Gawd you'll *git* pushed! If you wanta git along with 'em you got to take a firm stand."

* * *

THAT NIGHT we made another dry camp.

Wood—even cowflops—was in short supply but Jeff, no doubt as concession to our red friends, ordered Jones to spread himself and we had the best meal we'd been served in six nights. Jerked beef cut up in some kind of white gravy, spuds baked in the ashes with their jackets on, hot buttered biscuits and coffee strong enough to stand without a cup. And canned peaches to round things off.

True to what they'd been offered, Jeff gave each Indian a black uncreased Stetson, a small sack of dried beans, and tobacco. The chewing sort. In addition to this largesse the older man was ceremoniously presented with a good round dozen of Larrimore's thin cigars.

Before the rest of us turned in, Harry arranged for three shifts of men armed with rifles to patrol the perimeters and make sure none of the horses managed to get themselves lost. This possibly wasn't necessary but, reminded of the loss we'd already taken and a pair of Indians right in our midst, I couldn't blame Harry for trying to play safe. He had to see that Jeff remembered that a man without a horse in this kind of country was in mighty sorry shape.

It looked like being another hard night. I couldn't rid my head of the many disquieting notions continuing to churn up unwanted activity. Generally, I could put such things out of mind but certain faces in this outfit continued to plague me, not the least of which was Fern's.

I recalled how before the start of this jaunt I'd considered her a plain damn nuisance, arrogant and headstrong and like to be a pain in the ass insisting on having a part in this deal. Since then I'd learned she could grow on a man, no fool at all but a girl with real pluck and a heap more sense in a practical way than that dreamy-eyed Jeff with his talk of dead Indians and artifacts nobody else had dug up.

Thoughts of Hatcher and his deadly companions continued to rile and disturb me. For all the airs he put on, his talking talents and confident authority, it appeared to me dubious that if push came to shove he'd be at all able to control that pair.

First thing I'd done when we'd quit for the day was to take care of Gretchen and put-up Fern's tent. "Stay away from those Navajos," I told her, but all I'd got out of that was an odd look and laughter. She said, "That old man is no scalp-hunting redskin." A mischievous light danced round in her stare. "He told me his name— Johnny Two-Feathers. Isn't that quaint? The other one's Hosteen Joe— "

"It's that other one we got to watch out for."

"Johnny'll keep him in line. He's pretty well educated by local standards. Brought up by the Jesuits in mission schools, first in Tubac and again at Tucson; even knows a few words in Latin! Don't you hate to think of a man that old having to sleep on the ground?"

"Fern," I said, "he's been doing it all his life."

"You know what he calls you? 'Man-on-a-Mule.'" Her laugh tinkled again like silver bells in the sunset. "He calls Jeff 'Young Man Who Hunts Old Ones.' "

He had certainly made an impression on Fern—a notion I wasn't at all sure I cared for.

Just as I was finally about to drop off, young Jeff came over and squatted down for a chat. "You know," he said, "I believe I've caught up with the bee in Harry's bonnet. I heard him asking old Johnny about beads—"

"May be fixin' to do a little trading on the side," I told him. "Better get some sleep."

Jeff's mention of beads in connection with Harry became one more notion I didn't like the look of. But nothing happened in the night and once again we got off to an extra early start with old Johnny up there at the front of the line and Hosteen Joe and his surly scowls noplace in sight.

Hatcher dropped back and I brought this up. "I dunno," Harry said. "He's out there ahead of us someplace, making sure—according to Johnny—we don't run into trouble. Between you and me and the gatepost he's more like to stir it up and kick the lid off if he can."

Refried beans juned around in my stomach. Dust devils spun across the empty flats and heat waves shimmered and danced in the distance. Noon came and went without rest and no edibles, with the gritty shadow shapes of men and horses drearily toiling in dust-choked silence beside us.

As the afternoon wore on, the gray scarps of clay hills filled with shale began to lift and crawl with interminable monotony across the trackless landscape. There was no sign at all of the missing Joe, nor did he turn up for supper when we stopped at a seep to pitch camp for the night.

Harry growled at me bodingly, "That sonofabitch is up to something!"

But the night was got through without alarm or apparent mishap. For breakfast we had corn bread and another dose of refried beans. Plus some of Jones's Arbuckle. No one had much to say. We got away bright and early, Johnny Two-Feathers riding again with Fern at the front of the outfit, Clampas and Fletch flanking their progress about a hundred yards out.

The morning breeze wafting across that seared and blackened vista ghosted away within the hour and the molten disk of the rising sun began to get in its licks. Hatcher, swinging his mount in alongside Gretchen, gave me a brief unjoyous grin. "Don't blame them basket-makin' aborigines for getting the hell out of this place! Enough to cramp rats!" he growled, sleeving his face.

"Probably better when those cliff towns were buildin'. Expect they had more rain; Chaco was likely runnin' bank to bank. I remember Jeff saying they did quite a bit of farming down on the flats."

"What kind of boodle you reckon he's really after?"

I flipped him a look. "You know what he's here for. No secret about it; he's hopin' to unearth the Anasazi's beginnings and dig up enough evidence to prove—"

"You ain't swallerin' that hogwash, are you?"

"What's your idea?"

"I think he's after turquoise. Why else would his sister rope *you* into this?" Harry peered at me sharply as if to see how I was taking it. "Your old man runs a trading post. Among these redskins, from what I've seen, there's a big demand for them blue stones!" He let the silence stretch out, squirming round for a better look at my face. "Hell, some of them bucks would trade their women off for 'em! I been told," he said, watching, "it's been a prime source of feuding down through the ages—oldest gemstone known."

"Even so," I told him, "what you're thinkin' don't make a heap of sense. Jeff's an academic, a professor of anthropology. His notions in that field look pretty reasonable, I'd say. The man is after kudos, the kind of acceptance and undoubted publicity he could get overnight if he's able to dig up the kind of factual evidence no one has managed to turn up before. He ain't the first of his kind to put a dig on out here, you know. There've been others—the Wetherills, for instance."

Hatcher wasn't convinced. "Maybe. But you take it from me there's something besides old pots drivin' that dude. I've got a hunch he's stumbled onto something. Big an' blue and buried in that canyon!"

SIX

THE NEXT DAY WAS SUNDAY.

The night before, while I was putting Fern's tent up, old Johnny had sought me out to say he would soon be released from his obligation, that we should see the red cliffs before another night. This knowledge trickling through the camp had set up a certain amount of excitement, put a new look on the faces of our outfit.

To go with our breakfast coffee Jones gave us nothing but yesterday's biscuits. Harry paid no mind to the grumbling, as anxious to get moving as Jeff was himself. By six o'clock we were well on our way, myself as usual still riding drag with Fletcher and Clampas out several hundred yards ahead of the pack string.

Fern came back to swap a few words with me. I said, "Who had the ordering of grub for this outfit?"

"That was Harry's department. In his behalf I'll have to point out we've a better variety than Jones has dished up. There's quite a bit of tinned beef but Jones is afraid of it with all this heat. The cans aren't bulged; I believe it's all right." The roan mop of her hair was windblown and tousled. "What were you and Harry so earnest about yesterday?"

"He's got it into his head all this talk about Basketmakers is just so much crap, that your brother's after turquoise—"

"Turquoise!" she cried, eyes locked on mine widely. "Where did he pick up that silly notion?"

"He's been workin' on it. Only thing that makes sense to gents of Hatcher's persuasion is a whopping pile of dollars and the quickest way to get them. He simply can't believe two dudes from Chicago would come all this way just to dig up a bunch of old pots and such."

She bit her lip, looked worried. "That's ridiculous! Exasperating!" The blue-green eyes intently searching my face became anxious. "You don't believe that, do you? I swear it isn't true—for years Jeff has believed these earliest Basketmakers came to this region thousands of years before his colleagues can be brought to admit...he's been trying to get back far enough to prove it. This is something he feels very strongly about. If he can only dig up-"

"Yes." I nodded. "I'll go along with that."

She said in a burst of anger, "This idea of Hatcher's is utterly untrue! Oh—I'm afraid this is going to make trouble, Brice. If that notion gets around it could wreck this dig before it even gets started! I'm going to send Jeff back to talk with you."

* * *

JEFF LOOKED FLUSHED, and angry too, when some half hour later he swung his horse in beside me. "Fern's told me about Hatcher. I've just been talking to him; wasted breath!" he said bitterly. "The man's impossible! Just sits there and grins at everything I tell him!"

"That figures. Only thing he wants to hear about is profit. Did he threaten you again with taking the crew out of here?"

Jeff shook his head irritably. "No, he made me a proposition. The fellow's preposterous!"

"What kind of proposition?"

"The man's a mental case! Says he knows of a ready market that will pay big money for any turquoise we come onto, that if we find any gem-grade rough or mounted spiderweb we could make a real killing. He proposes we split, him and me, fifty-fifty. I reminded him again I wasn't looking for turquoise, that what he suggested was completely unethical. 'Who's talking about ethics?' he sneered. 'You better have your head looked at. I'm telling you this could be a goddam bonanza!' "

The look on his face was furious. "I tried to tell him it wasn't likely we'd come up with hardly more than a cupful of extremely old and crudely cut beads, and that whatever we found was going back to the university."

I said, "How did that strike him?"

"He just laughed. 'All right,' he said, 'you go dig up your pots and *I'll* hunt the turquoise and I'll be claiming every chunk that's found.' I was so mad I could hardly talk. 'Over my dead body!' I told him, and got another of those pitying grins. 'Wouldn't be surprised,' he said, 'if that could be arranged.' "

We looked at each other through an uncomfortable quiet. Heat writhed above the gray shale-covered ground and shimmered between the distant worn-down bluffs. We set off after the others.

"You'll be knowin', of course, you're not the first to come in here?"

"Yes." Larrimore nodded. "Simpson came here in '49, Jackson in '77. There were Hyde's expeditions of '96 and 1901. Artifacts were found; but what they uncovered, while extremely interesting, didn't even approach the beginnings of these people. What they took out was relatively modern, Basketmaker Three and Pueblo stuff. There's got to be more underneath—that's why I came out here. If there's to be any proof of the dream, I've been coddling it's got to be right in this area someplace."

He gave me an anguished, frustrated look. "What are we going to do?"

"Just now, nothing." I shook my head much as he had done. "Right now, if he's got the crew with him, we're crouched between a rock and a hard place. I don't believe more than three of those boys will side with him. I think we'll have Jones and maybe Alfredo. But if it comes to a scrap, that's pretty rough odds. He's going to have Clampas and Fletcher for sure."

Jeff's gone-white face was filled with despair. I peered off across the scarps of those shimmering bluffs and, twisting, swung my glance to where the blue and wavering peak of a mountain thrust above the trembling haze. Jeff abruptly caught hold of my arm. "Look!" he cried, pointing— "isn't that the Chaco?"

I nodded. "The south gap. But it isn't where you're

staring. What you're seeing's a mirage. Take a glance at your sister and that old man. You don't see them turning. They're goin' straight on."

Jeff sank back in his saddle. "What if I order—"

"You're not in a position right now to order anything. If Harry's passed the word, and you can bet he has, the greed he's built up in that pair of gunslingers could get you killed at the first sign of trouble. Leave it alone. I want to think about this."

* * *

THE BROILING HOURS DRAGGED ON. The sun sagged into its downhill slide. A little breeze sprang up, too hot to afford relief. When our shadows began to drop behind us the Navajo, riding with Fern perhaps a quarter of a mile ahead, pulled his piebald pony to a stop with lifted arm. The whole line stopped. A mumble of voices reached us in a faint jumbled sound.

Jeff cried, "What are they talking about? Why have they stopped?"

"Let's go find out." I tightened my legs against Gretchen's ribs and pushed her into a trot, Jeff's mount following. Harry, Fletcher, the old man and Fern had all dismounted, the first pair staring like they couldn't believe it into a huddle of blasted rocks where a seep formed a pool of unexpected water. Fletcher scrubbed a fist across beard-stubbled cheeks. "Heap good water," Johnny Two-Feathers said. And Harry with a jerked-up glance at the sky slammed his hat on the ground. "We're campin' right here—we've rode far enough!"

No one felt inclined to argue with that. Alfredo got

an armful of sticks and Turtle Jones began to build up a fire while a rope was stretched round the pack string and the crew began peeling off loads and saddles. In almost no time at all Jones was treating us to refried beans.

It was crowding six in lengthening shadows by the time tin cups and pans clattered into the washtub and those who cared for it began to light up. We were in a locality of old rocks and outcrops with night closing in and no prospects showing for a better tomorrow. Fletcher and Clampas with instructions from Hatcher went grumblingly away to take up stations with their sour looks and rifles; and it was at this moment, taking a final survey of our unenviable situation, that I saw Fern with Flossie making her way in my direction.

Hatcher's sharp stare had discovered this, too.

The grin fell off his face as the dog with lifted hackles, growling softly, bared her teeth. "You better keep that bitch in hand," he said, ugly, stopping in his tracks to stand and glower in my direction. Fern grabbed the dog's collar and Hatcher straightened up to send a scathing glance across her face before turning the full weight of his inspection on me.

"Things have taken a change in this setup. I can see you've been told," he chucked at me with a laugh. "From here on out, those who ain't with me are in line for bad trouble," and he went stamping off, muttering under his breath.

Gretchen waggled her ears and hee-hawed like a rust-clogged pump rod. Hatcher half turned like he was minded to come back but presently went off without further remark.

Fern sank down, legs folding under her, with an audible sigh. "Jeff's going about with the look of a zombie."

"He's come too far to give it all up now."

"But what can we *do?* He won't deal with Hatcher." There was a tremor in her voice. "He's just about lost all heart for this dig."

I had no doubt Hatcher'd meant what he said. He figured he'd got hold of his life's best chance and was going to stay with it come hell or high water. No use kidding ourselves about that.

"Maybe things'll look better in the morning." I put a hand on her shoulder and gave it a squeeze. She got wearily up with an attempt at a smile that came off so stricken I made an extra effort to promote a cheerful outlook, but what was there to say remembering Hatcher's ultimatum? I could probably get the drop on him, but with Clampas and Fletcher with the camp spread out under the snouts of their rifles, such a move would be worse than not doing anything. To effectively improve this situation at all, those two hard cases had to be near enough to Harry to hold all three at a decided disadvantage.

I watched her move toward the tent, Flossie ambling along beside her.

She'd made it apparent she was neither meek nor biddable. She might not be any beauty but I had learned she was a girl with a good bit of bottom, in the main optimistically good-humored and not one to find relish in a jaundiced view of things. A down-to-earth sort of person...

I hauled myself up with a muttered oath. This was

not a time for that kind of thinking. My sort of drifting held no place for a woman and nobody knew this with more conviction than myself. If she and Jeff were to have any chance of wresting the whip out of Hatcher's hands, it behooved me to do something pretty damn quick.

SEVEN

DAYBREAK FOUND us mounted and moving. By all the signs and signal smokes the next camp should place us in Chaco Canyon. I'd done a mort of thinking without latching on to the faintest glimmer of how to disabuse Harry of the notion he was boss. The fellow was much too cagey to be taken unawares or let himself be lured beyond reach of those gunslingers' rifles. Catching him off" balance was going to take some doing.

The molten arc of the sky showed not the ghost of a cloud. The sun crashed down with insensate fury and all about us appeared not to have known a touch of moisture since the Anasazi vanished. If other springs existed in this burned black flat, no one but Navajos knew of their location. If this drought-ridden country had any charm we had yet to discover it, a grim and empty place steeped in the stillness of the centuries. Burning sands and swirling dust storms, a hard land to picture as ever having been any different, yet it surely had; no people could have settled and flourished for hundreds of years in such desolation.

I was in better case than most of our outfit for I had crossed this waste before. Had actually encountered a few of these ruins Jeff and his sister had come to investigate and drearily discerned how little could be hoped from digging ground already disturbed. To provide Jeff's theories any chance of proof, he had to have ground untrod through intervening ages. No easy chore, though I reckoned it possible if we could find some solution to Hatcher's threats.

There was little to be gained by openly opposing him. Any such attempt must be a last-ditch risk, for he was obviously prepared for ruthlessly crushing any action we might launch. Any turning of the tables called for guile and much patience.

Needing to make Jeff understand this, I sent Gretchen forward. But Harry, catching this maneuver, came up at a brisk trot, forcing his horse in between Fern and Larrimore with a nasty grin. Ignoring him I went on to pull up beside Fletcher, hoping to start a bit of counter-irritation. "Has Hatcher mentioned his latest scheme?"

Fletcher's look crawled over me morosely. "Keep away," he growled. "I got nothin' to say to you," and shifted his rifle.

"The man's told Larrimore he's claiming any turquoise we happen to find. I imagine what he has in mind is beads or nuggets; you can generally find a few around any old ruin. Just wonderin' if he was intending to share with you boys."

Before the fellow had time to digest this or show

enough expression to afford me any lead, Hatcher loped up with an oily smile. "Won't do you no good trying your blarney on Fletch. Or anybody else. All my boys are in on this bonanza. Don't let me catch you suckin' up to 'em again."

Turning away with a shrug I felt his hard look following. "If you want to start trouble," he called after me, "just stir up them dudes and you'll get yourself a bellyful."

* * *

THE HEAT-BLASTED BLUFFS got closer and rougher as the morning dragged along. By this time, blue hazed in the distance, you could see where the south gap cut into the canyon and guess at the rubble that lay all around it. I was presently surprised, staring through the lifted dust, to find our old Navajo riding back in my direction. "How!" he hailed, swinging in beside me with a lifted hand. "Pretty soon I go."

"Thought maybe you were figurin' to throw in with us."

A faintly humorous glint briefly touched his glance. "White man's troubles like white man's whiskey. No good for Navajo. I got sheep to look after."

"You on your way?"

"Plenty soon. When you come to Chaco." He eyed me a moment. "You got message?"

"Heap smart Indian," I agreed with a grin. "Tell missy to keep her tongue between teeth. And tell her that goes double for her brother."

Watching his paint horse go loping back to where

Jeff and Fern rode at the head of the line, I wasn't at all hopeful he'd be allowed any private conversation. I saw Clampas gesture, saw Hatcher wheel and take a long crusty look. But contrary to my assumption, he sank back in the saddle and continued whatever he was laying on Clampas.

If only those dudes would take my words to heart I might have time enough to cobble together some means of forcing Hatcher to leave them alone, for it had to be Fern they'd level their spite at. It would be me they'd want to be rid of but might figure to keep me in line through the girl.

I kept cudgeling my brain without hitting on a notion that wasn't loaded with dire consequence should I fail to bring it off. That smart dog, Flossie, was sticking close to her mistress. The Navajo had left them to ride out a ways ahead, leaving the rest strung out behind; and Harry, abruptly beckoning Fletcher, turned his mount and swung toward me, the pair of them bracketing Gretchen.

Hatcher said belligerently, "So's you know where you stand in this, mister, I'm telling you now to stay away from my boys. You're not goin' to change 'em, they're all in this with me. You make any trouble you're going to get hurt—*bad* hurt. Savvy?"

I forced a false admiration into my look. "I can see you don't miss much."

"You better believe it! I've got the whip hand and I intend to hang on to it. First wrong move outa you will be your last—just remember it."

With a final hard stare he wheeled away.

Fletcher, bending toward me, thrust out a hand, a jeering derision taking hold of his face. "Fork over that rifle an' don't give me no back chat." Hatcher had stopped and was watching intently. I pulled the Remington from its scabbard and held it toward him, butt forward. "You're learnin'," he chuckled, and galloped off after Harry.

* * *

HATCHER ORDERED camp pitched in the south gap entrance to the canyon. Jeff hadn't toted a rifle, nor had Alfredo or Jeff's sister, but Clampas had lifted Jones's artillery. I was surprised they hadn't taken my pistol. Hatcher probably figured, now that he'd spiked any attempt at sniping, to extract it later.

The Navajo departed with several more of Jeff's skinny cigars, and the crew got busy unloading the pack string while I tended to Gretchen and put up Fern's tent. "Pin your faith on patience and don't start anything," I muttered as she ducked inside it.

Alfredo with sticks he had fetched from our last camp built up a small fire while the cook, with several tins stacked beside him, began beating up dough to put into his Dutch oven. I'd have hunted up more wood but there obviously wasn't any. What the Anasazi hadn't taken to put into roofs and ceilings the Pueblo builders had completely exhausted.

For supper, in addition to hot biscuits and lick, Jones had provided corned beef in abundance, saying he'd just come onto it and hoped we appreciated the effort. Nobody else said anything but all took copious helpings. When we had finished and dropped our pans and eating tools into Jones's tub, Harry asked Jeff where he was aiming to start his dig.

When Larrimore shrugged without answering, I took it on myself to say, "Not far from where we stand right now, just inside those walls, you'll see what's left of Una Vida. Lots of adders, rattlesnakes and gophers, but without an extensive dig I doubt if you'll be happy with anything you'll get. It's not one of the larger pueblos and there's not much left. I did pick up a handful of beads which," I added with a quick glance at Harry, "my old man managed to sell at considerable profit."

All that got from Hatcher was a grin. But Fletcher and a couple of the crew went off to try their luck. Harry said with curled lip, "Penny-ante stuff. Someplace hereabouts there's a big cache of stones that ain't never turned up—a whole goddam wagonful! That's what I'm aiming to get my hooks on. That or what Geoffrey here is goin' to find for me."

The gloat in his voice got under Fern's skin and the hot look she gave him would have withered an oak post, but Harry took it in stride with a satisfied chuckle. "Careful there, honey, you'll be poppin' a gasket." He rubbed a look across me. "Your old man trades in turquoise, don't he?"

"Expect he does when there's any call for it."

He dug in a pocket and tossed me a chunk about the size of a walnut. "How's that look to you?"

"I'm no expert."

"You must have seen enough to have some idea. Come on, be a sport. Fair, average, good or gem grade?"

I tossed it back. "About average."

Hatcher snorted. "That assayer at Ajo called it gem grade." His stare winnowed down to bright shining slits. "That's no way to get yourself cherished. Try playing along on my side of the fence an' you'll have a good chance of putting money in the bank."

I put in my glance a rapt admiration that drew a twinkle from Fern when I told him rueful-like, "With your flair and style you ought to own the bank by this time."

He kept the grin on his face but there was nothing to comfort in the cut of that stare. "Always the joker," he threw back at me smoothly. "When I drive that wagonload over to Half Step, your old man better figure to buy gem grade."

* * *

THE SUN WAS BEGINNING to turn the sky pink all along the east flank of the little still left of Una Vida time we got through with breakfast next morning. Harry appeared bushy tailed and, at least on the surface, his old hearty self when "Well, Jeff," he said, "what's the program today? You aim to clear some of the rubble away from this site or try someplace else?"

"I believe the sensible way to tackle this would be to have a good look at what's available first of all."

"You mean explore the whole canyon?"

Jeff nodded. To me he said, "You're the only one of us that's been here before, Brice. How many ruins are there?"

"Hell—I dunno. Ain't too much left of a lot of them. As I understand it these places were towns. Inside the canyon there probably ain't over five or six that look worth botherin' with and I expect every one of them has been pretty well pawed over."

Jeff said, "The two largest, I believe, are Pueblo

Bonito and Chetro Ketl that Simpson examined in forty-nine.

Hyde, too, did quite a bit of work at Pueblo Bonito just a few years ago I'm told. I'm not familiar with Wetherill's work or Putnam's, but Wetherill I think had a trading post somewhere in this area. Very likely he went over the best of these sites.

"I realize, of course, there may be more to uncover even in towns like Pueblo Bonito, but my time is limited. I'd probably do better tackling one of these sites like this one right here that appears too negligible to hold any interest."

"Let's get at it then," Harry grunted, rolling up his sleeves.

"I think I'd rather look at the rest first." He turned to me. "Wouldn't take over five or six days to see the lot, would it?"

"If it's just ridin' through without dawdlin' you can cover the whole canyon by nightfall."

"Will I see any cliff dwellings?"

"I can't recall any inside the canyon. There's places where the cliff walls are pretty well broken down with gulches leading off. Could be something back in there maybe."

"The point is," Jeff said in a thoughtful voice, "these pueblo towns mostly date back not more than seven hundred years. The earliest evidence of Basketmakers we know anything about—and precious little at that— indicate they were in this vicinity at least two thousand years ago. That's the period I'd like to put my dig in."

Hatcher said, glancing around, "Let's get the pack string loaded and be on our way."

During the next couple of hours it became fairly

evident he had no intention of allowing private conversation between the Larrimores and me. He had them segregated up at the front with Clampas cozily riding between them, while keeping Fletcher and myself accompanying him behind the pack string and crew as the best way to thwart any trouble we might attempt to kick up.

He mightn't be smart but he could be plenty cunning when he put his mind to it.

We passed quite a number of ruins without pausing. Several textbooks had been published, mainly based on the investigations of earlier expeditions and the work of persons such as Wetherill and Putnam who, whatever they may have found, hardly did much more than scratch the surface. Along the eastern seaboard it seemed there were quite a number of people who wanted to know more about such antiquities and the Indians who created them.

Hatcher said after a while, "Any fool who'd spend his life in this godforsaken place should have been shut up with a string of spools! Fair gives me the jitters—can't you feel it, Corrigan?"

"It is kind of depressin', sure enough."

"Depressing! Is that all you notice? By Gawd I don't look forward to spending a night here!"

"Guess someone must've filled you with them stories about the chindi."

"Chindi?" he growled suspiciously. "What's that?"

"Spirits of the ancient dead. Must be a heap of them around. Stands to reason. What the college crowd refers to as original Americans were tramping these localities at least six thousand years before Christ."

Fletcher gasped, goggling, "Jesus! I didn't know he'd ever been around here—"

"Oh, be still," Hatcher said, and brutally kicked his horse into a canter, in a hurry it seemed to catch up with the others. "What's the matter with him?" Fletcher grumbled. "He's been jumpin' around like the seven-year itch."

EIGHT

WE CAMPED that night at the canyon's far end where he had two of the crew with the sweat rolling off them go down into the wash and dig a monstrous great pit, deep enough pretty near to bury the whole outfit. We didn't know what Harry was after, but if it was water he sure didn't find any. By the time each horse had drunk a hatful out of our canvas sacks there wasn't enough left, putting them all together, to put out the puny fire Alfredo kindled. "By Gawd, that does it!" Fletcher snarled, glaring at Harry. "What the hell do we do now?"

"Guess you'll have to do without."

"I can open some canned pears," Jones offered with a scathing look at the skimpy fire. "I can open some corned beef but you'll have to eat it cold. I mean, just the way it comes from the tin."

I saw the amusement slide through Fern's glance as she took in the comical look on Hatcher's face. "Go ahead," he growled. "Be better than nothing." His stare swiveled irascibly. "In the morning," he told Clampas, "send a couple of the crew out with rifles and see if they can't scare up some fresh meat."

It was a sour-faced outfit that sought their blankets after wolfing down Jones's provender. Jeff's look, no matter the desert's heat, appeared five shades paler than it had that noon. I could understand his stunned expression for, on top of all the other tribulations, to find ourselves without water and no flowing stream nearer than fifty miles in any direction, everything he had planned was on the brink of disaster. These horses couldn't last long without water. He was faced with the ruin of everything he had hoped for.

"Damn it all," Hatcher muttered, "there's got to be water around here someplace. Along the sides of that wash you could see where floods had almost crept up to more than one of those ruins. Jones, you an' Alfredo get down in that hole and do some more digging!"

Nobody yet had gone out to hunt meat. I hadn't seen one rabbit in the last thirty miles but there were coyotes probably if you could manage to stomach them. I'd noticed signs of ancient irrigation at Una Vida and one or two of the larger pueblos we'd passed, and downslope east of where we'd come into the canyon there might be a spring, though it wasn't a heap likely.

"What about that fork where the canyon branched off in a gulch toward the west?" Jeff asked anxiously. "Perhaps we could find water there..."

It was possible of course; anything was possible. I had been intending, if we could shake Harry and his pair of trigger-happy hard cases, to slip Jones and the Larrimores down that arroyo and whatever tinned stuff we could manage to get out with. Branching off of it somewhere along the left side, pretty well hidden last time I'd been through, was another narrow trail with the kind of thing Jeff had been hoping for. Not a large community—perhaps thirty rooms—but in a pretty fair state of preservation and no evidence of vandalism. It even had a small kiva, or ceremonial chamber, I seemed to recollect. And a well you could reach with a long rope and bucket.

I peered around for Flossie. She was not with Fern or anywhere in sight. Jones and Alfredo, armed with shovels and a pick besides, had just reluctantly started for the wash when Fletcher said bitterly, "I'm goin' to git outa here—"

Hatcher swung round. "You'll go when the rest go!" Seeing the way they were glaring at each other I was mightily tempted to make the big push till I saw Clampas with those pale eyes fixed on me and that black-bored Sharps pointed right at my brisket. Clampas's gaunt cheeks twitched in that high flat face and I turned away, cursing under my breath just as Flossie, coming out of the wash, stopped to shake. Jones's yell came up after her. "Two foot of water in that hole!"

The next hour was spent filling up our water sacks and taking the horses, one by one, down to drink. When the pool cleared a bit I took Gretchen down under Clampas's watchful eye.

"Well," Harry said in his old hearty manner, "what's next on the agenda?"

Jeff still looked unsettled by this change in prospects, like he was finding it hard to pull himself together. "I don't know," he said vaguely, "most everything we've seen either entails more work than I have time for or has been worked over by somebody else. I'd thought," he said, looking north, "to try up there but it doesn't seem very promising..."

It certainly didn't: badlands far as the eye could reach, a vast desolation it would take weeks to explore. I couldn't see nothing for it but to take them on back to where that side gulch branched off and try our luck there.

I told him, "That side canyon we passed near that last big pueblo just might have something, or you could try that ruin. I don't think anyone's done a serious study there or done any sort of a scientific dig, though the refuse heaps have been pawed over and vandals—"

"Let's try that side canyon," Jeff said without hope; and Hatcher sent off the crew to pack up the supplies and get the pack string loaded. It was close to ten o'clock before we got out of there.

Every mile—sometimes less—along the canyon's north side there were ruins large or little, and only the most insignificant remains had been bypassed by persons who had been here before us. Since the publication of Lieutenant Simpson's *Journal of a Military Reconnaissance from Santa Fe, New Mexico, to the Navajo Country,* dude pot hunters and others had prowled through here in ever increasing numbers by what you could reckon from the look of these places.

Some of the towns had practically disappeared save what was left among the rubble of centuries, some battered and broken walls with scarce a foot or two showing above scattered rocks turned black from the heat with hardly a tuft of seared grass showing where once there must have been considerable farming. If the Anasazi had left anything from the time of their occupancy not taken away by those who came later, it would probably be in such near-obliterated remnants as these.

It was well past noon when we reached the branch canyon and started along it with skeptical glances sweeping across the bleak cliffs. "I don't think there's much here," Harry told Jeff with a disgruntled snort. "We better go back an' try one of them others."

Fern and Jeff exchanged glances near as hopeless as Hatcher's. Gretchen heaved up a sigh. I wanted to suggest Jeff should look a mite farther but thought better of the notion. Hatcher would send someone with him and not like to be me. I said, "Can't be sure, but around that next bend there's another ruined place I seem to remember that might not be too torn up."

Harry shrugged and we pushed on.

There *was* such a ruin and of pretty fair size. Jagged holes had been poked through the nearest wall where looters had busted through in their search for anything they figured worth taking. Harry dismounted, jerking his head at Larrimore. "Rest of you stay here, we're going to have a look."

They'd been gone about ten minutes when we saw them coming back. "Place has been ransacked," Jeff told his sister. "By the shards I picked up it's a long way from old enough to waste any time on. Basketmakers hadn't anything to do with it." He put his look on Harry. "You want to go any farther?"

Harry scowling at me, abruptly made up his mind. "Might as well," he grumbled, and climbed back into his saddle.

It was a twisty trail, half obliterated, the floor at this point not over a hundred yards wide with the walls closing in and no sign at all of travel. Stunted bushes cropped up here and there, prickly pear and cholla, an occasional ocotillo thrusting up its thorny wands.

Some mile or so beyond that demolished ruin we'd stopped at, the walls opened out again. A lot of rock was strewn about where great sections of the heat-cracked cliff had broken loose to fall among a scraggle of stunted iron-wood. Since leaving the Chaco we'd come four or five miles in what was now little more than a gulch when, greatly astonished, the crew stopped to gape. What we saw was another seep with a ten-foot pool of gleaming water shining under it and tamarisks and salt cedar stretching tall beside it.

Hatcher grunted with a pleased look around. "We'll make camp here an' start back tomorrow."

They got the horses penned after letting them drop their heads for a drink and got busy unloading the pack string. I watered Gretchen and rubbed her down and left her on grounded reins to limp over and help Jeff set up Fern's tent, Flossie watching with her tongue lolling out.

Just as Fern ducked through the flap, wiping the sweat off her cheeks, I told her brother as Harry started toward us, "There's a cliff house not two miles from where we're standing."

Hatcher came up with a suspicious stare. "You know this place was here?"

"Figured it was bound to be if it hadn't dried up."

"Why didn't you open your yap about it yesterday?"

"Wasn't too sure we could find it."

"Yeah. I bet." A nastier expression took hold of his mouth. "Don't push your luck, Corrigan. I meant what I told you. If you want to keep healthy, better watch your step." With an angry nod he strode off to join Clampas, who had his back to a rock watching cozily while Alfredo dug out tinned ham from the stores and Jones stirred up dough for the biscuits.

We had a good meal that evening and a medium-sized fire that we could loll around afterward, and the majority of us—except for a guard sent off to stand between us and the way we had come—took a thankful advantage of it. Smoke from hand-rolleds curled and fluttered among the bouquet from Jeff's slim cigar. Flames winked and danced above Jones's bed of ashes. No voice was raised in anger. Talk was sporadic, stretched out and thin until Harry, making a push to get Larrimore started, asked from his place between Fern and me what Jeff thought of the prospects.

"Well, all the ruins we've so far looked at were put up in at least three different time spans. I can't believe even the earliest of these had a great deal to do with the earliest Anasazi, the first influx of Basketmakers. My guess would be they most probably date from Basket-maker Three.

"One has to realize, of course, that all those far-back aborigines didn't come from the same mold—nor fit it. These prehistoric people arrived in this region in successive waves. The first group," Jeff said, warming up to his subject, "are the people I'm most interested in, the original tribe to cross the Bering Strait; primitive, with few skills, who lived in pit houses and built no permanent shelters."

The happy eagerness of Flossie's look as she lay by her mistress and hopefully watched me, occasionally waving the plume of her tail, was the pleasantest view I had seen in some while. Fern's head with its freckled nose and that mop of roan hair was obscured by Hatcher's shoulder between us.

"After them," Jeff went on, "came Basketmaker Two and Three as they're called. Following these at widely separated dates came the Pueblo peoples. The original Basketmakers were nomadic hunters and gatherers who constructed neither pottery nor permanent quarters. Understanding this, it becomes obvious at once that any Basketmaker remains in the Chaco are either deeply buried or the work of Basketmaker Three."

"And so?" said Hatcher.

"So," Jeff replied, "a dig under such considerations and with less than five weeks before I'm expected back in Chicago seems out of the question. An archaeologist of any repute is not one to throw dirt helter-skelter. Much as I hate to, any dig I make here will have to be left to some future date."

"Mean to say," Hatcher growled, "you're throwin' this up and taking off for home?"

"Not precisely. I will do whatever I can to find facts and leave from some point closer than Ajo."

Ears cocked, grinning face on paws and her behind in the air, Flossie was trying to encourage me to play. As Fern had said, the dog evidently liked me. "If that brute," Hatcher said, "tries jumpin' on me it's going to be her last jump!"

Fern took hold of her, pulling the dog back and showing in the scathe of her look a bristling indignation as it settled on Harry. "Meantime," Jeff went on, "the most I can hope to pick up in this manner are relics or artifacts from people designated as Basketmaker Three, which really isn't what I came for. And if you're thinking of burial sites," he told Hatcher, "it's been established on pretty good authority these persons also had gone by 1200 A.D., near enough."

There wasn't any of this what Harry wanted to hear and he studied Jeff dourly.

When it occurred to me to take enough stock to find out where the divers personalities of this field trip were placed in relation to the others, I couldn't see Jones and had no idea where Fletcher had got to until I heard him slamming his way through the tamarisks.

Red-faced and panting he came barging up, to gasp out at Harry, "There's a *cliff house* up this trail! Just a whoop and a holler beyond them trees!"

The whole crowd was galvanized. Hatcher jumped up with every other last thing fallen out of his head to go at an accelerating gait in the direction of that water-fed growth as though determined to be the next to see this marvel, the rest of us strung out in his wake and Flossie barking in a seventh heaven of excitement.

Nobody stopped to rope out any mounts and our exodus from camp soon resembled a rout. Fern, as I went past, caught hold of my arm. "Do you suppose that's true?"

"It's true enough. I was hopin' they wouldn't find out about it till your brother had a chance to go over it private."

"You think it's—?"

"Couldn't tell. I been hoping it would fall into the right age bracket—looks older than Moses, and I don't believe any vandals have got to it. Nine chances out of ten that kind of trash would never have pushed through those woods. Been content," I said, "with the discovery of that water and gone back the way they came."

She peered up at me anxiously. "What do you think will happen now?"

"I don't know. Try, if you can, to keep Flossie away from Harry. And away, particularly, from that prize pair of killers."

The goal that had drawn us all like a magnet was still some distance ahead of where Hatcher and Jeff spearheaded our invasion. Most everyone now had dropped to a kind of shuffling walk though the quiet habitual to this hidden place hung in shuddering tatters in the battering from voice sounds. Jeff's small torch threw monstrous great shadows that continually hopped around us like a band of frightened chindis.

"There!" Fletcher cried. "Right there! Do you *see* it?"

Not even those nearest, pressing forward in the awful grip of ungovernable excitement, managed to conceal this wonder from Fern's riveted gaze. There was a tenseness in her grip, the breath seemed caught in her throat. "It's magnificent!" she whispered. "Just the sort of place Jeff's been praying he could find!"

In the moving light, as the torch was flashed about, the sheer wall built against the cliffs red rock must have reared a full fifty feet above the gulch's passage, un-pierced in its lower dimensions. Larrimore, attempting speech through his emotion-blocked throat, was heard to say, "Tomorrow we'll have a good look at it; there's nothing we can reasonably accomplish tonight."

NINE

NO ONE LAY ABED or lingered beneath cover once the hours of darkness had passed. They were far too excited, too anxious to get inside that relic of ages and learn what sort of treasure had lain hidden here through uncounted years. Not one of the bunch even thought to complain at the retried beans Jones had hashed up to give body to his Java.

Harry, in the first bright shaft of the rising sun, appeared as innocently expansive as a con man in possession of his neighbor's billfold. Even Alfredo was grinning as he piled our used breakfast gear into Jones's wreck pan. And Flossie, dancing about, divided her attention between me and her freckled mistress.

All the world was agleam that morning.

Fletcher's muttered claim that he should be given no less than a finder's fee brought a general laugh. Not even Hatcher spoiled it. "What's the procedure?" he inquired of Jeff. "How do we tackle this?"

"First off," Jeff told us, "I think we'd better find some way to get in. And the most important thing to be borne in mind is for the rest of you not to touch anything till I've had a chance to examine the place. Should we move our camp? I ask because if we don't, someone is certainly going to have to keep an eye on it."

"Not me!" Fletcher growled.

"Me neither," spoke up Clampas.

Harry's roving eye pinned Alfredo. "You'll do. Give him Corrigan's rifle. Fletch—you stay here too. I don't want to come back and find this camp all over hell's kitchen."

Fletcher's cheeks locked into anger. Hatcher, ignoring him, bade me go break out a pick and shovel and step lively.

I passed these tools to one of the crew that I knew was too stupid to open his jaw and limped off to throw my saddle on Gretchen, after which I stepped into it. And heard Flossie growl as Harry brushed past her. But Fern had a hold on her so Hatcher went on, increasing his step to catch up with Jeff. "How," he asked, "do we get into this place?"

I kicked a foot from the stirrup and hauled Fern up behind me. "No sense in you walkin' like the rest of these peons." Felt pretty good having her arms around me, and I thought to myself I'd better try this again. We could see that place a lot plainer with the sun up. Against that red rock it was even more impressive than it had seemed the night before, the whole towering face of it built up from little flat stones. And no openings at all in the lower two thirds of it.

Jeff, standing there with Harry, thoughtfully eyeing it, said, "Looks like we'll have to go in from the top unless we can make out to rig up a ladder—"

"Can't we just knock a hole in it someplace?"

The turn of Jeff's head showed what he thought of that. Fern got off Gretchen's rump and I got out of the saddle, letting go of the reins to stand with the others peering up at that sheer wall.

Trouble was we hadn't any ladder and, as Harry pointed out, no trees tall enough to make one that would be long enough to reach those openings.

Jeff said, "We'll have to send someone up to have a look on top. Bound to be some way of getting inside it. Anyone care to volunteer?"

Nobody clambered over the rest to become the first to get his name remembered.

Hatcher said, "We'll all go then. It's a cinch there won't nobody get in from down here."

"Time's a-wastin'," I mentioned. "Which way do we go?"

"Straight ahead," Jeff answered. "No way up back there."

I left Gretchen hitched to the ground, glad I'd remembered to throw some oats into her, and took off after the rest of them, expecting to have a pretty stiff hike. Without finding some kind of stairway we'd have to keep on till we found a spot where a section of the cliff had broken off to give us handholds.

It took an hour to come onto one.

And a pretty depressing sight it was, with great chunks of rock tumbled hell west and crooked, just about choking off what was left of this gulch. Catclaw and cholla grown up in tangles all through it. Hatcher led off, warily picking his way with Jeff right behind him, the rest of us strung out and myself helping Fern as seemed only natural at the end of the line.

Getting up took the bulk of another half hour with

the sun hammering down and sweat rolling freely to mix with the dust raised by those ahead. "And it looks like," I muttered, "we'll come back the same way!" But one good thing, I thought to myself, at least some of these rannies would have had a bellyful.

We now found ourselves on a kind of plateau with a wide sweep of country stretching off a far piece to a haze of blue hills slithering out of the distance. "Wake up," Fern exclaimed. "Let's not get left here!"

On this high scarp we trudged after the others, presently catching up to hear Hatcher wanting to be told how we'd know when we got there. It was a fair question. The serrated lip of this bluff sure as hell wasn't posted. "I guess," Jeff answered, "we'll have to keep looking over."

Harry, snorting, caught hold of one of the crew and with a shove sent him forward. "Get on up ahead an' find that place, Frisco."

Eventually he did. "Right under me now," he called, going abruptly motionless in his crouch above the rim. Hurrying forward I followed his look. Down there beneath us in a scrambling tug of war was a hatless Fletcher on one end of her reins and Gretchen on the other setting back with bared teeth.

"Get away from that mule!"

Fletcher's head spun around, glittery eyes trying to find me. "Up here," I called, and shoved off an egg-sized rock to nudge him. He let out a yell, eyes big as a bull's when he spotted my pistol about to open him up. He let go of those reins in such an explosion of hustle he tripped over his spurs and went down like a tree with all branches crashing.

"D-Don't shoot!" he gasped, a quivering bundle of terror. "Lemme tell—"

Gretchen's raucous complaint sawed the rest of it off just as I felt three-four others crowding back of me, and Hatcher told his henchman, "Never mind the windies!"

Fletcher's weather-roughened features ran together like sloppy dough. "But I come after that mule t' help me find you fellers—"

"A likely tale."

"Like or not," Harry's hard case shouted, "Alfredo's all spraddled out like a bunch of old clothes with a knife buried back of his wishbone. An' I'm tellin' you, by Gawd, there ain't a horse left in camp!"

TEN

YOU'D HAVE THOUGHT we were figures chopped out of wood.

No telling how long we stood clamped in this paralysis staring at the horrid thing that was now spelled out in front of us. Locked in this catastrophe it was Hatcher's snarl that broke our shackles. "Stay right there!" he bellowed, and took off pell-mell over the way we'd just come, the whole crew but Jones going hellity larrup after him.

I found my look on Clampas, who gave me back a cynical grin. "If them broncs are gone they're gone, that's all, and the boys'll hev to chase after them. Me, I stick with the main chance, mister. Right here with the professor."

Jeff, turning away, said, "We've got to find that entrance."

"But Jeff..." Fern cried. "If the horses are gone?" She appealed to me with her eyes seeming black against the pallor of that freckled skin.

"Like Clampas I'm stringin' along with Jeff." I

dropped a hand on her shoulder. "Buck up. We're like to be here a right smart while before those horses become important."

She eyed me uncertainly. "That poor man..."

"Very sad." Clampas nodded without visible grief. "These things happen. A business of this sort is hazardous at best."

She twisted around to have a sharp look at him. He stood there smiling in the best Hatcher fashion but making no attempt to dress it up in fine linen. "One learns to adjust."

Quite true, I thought, but no need to be so blunt about it. Fern moved closer to me. "But how could it happen? Who do you suppose killed him?"

"You want it tied up in pink ribbons?" Clampas shifted his weight. His glance touched mine. "I wouldn't put it past Fletch..."

With a look of abhorrence, she turned her back on him. But it came over me, there'd been no one else down there. Still, in a larger view, this *could* have been something handsome Harry dreamed up, using Fletch for the cat's-paw...

Jeff, with no heed for us, was down on one knee picking at the cliffs edge with his silver-handled jack-knife. Grunting now he stood up, slipping the knife back into his pocket. "I believe this end has been built up with masonry. Take a look at it, Brice. Built up and smoothed and made to look solid rock with some kind of reddish mud plaster."

Now that I looked closer, I could see what he meant. The top of the bluff where we stood, the end nearest Chaco Canyon that is, for eight or ten feet felt different to the touch. "Let me have that shovel," Jeff said, and proceeded gingerly to scratch at the surface.

He'd guessed right. It was some sort of mud mortar artfully plastered over a cunningly contrived sheet of masonry. Long ago it seemed likely a fairly large chunk had fallen out of the cliff at this point. "This has to be where the entrance was—there's no other place for it," Jeff panted, busily scaling off that whole stretch of plaster to uncover the work of men long gone. "When they quit this building, they did their best to conceal the way in. Look there," he pointed. "It's a kind of blind window they've laid up across what used to be the doorway. When everything was ready they simply filled this in."

It seemed plain enough now he'd pointed it out.

"You'll notice," he said, "when they sealed this up they set the rocks in vertically instead of crossways like the rest of this stretch; it proved handier I suppose."

"How you reckon to get in there?" I asked.

"We'll have to be careful. I certainly don't want to break this up. What we need right here is something we can use to poke out the mud between those upright stones. A case knife or bowie—"

"I've got a bowie," Jones said, stepping forward. "Let's have a look at that."

Jeff made room and Jones, kneeling, began to pick at the binder. It appeared to have hardened considerably through uncounted ages, though in some spots it had deteriorated noticeably. After about twenty minutes of steady digging, the rock he was working on let go and fell with an echoing rumble and clatter into whatever lay directly beneath.

Jeff motioned Jones aside to put his face to the hole.

"Blacker than pitch," he said. "I can't see a thing. Try the next stone," he muttered, getting out of the way. "You'll have to admit," he remarked as Jones resumed his labors, "those old boys were indefatigable workers. They must have quarried, transported and tediously shaped several million stones in the building of this place. A prodigious task with the primitive tools available to them; at least as difficult, I would imagine, as the construction of the Egyptian pyramids."

At the end of half an hour Jones had three more stones out, the last pair caught and gruntingly laid to one side. "Not quite so dark down there now."

Jeff, taking his place, peered into the hole for a nerve-rasping spell. Fern asked, "Can you see anything?"

"Not much," Jeff muttered, getting up to stretch his back. "Near as I could tell, there's a five- or six-foot drop. Probably know more about it once we get the rest of these stones lifted out."

"Let me take a whack at it," I said, and Jones passed me the knife.

It soon became evident that, because of the weight and the awkwardness of how we had to go about it, you couldn't remove but one stone at a time without risk of damaging whatever was below. Between us during my stint with the knife Jones and I managed to get out three more of the stones used to seal up the entrance. This left only four more in place when we moved back to give Jeff another look.

"Well," he told us as he got to his feet, "what we're faced with is a narrow room some four feet high, every wall of which is plastered and without any sign of an opening except for the one we've just made."

"Oh dear," Fern exclaimed. "You mean it doesn't go anywhere?"

"There'll be a door, I'm sure, or another blind window, but we're going to have to hunt for it." He considered it, frowning. "We're not going to get into that place today." He took a squint at the sun. "We'd better get back to the camp while there's still light."

* * *

WE BUILT up the fire while Jones dug a hole in the dwindling pile of our supplies and Flossie quartered the site with her nose to the ground, dashing first one way and then off at a tangent. I led the hee-hawing Gretchen to the pool for a drink, then fetched her back and hung a nosebag on her. Hatcher and his horse hunters weren't anywhere in sight, nor was the corpse of Alfredo, which I reckoned they must have buried.

Jones opened several tins of ham, got out his Dutch oven and started working up dough for his biscuits. Fern peeled potatoes and sliced them into a bowl while Jeff sat figuring on a page of his blue-backed notebook. The sun was gone and it was getting dark fast when a strengthening sound of travel pulled all eyes in the direction of the trail.

Looking pretty well beat, Hatcher and his helpers came up to the fire. No one ventured to prod them with questions for all could see there were no horses with them. Hatcher said finally, "No we didn't find them. I reckon them ponies must've run halfway to the canyon."

You couldn't hardly call Jones's fine supper a hilarious occasion. Hatcher perked up a mite when told we'd uncovered the entrance to our objective. No one sat around the fire once the meal was finished. Off to one side Clampas beckoned Harry for a low-voiced conversation with several frowning looks in the direction of Fletcher, and a short time later—Harry having put two of the crew on guard with Clampas—the rest crawled into their blankets.

Despite the daytime heat, which must have been topping out at close to a hundred, the nights were cool and, toward morning, often rightdown chilly. Though strongly tempted to hitch Gretchen, in the end I did not do so but fetched her under the tamarisks and there made my bed. Not that I expected to get a lot of sleep.

A jumble of thoughts juned around in my noggin, fleeting visions of Fletch in his various attitudes interwoven with sundry pictures of Harry. Having Gretchen, thoughts of the horses did not unduly worry me. For once Jeff made up his mind to depart, we could strike out for Farmington on the Denver & Rio Grande, not over fifty miles away. About two days by shanks' mare. I could put Fern on Gretchen.

I probably dozed, off and on, but in more wakeful moments I kept coming back to the unexplainable raid on our horses. Who but Fletcher could have set that in motion? The man was mercurial enough for just about anything, yet the suspicion kept nagging me that Hatcher might have been back of it, that a couple of those nags might not have left with the rest. Once Harry got his hands on any loot of real importance, he would be long gone in one hell of a hurry.

If any off-color business got afoot during the night, I certainly wasn't aware of it.

I did not wake at the crack of dawn, but came alive

shortly after to the aroma of coffee and the sight of Turtle Jones hunched over his fire-blackened skillet. Jeff and Clampas were already stirring and it looked like being another hot day.

Gretchen was happily browsing on such tufts of grass as she could find about the pool and, looking around with lifted head, gave me a cheerful gate-hinge greeting which could hardly have failed to rouse the whole camp. "Well," Hatcher groused, untangling himself from his bedroll, "does that godforsaken critter have to wake us every day!"

Flossie slipped out of Fern's tent and with great aplomb came to a squat behind the closest bush. She then cantered round with her nose to the ground taking inventory of any new smells the night had left behind, vigorously flailing her tail when she caught sight of me, further expressing her delight by hustling over to jump about with much enthusiasm, never quite touching me. "Good girl!" I said, and she ran off to find Fern.

Jones yelled, "Come'n get it!"

We wasted no time in putting it away. Returning from dropping our tools into the washtub, Jeff said to Hatcher, "Off to more horse hunting, are you?"

"Not me," Harry declared. "That bunch—if they ain't been stole and spirited out of the country—will probably wind up makin' Navajo stew!" His glance checked Jeff's face. "I been talkin' to Clampas—think you'll get into that place today?"

"The date of our entry," Larrimore told him, "could be anybody's guess. People who put up that apartment house went to some pains to close it up when they left. All of yesterday's work didn't get us any farther than a completely sealed room."

"Don't pay to be too particular. Bust a hole through the wall and you're on your way."

Jeff shook his head. "I wish it were that simple. I think I'll borrow Jones again if you've no objection."

"Good worker, is he?"

"Opening up that house in an acceptable manner," Jeff said, "requires skill and know-how, not just muscle. Far as I can tell, no looters or pot hunters have got inside yet. Which makes it imperative," he went earnestly on, "that I allow nobody in there but authorized personnel." He stopped to give Hatcher a very straight look.

Harry gave it back to him. "Suits me," he said, and grinned. "I authorize Clampas to be your chief helper."

Young Larrimore showed him a wintry smile. He knew as well as Harry there was no getting around it, that whatever Hatcher wanted there was nothing to stand in his way.

He took a deep breath. "Do I get Jones, too?"

"Sure. Take anyone you want. I think we understand each other," Harry said smugly.

Fern, coming up, asked, "Couldn't someone manage to construct a ladder? With all those trees..."

"Yes, ma'am." Harry trotted out his charm to affably assure her, "I'll see what I can do."

As before, I took Fern up behind me on Gretchen; Clampas, Jeff and Jones took to hoofing it. And once more, as before, I left Gretchen standing below the great wall and limped on with the others to the place of fallen rock. It must have been about nine by the time we stood before the hole we'd made in the entryway yesterday. There were still the four stones we had yet to prize out of it. Jones picked up his bowie and went methodically to work.

"What is Harry," Jeff said to Clampas, "going to do about those horses?"

"What *can* he do?" Clampas shrugged with spread hands. "When you're ready to go we'll just have to walk. We can probably make Farmington in a couple of days. You can catch a train there." He eyed Jeff curiously. "What I can't savvy is why you picked Ajo to take off on this jaunt."

Larrimore said grimly, "I left the arrangements up to Harry."

No more breath was wasted on talk until Jones and me had got those four stones out and carefully laid them outside the hole. At that point Jeff said, "You go first, Corrigan."

Not sure how much of a drop there might be in that uncertain light, I took my time and went in belly down with considerable care, remembering the stones we'd dropped in there yesterday. "How's it look?" Jeff called with his head through the hole.

"Not much room to work in down here. Anybody think to fetch that bar?"

"We've got it right here." He passed it down and I handed up the loose rocks that cluttered the floor. Jeff said, "I'm coming down," and stood a few moments after he had joined me, taking a long look around. "Not much headroom," he grunted.

"No. You'll have to watch out for your head. They did a good job—not a crack in these walls. Where do we start?"

He stood awhile, cogitating, mulling it over. "Let's see...that left-hand wall will probably open into space.

Chances are we'd best tackle this one. And low down, Brice—about two feet up from the floor and close to this end where it connects with the cliff."

I picked up the bar, driving the chisel end into the plaster. Nothing came of the impact other than the merest splatter of dust and the negligible mark the bar had left on the wall. I looked at Jeff. "Go ahead," he said. "Try it again. A little more to the right."

Same story. "Feels like solid rock."

Jeff nodded. "Probably is. Try a bit higher."

I did, but no improvement. I banged the bar into it again, lower this time. It went in about two inches and when I jerked it out about twelve inches of plaster flaked off. No seams showed behind it. "They've set a single rock upright," Jeff said, "to seal off the passage. See if you can scale off some more of that plaster."

Starting at floor level and working upward, I cleared a space some three feet by five and when the dust finally settled we had ourselves a look. What they had done was plain enough now. As Jeff had surmised, they had set in an upright slab of rock measuring two feet by three. "Be just about big enough," I said, "to let us squeeze through. Once we've got that slab pried loose."

"Hey, down there," Clampas called. "How about givin' me a turn with that bar?"

"You bet!" I said and, with the sweat dripping off my chin, was glad to climb out. "Whew!" I puffed, flipping Jones a wink. "You can have my next turn. Talk about Turkish baths—that's got them all beat!"

"Not much room." Jones grinned.

"Toss down that knife," Clampas grunted. "I've got to loosen this mortar."

Pretty soon Jeff said, "Try it now." We could see

Clampas laying into it with that forty-pound bar, bent over like a gnome to keep his head off the ceiling. He'd got out of his shirt and even in that half-light you could see the gleaming roll of huge muscles and the way they jumped every time that bar slogged home. A steel-driving man if ever I saw one.

"Stand back," he grunted some five minutes later. "I think it's moved—couple more whacks and it's goin' to come out of there." He spat on his hands and took a new grip.

"A genuine pleasure," Jones breathed in my ear, "to be up here watchin' that feller at work."

"You bet," I said, "and it's something you ain't like to see every day. I'd admire to give Fletch a dose of the same!"

"*Look out.*' "*Clampas* hollered. There was a grating wrench and a resounding crash and through the dust I could just make out that great whopping slab laying flat on the floor.

"Bravo!" Jones cried, and we both clapped hands.

Clampas grinned up at us. Jeff pulled his head back out of the new hole. "Can't see a thing. Pass down that torch."

Jones put it in Clampas's lifted hand and he and Jeff moved over to the opening, pointing the light on whatever lay beyond. They took a good long look, so long Jones growled impatient, "Hell's fire! Cat got your tongues?"

Jeff shook his head. "Another empty room. Bigger than this but otherwise just like it."

I guessed he was pretty disgusted after all that work and so little to show for it. "Go ahead—take a look," Jeff said. Clampas wiggled his length through the hole he'd just opened, disappearing from sight. Jones lit a smoke. Jeff stepped over to the hole. "Just the same?" he called.

Clampas's voice when it reached us had a faraway sound. "Just the same, except size. Plaster on every wall. Not a crack showing. What the hell time is it?"

I consulted my shadow. "Round about three." Jones looked at his watch. "Three-twenty." I said, "Where's Fern?"

"She went back a couple hours ago. Guess she got hungry—which reminds me," Jones said. "I prob'ly better be gettin' back too."

"Guess we all had," Jeff said as Clampas rejoined him. "Too late to get through another wall today. Anyway this torch needs fresh batteries."

* * *

SOME THINGS, I thought, can't hardly be mistaken.

We were bound for camp, picking our way through the catclaw and cholla garnishing that fall of tumbled rock, grim of eye and thin of lip, nobody opting for conversation, each of us turning things over in private. Peering at Jeff as we moved along, one could not help noticing the harried expression that in the past several days looked to be coming habitual. I suspected this sample of life in the real world had descended on him as a pretty rugged jolt.

He must have found Harry a rude disappointment, to have discovered in the man an unscrupulous schemer where he'd looked for a knowledgeable enthusiastic friend. To realize he'd hired a purveyor of illusions must have been a sad shock. Even more than the affront to his self-esteem had been the growing conviction his whole trip had been wasted unless something of value could be dug out of this cliff house.

Clampas, I reckoned, would have been a pleasant surprise. The way the man had pitched in, the prodigious work he had done could have given Jeff assumptions which had no basis in fact. Absorbed in his own concerns, determined on the renown which must so far have eluded him, Larrimore was in no condition to see Clampas as I saw him—hard, twisted, coldly calculating, a man without sentiment who would kill even quicker than that lout of a Fletcher if it suited his purpose.

I was glad I didn't stand in Hatcher's boots.

We were back at camp, pushing through the tamarisks about the pool when Jeff in the lead stopped with such suddenness Jones banged into him. No need to search for the cause of their astonishment. It was there in plain sight.

The horses were back.

ELEVEN

BACK, too, was the Navajo, Hosteen Joe, the man who had left our hospitality in fury, that brash young buck who had wanted Clampas's rifle.

Hobnobbing with Harry, plump with smiles and self-importance, proudly fastened to my confiscated Remington, Joe had the strut of a visiting chief. Harry, too, looked to be in fine fettle as he beckoned us forward in his heartiest manner.

"Look who's here and see what he's fetched us— every last pony that departed this camp!"

No mention, I noticed, of poor old Alfredo.

"What happened?" Clampas asked. "Couldn't he find a buyer?"

"That's no way to make a man welcome," Harry chided. "Took him three days to get these broncs rounded up."

"Yeah," I said. "What's he doing with my rifle?"

"Not to worry. We gave him that as a very small token of our appreciation." Turning to Jones he said,

"See if you can't dish up something extra special tonight. You know— in honor of the occasion, eh?"

Jones without answering went off toward the fire some jubilant soul had thoughtfully built up for him and began rattling round among his pots and pans.

Fern with Flossie scampering alongside came over to ask her brother what he'd found. "Well," she remarked after his unenthusiastic answer, "that's encouraging, don't you think? They'd hardly have gone to so much trouble if they'd left nothing behind other persons might value."

"Perhaps you're right," Jeff nodded dourly, and tried then to show a more cheerful countenance. "It's not the work of the original Basketmakers, but it may well prove to have been constructed by some of the descendants not too far removed. It doesn't have the appearance of Pueblo work."

I sensed an anxious look of foreboding in her glance as Clampas came up to consider her blandly. "Not worrying about the chindis, are you? After all these years there shouldn't be much left of them."

* * *

JONES OUTDID himself with supper that night. Baked potatoes and ham, johnnycake and Java hot from the coffeepot with juicy canned Bartlett pears to wind up with. Harry pronounced it a feast fit for kings.

Hosteen Joe was feeling his oats. "By myself I catch these horses. Not many peoples could do such thing— you know that? Me, I'm one smart Indian, no?"

"You're a wonder." Clampas smiled.

"That hat still fit all right?" Jones asked.

I went off to palaver with Gretchen. Before I got out of earshot Hatcher told Larrimore, "Tomorrow I'm going up there with you. We'll leave Clampas in camp to keep an eye on our belongin's." When Jeff made no comment Harry divulged as though dispensing a favor, "We'll take Fletch along to take care of the rough work."

Gretchen cocked an ear when I stopped beside her and twisted her head to nuzzle my pocket, pulling back her lip while ogling me with great expectation. "Such a moocher," I said as she lipped the sugar lump off my palm.

But I was bothered in my mind, uneasy as Fern, thinking about that Indian fetching back our horses. It seemed a most unlikely action. Why had he done it? What was he up to? I reckoned we'd find out before we got done with this. But, I remembered as I got into my blankets, it was the Sharps Joe had wanted...

Had Joe killed Alfredo? Then stampeded the horses?

It didn't appear to make any great amount of sense to do these things and then fetch them back again. Could he have brought them back to make Hatcher feel beholden? Hatcher was pleased enough to give him my rifle. But it hadn't been mine Joe had taken such a shine to...

Much as I distrusted Clampas, I could think of no way he could have mixed into this. He'd been with us up there on the cliff top when those broncs had left camp and Alfredo at that point had certainly been alive. Now the horses were back and that Navajo with them. And if Harry had sense enough to pound sand down a rat hole, he'd surely be bright enough to watch that Indian.

I was back in my thinking to that notion Clampas had pushed out for our scrutiny, that Fletcher was the one we should have had our sights on. Had Fletch driven off our caballos on orders from Harry? Then again, if Hatcher'd had no part in it what could Fletch have hoped to gain?

It must have been about there that sleep overtook me.

Next morning, after getting outside Jones's refried beans, I took Gretchen along to the pool for a drink. Coming back with a bucketful to leave outside Fern's tent, I stopped to exchange a few words with Jeff and asked if Fern was going with us this morning. Jeff said, "I suppose so," and frowned. "Must get pretty tedious for her up there but she's refused to stay in camp if that hard-eyed gunslinger is going to be staying here—says he makes her skin crawl. You don't think he'd—?"

"Clampas," I said, "has got his sights set on loot. Same as Harry. It's occurred to me, Jeff, we should have been posting a guard up there."

He peered at me wide-eyed and vigorously nodded. "You're absolutely right. We'll do it hereafter." He stood there thinking about it, then said with a grimace, "Here comes Harry. Guess we better get up there."

"You go ahead. We'll come along as soon as Fern's ready."

It didn't take long to put the saddle on Gretchen. I knew she was not real keen on carrying double but reckoned another sugar lump would improve her outlook. When Fern came out of the tent to join us I could see she was troubled. She said, "I've this frightful feeling we're heading into something that had better been left alone. Do you suppose, Brice, it was never intended that we should get into that sealed-up place?"

"It's just the strangeness—"

"I feel so alone," she said, looking out over the sunlit surroundings. "This landscape's so big, so bare, it depresses me."

There didn't seem to be very much I could say to that. Flossie then came gamboling up and we got aboard Gretchen and took off for the cliff house, catching up with the others just short of the rockfall.

"Didn't you mean to leave Gretchen back—"

"I'm going to leave her up here where there's something she can browse on. You go ahead. I'm goin' to take the saddle off. Give her a chance to roll if she wants to."

She went off with Flossie eagerly beside her. Jeff, Harry, Jones and Fletcher were halfway to the rim when Fern with a scream abruptly froze in her tracks. I made a pass at my hip and shot the head off the rattlesnake coiling on the sun-bright rock just ahead of her. "You're not going to faint, are you?" I kicked the wriggling mass off the rock.

"No..." She looked kind of peaked. "No—of course not!"

"I'll go ahead," I said. "You step where I've stepped."

Jeff, alarmed by the shot, had stopped and was looking back at us. "Snake?" Harry asked, and I nodded. "He didn't get a chance to strike," I assured Jeff. "Gave her a turn—she'll be all right."

* * *

AT THE SITE of our labors Jones and Fletch were looking things over, Fletch wanting to know how far we had got. "Then you haven't found anything yet," he sneered. "If," he said, "there's anything to *be* found."

Jeff ignored this. "Jones, I expect you remember how we tackled that first room? I want you and Fletcher to get into that second one and get enough of that plaster off to find us a door."

Jones picked up the shovel and followed Fletcher into the hole, then reached up a hand. "Might's well take that bar along, too. We're sure goin' to need it."

It was not long before we heard the shovel flaking off plaster and Hatcher demanding to know if we aimed to spend the day improving our tan. Jeff gave the Fellow a very cool look and suggested if Hatcher wasn't entirely happy to be an onlooker on this important occasion no one would insist that he remain standing about.

A startled, half-furious expression skidded across Harry's widely opened stare. A flush, rapidly darkening, crept above his collar as he backed off a couple steps, mouth opening and shutting but with nothing coming out.

Larrimore turned away. "How's the dust down there?" he called into the excavation.

"Not too bad," Jones called back. "There's room enough here if you want to come down. We've got the baked mud off two off the walls." His voice grew less intelligible. Then, much louder, he informed, "Fletch is clearing the wall to the right on our opening—*I believe we're on to something!*"

Flossie barked and disappeared into the clifftop opening. "I'm going down," Jeff said, and followed the dog. "Oh—I do hope they've found something," Fern declared excitedly.

Harry, bending, tried to discover what was going on below. I said, "You can't see where they're at from up here; the place we pulled that slab from is at right angles to the hole you've got your head in."

Fern's hand gripped my arm. Jeff called up, "They've cleared the third wall and there's a real five-by-two-foot door just waiting for us to get at it. Come down if you want to have a look."

Hatcher wasn't one to step aside for women and children. Thrusting a leg through the hole he lost no time in dropping onto the next level, the four-foot-high room we'd got into a couple days ago. Not wanting her to skin a leg or otherwise collect a hurt I reached up and brought Fern safely down, observing the excited look on her face. "Watch out for your head in this cubbyhole," I muttered, noticing with pleasure the way her nose wrinkled up beneath that mop of roan hair.

Jeff was in the next room with Jones and big Fletch with Harry just beyond the hole we'd made yesterday. "Move over," I told him. "We'd like to see, too."

When we'd all got in there Jeff gestured toward the sealed wooden door they had just uncovered. I was surprised to notice that while it showed considerable age, as might have been expected, it was still a sturdy obstacle. Jeff said, "You're probably about as curious as I am, and I'll admit the desire to tear down this door and get beyond it is almost irresistible. But no reputable archaeologist can afford to give in to that kind of action. There's a meticulous discipline to the way we do things."

He gave Jones a nod and our cowpuncher cook un-limbered his bowie knife and with tedious care began chipping away at the ages-old mortar that held the door shut. "When this was set into the wall," Jeff informed us, "hinges as we know them had not been invented, nor had iron been discovered. What we have here is a solid sheet of wood chopped from a tree with some sort of stone implement, set into the opening and held in place by wedging it with a mud-base mortar filled with tiny pebbles. Once that's been removed the door can be lifted out."

You could see the impatience on those watching faces and I could feel it in myself. It put a strain on our tempers, honed our expectations. By the time the door moved and was brought away in Jones's hands every one of us, I guess, was about ready to pop. First through the opening was Flossie, then Harry Hatcher. We were all crowded around the opening, staring with an inten-sity that must have been laughable to anyone not caught up in our emotions. The frozen expressions on those roundabout faces were as plain as they were comical. There was nothing to be seen in the uncertain light and that tomblike quiet but another empty room with an open doorway off the left wall.

"Jesus!" Hatcher said. "I might's well have stayed in camp!"

Jeff, stepping forward without remark, crossed the room to the open doorway, through which Flossie had just disappeared. And there he stopped.

To the rest of us, watching in that unearthly quiet broken only by the patter of the dog's clawed feet, there was an arrested quality in Jeff's stance that put, I think, a quivering chill into all of us.

Frustration thinned Jeff's voice when he said, "Nothing in there but a pile of loose sand and off in one corner a hole in the floor."

TWELVE

HATCHER CROSSED the room with Fletch at his heels, roughly shouldering Jeff out of the way. The dog barked somewhere as they passed out of sight. "Here, Flossie!" Jeff called as the rest of us joined him, but the dog didn't come. We could see Fletcher and Harry crouched over the hole, light from below shining bright on their faces, on dropped jaws and bulged eyes. "Oh—what is it?" Fern cried. "What are you staring at?"

In a stunned tone of voice Harry said, "Damned if I know... a lot of stuff down there, all piled up in a corner. Bunch of different-size pots..."

Jeff looked disgusted. "The Basketmakers weren't potters." Fern pushed past him. "Do you see Flossie?"

Harry said, "Yeah, she's down there."

"Is she all right?"

"Looks all right to me."

"Let me have a look at those pots," Jeff grunted as we all ganged up behind Fletch and Harry. "What color are they?"

"Black on white," Fletch mumbled.

I said, "Looks to me like they're all Anasazi. They weren't made yesterday, that's for sure. I see a couple of storage jars and what seems like a wedding pot. There's a low flat bowl—maybe these people were Mogollons or some of the late Cochise people. That bowl looks to be about half full of corn."

Said Jeff, like he was turning it over, "Might possibly be Cochise. They made pottery after contact with some of the Mexican Indians."

"How," asked Fern, "are we going to get Flossie out of there?"

"That's about a five-foot drop," Jones said. "We can easy make a ladder—"

"We'll probably have to make several ladders," Jeff said, looking around, "if we don't come across some, which we probably will. We'll have to have short ladders to find out what we've got here. Must be at least five floors to this place."

Fern said to me, "Can't you get Flossie and hand her up?"

"You bet," I said, but after I dropped down there Flossie proved elusive. She'd come up to me and sniff in what seemed a friendly fashion, but each time I tried to get a hand on her she'd duck away.

"You go," Fern said to Jeff. "She'll let you pick her up."

"We'll get her tomorrow," said her brother. "Spending the night here isn't going to hurt her. Tomorrow we'll have a ladder."

I said, "What time you got, Jones?"

"Pretty close to two, about three minutes till."

Harry, catching on, said, "Fletch, you hike back to camp and fetch us a ladder."

There was very little enthusiasm in the scowl Fletcher showed but muttering under his breath he went back through the hole we had taken the door from. Yet, oddly enough, his departure did not erase the anxious look from Fern's face.

This room I was in was lighter than the upper ones by reason of the window hole that was in the outside wall. There was an elongated shaft of sunlight on the floor and Flossie with her tongue lolling out was sitting in this watching me. "Come on, Flossie," I said, bending toward her. I held out a sugar lump. Her tail thumped the floor but she showed no intention of coming any nearer.

Jones said, "Reckon I better be gettin' back too. I ought to go over that tinned stuff. All this heat...you never know. Maybe I can help put together that ladder."

Jeff gave him rather detailed instructions and some ten minutes later he set out. "Keep a lookout for snakes," Jeff called after him.

Fern, still with that anxious look in her eyes, appeared to be keeping a close watch on Flossie, who had gone back to sniffing around that bunch of old pots. Larrimore heaved a despondent sigh. I said, "This place looks to be in pretty good condition. No sign of them—I mean the folks that built it—having been attacked or driven out. If they'd been hit by a plague—"

"It doesn't seem to have been that," Jeff said, shaking his head. "If it's corn in that bowl it couldn't have been lack of water. Perhaps they had a lemming complex, or just an itch to move. Let me look at that bowl, Brice."

I limped over to where Flossie was still nosing the

collection, picked up the bowl and passed it up to him. "It's corn. Hard enough to be petrified."

But it wasn't the corn that concerned Jeff. It was the container he was studying.

"Does the design tell you anything?"

"Not really. It was obviously made a long time ago. It's a lightning design repeated with variations through hundreds of years; you'll still see its use in some of the pueblos. It's Anasazi ware, you were right about that. We might get a relative date from that corn."

"How many rooms do you reckon we've got here?"

"Possibly thirty. I wouldn't guess more than that. Probably less."

Flossie came over, stretched out a yawn and sat down beside me, thumping her tail as we exchanged looks. Then she was up again, moving off a few feet to stand intently staring at the door hole opening out of the west wall. Just above a whisper Fern said, "She's listening to something. You don't suppose there's anyone...?"

"Not unless," Jeff said, "there's another way of getting in that we haven't found."

While he was talking, I started toward that across-the-room doorway. This was all the encouragement Flossie needed. At a bound she was off and through the opening, the sound of her flying feet rapidly fading. I passed through after her and through three more, pulling up, gun in hand, before a fourth doorway hung with strung beads.

In the breathless quiet I caught the sound of her again, growing plainer. I heard her shake. And then there she was coming out of the beaded doorway, giving a wag of her tail as she sighted me. "Good girl!" I said as she stood looking up at me. "Guess you must've been chasing a chindi."

Jeff, when we got back, was down in the room below Fern, looking over that pile of pots with an expression I felt was unduly thoughtful. "Each of those two largest storage jars," he said, pointing, "are filled with white and black beads. And that pitcher is filled with blue ones."

I picked up the pitcher and poured out a handful. "Fossil turquoise, and enough of it here to gladden Harry's heart. Prime grade, I'd say—and, by the way, where *is* Harry?"

"He went up top to watch for the ladder."

I poured the handful of turquoise back where it came from. "What do you want to do? Let Harry and friends get a look at this and we're going to have trouble."

"Yes." Jeff grimaced. "Throw a handful of those white beads on top of them and put that pitcher at the back of the pile. We'll have to figure some way to keep them out of sight."

Hoisting myself up till I got a knee hooked over the hole's edge, I climbed out onto Fern's level. "Poor Flossie," Fern said, looking sorrowfully down at her. "Poor, poor Flossie."

"Yes," Jeff said. "Well, shall we go outside? If we had Clampas here he would say his heart bleeds for her."

"You staying down there?" I said.

"I want to poke around a bit. And if you've no objections I'd like you to count on staying here tonight. If we can keep them from it, I'd like to keep the vandals in our party from taking over."

I looked up at the sound of running steps approaching. I could feel the whole length of me tightening up. Was this what Fern felt? This queer foreboding? It was like receiving a telegram just as you're about to tuck into your supper. It was Harry, of course, and one glance at his face told us this was no joke.

The words tumbled out of him. "I sent Jones on to camp. Fletch is down in that rockfall with an arrow in his throat!"

THIRTEEN

I LEFT Fern with Hatcher and went hurrying along the clifftop, grimly wondering if this was a second installment of what had been started with Alfredo's death and the stampede of our horses. I wasn't far into those rocks when I found him, face down in the hollow between two large boulders.

You generally know when you're looking at death. There's something about it that makes itself manifest. I knew at first glance Fletcher'd cashed in his chips. I climbed down there and turned him over, wondering what had given Harry the notion an arrow had done for him. Then I saw it and guessed you could call it an arrow if that suited you.

It was there in his throat just below the Adam's apple, a slender shaft no more than eight inches long, almost certainly propelled from some kind of blowgun. There wasn't much blood.

I took Fletcher's pistol, thrust it into my waistband. No sign of his rifle. If an Indian had done this there wouldn't be. But what kind of Indian around here used a blowgun? Clampas would have said, "Must've been one of them chindis."

This wasn't going to help Jeff's hunt for glory. Our three-man crew was like to cut for the tules when they glommed on to this. If they'd take that smartass Navajo with them...A small palaver with Hosteen Joe, it occurred to me, would be at least a possible move in the right direction. Given his makeup...We knew nothing at all about the bugger...Well, I knew in my own mind Joe was a troublemaker, a rebel and misfit who felt he had been shortchanged in life's lottery. Joe in a number of ways looked cut from the same cloth as Harry—out for anything he could get. And not particular how he got it.

If I'd been bossing this deal I'd have run him out— him, Harry and Clampas—and the sooner the better.

I left Fletch where he was and limped down to see about Gretchen. She didn't like showing it but I could tell she was glad to see me. I gave her a sugar lump and threw on my saddle and, after rummaging my notions, climbed aboard and headed for camp. And got there just as Jones, toting a short ladder, came bucking his way through the tamarisks. "I'll take it," I told him. "Guess the camp's fair buzzin' with the news of Fletch's passing."

"Ain't too much bein' said but plenty wild looks are bein' chucked about." Jones grinned. "Clampas allows the chindis must've got him."

"I thought he'd get around to that. Well, keep your eyes skinned. I'll be stayin' up top tonight, me an' the mule here."

"What about grub?"

"Won't be the first time I've missed the wagon." I

hooked an arm through the ladder and gave Gretchen the go sign.

When we reached the rockfall I got down with the ladder and looped the reins around the horn. "You're a smart enough critter to get up there if you've a mind to," I told her. "Just watch your step and follow my lead."

She hee-hawed a couple of times, then took after me. Figuring he'd earned it we bypassed the place where Fletch was resting. I guess she found it rough going but five minutes after I came out on top Gretchen joined me, nuzzling my pocket like she understood her due. Wrapping her lip around a sugar lump beat everything.

She kind of rolled her eyes when she came up to the entrance we had made in that cliff house. You didn't have to spell things out for her; she could read body language and was quick to catch on. I called out to alert the Larrimores, and then told Gretchen, "Browse up here anyplace you've a mind to," and stripped off my gear and cached it just inside that four-foot room that once had served as an entryway.

I found Fern and Jeff in the room above Flossie and set up the ladder. "Be a little careful with this thing, it's not an A-1 job. When the red brothers set out to put a ladder together they lash each joint with a strip of wet hide. Once that dries, you got a real foundation. Well, there you are."

"Jeff," Fern said, "go fetch up Flossie." Then, to me she said, wrinkling up her freckled nose, "I can't stand this place. There's something about it that makes me squirm."

Her brother fetched Flossie up and set the dog

down. She went straight to Fern, wriggling all over, tail threshing ecstatically.

"I'm going to leave this torch with you," Jeff said, putting it into my hand. "Who do you suppose killed that fellow? And with a blowgun! I never heard of our kind of Indians—"

"You never heard of Hosteen Joe till you came out here and met him. I'm not sayin' he did it. Jones tells me Clampas has been laying it on the chindis. First thing you know—Well, never mind that."

"You think he believes it?"

"No. Local tradition tends to back him up, though. You'll find these abos set a great deal of store on that sort of thing. Good excuse for pretty near anything."

Jeff shook his head. "Next year," he said with a determined glance, "I'll come back and find out where these people went. And I'll be bringing my own crew with me!"

"They'll be your kind of people and that makes sense. Have a better grasp of what you're tryin' to accomplish."

He rummaged my face with a sharpened glance. "You've had an education—"

"Sure. School of Hard Knocks. My old man had his own set of notions, didn't subscribe to such dodderin' thoughts as all work and no play makes Jack a dull boy. I got the hell away from him quick as I was able."

"Still," said Jeff, running a thoughtful tongue across his mouth, "some of his lore must have rubbed off on you. That turquoise we found..."

"Fossil stuff. Formed as a mineral replacement in reeds, pithy sticks and the like. It's tubular—fine stuff for makin' necklaces."

"Valuable?"

"Rare," I said, "and like most rare things at the changing of hands the price goes up and it's strictly hard cash. How are you figurin' to go over this place? An overall look to see where you're at, or room by room?"

"In the time available I think I'd better see the whole layout first."

"All right then; I'll see you in the morning and we'll get right at it."

Fern's look lingered briefly and then they were gone.

* * *

I WENT out to see how Gretchen was doing, then sat for a while with my legs idly swinging in the entrance hole, staring off at the purpling shape of a distant range showing low against the far horizon. There were bushes enough up here I reckoned to keep a mule happy for most of the night.

It was fortunate Jeff had been stupid enough to give me this chance to have a good look around, even leaving me the bonus of a torch to do it with. I say 'stupid' because that's just what it was. He didn't know enough about me to have the least basis for such reckless trust. His own sister when she'd hired me out of desperation had put me in the same class as Fletcher and Clampas, a man who lived with a gun. And she had pegged me right. More right than she knew.

Pushing off my perch I dropped into the house Jeff had claimed for his own. It was hard to picture this place as the seat of a community, filled with the noise of a people going about their everyday affairs. They might not have been the ape-men Jeff hunted, or even very close to the beginning of things, but primitive enough to be an unwelcome sight backed into a corner in the dead of night.

I'd a hunch Fern was right in her distrust of this place. I didn't like it either though I couldn't uncover any practical reason. Just a feeling, that was all, a kind of aura that reached out to curl about one. A sense of watchful, breathless waiting as if the place were about to gobble one whole. Damned silly, of course, and I knew it, but knowing didn't chase the feeling away. I went forward again, pulled along by remembrance of that beaded doorway I had seen hunting Flossie.

A thing like that didn't belong in this place. No Indian I had ever brushed up against would have hung a bunch of beads across any doorway. Someone else must a taken over this dwelling after the original inhabitants had departed. And if this was the case it had to have been this later group who had so meticulously sealed the place up. Some of Clampas's chindis?

Such bead-hung doorways were not uncommon in Mexican houses.

Thinking of the way this place had been sealed I felt reasonably certain the ones who had been here after the builders had gone must have come and departed many hundreds of years ago. The stillness of centuries hung over these rooms. As I've said, you could feel it.

I switched on the torch and went down the ladder up which Jeff had fetched Flossie.

The pots and bowls still sat where we'd left them and I moved on through three rooms to stop and stare at the preposterous sight of that bead-hung doorway.

The vastness of this quiet seemed to hover just beyond me in those jet-black shadows retreating before my light, before the sound of each step. I was tense with excitement, with a feverish anticipation and with the prickling dread with which we face the unknown. I kept telling myself there was nothing to be afraid of and, trying to bolster this belief, wouldn't let my hand touch the pistol at my hip.

With the torch aimed dead ahead of me I pushed through the beads with a muttered oath. No one grabbed me. I was faced with nothing but an empty room with a floor hole black before the left-hand wall.

I limped back and got the ladder.

Dropping the heavy end of it through the hole I climbed cautiously down to get off it onto a lower floor which offered little reward for the effort it had taken. A couple of moth-eaten goatskins lay in one corner beside a crude wooden flute. And a handful of pebbles that shone blue in the light.

A few more of these lay scattered this side of the archway giving onto the next room as though dropped in hurried flight or fallen from a burst sack in someone's clumsy fist.

Picking a couple of them up I gave them a closer look. Turquoise nuggets. Good but not gem-grade. All right for beads. I strode on through the arch and stopped with caught breath.

FOURTEEN

THE SUN WAS close to two hours high before sounds on the trail below warned that someone at last was approaching from the camp. With a frowning impatience I looked down from the cliff to see Jeff, Fern, Harry and Clampas riding toward the rockfall and, strung out behind them, Jones with six laden packhorses.

I collected Gretchen, flung on my saddle and headed in the same direction, busting to know what the hell they were up to.

When I reached the top of the rockfall the cavalcade below was just coming up to the trailside end of it. Harry, spying me, flung up a hand. "Come down here, Corrigan!" he called like he owned me.

If Gretchen hadn't been all night without water I might have ignored him. In the end with clamped jaws I sent the mule into that jumble of rocks and, sitting back like I was Lord of the Mountain, let her pick her way through them. We came out into the trail and I fastened my stare on a pale-faced Jeff. "What's the idea? You shiftin' camp?"

Jeff looked sick, Hatcher angry, Clampas amused, and Fern about ready to throw in the sponge. "Crew slipped away during the night with that goddam Navajo and better'n half our tinned stuff!" Harry snarled like he eyed it as a personal affront.

"I don't guess he left my Remington, did he?"

Hatcher snorted. "Clampas—who was supposed to be on guard—fell asleep! It's a goddam wonder we didn't all get our throats cut!"

"So we're moving camp," Jeff said tiredly. "I thought if we set up atop that cliff, we'd be in a position to keep our eyes on things—"

"And what did you figure to do for water? Pipe it up there?"

Jeff looked embarrassed. "We hadn't thought of that," Fern said.

"You better think of it now." I directed some of my irritation at Clampas. "Why didn't you tell them they'd be killing half the horses trying to get 'em through those rocks?"

Clampas shrugged. "Harry ain't partial to advice from hired hands."

"I can see that," I said. "It's about time someone told Harry where to head in at. Any kid just out of diapers could have made a better job of this than he has." Catching hold of my temper I told Jeff bluntly, "If I was in charge of this, I'd damn quick show Harry where he belongs—at the foot of the line, stripped of all authority."

I saw Larrimore wince, but Fern coming to life said approvingly, "You *are* in charge."

"You can't do this to me!" Harry shouted. "I got a contract with you!"

"Not any longer," I said. "It's been canceled. From here on out you're just one of the hands. And if that doesn't suit, you can spin your bronc an' light a shuck out of here."

Spluttering, frothing, Hatcher was so pissed off he couldn't get a word out. He finally slammed a hand at his gun. Then let go of it like it had scorched him when he found himself staring into mine. I said, "You brought Fletch into this. Now get up there and bury him!"

I watched the man fling out of his saddle and go stomping off to the packs for a shovel. "If I were you," Clampas said with his glance gone solemn, "I'd keep a spare set of eyes in the back of my head."

* * *

THE LARRIMORE EXPEDITION was now reduced to a party of six. Knowing the risks of trying to get flatland horses onto the clifftop through that jumble of rocks, I'd have sent the whole lot of them back to the pool had Fern not volunteered to see to their water needs. "I'm afraid it will take up most of your time, Fern."

"Oh, I'm used to commuting. One of the primest facts of life in Chicago. Don't look at me that way—I'll be all right. Don't you think you were just a bit rough on Harry?"

"Man's a born schemer; you should never have employed him."

"I didn't employ him!" she came back angrily. "He was Jeff's idea." Then, more quietly, "You have to realize my brother has little experience outside of the classroom. Most of his life has been devoted to archaeology. After trying for years to get a full professorship he hoped, coming here, to uncover new facts of indisputable significance, credit for which no other scientist would be able to minimize or take away from him." There was a pleading in the smile she tried so desperately to show me. "He knows nothing at all about people like Harry."

"I can understand that."

"Can you understand what he's been hoping to accomplish? Our earliest ancestor, Mousterian Man, has an accepted existence of approximately sixty thousand years, a nomad cropping up in many and diverse places. Now these Basketmaker people of the Anasazi are generally believed to have come into this region some twenty-five thousands of years ago. What Harry hoped to do—and *will* do if he can come up with sufficient evidence—is to connect these two up. Don't you think that's worth doing?"

"I'm just an ignorant country boy, Fern. I wouldn't know up from down about such things."

Jeff, coming over to us, said impatiently, "Hadn't we better get up there, Corrigan?"

I nodded, still choused around in my mind by Fern's pitch. All that kind of guff was so much ancient history, I couldn't see how it could matter today. It was today I'd stuck my neck out to deal with, a time full of danger I could easily recognize. I knew a lot more about what lay ahead of him than Jeff did, and what I knew he wasn't going to like. "Who do you want up there for a helper?"

"Oh, Clampas, I guess. He was certainly a help getting us into this place."

You couldn't fault that. "All right. Take him up with you. I'll be along soon's I've tended to Gretchen."

I would rather have had Jones. Not so smart but reliable.

* * *

WHEN I CAUGHT up with them Jeff and his helper had just got as far as the room with the pots he'd had to carry Flossie up from. The pair of them were standing there peering at that collection of relics. I was forced to decide quickly which figured to be the lesser of two tough choices, and said, "Why not start right here?"

"But I told you yesterday," Jeff remarked with surprise, "I'd prefer to go over the whole area before attempting to evaluate anything."

"You're the boss," I nodded, and to Clampas, "Better fetch that ladder along."

"I can see," Clampas grinned, "you're not one to overlook the natural advantages."

"You look strong enough to carry it," I said, motioning him on after Larrimore.

Each of the empty rooms we went through appeared to deepen the gloom that showed so plain on Jeff's face. "What happened," I said, "to that Mousterian tribe?"

He looked at me in some astonishment; then, catching on, said, "I guess Fern's been talking shop. As a matter of fact there are a number of theories but no substantive evidence."

"Just disappeared like our Basketmakers?"

"That's about the size of it."

The bead curtain now was just ahead of us. Both

men stopped to stare, neither liking it. Clampas's eyes jumped at it. "What's that thing doin' here?"

Jeff looked appalled, licked his lips like he couldn't believe it. "Someone's been here..."

"Not since that entrance was sealed," Clampas objected.

"The people who built this never added that touch. Someone's been in here since the builders departed."

"You reckon they cleaned the place out?"

"I don't know," Jeff said bitterly, "but even if I find it the evidence, I'm hunting will be open to doubt. Who's going to say now when and how it came to be here? Not with two sets of people running in and out of here."

"Maybe," I said, "we better hunt another site."

"No time for that now," Jeff said miserably. "Might as well get on with it."

He pushed through the dangling strings and stopped, much as I'd done, eyes going to the goatskins and the scattered beads. "Harry," smiled Clampas, "will be happy to see those."

"Harry," I said, "has pretty well lost whatever edge he was countin' on."

Clampas's glance twinkled amusement. "Time will tell," he said blandly.

"Take this," I told Jeff, handing over Fletch's pistol. "You may find a use for it."

"That's right," Clampas nodded. "Place like this, who can say what might happen?"

"I can tell you what won't," I said. "None of this turquoise is going to wind up with Harry!"

Clampas looked at me and shrugged. Jeff, walking into the next room, swore. Clampas hurried after him and I went in on Clampas's heels. "Jumpin'

Jehoshaphat!" Harry's gunfighter cried. "Looks like the hideout of the Forty Thieves!"

It did indeed. A great assemblage of pots and relics — Jeff called them artifacts—was heaped about the walls in astonishing profusion. One two-foot jar of the storage variety was filled with a miscellany of spear points and arrowheads.

Several others of equal dimensions—as I'd already discovered—were filled with rough spiderweb turquoise. Eight others were filled with strung beads, also turquoise. Quivers of arrows. A considerable pile of bows of diverse styles and vintage were piled alongside. There were hide shields and wooden spears, scrapers, metates and forty-eleven other items too varied to enumerate.

I noticed Jeff staring at something he'd picked up and Clampas, ogling those jars of sky-blue stones, chucked a wink at me with an enchanted grin. "I ain't no authority," he declared with a chuckle, "but what we've got here oughta easily ransom any king those Conquistadores managed to overlook. Congratulations, Larrimore! Looks like you hit the jackpot."

FIFTEEN

THERE WAS SUCH A PETULANT, resentful twist to Jeff's features, I could almost have felt sorry for him if he hadn't made such a mishmash of things.

"What's that you're holding?" I said to him brusquely, and he dropped into my hand a small stone lamp—leastways that's what he called it. To me it was nothing but a rock with a hollow worn into it and a more or less flat bottom, maybe two inches thick and three in diameter. "Valuable?"

"Hey!" Clampas said. "That looks older than Moses."

"Quite a bit older," Jeff replied with a sigh. "Not that it matters. After being found here its age, like its value, has little significance. With two sets of tenants calling this place home, nothing I discover will be worth a plugged nickel."

"In that case," Clampas hurried to assure him, "you can give me the blue stuff and forget you ever saw it."

"Well, come on," I said, "we might as well get on

with it. We've still got a couple dozen rooms to get through."

"Sounds like Christmas," Clampas chuckled, giving his hands a promotional dry wash.

Jeff gave him one hard look and thereafter ignored him. He set off for the next room in line, but instead of discarding that 'worthless' stone lamp I noticed it went into his brush jacket pocket.

Any freebooter would have found in this trek through the cliff house a quite ample compensation for the time expended. The next eight rooms provided three moth-eaten goatskins, a discarded wooden flute, a scatter of mixed black and white beads, three broken pots, an elegant pitcher with a broken snout, three bundles of corn shucks and not another thing.

Jeff sent Clampas back for the ladder.

When the gunfighter returned with it we canvassed two additional rooms, both empty. The first of these, however, had a hole in the floor, and into this Jeff had Clampas drop the ladder. When the man stood aside Jeff motioned him onto it. Clampas looked Jeff over with a speculative stare. "You wouldn't be thinkin' of leaving me down there, now, would you?"

Jeff with a grimace motioned him on, stepping onto the ladder as soon as Clampas got off it on the floor below. So there we were, all three of us, in another empty room. As it eventually turned out every room on this level was empty, much to Clampas's disgust. "How much longer am I totin' this thing?" he growled, giving the ladder a slap with his gun hand.

"Till we're through with it," Jeff said. "Now put it down that hole and let's see what's below."

This next level, I'd been thinking, would likely be

the last, so after we'd gone down it I told him to leave the ladder where it was. There were more rooms down here than on any of the upper levels. "How many people," Clampas asked Harry, "do you reckon lived in this place?"

"I'd say about five hundred."

"At one time?"

"Certainly." Jeff produced a wan smile. "To the people using it this place represented a complete community—a town. Each family had a room."

It was plain such an arrangement held little charm for Clampas. The next fourteen rooms we toured held nothing but discarded odds and ends apparently not cherished by those who had abandoned them, except in the fourteenth where Clampas picked up a rather bleached-looking turquoise ring and two bracelets, all of crude workmanship. Dropping the bangles in his pocket Clampas threw the ring away. Jeff, however, retrieved it, saying, "Keepsake."

The fifteenth and last of the rooms on this, the bottom level, turned out to be an eye-opener, extending into the cliff itself for a distance of possibly some forty feet. "Originally," Jeff told us, "this was probably a cliff shelter, in use sporadically for several hundred years before it was hidden behind this building. One would have to do quite a bit of digging to uncover and date the successive layers of use."

We'd been using the torch on the last couple levels and there wasn't much left in it. I said, "We had better vamoose before we find ourselves stumbling around in the dark."

* * *

THEY'D SET up camp just below the rockfall and, time we got down there, Fern was just returning from the pool with the last group of horses she had taken to water. When he saw she was back, Jones beat on his washtub and advised us to come and get it. Advice which no one disregarded.

The main course was beef stew supplemented by corn-meal muffins, java and retried beans. To all of which they did full justice. "Well, how'd it go?" Harry asked, trying for a show of his old hearty charm. "Find anything worth carting home?"

"Been more'n one bunch living there," Clampas told him. "Jeff looks about ready to blow the whistle."

Jeff said nothing, just picked up his eating tools, stepped over and dropped them in the tub. Fern said with obvious concern, "Didn't you find a thing?"

Jeff put the stone lamp into her hands. "Why, this is marvelous!" she cried, turning it over and over. "It must be quite the oldest artifact you've ever found."

"It's old enough, all right," he said glumly, "but how do you prove how it got where and when? I can date it. That's not the point. The problem is provenance. How can I indisputably prove it appeared with the builders, not with those who took over after they left?"

She pushed it around through her head, suddenly smiling in a way that lit up her whole face. "Tree rings," she cried. "We can date the building by the age of the timbers —the roof poles, the wood they put into those ceilings."

"Sure." He nodded. "I thought about that. But what if the age of the stone doesn't match? And it probably won't."

"But if the stone should be older than the timbers—"

"You forget. It's the people, the builders, I'm trying to put dates to. With two different groups having used this place, who's to say which of them first had this lamp?" He thrust it back in his pocket with a lugubrious look. "It may even have been found here, and probably was. In which case, being older than this cliff house, it's of no use at all."

"What do we do now?"

"Tomorrow," Jeff said, "I'm going to have another look at certain features I didn't take the time to study properly. Also I've got to decide which of the pots we'll want to take back with us, for we certainly can't spend more than another week here."

"I'll go with you and help," Fern said. "I don't believe we've enough horses to remove very much. We'll have to box any pottery we take..."

"Let's have Brice up there with us," Jeff surprised me by saying.

"Maybe," I said, "it would be better to take Jones. He's pretty handy."

I could feel the probe of her swung-around stare. I'd no idea what she felt about me. For my own part I reckoned I'd been seeing a sight too much of her, one reason she was hard for me to talk to. We had nothing in common. She was big-city, long used to things I knew little about, nor wanted to. My sort of life—if she could have had a good look at it—would have appalled her. The men she knew didn't go around strapped to a shooting iron.

"Don't you want to go with us?"

"Not particularly."

Biting her lip she continued to consider me, almost as though she thought me willfully stupid. Catching hold of my arm she drew me aside. "What is it with you? Don't you know my brother is counting on you?"

"In a way, perhaps—"

"In every way! You saw how things were. Harry running roughshod—why don't you get rid of him?" Her glance sharpened angrily. "I expected when I gave you Harry's job things were going to be different."

I said, "They are different. Giving me that job has made a prime target out of me!"

Having seen how upset she was I probably shouldn't have said that. A startled look came over her face. Then, flushed and furious, she lashed back. "If you're afraid of him—"

"Don't talk like a fool! What's left of this outfit's about ready to explode. With this goddam heat and all that guff about chindis it'll take damn little...Point is until we know—and I mean *know*—which of those buggers is throwin' the wrenches..."

"It's your job to find out!"

I gave her a hard look and turned away. I hadn't figured right now to bring things to a boil, but if she thought—Ah, to hell with her! Finding Hatcher watching with that sly smirk on his puss I snarled, "Get a horse and a shovel and don't keep me waiting!"

I tossed my saddle on Gretchen, kneed the air from her belly and cinched her tight. She gave me no argument, knowing I was in no mood to be trifled with. I slipped the bit through her teeth and climbed aboard and, picking up my ex-boss, headed for our previous camp.

"What's up?" Harry said and, getting no answer, buttoned his lip.

When we got through the tamarisks I said without beating around no bushes, "If you found it convenient to get rid of a body, what would you do with it?"

Harry's cheeks turned the color of pummeled dough. "I...I—"

"Never mind. I reckon I can find it," I said with a curse, and sent Gretchen over to where Jones had had his fires. I got down, kicked the circle of stones aside and put my eye on Hatcher. "Start diggin'."

With a pasty face Harry bent to the task.

I could tell by the ease with which the shovel bit into that fire-blackened dirt we had got the right spot. With the sun not yet down, it looked like pretty hot work. He didn't have to go far. I could tell when he straightened, looking sick, he had put his shovel on something that yielded. "Careful now, I don't want him dug up. All I want is a look at his face."

"Wh—Who d'you think we're going to find?"

"Hosteen Joe."

Squatting down, having motioned him out of the way, with my hands I brushed back enough of the loose sandy soil to see that the cadaver had been planted face down, to make out the dried blood and powder marks on his shirt. "Shot in the back close up. With a pistol. Turn him over."

Harry's sweat-shiny face was a picture of horror. Shaking like a leaf he drew back in repugnance. "For Chris-sake," I said, "he's not goin' to bite you!"

I caught hold of the hair, jerked the head up enough for him to see it was Joe, then let it fall back. "All right. Cover him up."

SIXTEEN

WE HADN'T MUCH MORE than got through the
tamarisks on the way back to camp when, rounding a
bend, we found Clampas riding toward us.

"Ah, the Mule Man and stooge," he hailed, combing
us over with his sardonic look. "Much as we'll regret the
loss of your company, if I was you, Harry, I'd trot right
along."

Hatcher, with the look of a frightened rabbit,
appeared only too glad to be let off the hook.

Clampas's gaunt face swung back to me. "Where
the hell you been? They're all out huntin'—figured the
chindis had got you."

I just stared at him, not saying anything. He
laughed. "So you found him. Kinda figured you would.
Takes one to know one." He looked amused. "That
Harry," he chuckled. Then his brows drew down. "You
don't believe it?"

"He hasn't the stomach for that kind of thing. You
were using that smartass buck all along, right from the

time he showed up with old Two-Feathers. What'd you promise him—that Sharps? It was you put him up to makin' off with those horses. You probably used him to get rid of the crew."

"Sure. I had to figure some way of cuttin' down the odds." Clampas grinned. "Hell, Fletch was no loss, an' I won't shed no tears if something happens to that mealy-mouthed Harry. You been around. Quit usin' your head for a hat rack. Comes to that, your friend Harry proposi-tioned me two days ago, wanted us to team up and split that turquoise right down the middle!"

I felt an almost overmastering impulse to go after him right then. "Guess you allowed you didn't need his help."

Clampas smiled. "Not likely. If I'd said anything like that he might of taken the notion I aimed to grab it myself."

"I suppose that never entered your mind."

"Oh, I've thought some about it—of course Hatcher doesn't know about that pile we saw this morning. If I was figurin' to team up with anyone it sure wouldn't be with no chump like Harry."

"Guess you'd want a man you could count on."

"Now you're talkin'."

"Don't look at me. I like this layout just the way it is."

"Here," he said, tossing me a penny. "Flip it—I'm going to show you something."

Almost before the coin left my hand Clampas's gun flashed up. It coughed just once and the penny disap-peared. "Kid stuff," I said.

I could see he was graveled. "Corrigan," he said, "you amaze me."

"Just be careful that shooter don't point in my direction or you ain't going to care whether school keeps or not."

He didn't like that either. He looked me over for a while before he said, "How's Burt Mossman getting along these days?"

"Haven't seen Burt since I quit the Hashknife."

"No accountin' for tastes," he said lightly. Then he fetched out that bullypuss smile once more. "Just do yourself a favor and stay out of my way."

* * *

NEXT MORNING, with the promise of another hot day, I heard Jeff telling Jones to take over Fern's watering chores, that she'd be going with him to decide what relics they wanted out of the cliff house. When Jones turned away to get this work started, I led Jeff off a piece and told him bluntly, "You better take Harry up there and leave me in camp."

"I don't want Harry up there."

"It ain't a question of what you want but what you can afford. I don't think you'd be real smart to leave Hatcher and Clampas here with no one to keep an eye on them."

"Not sure I get your point," Jeff said, frowning.

"All right, I'll spell it out. How do you aim to get whatever artifacts you want back to your headquarters in Chicago?"

"I'm intending to use those horses."

"And when you're ready to go suppose there ain't any horses?"

"You think Harry—"

"Harry," I said, "is under Clampas's thumb. He's scared to death of that bucko."

"Why would Clampas want to tamper with our horses?"

"He's already tampered with them once through Harry. You think Clampas was asleep when your crew took off? Wake up, Larrimore. You're dealin' with the *real* world here! Clampas saw that turquoise yesterday, damn near a wagonload, and I'm telling you fair and square he has no intention of seeing it wind up in some university."

"What makes you think—?"

"Hell, he as much as told me. Said Harry had offered to split with him. Be no problem at all to run off those horses and cache them out of sight till you and your sister have started hoofin' it for the railroad."

Jeff stared at me, shaken. "You want me to make them a present of it?"

"All I want you to do is face the facts and make it no easier for them than you can help."

I watched him go off and beckon Harry. When I swung around there was Fern with a tired look to the set of her shoulders. "So you're not going up with us?"

I shook my head, not wanting to get trapped into another unprofitable argument. But she wouldn't leave it like that. She said, coaxing, "I'd feel a lot safer if—"

"Fern, believe me, it won't do to leave Harry and Clampas down here together."

She kept searching my face with that blue-green stare, the rising sun in her hair like copper. She was not a person easily put off. "Look," I said, "both Harry and Clampas are bustin' to get their hooks on that turquoise. Harry's soft—we can handle him. But Clampas is something else again. He's got no more scruples than a goddam snake."

"You don't have to convince me; I had a feeling about him as soon as I saw him. I told you that. It's why I wanted you to come with us. But I'm just as upset by those rooms up there. I've a very bad feeling about that place every time I step into it. It isn't anything I can easily explain; there's something evil about it, a feeling of menace as though something horrible had taken place there and was waiting—just waiting like a spider in its web—to happen all over again."

She put a hand on my arm and I could feel her tremble with the freckles standing out against the pallor of that tipped-back face as she stood there looking up at me with the need so apparent in those searching eyes. "At least come with us—"

"As I've just pointed out to your brother, if you intend to take anything away from this place you can't afford to lose those horses, Fern. Jeff may not have found what he hoped to but the things he *has* found are commercially valuable, enough to pay for more than one extensive dig. He can't want to throw all that away through losing the means of taking it out of here."

I could see these things weren't touching her at all. I'd been throwing my words against a locked mind, a stubborn conviction it seemed nothing would loosen. What she wanted, I thought, and really needed, was a man of her own, and she had fastened on me.

Her next words proved it. In a voice gone husky, her hand tightening its grip, those near-whispered words banged against me like fists: *"If you care at all for me, Brice..."*

I jerked myself free. "It's no good, I tell you! Stay

away from me, Fern. I wouldn't fit into your life. Nor you in mine!"

SEVENTEEN

AFTER FERN, her brother and Harry went into the rockfall on their way to the cliff house entrance I sleeved the sweat off my face and looked around for Clampas. Jones was just coming back from a trip to the pool with the first batch of horses he had taken to water. I hailed him to ask if he'd seen the fellow. "Clampas? Sure. He's down at the old camp."

"Doing what?"

Jones said dryly, "I didn't ask." Something in my expression apparently spurred him to say, "You want I should tell him to get his ass up here?"

"No, let it go. What I've got to say to him can wait a while longer."

I rolled me a smoke while he penned the horses he had just brought back and set off for the pool with the rest of our stock. Which reminded me that Gretchen hadn't been watered yet. "You'll just have to wait a bit," I told her. "I ain't about to go off and leave them critters unguarded till I've had me a little chat with that bugger."

God but it was hot. Seemed like each day was even hotter than the last. And by the looks of that sky there was no relief in sight. I felt mean about Fern but it was one of those things you had to nip in the bud, and I reckoned I'd done the right thing if I could stick to it.

I looked around for Flossie and then remembered she'd gone with Fern. I hoped that ladder Jones had put together for us wouldn't decide to come apart while somebody was on it. Seemed like I was working up a fit of the dismals. I wasn't the kind to set around and do nothing. Aside from keeping an eye on the penned horses, which I got to admit was becoming monotonous, what was there to do?

Jones came back with the last of the watered stock and after he'd penned them came over and hunkered down on his bootheels. He picked up a stick and made doodles in the dirt. "When's the professor pullin' out, do you know?"

"Within the week I guess." I shifted my weight. "Clampas still down there?"

Jones nodded. "What happens to us when they get to the railroad?"

I looked up without interest. "Reckon they'll pay us off."

Even in the shade sweat was all over us and the goddam flies wouldn't let us alone. I finally got up and just about then horse sound swiveled our heads toward the trail.

As expected it was Clampas. He swung off his horse with that sardonic grin, stood looking at us with the reins in his hand. "Still up there, are they?"

Neither one of us bothered to answer. With a shrug

he went off to put his mount in the pen. "Wonder," I said, "what he was doing down there."

"Wasn't doin' nothing. Just settin' there under them tamarisks."

"Hatchin' up more devilment probably."

He came back after a while and bit himself off a chew from his Picnic Twist. "I see Harry comin' down but no sign of the others."

When I heard Hatcher's boots coming out of the rocks I turned around for a look at him. He wore the shine of sweat on his troubled face. When he got back his breath he said, "I couldn't take no more of it. That's the scariest place I ever been into."

"See any chindis?" Clampas grinned.

"No, but I sure seen a mort of turquoise." Naked greed gleamed out of his stare. "You reckon he's sure enough aimin' to pack it all back to that fool university?"

"It ain't got there yet," Clampas mentioned, and swiveled his glance for a look at me. I paid him no heed. "Have they made up their minds what stuff they're going to take?" I asked Harry.

"I guess they're takin' six or eight of them pots. And the turquoise." He scowled. "Sure makes me sick to think of it. If we had any gumption we'd take it away from him."

"Watch out," Clampas drawled. "That sort of gab don't set well with Corrigan."

Hatcher eyed me, disgusted.

"When are the Larrimores comin' down?" Jones asked. He slanched a look at the sun. "Mebbe I better wrassle up some grub."

Harry kicked at a horse apple. "Jeff allows he's goin' to spend the night up there."

Clampas chuckled. "Figures to keep his eye on the turquoise, I reckon." He spun the rowel of a spur. "Wouldn't want anything to happen to him...Maybe I ought to go up an' keep him company."

I reckoned he was trying to get a rise out of me.

A shadow crossed my lap. I looked up and saw Fern coming toward us. "Hi," she said, flushed of face and looking straight at me. "Hi," I said. "That right about Jeff? He's really fixin' to stay up there?"

"That's what he says. He wants Jones to fetch him some food and a water bag when it's ready."

Harry said, "I wouldn't spend a night in that place for all the gold in the Denver mint!" And Clampas said solemnly, "Ain't likely, Harry, they'll offer it to you."

After we'd eaten, Jones with a water bag slung from his shoulder took a pan heaped with grub and set out for the cliff house. Fern said to me with an expressionless face, "You meant that, didn't you?"

"Yes. Where's the dog?" I saw the whole shape of her stiffen, but whatever she felt it wasn't being advertised. I thought for a moment the breath had caught in her throat; her eyes never left my face as she replied, "She's staying up there with Jeff."

It seemed to be awful quiet for a second. Then she turned, moved away toward her tent, and I found Clampas watching from between the two pens Jones had put the horses into. In an effort to put Fern's look out of mind I walked up to him grimly and stared him in the eye. "You're not going to get it, Clampas. Make up your mind to it. And if anything should happen again to what's left of our remuda you can look for big trouble."

* * *

JEFF WAS BACK in time for breakfast. Flossie, too; and the first thing she did was make a beeline for Fern's tent. When Fern came out with her a few minutes later it was with her usual calmly competent appearance despite the dark smudges I saw under her eyes.

After we'd eaten Jeff drew me aside and speaking under his breath said, "There was something up there— must have been about four o'clock. I'd been dozing I guess and had forgot to turn off my torch. It was pretty weak when I jerked open my eyes and saw this shape slipping out of the room. Just as it seemed about to fade through that arch I yelled. The top part of it turned and I was staring at the most terrifying face I've ever seen in my life. Great ringed eyes beneath fluttering tatters of ropelike hair, and a leering mouth parted over two teeth behind lips that must have been at least an inch thick."

"Sure you weren't dreaming?"

"I wish I could think so, but when I saw that horrible face peering at me I was wide awake. Believe me I was! I can see it now, grinning around those two teeth!" He swallowed convulsively. "You think it was a chindi?"

Some of what he felt must have rubbed off on me. The sweat grew cold on the back of my neck. I stood motionless, not answering, trying to control leaping thoughts, my eyes fastened on Clampas. "No," I said, looking again at Jeff, "I think you saw an illusion—"

"Damn it," he growled. "I *saw* it, I tell you!"

"Of course. I'm sure you did. I'll stay up there tonight and see if I can catch a glimpse. Were you in that room with all those jugs of turquoise at the time this happened?"

Jeff nodded. "I was trying to make up my mind how much of it we could pack."

"All right," I said. "Keep your mouth shut about this," and limped off to saddle Gretchen.

* * *

RIDING up through the rockfall I left the mule outside the cliff house entrance, wriggled my way through the hole we had made and set off to find if there was anything I could discover. Like, for instance, if there was some other way of getting into the place. I figured Jeff had been too shaken to make any kind of thorough hunt himself. Of course we'd already canvassed the place but I had an idea I wanted to check out.

Down the ladder I went and into the room where we'd found the first pots. Jeff had separated a few of these and set them to one side, possibly the ones he was figuring on taking. He'd fetched up and put with these that pitcher with the broken snout. I hadn't thought to bring a torch so there wasn't much point in going stumbling about through the dark of those lower rooms scratching matches to see with.

This being the level with the occasional apertures left in the outside wall for windows, I was about to head for that room behind the strings of beads when a swift patter of feet wheeled me around to see Flossie happily wagging her tail in the doorway behind me. "Where's Fern?" I said, and Fern answered for herself, coming to stand beside the dog and holding out a torch. She said, a bit uncertain-like, "I came up to fetch this for you. Didn't think you could do very much without a light."

"Too right," I said. "I tore off in such a hurry I forgot to bring one with me."

I expect I felt more awkward than she did, remembering the things we had said to each other. "If—if you'd like to come along, I want to check on that turquoise..."

"If I won't be in the way."

"You carry the torch," I said, watching Flossie scamper eagerly ahead of us.

Still with an occasional window hole lighting the way, we came to and pushed through that bead-hung doorway and came into the room with the pair of old goatskins where a handful of turquoise had lain scattered on the floor. "We picked that up yesterday," Fern said, and we moved on through the arch, stepping into the room where we'd found what Clampas had termed the "chindis' hoard." There were changes here too.

"We picked out what we thought was the best of it and piled it over there," she said, pointing. "Neither one of us, however, knows hardly anything about turquoise. We'd be obliged if you'd go through it and weed out the ordinary stuff. It's going to be a real weight problem taking very much of it, I'm afraid."

"If we all went on foot you'd have six more horses you could pack," I pointed out. "And if you don't take it out—all of it, I mean—by the time you're able to return somebody else will have scooped it up."

She looked at me tiredly. "I guess you mean Harry and Clampas."

"You bet. One of them anyway. When's Jeff figurin' to leave?"

"He says tomorrow." She sighed. "I don't think we can be ready by tomorrow. Too much to pack up and all that carrying down through the rockfall. I dread to think of it."

"Speaking of dread," I said, taking a look at her, "do you still have that feeling about this place?"

"Yes. More than ever. I'll be glad to see the last of it."

"I remember you thought something terrible must have happened here, that these rooms were waiting for it to happen again."

"Yes." She shivered. "I still feel that way."

"I've had a few uncomfortable thoughts about the place myself. There's a brooding, sinister sort of atmosphere I find it hard to explain away. More than just this tomblike quiet. It's as though the very mud and stones have soaked up the horror and anguish—"

"Don't talk about it, Brice. I'm just about ready to scream right now."

She looked it, too.

"All right. Let's go—where's Flossie?"

Fern whistled. Away off somewhere down below a dog barked. "Here, Flossie!" Fern called, and the dog barked again. "She's on a lower level," I said. "Stay here. I'll fetch the ladder."

"I'm coming with you," she said, hurrying after me.

* * *

I HOOKED the ladder over my shoulder and we started back. When we got to the hole I dropped the ladder into position. "Throw some light down there." When she did we saw Flossie, tail wagging and looking proud as Punch with a long bone sticking out from both sides of her mouth. I said, "Good girl, Flossie," and to Fern: "How will we get her up? Can you carry her?"

"I don't think so, not and climb that ladder. She's pretty heavy. I better get Jeff."

I said irritably, "You'll have to have the ladder to get onto the next floor." With exasperation mounting, I hauled up the ladder and manhandled it back where I'd got it. When it was in position she said, "You keep this," and handed me the switched-off torch.

The sun coming through those window holes made it plain it would soon be dropping out of sight. In this kind of country black night wouldn't be long delayed. It was odd we hadn't found any Indian-made ladders. By the time I'd quit wondering about this I was back in the room above Flossie so I switched on the torch and there she was, still chomping that old bone she'd dug up.

With the torch still on I remembered the notion that had fetched me up here. Squatting down put me under the sun glare coming in from outside and I switched off the torch, juggling that notion around and thinking it had to be sound. Because, unless Jeff's apparition turned out to be a permanent resident, it someway had to get in from outside, and the only feasible way it could do this was through one of these top-level window holes. And that meant a rope with an anchor at one end of it.

Why not, I thought, go and look for it now? There ought to be time before Fern brought Jeff up here. I shoved to my feet and walked into the next room— nothing there, nor in any of the others on this level until I remembered I hadn't thought to check the three rooms on the downtrail side of that bead curtain.

Well, I expect you guessed it. Our chindi had climbed into the turquoise room; there was the rope coming in across the sill of the window hole, held in place by the metal bar it was tied to—only, by grab, it was no metal bar but the dismantled barrel of my given-away Remington!

EIGHTEEN

JEFF WENT DOWN and brought up Flossie, bone and all. He did not appear too happy about it; I expect he felt considerable put out, dragooned into playing errand boy to a dog. Flossie fetched her bone over for Fern to admire and was visibly delighted by Fern's lavish praise.

Jeff, looking at me, said, "You want to check this turquoise for me? Seems to be all I'll have to show for this trip."

"You've got that Stone Age lamp in your pocket."

"Well, yes," he nodded, "but I can't tie it in to what I came here for. Offhand, how much of this mineral would you say is worth moving?"

"Offhand, I'd say all of it. And by walking the forty miles between here and the railroad you'll have enough horses to tote it. You've got a king's ransom here if you can manage to get out with it."

"I hope you know what you're talking about," he muttered, perking up a little.

This was my hope, too, but getting it to Chicago was like to take a heap of doing.

It was just about then I saw him suddenly stiffen, startled stare clamped intent on the bone Flossie was gnawing. "Here—let me see that," he grunted, bending over.

Flossie growled, backing off.

"Let me have a look at that," Jeff said warily. And Fern said, "He isn't going to keep it. Here—let me have it."

The dog, distrustfully dancing about, reluctantly surrendered her coveted prize.

Peering over his shoulder I said, "Doesn't much look like it came off a steer."

Looking immensely excited, Jeff looked up to say, "It's a human leg bone, what there is of it. I'll have to get it dated, but near as I can tell it's about the same age as that stone lamp I found."

"Good girl!" Fern told Flossie. "Let's go find another, shall we?"

Flossie, thus encouraged, straightaway leaped to the floor below and was off like a bat out of Carlsbad. "Come on!" Jeff cried, and went hurrying down our makeshift ladder. With a deal more care Fern and I followed. But the dog was no longer on that level. "She's making for that cave shelter," Jeff declared excitedly.

When we reached it Flossie, half out of sight, was making the dirt fly. In less than two minutes she came scrambling out with another aged bone, an arm bone this was, and Jeff looked even more excited than she was.

Peering into the excavation with the aid of the torch we could see a number of other half-buried bones and the lower two thirds of a badly smashed skull.

Fern, looking sick, backed hastily away. Eyes bright, Jeff said, "I'll have to get a shovel—"

I caught hold of his arm. "We forgot to fetch the ladder."

But there was no holding Jeff. "Wait here," he growled, and took off at a run. Looked like Flossie's find had made a new man of him.

* * *

FERN, I could see, did not share his enthusiasm. With waxen cheeks and worried stare she followed me into the part of the room that was not under the fire-blackened overhang. Recalling the look of that smashed skull I couldn't help wondering how many other mangled bodies had been buried here. Fern tried to get Flossie to leave the bone alone but, having been robbed once, the dog had no intention of giving up this newest prize.

My thoughts shifted to the man who had climbed that rope with the aid of my dismantled Remington, a dangerous feat exposed as he must have been against that sheer wall. He could not be seen from our present camp but he risked at the least a very nasty fall in the event the rope broke or any portion of that wall collapsed. Was this the man with the horrible face described by Jeff?

I reckoned Jeff was into the rockfall by this time. Even without the ladder, getting out of this place offered no great problem; I had done it myself without any ladder. Be different of course for Fern and the dog.

In the creeping breathless quiet the sound of approaching steps carried plainly and Clampas came into our cave-shelter room on the heels of Jeff and the shovel he'd gone after. I could see Flossie bristle. Clampas reached for the shovel. "Just show me where and I'll do the digging. Expect you've already seen all we're likely to find."

But he was wrong about that. In little more than half an hour's work he uncovered six skeletons, not counting Flossie's find, and the heads of each had been smashed like the first. "Looks like they been poleaxed," he said. "No jewelry. You want to clear any more?"

"I guess we've seen enough," Jeff allowed. "We better get back to camp. You all right, Fern?"

"I've felt better."

Jeff picked up the shovel. Flossie picked up her bone and hustled after Fern.

"Don't you think," Fern said, catching her brother's arm, "we ought to cover them up?"

"They're not goin' to object," Clampas said. "But here's the shovel if you don't feel right about it."

By the time they'd moved the ladder twice and twice lifted Flossie onto the next level, Jeff's feeling that all was well with his world looked to have dampened down somewhat. The sun was nearing the horizon when we came out on the clifftop and Fern, Flossie and Jeff up ahead were again debating their time of departure. Clampas, several yards behind, showed a mocking smile when I caught up on my faithful steed.

"You're goin' to wear that goddam mule to a frazzle if you ain't careful," he said.

"She paces herself—got more sense than a horse," I told him. "I been wonderin' about the way Fletch was killed—with that dart, I mean. You got any idea where it came from?"

"Hell," Clampas said, "I just retched up an' jabbed

the thing into him."

"I wouldn't put it past you."

Clampas looked amused. "Come off it, Corrigan. You must think I'm some kinda one-man exterminator."

"Jeff had a bit of excitement last night. While he was up there sleeping with that turquoise some cat-footed jasper in a ceremonial mask slipped into the room trying to give him a fright."

"That so? Was he frightened?"

"Reckon it startled him some. They're not used to chindis in Chicago. I gave him Fletch's six-shooter, told him next time he sees one to salivate the bastard."

Clampas laughed. "By the way," he said, "didn't it strike you as odd there wasn't no jewelry on them guys we dug up?"

"I doubt if them Basketmakers wore any gewgaws. If they did they were probably stripped before they were planted." We went along a few mule lengths without any more chitchat. Then I said to him casual, "I'll be staying up there tonight. Happen you run into that venturesome chindi you can tell him he needn't risk his neck on that rope. I'll leave the door off the latch and he can walk right in like he's one of the family."

* * *

WE WENT DOWN through the rockfall and put on the nosebags.

After we finished feeding our tapeworms, and I got back from getting Gretchen a drink at the pool, Fern waylaid me before I could start once more for the cliff house.

"Do you feel you really have to spend another night

up there? Why don't you just forget that turquoise—surely you can't believe it's worth such a risk. Now that Flossie has discovered those bones..."

"Those bones," I said, "if they pack the right date, might well put Jeff where he's achin' to be, right up at the top of the archaeological totem pole. And if he can get that turquoise back to Chicago he can be almost certain of coming back here next year; no one could afford to stand in his way."

"But why should—Brice, why should you care whether he comes back or not? I'm afraid of that place. I don't think you ought to stay up there—it's dangerous!"

"Aren't you forgetting? Danger's my business, my stock in trade. As for carin' whether or not your brother comes back...hell, I'm countin' on him hiring me at double my present wages."

I endured a long look, hoping she wouldn't bawl. With the orneriest grin I was able to dredge up I pointed Gretchen into the rockfall, still feeling the drag of her stare on my back.

At the cliff house entrance I pulled my bridle and tack off the mule and turned her loose to forage for herself, pretty sure she'd come running if she heard me call. Then I went inside, picked up Fern's torch, went down the ladder onto the next level and listened to the rasp of my spurless boots stalking through the piled-up silence of centuries. I had the same creepy feel the place had given me the first time, but I was no silly girl to let it build fantastic fancies.

Reaching the turquoise room I limped across to the window hole, pulled up that rope and untied it from the barrel of my stockless Remington. The barrel had some fresh scratches but near as I could tell no further

damage. I guessed it would still shoot and made sure
that it was loaded, taking out the cartridges and dropping them in my pocket. Then I took the barrel with its
still workable mechanism into the next room and laid it
down in a corner where I hoped it wouldn't be noticed.

I got the rope then and tossed it down onto the floor
below, not caring to give Clampas's chindi the least bit
of aid I was able to avoid. With this same thought in
mind I went back and removed the ladder from where it
had rested against the floor above. Now, I reckoned,
chindis or not they could hardly drop in without me
hearing them. But just to make sure, I moved back out
of sight and sat down on the floor with my back to a wall
below the hole I'd just taken the ladder from.

After my recent talk with Harry's gunfighter I was
not at all sure I would have any visitors. I didn't think
Clampas would intrude on my vigil. Dangerous he was,
I'd no doubt about that, but men of his stamp preferred
the odds to be with them. They didn't like going up
against a pat hand.

I was a long way from making up my mind about
Harry. I had him figured for a slick-talking con man and
all I had seen of him bore this out. Ruthless enough
with things going his way, but when push came to shove
he had twice backed off. And he had certainly appeared
to be afraid of this place. Had this all been an act? Was
he at rock bottom a lot tougher than he looked? Appear-
ances for sure could be almighty deceptive.

It seemed three times as quiet now as it had when I
came in here. The same breathless hush that had raised
my hackles before, the same sense of unspeakable evil
Fern had felt to be cooped up in these ancient walls
seemed abruptly less than a hand's grab away.

I advised me not to let myself run away with any such preposterous notion but it did not take the curse from this quiet that seemed to be soaking right into my bones. Outside in the heat of a blazing sun a man could scoff at such nonsense, but as the cold of the night settled into these rooms nothing appeared too outlandish to seem possible. Not even chindis.

I would have liked to have had my pistol in hand but was too keyed up now to risk the least movement. Twice I thought to have heard a stealthy foot; once I'd have sworn I'd caught the slither of cloth brushing unseen against something in passing.

I was fast becoming a bundle of nerves.

With no idea how long I'd been rooted there with muscles cramped and ears about ready to fall off with listening it took a real effort to get off my behind. Every joint in my body was stiff with cramp, so locked in position I fully expected to hear them creak with the strain. But eventually, by degrees, I got onto my feet, feeling like I had been dragged through a knothole.

The place was as still as the night before Christmas, and if anything was stirring I sure didn't hear it. When I felt I could move without breaking apart I crept into the next room and over to the window hole for a look at the night. The moon had got up, but although not in sight the argent gleam of its presence lay wraithlike along the opposite wall of the gulch.

Pulling off my boots to cut down the racket, I slipped through the bead strings and over to the door hole that let into the room where the king's ransom lay. Someone a long time ago had assembled it there and never come back for it.

Would Jeff's luck be any better? I wondered.

NINETEEN

IT MUST HAVE BEEN PRETTY WELL along toward morning when I got to remembering my days on the trading post at Half Step. I didn't think of them often. Growing up as a kid, every day had been an adventure —learning to ride and seeing new faces, getting to know a lot of interesting Indians, admiring the jewelry they brought in to trade or leave as pawn when they ran short of cash. But when I reached my teens this was all old stuff and hanging around that place bored the hell out of me and going off to school, after the first couple of years, seemed just as bad. I was probably fiddle-footed. What I wanted was excitement and I found it with Burt Mossman. He had the coldest eye I have ever looked into...

Of a sudden I found myself bolt upright, listening into that brooding silence, staring wide-eyed into the dark around. Something, I thought, had shifted its weight. But what? And where?

Motionless, listening, I snapped on my torch, aiming it into the black hole of that doorway, thinking to see a faint blur of motion. I couldn't pick it up; the light was too nearly spent to give any definition. I lunged to my feet and tore into the room where the two goatskins lay and found nothing but shadows that drifted away in the fading dimness of my torch. All I could hear was a wild thudding inside me. Then a sound like a fast freight car passing and something whacked into the wall behind me and I threw the damn torch in a passion of cursing. No grunt or cry came out of the shadows, nothing but the clatter of the rolling torch.

Strangely enough as I crouched there panting I had a vision of that dart in Fletcher's throat and sensed it must have been sped from an ordinary peashooter. And there was nobody near me and I knew for sure that except for myself this room was empty. No one had left by that moonlit window hole.

I pulled in a fresh breath and straightened out of my cramp. I turned back to the doorway I'd come through so reckless and felt along the wall but there was no dart there. What I jerked from the wall was a feathered arrow.

*　*　*

IT WAS GETTING light fast with the night all but gone when I limped back to cautiously examine the window hole. No rope nor any mark of one. What the lift of my stare discovered outside was a deal more startling. Spread along the rim of the gulch wall opposite were the motionless shapes of a long line of horsemen, black against the brightening sky.

Indians!

I tore out of that room through the dangling beads

and through three more and straight up the ladder and squeezed through the holes we had made getting in here and out on the clifftop and, not stopping for breath, flung my saddle on Gretchen and took off for camp.

Only Jones was afoot, building up his fire, when I went down through the rockfall in a clatter of hoofs with six-shooter lifted, belching out the alarm. "Indians!" I yelled, pulling up by the fire in a splatter of dust. "Not two miles away—must be half a hundred of 'em!"

Clampas and Harry came running with rifles and Fern and Flossie tumbled out of their tent just as Jeff appeared, struggling into his shirt. "Where?" Harry cried with eyes so bulged I thought they'd roll off his cheekbones.

"They were on that wall across from the cliff house—"

"But there's no place to hide! We'll be slaughtered like sheep!" Harry jittered.

"Not if you can get yourselves into the cliff house."

"But the horses!" Jeff wailed. "They'll—"

"Hell with the horses!" To get them moving, knowing better, I snarled, "If you don't want to find yourselves over a fire, for Chrissake get out of here! Pronto!"

"Too late," Jones muttered, throwing out a pointing arm.

I wheeled. He was right. Whatever the outcome we were trapped here now. Both cliffs were black with jostling horsemen. Spears, bows and a miscellany of rifles were plainly visible as were many of the faces. Navajos, all of them, and not to be trifled with.

* * *

NOW, on the opposite wall, the ranks opened up and a commanding figure put his pony down the precipitous slope on skidding hind legs to pull to a stop less than twenty feet away. The vicious slam of a shot ripped the sudden silence and I whirled to find Harry staggering backward off balance. Clampas, his face gaunt, had wrenched the rifle from Hatcher's grasp and thrown it into the brush. The Navajo—it was old Johnny Two-Feathers—sat his mount imperturbably, making no move at all.

"I will talk," he said, "with Man-on-a-Mule."

"Go ahead. I'm listening."

"This is bad thing you do. Going into the house of the Anasazi, stirring up the chindis. Taking away things that do not belong to you. Bring very bad trouble."

He studied me awhile. "Where Hosteen Joe?"

A very sticky question.

"Dead," I said finally.

"So," the old man smiled thinly. "You admit it."

"I don't think you'd care for a lie."

"Where?"

I said, "Matter of fact we thought he'd gone off with the boys who deserted our crew one night..."

"We talk with crew. Joe not with them."

I could see what was coming, but no way around it.

"You show," he said.

"Joe's at the old camp. By the tamarisks."

Johnny Two-Feathers nodded.

"Come," he said. "You show."

I could feel the sweat trickle down my back. But

there was no way around it, not without bloodshed, and most of the blood would damn sure be ours.

"All right." I put Gretchen onto the trail and the old man swung his horse in behind. A grim and talkless ride. Some awful thoughts churned through my head, but nothing I could dredge up offered so much as the faintest glimmer of any way out of this.

I put Gretchen through the trees. The old man on his horse came through behind me. "Where?" he said. "Where you put Joe?"

It was plain no explanation I might make could wash away the fact of that bullet through Joe's back. "I should have fetched a shovel."

He waved that away. I pointed out the place, thinking maybe he wasn't minded to have Joe disturbed, a forlorn hope that didn't last any longer than it took him to walk over there. He shoved away the stones, began scuffing at the soft dirt under them.

When he was down about a foot he got onto his knees and began scooping the dirt out with his hands. It didn't take long before Joe's shirt came into view with the dried blood still showing. The old man stared a long while at that sight without opening his mouth.

When he presently got up he considered me grimly.

"Who shoot Joe?"

So I told him how I'd wondered if after all, as we'd supposed, Joe had really ridden off with our crew, and how I'd come down here on a hunch to have a look. And found him. Not putting any name to the man who'd come with me.

But I could see straightaway it wasn't going to be enough. Still holding me with that bitter bright stare, "Who shoot Joe?" he said again.

"I wasn't there—how could I know?"

That bleak brown stare stayed on my face for an interminable while, then abruptly he said, "Paleface say one eye for an eye. You no tell I pick someone. Navajo have roast brain for breakfast." With a teeth-showing scowl he climbed back on his pony and rode through the trees.

* * *

IT LOOKED like Larrimore's ill-fated expedition was in for more trouble than it could happily stomach. If I didn't divulge my suspicions of Clampas...It just wasn't in me to play that game. I could, without regret or compunction, kill that devil if it came to a showdown, but turn him over to be tortured by these Indians I simply couldn't do, even though I'd Two-Feathers's word somebody was going to have to pay for Joe's murder.

When we came once again into a camp gone silent as that damned cliff house, the old man, staring like a graven image on his piebald pony, held up both arms and wasted few words. "A young Navajo man has been killed at your campfire. The People have suffered much and long from the white man's duplicity. You will take nothing from this house of the Anasazi. You have until sunrise tomorrow to give up man who kill Hosteen Joe. I have spoken."

With no more talk he drove his colorful mount up the opposite slope.

You can imagine the result of those remarks once he'd gone. The stupid uproar, the fright and the bluster, everyone trying to shout down the others. When I'd heard enough of it I said sharply, "If we refuse to dredge up a sacrifice for him he'll do the picking. This camp is not defensible. We're sitting ducks."

"Why don't you do something?" Harry demanded of me, and there were nods all around; the only dissensions being Flossie and Fern.

"I intend to," I said. "Soon as it's dark I'm going up to the cliff house and if the rest of you want to stay alive a little longer you'll do the same. Up there, until we run out of ammunition we can probably hold them off."

"And what about our horses?"

"The Navajos have gone," Hatcher cried. "I say let's make a run for it!"

"They haven't gone. They've only dropped out of sight. There's no way they'll be leaving this place till they've got what they came after. They'll be satisfied with that and our empty-handed departure. But you try to slip out of here and you'll be dead before you've gone a half mile."

"We ain't givin' nobody up!" Harry howled.

"They're not after you." Clampas grinned. "I'll lay you forty to one it's the—"

"Shut your damn trap!" I snarled at him, but Fern had already sensed it was her they'd demand. "Put it to a vote," Jones suggested, and I nodded. "All those in favor of letting them have Fern—if that's who they ask for—stick up your hands."

Harry's hand went up like a shot. No one else moved, but the look in their eyes showed what they thought of him. Clampas said, "Corrigan should have told that Injun it was you killed Joe."

Jeff came enough out of his trance to want to be told where the cavalry was, and Clampas laughed. "Settin' around in their friggin' barracks, of course." He threw a look at me. "Sure goes against my grain to pull out of this place without them stones the chindis been hoardin'."

"Surely," Jeff said, trying to pull himself together, "some of us could break through if we made a concerted rush for it?"

"You're welcome to try," I said dryly. "It's going to cost them something to lift my scalp." I looked them over once more. "If the one who killed Joe doesn't give himself up there ain't one of us going to leave here alive."

* * *

AS SOON AS it got dark enough to hide our movements we slipped one by one into that jumble of fallen rocks to make our attempt to get into the dubious safety of the cliff house. Each moment of that climb I expected to hear or feel the slap of a bullet and had little doubt the others felt likewise. We were fetching what stores we were able to carry. Way it turned out none of us had thought to bring up any wood. I had purely hated to leave Gretchen behind, but in the interest of harmony had turned her loose without saddle or bridle to fend for herself.

It was a nerve-racking climb but we got to the top of the cliff without incident. Flossie, eager as always, was the first one in. Lathered with impatience the rest of us wriggled our way through the entrance Jones and Clampas had opened, though not in some cases without second thoughts.

Fern and I were the last ones in and she said, voice

husky, "I'd give a good deal to be somewhere else. Do you think we've any chance of ever getting out of this?"

"Do you know if anyone thought to fetch a torch?"

"I brought one. I think Clampas fetched two. You haven't answered my question."

"The probabilities are self-evident. Even," I said, "if by some sort of miracle we do manage to get clear, it doesn't seem a heap likely we'll get as far as the railroad."

To the others I said, "Let's not show any lights. Longer it takes them to discover we're up here the more chance we'll have of staying alive."

"We can't stumble about this damn place in the dark!" Harry snarled.

"We're going down to the next level—the one with the window holes—and that's where we'll stay. Careful now on that ladder. If you've got a pistol, Jones, I wish you'd stay up here for a bit till we're sure those Indians haven't found out we've come up here—but don't shoot anybody without you have to."

"Okay," Jones said, and edged past me. "It's blacker in here than the gut of a camel; can't see a hand in front of your face!"

"What good would it do you if you could?" Clampas asked from below.

"Can you catch hold of that dog, Jeff?" I called when he'd joined Clampas. "All right, Harry, you're next on the ladder. Now you, Fern," I said when Harry got off.

I left the ladder where it was after climbing down myself. "Have you got hold of Flossie, Jeff?"

"I've got her," Fern said.

"We don't want her running loose down below.

Everything we want is on this level so keep a good hold on her till I scout up something to put over that hole."

Trouble was I could not recall seeing anything that would cover a hole three feet wide; the tent I reckoned would do very nicely but we hadn't fetched the tent. "Be better," Clampas said, "if we spread out, don't you think? Each of us pick out one of them window holes so we'll know where we're at. I'll take the one beyond the room with the chindis' hoard."

We could hear him moving off. Harry said, cutting through the boot and spur sound, "I'll take the room this side of him," and went tramping off through the dark in the wake of his gunfighter. And this was when the dog slipped her collar and went scampering off in the same direction. "Flossie!" Fern called. "Come back here, Flossie!"

"I'll get her," Jeff growled and, when she refused to heed his whistle, went irascibly after her, muttering under his breath.

"Oh dear," Fern sighed. "She can be an awful nuisance..."

"Stay here," I said in the sudden grip of an unwanted thought. "Let me have that torch. Where are you?"

"Here—" she said, and put it into my hand, but before I could move we heard a yell and a thump and pitiful whimpering sounds out of Flossie.

TWENTY

FERN STARTED off but I grabbed her. "Wait!"

"No!" She jerked loose of me. "Flossie's hurt—she needs me!"

I was too impatient, too crammed with the bitter black thoughts whirling through me, to waste time arguing. I switched on the torch, went dashing through rooms, and to hell with the noise, caring only for getting there in the shortest time possible. Through the clattering beads, through the dark doorway, past the chindis' hoard and up to the floor hole where Harry and Clampas crouched peering into the black pit below.

I played the light down there, my worst fears realized, staring aghast at Jeff's crumpled shape and the dog whining beside him. "Looks," Clampas said, "like he's broken his neck."

I grabbed hold of Harry. "How'd it happen? Quick — tell me!"

But the man was too hysterical to get any sense out of him. I put the light onto Clampas. "It was the dog,"

Clampas said. "He was trying to catch hold of her and missed his footing..."

I looked a long while at him, hearing Fern come up and her gasped "Oh, God!"

Clampas said, quietly grim: "He *fell*, I tell you—I didn't push him. I was at the window when Flossie dashed past with Jeff racing after her and me diving after them, too late by ten strides. He was already down there when I got to the hole."

I blew out my breath, put an arm around Fern. She was trembling all over, trying to stifle her sobs against my shoulder. I said, hating the necessity, "We'll have to leave him down there—for right now anyway. I'll bring up the dog." I slid my legs through the hole and let myself drop.

After making certain that Jeff was dead, and not just badly injured, I turned to the dog.

Flossie, still whimpering, must have understood more than you'd normally allow for, making no fuss when I hoisted her into Clampas's reaching hands. Clampas passed her to Fern and reached down for me. I got a knee over the hole and heaved myself up.

I thought later I should have shown Fern more sympathy in the shock of her loss, but at the time, right then, my head was too filled with the consequences and the needs they forced on me. At any moment now, with dawn scarce an hour from bursting over the horizon, that old man would be coming to demand a victim. I had to find some way to get us out of this trap; and I could see no way without a distraction.

I finally came up with a harebrained expedient, a notion so wild I damn near threw it away till I recalled Two-Feathers' words about the Navajos' sojourn at

Bosque Redondo. Latching on to no alternative I reckoned it was better than nothing; not much but worth a try.

To Clampas I said, "Somewhere in one of the rooms on this level you'll find the barrel of my rifle and a coil of rope. Get them. There's an Anasazi flute, too; fetch me all three of them and don't waste no time."

I saw the speculative look that slid through his stare. He wasted no words but went off at once. Harry, I could see, would be of no use whatever. Fern was still holding Flossie when Clampas came back with the things I had asked for.

"Take a look out that window hole," I told him and, while he was doing it, I knotted one end of the rope round the rifle barrel, the way it had been when I found it. "How does it look?"

"Can't see anyone. You goin' down that rope?"

"If we're to get loose of this we've got to have some kind of distraction. Don't any of you try to leave till I come back. If I don't show inside of an hour you'll be on your own."

With the rifle barrel wedged the way I had found it I tossed the rope out the window. "Don't do it, Brice," Fern cried, her voice filled with alarm and her eyes big as saucers. "If you're seen they'll shoot you!"

"They're like to shoot all of us unless I'm able to come up with a diversion."

I thrust the flute in the grip of my waistband and catching hold of the rope thrust my feet through the window. Swinging around with feet keeping me clear of the wall I started down, hand under hand. Forty feet on that rope seemed more like forty miles with the expectation of being shot any moment. The horses in their pens were on my mind likewise but they were two miles away and almost certainly were watched.

Ten feet from the ground I let go of the rope and took off in great strides in the direction of the pool, flute in one hand and my shooting iron in the other. I was anxiously conscious of passing time but didn't dare run until I'd gained more distance. Fern was too right. If I was seen I'd be shot. When I figured I'd covered enough ground for safety I broke into a run.

I went through the trees around the pool without stopping, but slowed to a walk trying to catch me some breath and ease the cramp in my side. Five minutes later I stepped up my pace and, pretty quick then, I started running again. It seemed like when I quit I must have covered about five miles. I stretched out on the ground till I caught up with myself, rummaging my memories, recalling my youthful admiration of the boys in blue.

When I got my wind back I scrambled erect and, grabbing up the flute, blew the cavalry charge. Loud and clear it sailed through the dawn, not quite like a bugle, but near enough for a Navajo. Then at a limping run I started back and ten minutes later with the sun throwing my shadow long ahead of me I sounded the cavalry's get-up call.

At last, within two miles of the cliff house I put the Anasazi flute to my lips and blared out the cavalry charge again.

* * *

I MOVED with a deal more caution now, eyes skinned sharp for the first hint of trouble. I had done what I could but was afraid deep inside it would not fool an old man sharp as Johnny Two-Feathers. I watched every rock, every bush and shadow, eyes strained to catch the least blur of movement. I still had the flute and the sweat creeping cold down the length of my spine when I rounded the last bend and saw the cliff house before me.

Clampas spotted me at once and came sliding down the rope. "Corrigan, you're a wonder—you really are! That flute cleared them out of here, lock, stock an' barrel!"

"How about our horses?"

"They didn't stop to grab 'em. I sent Jones out to look."

"We've got a chance then," I said, "and that's all we've got. No time to fool around. They'll be back just as soon as they discover they've been tricked, and they'll be looking for blood."

He considered me brightly. "What about that turquoise?"

"If it was up to me I'd leave it. After losing her brother I guess Fern will not be wanting to leave any of the stuff that cost him his life. They brought a bunch of sacks, I remember. We'll take whatever they'll hold and no more. When they're packed we'll let them down on that rope, pick 'em up here after we get the horses."

* * *

I WAS RIGHT ABOUT FERN. She wanted the pots they'd set aside, all the turquoise and several bones. I said, "Be reasonable, Fern. We can't take all that stuff.

We oughtn't take any of it. Those Indians will be back, and damn soon probably."

Ignoring this she said, "And I want that stone lamp Jeff's been carrying in his pocket—we'll have to take him, too."

I shook my head, seeing the futility of argument. "We'll put the stuff in those burlap sacks—"

"You can't put Jeff in a sack!" she flared. "Anyway there are no sacks up here."

I reminded myself of her loss and the shock and kept my temper where it belonged. Just the same, with my experience of Indians and time running out, I was just about ready to jump out of my skin.

Jones came down from his lookout. "You want I should fix us some grub?"

"We got no time to be lallygaggin' around. Go fetch me those sacks from the stores we carried up—and I mean right now. Stir your stumps!"

"Where's Flossie?" I said to Fern.

"She's around here somewhere—"

"Damnation!" I swore as my glance lit on Harry. "What the hell have you got in your pockets?"

He backed away from me shaking. His left eye twitched. "I only done what Clampas told me—"

"You turd!" Clampas snarled. "Anything I want I'm big enough to carry!"

Fern, paying no attention to this, was moving jugged turquoise from one place to another. Exasperated I said, "Never noticed before that you were into Jeff's line—"

"Enough of it's rubbed off for me to know what's worth saving...I want that flute, too! If we could I'd take back one of those skeletons; never mind how I feel about them. Bound to be a demand for anything that old."

"Most of the horses we're going to have to use aren't pack animals. They'll be the devil to load and there's a limit to how much they'll carry. We'd do a damn sight better to be riding them."

Clampas, I noticed, was eyeing Fern distastefully. I said, "Get over to that aperture and keep your eyes on the prowl for them Indians. You better pull up that rope..."

Jones came in with an armload of sacks. "Fine," I told him. "You can help Fern fill them," and catching up one of those burlaps myself I began dumping jugs of turquoise into it. "You'll have that all mixed up!" Fern cried censoriously.

"We haven't the time to pick and choose—you should have done all that yesterday! Can't you get it through your female head a Navajo's just as human as you are? They'll be back here full of sound an' fury—"

"Company comin'," Clampas called from his aperture. "Good God A'mighty! Come look what's down there!"

I flung over there. Some jasper was sitting down there in a buggy like a syndicate ranch boss, all togged out in his big-city duds. "Who the hell's that?" I snarled at Clampas.

"Hello up there!" this dude chucked at us. "What do you people think you're doing?"

"Fishin'," Clampas told him. "What's it to you?"

"D'you know who I am?" He sounded plumb riled. "Happens I'm the Inspector of Antiquities for the sovereign people of New Mexico. How'd you get into that place? It was sealed up tighter than a boar's ass! Don't you know you're violating the law?"

"Do tell," Clampas said.

"I'm gettin' out of here!" Harry declared through chattering teeth.

"Get down on your hunkers and help fill these sacks!" I gave him a shove. "And you can empty those pockets into one of them, too."

"That joker still down there?" I snarled at Clampas.

"Sure is—can't you hear him?"

"Them horses," I told Jones, "must be bustin' for water. Get down there and see to it."

I had so much on my mind I couldn't think straight. That jasper in the buggy called up to say, "All the old ruins in and around Chaco Canyon have been declared off-limits to vandals and all you pot-hunting buggers. By rights I ought to take you people—"

"By rights," I yelled, sticking my head out the aperture, "if you don't get out of there in one tearin' big rush you're like to find your hair on a Navajo lance!"

"New Mexico's at peace with the Navajo Nation. Those redskins have been pacified—"

"Stick around awhile and you'll learn how peaceful and pacified they are." I told Clampas to get that rope tied around a couple sacks and start them on down. "We've got to hustle this up and get out of here"

That old fool in the buggy was still shooting his jaw off. "Breaking into this property will probably get you three to ten with—Here, you! What's on that rope? You can get ten years if you're caught looting a ruin—Haul that back up!"

"Get it down there," I told Clampas, and stuck my head out the aperture. "Be a gent for a change," I told the goggling bureaucrat, "and unloose that rope so we can pull it back up. We got a lot more to go and time's gettin' short."

He peered as if he was staring at a two-headed calf. "Get at it," I said, "before you catch a blue whistler," and thrust the front end of Clampas's Sharps out where he could see it.

He couldn't believe it. I shifted the muzzle till it was looking right at him. Red-faced and spluttering, he got out of his buggy and bent over the sacks.

I hauled up the rope and lashed a couple more onto it.

It was while this second batch were on their way down that Fern clamped a hand on me. "Listen!" she cried, the freckles showing up like splatters of paint. "Don't you *hear* it?"

"I hear it."

In the blazing wrath of that midday sun there was a quality that made the blood run cold in the sound of those throbbing drums.

TWENTY-ONE

"NAVAJOS?"

"You bet." I yelled at the dude, "Catch hold of that rope and we'll haul you up."

He stood there like something built out of matchsticks. Fern shook my arm. "What are we going to *do*?"

"They're comin' back!" Harry gasped. Way he was shaking it was a wonder he was able to stay in his clothes.

I called down to the dude, "Tie the rope around you under your arms and grab on to it." He was about as stupid as a newborn sheep. "Hurry it up!" I yelled; when he finally got fixed we started reeling him in. He was no featherweight with all that soft living but we got him up with a face like spoiled putty, and Clampas hauled him in through the aperture.

Fern shook my arm again. "If we left right now couldn't we still get away?"

I said with some hope, "We'd have a chance anyway. Grab your hat and—"

"But I've still got some of those things to be packed and somebody will have to fetch that stone lamp and—"

"You can't leave right now and do forty'leven other things! Make up your mind. It's either one or the other. Forget the rest of it. You'll have enough turquoise—"

"Oh, I couldn't—How could I abandon the result of all Jeff's work! How can you ask me to?" She looked around distractedly. "And I *did* want to take poor Jeff with us. If I can't he'll have to be buried...I hate to leave him in this horrible place..."

"All right. Now we know where we're at, I hope. Best chance left is for the jasper who croaked that smartass Indian to own up to it and take his medicine." I looked at them, disgusted when no one rushed forward to take the blame. "Then all that's left if you want to keep breathin'—"

The dude, looking horrified, broke in to say, "Did I hear correctly someone needs to be buried?"

"My brother," Fern said.

"What did he die of? —By the way, my name's Witherspoon."

"I understand he fell through a hole in one of the floors," I told him, impatient.

"Broke his neck," Clampas said.

Jones came through the doorhole this side of the beads. I said, astonished, "Thought you'd gone to the pool with the horses?"

"Well..." Jones fetched up a sick-looking grin. "When them drums got to poundin' it didn't seem advisable to get that far from shelter. I used up what we had left in the water bags, lettin' them guzzle it outa my hat."

"You see any Navajos?"

"Didn't see any, no; but I bet they seen me."

"See Flossie anyplace?"

"Came past her in that room with the sand pile; didn't see no cat but she was diggin' like she figured one was in it."

"Come on, Fern." I gave her a nudge. "We'd better get hold of her."

"I'll go with you," said Witherspoon promptly, and ran a jaundiced look over me. "I gather you're the head of this 'scientific' expedition?"

"Just a hired hand."

"My brother, Professor Larrimore, was head of it," Fern told him. "This dig was—"

"Just where *is* this dig? You been digging in *here?*"

"Jeff never got around to—"

"We've had a heap of hard luck," I butted in to say. "One damn thing after another. Now, with you jumping in—"

"Great Scott!" Witherspoon gasped, staring in astonished dismay at what our Flossie had uncovered in that sand pile. I wouldn't be surprised to learn my own jaw dropped. For there in the midst of that pile of loose sand stood three medium-sized jars of perhaps the finest cut stones of spiderweb turquoise I had ever laid eyes on.

"Get a sack, Brice," Fern said crisply. "The regents will be delighted with the display they can make of this. And these Anasazi jars—"

"I forbid you, madam, to remove one piece of that off these premises!"

That hoity-toity dude was all swelled up like a carbuncle, crammed with the righteous wrath of his office. "I will remind you of the law. The law unequivocally states that any person digging or carrying off relics and/or artifacts of any nature whatsoever from terrain protected by the State of New Mexico—"

I caught his eye, jerked my head toward the door, beckoning him after me into the next room. He came reluctantly and even more reluctantly listened eventually to what I decided to tell him. It was plain he didn't like it and stood there spluttering like a batch of damp firecrackers. "I don't care at all for your attitude, young man, and if that's a threat..."

"Just a promise," I said, and went to fetch Fern a sack.

* * *

IT WAS ASTONISHING the way that girl had recovered from the loss of "poor" Jeff. She appeared to have taken on a whole new character, I thought with just a shade of resentment. Doubtless this was just her real self-emerging after years of standing in the shadow of an ambitious brother. Looked like she had made up her mind to step into his shoes and reap any credit she could from this trip.

This didn't come over me all at once, you understand. The notion just sort of grew on me. Right then I wasn't doing much thinking with the sound of those drums steadily banging through my head. I reckoned to have Wither-spoon stymied for a spell, but getting around old Johnny and his braves was a horse of a different color.

On the way back to Fern with the sack Jones caught hold of me. "You set that gasbag down in a hurry." Still eyeing me curious, he asked, "Are we goin' for the broncs? I'd like to get the hell out of here."

I sighed. "So would I."

"That girl got the bit in her teeth?"

"Looks that way. She wants to take all the pots and at least a few bones. Fact is she's honin' to pack one of those dead Basketmakers Clampas dug up down in that cliff shelter—"

"We can't take the time to pack—"

"What I told her. Be lucky to get away with that turquoise, but she's some set on it."

"Why don't you put your foot down?"

It didn't come easy but I managed a grin. "Want to try your luck?"

"I'm just the cook. She wouldn't pay me no mind."

"Me neither," I said. "Grab up a couple more of them sacks."

When we got back to Fern she said, "I'm glad you fetched those extra sacks. We'll wrap them around these jars and leave the stones inside them."

We did just that. I gave the sack to Jones and told him to send it down on the rope. "Then you and Clampas head for the horses—"

Fern said, "Don't forget that stone lamp Jeff's got in his pocket."

"Yes, ma'am. I'm going down right now to pick it up." Giving her a servant's look, I inquired, "Will there be anything else? How about one of those skeletons?"

She gave me a rueful smile. "I'm reasonably sure those skeletons are the most important finds we've made. I hate not being able to take at least one."

Clampas, at that moment joining us, said, "Them

Injuns might be downright uncivil if they caught us luggin' off one of their ancestors."

She appeared a bit startled. "I hadn't thought of that. Anyway it doesn't seem practical...unless Mr. Wither-spoon would take it in his buggy."

"Better ask him." Clampas smiled. "Seems to be a real obligin' sort."

I limped over to the floor hole and down the ladder, dug through Jeff's pockets and, lifting his wallet in addition to the lamp, fetched them back to Fern with another of the bones Flossie had been playing with. "Let's go."

* * *

OUT ON THE clifftop with the sun bearing down and that goddam drumming still banging up a storm, the only movement I could see came from Jones, Clampas and that fatass Witherspoon picking their way down through the rockfall. No sign of a redskin, I was relieved to note. I couldn't set much hope on that since you seldom ever spot one till they're about to lift your hair.

Ten minutes later Fern and I reached the rockfall and, at that precise moment, the drums went silent. A whole flock of wild thoughts fluttered through my head and the sweat turned cold underneath my hat.

"Look!" Fern cried.

I didn't need any coaching. I'd already seen them. Half the Navajo Nation, it looked like, spread out across the opposite bluff.

TWENTY-TWO

"NEVER MIND," I said. "I'll get you out of this."

She twisted her head about, looking appalled. "Brice—I can't let you *do* this!"

"We'll see. Just remember one thing: when you're free to go, by God you go. Understand? No lallygaggin' round. You make one stop. At the tamarisks, and don't let those caballos drink too much. Fill the water bags and get the hell out of there."

She looked rebellious with her chin up that way. But I nudged her along. "Worst thing you can do is let those Navajos think you're afraid. Remember how upset you were to think that old man had to sleep on the ground?" I managed a laugh, and nudged her on ahead of me, wishing I felt as confident as she thought me.

Old Johnny was waiting for me there by the pens.

Before we could speak the fat Inspector of Antiquities came bustling up to him, puffed up with importance and the authority of his office. "My name's Witherspoon. I guess you know I speak for the Government?

Yes—yes indeed! Our Great White Father up in Washington has much admiration for our Navajo friends and has appointed me to look after their best interests ..."

"Lucky Navajos!" Clampas muttered in back of me someplace. Myself, I was trying to think how best I could put what I had to say to this red brother who was a heap less simple than Witherspoon thought him. One thing was sure: this old rascal hadn't forgotten what he had come for or how he'd been balked of his prey once already.

With an expressionless face old Johnny sliced through the rhetoric with a lifted hand. "My business here is with Man-on-a-Mule."

Fern and Flossie, I saw, were with Turtle Jones some thirty or forty feet back of Clampas—far enough off, it was my devout hope, not to latch on to what I aimed to say. I didn't want it spoiled by any words out of her. Two-Feathers faced me with some asperity. "Speak, Man-on-a-Mule!"

"You're here," I said, "for the man responsible for the death of Hosteen Joe. We're prepared to give him up if I have your assurance the rest of our party will then be free to leave this place."

"Where this man?"

"Do I have your assurance?"

I watched his glance passing over our company and settle on me with a long, searching look. And at last, reluctantly, he nodded. "Where this man?"

"He is in the old cliff dwelling."

"Why you not bring?"

I could read the suspicion abruptly staring from his glance.

"Well..." I dredged up a sigh with a rueful look. "I couldn't get him out of there."

"We get. You show."

He looked again at Clampas, at Jones and the girl with her hold on Flossie's collar. Once more he nodded, and to them said, "You go." And then, as an afterthought: "One horse each."

"Two ponies," I said, shaking my head.

Despite what I'd told her, Fern of course had to put in her oar, stubbornly declaring, "I'm not about to go unless you're going, too!"

"Be quiet," I growled, scared the whole thing would start to unravel. "I'll catch up with you later." To the old man I said, "Two ponies. They're going home—have to catch iron horse."

Those Navajo eyes never left my face but thin of lip he nodded. "Agreed."

Clampas, Jones, Witherspoon and a whey-faced Hatcher went into the pens and fetched out ten horses, on one of which, under Johnny's watchful eye, they packed a sack of tinned food, our eating tools, and the washtub. Then they all mounted up and with Flossie in the lead started off down the gulch on the trail to Chaco Canyon.

* * *

BECKONING several of his warriors down from the bluff, Johnny eyeing me reflectively commanded, "You show. Now."

So I limped off on foot up the climb through the rockfall nervously wondering if this would be the last time. I couldn't hear those redskins but knew they wouldn't be far behind. "Who this man?" grunted Johnny, directly back of me.

I told him it was Larrimore, boss and organizer of this field trip.

"The great scientist friend of the Navajo?"

"Yeah."

"Why he shoot Hosteen Joe?"

"Joe had a rifle one of the others had given him. Larrimore didn't like it."

"For one rifle he kill Joe?"

Pretty weak, I thought, but said, "Looks that way. He's no great hand for explanations."

When we got to the entrance we had made getting in there the old man motioned me into the lead, alertly following my snug passage through the hole. "Bad. Bad," he grumbled. "Chindis not like."

When I mentioned we had no torch he gobbled out something unintelligible to me and one of his clan disappeared to return with an armful of creosote brush from which several torches were speedily fashioned. Each of these men he'd picked to accompany him had a rifle and three of them wore bandoliers of cartridges. I reckoned he was determined to exact his due, and again the cold chill of this place crept over me, not lessened in the least by the thought of his outrage when he finally confronted the man I had promised him.

I took as long as I could guiding him to this denouement. When we got to the hole through which Jeff had plunged he ordered a torch lit and in its flare stared, it seemed like forever, at the crumpled shape below.

TWENTY-THREE

AT LAST HE looked at me. "White man cheat."

I'd had plenty of time to think about this and, for what it was worth, had my answer ready. "Not at all," I said. "You demanded Joe's killer but nothing was mentioned about him having to be alive."

"Why you kill?"

"I wasn't there when he died. I was told he'd been chasing the dog, lost his footing in the dark and plunged through the hole."

"This is true?"

"I can only say they didn't want the dog in the lower levels. It seems logical to believe it might have happened that way."

He looked at me hard. "What you do with these people? Why you not with Ranger?"

"Ain't Ranger now—leg caught a bullet. Was on my way home when I ran into the Larrimores. They were afraid of the crew hired for them by Hatcher." A little edge of bitterness got into my voice when I said, "They thought I could protect them."

He told the rest of them what I had said and it was plain by the angry sound of their gobbling they were determined I should pay for my duplicity. Strange as it may seem the old man stood out against them. When they finally buttoned their lips he said to me with an unshakable dignity, "The Navajo is an honorable man. I not like what you do, Man-on-a-Mule, but my word is good. This time you go. I have spoken."

* * *

THE SUN WAS low down above the western rim when I got back to the camp and limped over to the pen and dropped my hull on her, kneed the air from her belly, yanked the girth tight and climbed wearily aboard. There was a saying among Mossman's men that a Ranger was a man who never looked back. I set my jaw and put Gretchen down the trail.

Pausing briefly at the pool by the tamarisks I let her have a short drink and then sent her along at her rough-gaited trot with little expectation of overtaking Fern's party this side of night.

There had been no sacks below the cliff house when I'd passed, with them so burdened it seemed fairly obvious I'd come up with them at my faster pace before they reached the Chaco.

About an hour after dark I heard the rattle and skreak of Witherspoon's buggy not a great ways ahead of me. When we drew alongside I motioned for him to pull up and, when he had done so, asked if he'd any oats under the seat.

"Well, yes," he admitted, "but not any more than I'll be needing myself."

"Pass them over. My need," I said, "is greater than yours and Mossman will reimburse you on my note of hand."

"You're way out of your jurisdiction, Corrigan."

I scribbled him a note and tossed it into his lap. "Reckon that's so." I gave him a look at my pistol. "Let's not waste any time over this."

Grumbling and spluttering dire threats he surrendered the sack. Settling it in front of me I told him I was obliged and left him still fuming.

Fern and company had made better time than I'd ever expected, packing all the weight of that turquoise. Flossie let out a wild series of barks before I caught sight of them in the moon-dappled shadows perhaps two miles short of the canyon. The others pulled up in a bunch when the dog ran to meet us with Fern right behind. And the first thing Fern said was, "Brice! How'd you ever get away from them? Of course! You must have given them Jeff ..."

"Yes. He was the only one they couldn't reach."

"But wasn't Johnny furious?"

"I expect he was; but with Navajos, Fern, a deal is a deal and the old man was stuck with it. Where's Clampas?"

"Gone," she said. There was a world of bitterness in that bleak voice. "Gone with every last ounce of our turquoise!"

Well, I thought, I should have expected this. "How long?"

"Pretty close to an hour..."

"Never mind. I'll catch him. He'll be heading for the railroad at Farmington." And without further words I set out after him.

With any kind of luck I reckoned to overtake him before he was able to get out of Chaco Canyon. That was the first thing that crossed my mind. But before I had gone more than a whoop and a holler other thoughts latched on to me. Like he might, at this point, have no intention of busting out of the canyon. He was sure to figure I'd be right on his tail.

Given this situation what, I wondered, would I do in his place? He had all the advantage, knowing me as he did. Always big Clampas was a man for the edge. Brave as a lion, audacious but never reckless. Slicker than slobbers. I could see, thinking that way, he was going to hole up. Hole up someplace with that goddam Sharps and let me come to him.

Without hideous risk I'd no way to get near him. Long as he could keep me out of pistol range he could tease me the way a cat does a mouse, and enjoy every minute of it. Even if I waited for the others to come up it wouldn't change the odds enough to matter. Harry, back when he was riding high, had taken the rifles away from us peons; and then, after Fletch had been killed, Clampas had become the he-catawampus and leached all the courage Hatcher'd ever had out of him.

I had known all along Clampas was the deadly one. Even though, for my money, he'd eliminated Alfredo, Fletcher, Hosteen Joe and then Jeff, I'd nothing but my own belief—not so much as a scrap of proof. Which was why he'd been getting so much pleasure out of me. He'd known I was on to him, known I couldn't touch him. And he hadn't made the least effort to conceal from me that no matter the odds, he meant to have every bit of that turquoise. And now he had it!

I found it a mighty humiliating fact.

Nor was I able to work up any great enthusiasm for playing six-shooter tag through some ruin's empty rooms, for there again all the edge lay with Clampas. Ambush was his stock in trade.

As was happening all too frequent of late a picture of Fern with her roan hair and freckles came into my mind with a poignant clarity I could not deny. I thought if things had been different...and dismissed such empty dreams with an oath.

I kicked my thoughts back where they belonged, centered squarely on Clampas. A glib, wryly humorous, slippery villain to whom fair play was nothing but a laugh.

Already Gretchen had carried me past several ruins and a glance at the heavens assured me it would not be long before daylight would give him, with that Sharps, an additional edge. I began watching for tracks that turned away from the trail, went the best part of another mile before locating any that seemed sufficiently fresh. When I did come on to some they went angling away toward another ruined pueblo. He'd be holed up inside, squatting like some obscene spider, waiting for me to come into his sights.

I thought there had to be some other way to get at him, some way to cut down the advantage of that Sharps. If I could find his horses...

I cut away from his tracks, aiming to circle this ruin —it was one of the larger ones—at a distance hopefully sufficient to ensure my safety. I was thinking also of Gretchen; I couldn't afford to lose her in so desolate a place.

We got about halfway around those crumbling walls, towering in some spots almost fifty feet high, before in a patch of still, deep shadow I made out what I took to be the horses I was hunting. Those were horses all right; a questioning whinny confirmed this. Before she could answer I clamped a hand on Gretchen's nostrils.

Now what to do?

It was entirely probable Clampas was as aware of that whinny as I was. He might not be able to see me yet. Should I make an attempt—with the attendant risks —of trying to drive those horses away? Leave him afoot and force him to move? But with the size of this place I could see right away such a notion was foolish. Then another occurred to me that seemed a heap better. Grab the horses if I could and light out for the railroad, reverse our positions and force Clampas to be the hunter.

There was, I figured, considerable merit in this notion. For unless he could get himself mounted again I could be at the railroad a good piece ahead of him.

But the thought of that Sharps in this growing light put a cold chill through this jubilant thinking. That sonofabitch would knock Gretchen from under me sure as God made little green apples! Fond as I was of her, it wasn't this that deterred me but the knowledge he could then pick me off at his leisure.

Any jasper who could shoot a flipped penny into oblivion was not to be taken lightly.

Turning Gretchen ever more away from where those whinnying horses stood I went on with the circling inspection I had started. In about ten minutes the sun would be up. Whatever I decided was going to have to be done quickly. I could picture Clampas crouched in there someplace grinning over the sights of that Sharps, chuckling while he waited with Indian patience for me to move into range.

Some forty yards farther along I saw a whaleback rock with a fringe of greasewood some thirty feet closer to the battered walls than where I sat Gretchen, and the sight of this put a new aspect before me. The rock rose perhaps two feet above the shale-strewn surface of the ground all about it.

The possibilities this opened up were simply too tempting for me to resist. I got off the mule and considered it some more while I ran a hand across the loops of my belt, finding plenty of cartridges for what I had in mind.

The next step, of course, was how to reach it alive and in reasonable working order.

I didn't want to sacrifice Gretchen. Nor did I want to catch one of that Sharps's blue whistlers. I thought about it some more and moved Gretchen back a bit and sat down cross-legged to study it in depth, hoping these tactics might prod Clampas's temper or maybe stretch his nerves a little.

I gave it another five minutes and without more ado, with the rock between me and where I hoped he might be, I got over on my belly and began to wriggle toward its shelter.

Wham! went the Sharps and a lead plum went skittering off the rock's rounded top. He tried a couple more with no better result and by that time I was snuggled up against it. I blew out a held breath and sleeved the sweat off my forehead.

I had him placed now, but no guarantee he would stay there. Near as I could tell, without seeking a new and even more distant position, there seemed no way he'd be able to flank me. Breaking off four or five of the greasewood shoots, in time-honored fashion I edged the crown of my hat a very tiny way above the rock and Clampas promptly drilled it. He must have guessed the hat was empty; just wanted to show me what he could do. Or perhaps he was getting a little mite edgy. After all, he had to know the others would soon be along and he couldn't watch more than one place at a time. While Clampas was dealing with me, Jones and possibly Harry could slip into that ruin and make his position untenable.

While these thoughts were scampering around I had worked off my shirt and stuffed the top part of it with greasewood branches. Shoving another down through these I set my hat on it and poked this scarecrow enough above my shelter to entice two rapid reports. Both shots scored and as the dummy collapsed I let out a scream that should have sounded pretty desperate.

With much care I got back into my shirt and composed myself to wait for his footsteps.

But Clampas, too wily to let go of his advantage, put in no appearance.

The sun climbed higher. It began to get hot. My ears ached from listening for sounds that never came. An almost irresistible impulse urged me to move and only the knowledge of what it might cost kept me motionless. Certainly I could show as much patience as Clampas so long as those horses stayed where I could see them.

I could, I supposed, afford a bit more. Bothered by flies those horses were beginning to get restive and Clampas must know this; he must know too that the companions he'd robbed at gunpoint were bound pretty soon to be coming along.

I wasn't surprised when those fretting horses began to drift off. Now, I thought, he's going to have to make a move. With extreme caution I took a quick look around the end of my rock. Nothing happened, nor did I see him. My exploring hand found a piece of flat shale—the kind we used to skip across ponds—and scaled it, cursing, at the ruin's nearest wall.

TWENTY-FOUR

EVERYTHING SEEMED to happen at once.

A rumble of hoofs came up from the trail. Clampas crashed another shot whining off my rock. The confiscated horses he had lifted from our outfit, filled now with a whinnying excitement, went tearing off to rejoin their companions, turquoise and all. Clampas came over the broken wall of his refuge as though flung from a catapult, making straight for me, triggering that Sharps at every jump. How he missed hitting me I've never been able to understand. Only Burt Mossman's drilled-in discipline kept me rock-steady in the face of that charge. When he got near enough I fanned off one shot which must have caught him head-on. Arms flung out, he spun half around and collapsed in his tracks.

I saw Fern's mop of roan hair driving through milling horses, Jones's rigid face and Harry's frightened one, and then they were around me, all talking at once, and creating such bedlam it made my head swim, and I thought this must be what hell was like.

When finally I began to function once more I began

looking for Gretchen and found her trying to lift her head off the ground. As through a fog I stumbled over to where she lay with those great loyal eyes staring up at me. I fumbled a sugar lump out of my pocket and patted her shoulder. "You were a real lady, Gretchen," I told her, and put my pistol against her head.

When my surroundings came into true focus again Jones was putting my saddle on one of the horses. "Guess we're about ready," he said handing me the reins. "I've put the sacks on three of our spares. You want to lead off?"

"I suppose so. Keep your eye on Harry—he doesn't have a gun, does he? Good. You and him better ride drag; we don't want to lose any of those loose mounts between here and Farmington. We've got thirty-odd miles still ahead of us."

I rode more or less like I wasn't all there till Fern came up with some more conversation, none of which registered till she said, looking around at me, "I guess you couldn't have saved her?"

I didn't want to gab about it. "She got one of those slugs in the neck. Another broke a leg."

We rode for a while without further talk, which was one blessing anyway. But she was too full of plans and excitement to have kept her notions to herself for long. She kept twisting her head with her blue-green eyes slanching probing glances in my direction and then, unable longer to remain bottled up, declared, "I haven't yet thanked you for saving that stuff—"

"No thanks necessary," I cut into it brusquely.

"Well, you needn't bite my head off! How long will it take us to get to the railroad?"

"It's around thirty miles from where we are now.

We'll have to camp out tonight. With a good deal of luck we might reach Farmington tomorrow—late."

"Couldn't we just push right on?"

"These horses," I said, "ain't made of iron, Fern. They've got to have rest."

"But with these spares to switch off on—"

"Unless you're prepared to hoof it and leave all your booty."

"Oh, I couldn't do that—I mean give up that turquoise, those bones and the lamp."

"Then we camp out tonight," I said with finality. And that's what we did.

Seemed like we were all more worn out than we'd been ready to admit. The sun was just creeping over those distant hills with Shiprock looming blue-gray against the brightening sky when Jones roused us out to eat our retried beans, sloshed down with Java.

We were loading the horses when Jones grabbed my arm, swinging me around to follow the lift of his hand toward where a column of smoke pale gray in the sunlight was rising above a distant mesa. Even as we watched we saw the smoke cut off. Then three quick puffs shot skyward after it. Flossie was looking up at us nervously.

"Signals?" He looked to be in a state of shock. I met his rounded stare and nodded, telling myself I wasn't filled with the jumps but knowing damn well I was and couldn't help it. I was about to tell him to keep his mouth shut, but Harry's alarmed cry caught Fern's attention and I saw her cheeks turn gray as she took in the last of that disappearing haze.

"You don't suppose that's Navajos, do you?"

"Could be Pueblos," I said with professed indif-
ference.

But she'd spotted another smoke off to the west and
conviction showed in the shape of her stare.

I said to Jones, "Let's get this outfit on the road,"
and we hustled things up and presently were riding into
the morning's strengthening heat. No one but Harry
felt inclined for gab. With a twitch in his cheek and his
eyes looking wild, he yelled at me, "I thought you'd
fixed things up with that sonofabitch!"

"We don't know that it's them. Even if it is, those
puffadillies may not concern us at all."

And Fern said, hopeful through stiffened lips, "If
Johnny's bunch had changed their minds they'd have
caught us up hours ago. Before we had even got out of
the canyon."

"That's right," I put in, but couldn't help thinking
Johnny's mind had been changed for him, remembering
those furious faces at the cliff house.

The morning wore along with the sun glaring down
with increasing malevolence and me holding the horses
down to what they could handle in this increasing heat
and given our shortage of water.

Now and again we saw additional smokes in the
hazy distance and when Fern's look grew agitated I said,
"They're just making sure we get out of the country."
But I didn't believe it and she didn't either.

We stopped at noon to shift the loads and Jones
broke open two tins of corned beef, the contents of
which we choked down in silence while all of us
covertly kept tabs on the skyline.

"You know what it is," Harry kept muttering,
"they're after the chindis' horde, that's what!"

At last I said, fed up with his whining, "If you reckon you can do better, cut loose and take off."

I could see the hate shining bright in his stare. "I ain't leavin' without my pay."

"Your performance with this outfit doesn't merit any pay. You've been nothing but a drag ever since you signed, not to mention your sundry treacheries!"

Fern dug out Jeff's wallet. "I'll pay him—"

"Pay him nothing," I growled, and we rode on through the heat and the vast silence of this waste that grew nothing that lived but the gray wands of wolf's candle.

The hours dragged. The heat pulled sweat out of us that was dried by the oven-like atmosphere before it could drip. By midafternoon with the sentinel peak of Shiprock much plainer, Harry, forever twisting for frightened looks behind, suddenly cried in a panic, "There's a dust back there!"

Without bothering to look I said disparagingly, "Nothing but a twister. What you dudes call a dust devil. In this kind of country you get 'em all the time."

"I don't think so, Corrigan. I been keepin' my eye on it. Them's horses that's stirrin' it." He took another look. "Might be cavalry."

"Might be jumpin' beans," I said, disgusted.

Fern said, "Can't we go a little faster?"

I licked dry lips. "Whatever it is we're not going to lose it by killin' these horses. If it's Navajos they know this region a sight better than we do. They ride light. They don't pack forty-pound saddles or half a ton of turquoise —not to mention pots and bones!"

TWENTY-FIVE

KNOWING it was useless but under pressure from those hairy looks I did step up the pace a bit and on we went, worried, brooding, our anxiety increasing with each passing mile.

The horses were beginning to show the strain, especially the ones burdened with packs, all of them seeming more gaunt than I liked. We weren't, I figured, above six miles from the rails but it might as well have been sixty when Harry cried out, "It's them Navajos—I *knew* it! I can see them plain!"

Stood to reason, of course. But, I thought, if we could manage to get within sight of the town there was still a thin chance they'd give it up and pull off. I was coddling this notion when Jones growled on an outblown breath, "There's dust up ahead—they've cut us off!"

"It doesn't have to be Indians," Fern said, voice reedy, and slung a look at me. "Couldn't it be cavalry?"

"Not again," I said; and Jones, in no mood for a laugh, told her, "Ain't no cavalry around these parts."

I said, "We've pretty near run that dog off her legs. We might's well stop and get it over with."

Nobody liked it but only Jones spoke. "Might's well," he said grimly.

We pulled up. "No gunplay," I said.

"I guess," Fern admitted, "this dig of Jeff's was star-crossed from the start," and I nodded. "Sure does seem so, looking back. An exercise in futility, doomed from the time he signed Harry on."

"I wish," Fern said, "I'd thought to keep out that stone lamp, or one of the bones Flossie dug up to play with. If their dating coincided with Jeff's theories the regents might allow me to return next year, even if they put someone else in charge. Those seven skeletons—"

I said, "I guess we can give the poor dog a bone." Dismounting, I limped over to the horse that was carrying the lightest pack, the one she'd put those three jars into, fished out the leg bone and tossed it to Flossie. Though she made no move to catch it, and with her tongue lolling out a foot and forty inches, she did condescend to drop down beside it. Thoughtfully eyeing me, Fern said, "I wonder if I could someway manage to hang on to those jars..."

I shook my head, too used up even to grin.

* * *

IT DIDN'T TAKE the Navajos long to surround us; I'd have been glad right then of a few covered wagons, considering the uproar. They closed in from all sides waving a miscellany of weapons, gobbling up a storm. Old Two-Feathers let them holler, then shut it off with a lifted hand.

Looking over our sorry company, looking especially and longest at the horse I was hunkered by, he said, "Man-Without-Mule, we meet again."

"Ain't that a fact? Thought you told me we were free to go?"

"To go, yes. But not with things that belong to the chindis. I personally, as our white brothers say, will care for these venerated relics," he smiled, "as though they were my own."

I smiled too. "I believe you will."

Johnny Two-Feathers nodded. "Make much jewelry."

Then he waved a hand and the whole band headed back to the Chaco with our packhorses and packs.

"Well," Fern said, "we've still got each other," and Flossie, bright eyes peering up at us, wriggled and wagged in plainest approval.

A LOOK AT: QUICK-TRIGGER COUNTRY AND G STANDS FOR GUN
A WESTERN DOUBLE

From Spur Award-winning author Nelson C. Nye comes two classic action and adventure Western novels packaged together for the first time.

In *Quick-trigger Country*, Turk was just a kid when he got hooked up with Curly Bill Graham's outlaw gang, but quickly made a name for himself as a fast and fearless gunslinger. Membership in the Graham gang brought Turk every bit of the action and excitement he'd always craved—until the border raids turned into an excuse for senseless killing. When the range war flared, Turk and the Graham gang found themselves on opposite sides. He'd fight to the death to get back on the side of the law, but if he wound up on Boot Hill, he'd sure as shootin' take Curly Bill with him!

In *G Stands for Gun*, Sudden Shane rode through the moonlight, his guns ready for the final showdown with Jarson Lume, the merciless gun-boss of Tortilla Flat... Lume had made a hell-hole out of the town from the very moment gold had been discovered in the mountains. Now all law and order had vanished—the killings were so numerous people had stopped counting.

But Sudden Shane wasn't the type of hombre who took things lying down. His guns were as fast as the next man's. When the smoke cleared, either he or Lume was going to be dead...

Nelson Nye's award-winning westerns: *"Start at top speed and keep going hell bent-for-leather through to the smashing finish. The tempo of his stories is breakneck from start to finish. With*

AVAILABLE JUNE 2022

ABOUT THE AUTHOR

Nelson C. Nye (1907–1997) was an American author, editor, and reviewer of Western fiction, and wrote non-fiction books on quarter horses. He also wrote fiction using the pseudonyms Clem Colt and Drake C. Denver. Nye wrote over 125 books, won two Spur Awards: one for best Western reviewer and critic, and one for his novel *Long Run*, and in 1968 won the Saddleman Award for ""Outstanding Contributions to the American West."

Nelson Nye was born in Chicago, Illinois. Before becoming a ranch hand in 1935, he wrote publicity releases and book reviews for the Cincinnati Times-Star and the Buffalo Evening News. He published his first novel in 1936 and continued writing for 60 years. He served with the U.S. Army field artillery during World War II. He worked as the horse editor for Texas Livestock Journal from 1949–1952.

In 1953 Nye co-founded the Western Writers of America and served as its first president during 1953–1954. He was also the first editor of *ROUNDUP*, the WWA periodical that is still published today.

9 781639 779512